SIR WALTER SCOTT
NOVELS

ROB ROY

VOLUME I

Introduction by Malcolm Elwin

HERON BOOKS LONDON

LIST OF ILLUSTRATIONS

INTRODUCTION

From its publication on 31st December 1817 as the sixth of the Waverley Novels, Rob Roy *has held its place among the most popular of all Scott's romances. Perhaps, as Mr. Walter Allen says, it is not his best, but it remains eminently readable in possessing all the ingredients of historical romance –abundant action, swift changes of fortune, engaging characters impressive in their reality, both comedy and tragedy, a web of intrigue, a dramatic battle-scene in the ambush at the pass of Loch-Ard, a charming and vital heroine, and in Rob Roy himself – subtle but loyal, courageous yet cunning, always arriving opportunely to turn the scales in a crisis – the forerunner of Dumas' D'Artagnan.*

As in Waverley *and* Redgauntlet, *the story opens in the humdrum world of law and order to emphasise how political intrigue and ruthless violence may be lurking round the corner from the most peaceful thoroughfare. But in* Rob Roy *the scene shifts more quickly, and the opening immediately engages the reader's sympathies with Frank Osbaldistone in his spirited refusal to step into his father's shoes by tamely following a business career. On Frank's journey to the north there is no hint of impending fate beyond his fellow-traveller's fear of being robbed; at Osbaldistone Hall he sees nothing sinister in the rustic habits of the old squire and his sporting sons, but soon becomes aware of mysterious practices involving not only his cousin Rashleigh but also the beautiful Diana Vernon and the enigmatic and redoubtable Rob Roy.*

Diana Vernon is rated the most attractive of all Scott's heroines – even to being ancestress of that other Diana in Meredith's Diana of the Crossways. *She is the only one one of his ladies allowed to express herself as a woman and to take an active part in the story; Scott seems to be apologising for his own indiscretion in causing Frank Osbaldistone to be at first a little repelled by the unfashionable frankness of her manner. As Walter Bagehot remarked in his essay on the Waverley Novels, Scott himself had "never led the life of flirtation from which Goethe believed that he derived so much instruction," and so usually hurries over love scenes as in embarrassment. He comes nowhere else so close to expression of passionate emotion as when Diana parts from Frank on his leaving Osbaldistone Hall and when she stoops from her horse at their parting on the moonlit moor to brush his lips with hers.*

The idea of Rob Roy *may have been suggested by Byron's remark that he wished the story of* Waverley *could have begun further back in history to have revealed the roots of Jacobitism. For, while the events of the story take place immediately before the first Jacobite Rebellion of 1715, reflections on the past lives of Sir Hildebrand Osbaldistone, Bailie Nicol Jarvie, and Rob Roy himself illustrate the development of political emotions leading up to the rebellion even from the days of Claverhouse and the Covenanters.* Rob Roy *is thus the first part of a Jacobite trilogy, of which*

INTRODUCTION

Waverley *is the second and* Redgauntlet *the third and final part.*

Constable the publisher chose the title, urging that "the name of the real hero would be the best possible name for the book," to which Scott replied, "Nay, never let me have to write up to a name. You well know I have generally adopted a title that told nothing." But after they had dined, he was persuaded, and Constable related, "I never had found him so disposed to be communicative about what he meant do do ... he continued for an hour more to walk backwards and forwards on the green, talking and laughing – he told us he was sure he should make a hit in a Glasgow weaver, whom he would ravel up with Rob," *and embarked on "an extempore dialogue between the bailie and the cateran – something not unlike what the book gives us as passing in the Glasgow tolbooth."*

It seems evident that Scott had been pondering the subject for a long time before he began the writing of the novel in the spring of 1817. In his youth he had talked with the grandfather of a college friend, George Abercromby, who had actually visited and supped with Rob Roy in his cave. On 4th April 1812 he informed a correspondent, "I have got Rob Roy's gun, a long Spanish-barrelled piece, with his initials, R.M.C., for Robert Macgregor Campbell, which latter name he assumed in compliment to the Argyle family, who afforded him a good deal of private support, because he was a thorn in the side of their old rival house of Montrose." Finally in May 1816 a friend made him a present of Rob Roy's sporran, with its elaborate safety device, which is minutely described when Rob pays his debt to Bailie Jarvie.

INTRODUCTION

Presumably the scenes at Osbaldistone Hall had been written by July 1817 when Scott "made an excursion to the Lennox, chiefly that he might visit a cave at the head of Loch Lomond, said to have been a favourite retreat of his hero, Rob Roy," and went thence to Glasgow to study "localities of the birthplace of Bailie Jarvie." If this visit to Glasgow gave him the idea of Bailie Jarvie, the city may claim the inspiration of one of Scott's greatest characters, rated by Hazlitt among no less than five figures in this novel ranking as "perfect representations of human character or fanciful belief... Rob Roy (like the eagle in his eyry), and Bailie Nicol Jarvie, and the inimitable Major Galbraith, and Rashleigh Osbaldistone, and· Die Vernon, the best of secret-keepers."

"When I light on such a character as Bailie Jarvie," wrote Scott in the Introductory Epistle to The Fortunes of Nigel *(1822), "my imagination brightens, and my conception becomes clearer at every step which I take in his company." The reader will see that action and dialogue are equally lively from the moment of the Bailie's joining Frank's adventures, comprising some of the best chapters that Scott ever wrote.*

Yet he was handicapped at this time by agonies of stomach cramp – caused perhaps by duodenal ulcer – and by lassitude induced by taking opium, then the only available painkiller. When his friend and printer, James Ballan- tyne, exclaimed on finding him with a sheet of blank paper before him, Scott retorted, "Ay, ay, Jemmy, 'tis easy for you to bid me get on, but how the deuce can I make Rob Roy's wife speak, with such a curmurring in my guts?"

INTRODUCTION

Perhaps the book benefited by being written more slowly than according to Scott's usual habit. None of his novels presents a series of scenes more dramatic than the night visit to the prison, the expedition to the Clachan of Aberfoil, the meeting with Galbraith in the alehouse, the ambush in the pass, the fury of Macgregor's wife, Rob Roy's escape from his captors, and Frank's encounters on the moor. Some critics have argued that Rashleigh succeeded too readily in imposing upon a businessman so experienced as Frank's father and that there is no explanation of how the solvency of the Osbaldistone firm was so easily overset and re-established, but the story is concerned with the effects and not with the methods of Rashleigh's scheming.

Rob Roy *is the novel chosen for particular examination in Walter Allen's excellent appreciation of Scott in his study of* The English Novel, *1954. The facts about its writing will be found in John Gibson Lockhart's classic* Life of Sir Walter Scott.

MALCOLM ELWIN.

ROB ROY

For why ? Because the good old rule
  Sufficeth them ; the simple plan,
That they should take who have the power,
  And they should keep who can.
              Rob Roy's Grave.—WORDSWORTH.

ADVERTISEMENT

TO THE FIRST EDITION

WHEN the Editor of the following volumes published, about two years since, the work called 'The Antiquary,' he announced that he was, for the last time, intruding upon the public in his present capacity. He might shelter himself under the plea that every anonymous writer is, like the celebrated Junius, only a phantom, and that therefore, although an apparition of a more benign, as well as much meaner description, he cannot be bound to plead to a charge of inconsistency. A better apology may be found in the imitating the confession of honest Benedick, that, when he said he would die a bachelor, he did not think he should live to be married. The best of all would be, if, as has eminently happened in the case of some distinguished contemporaries, the merit of the work should, in the reader's estimation, form an excuse for the author's breach of promise. Without presuming to hope that this may prove the case, it is only further necessary to mention, that his resolution, like that of Benedick, fell a sacrifice, to temptation at least, if not to stratagem.

It is now about six months since the Author, through the medium of his respectable Publishers, received a parcel of Papers, containing the Outlines of this narrative, with a permission, or rather with a request, couched in highly flattering terms, that they might be given to the Public, with such alterations as should be found suitable.* These were of course so numerous, that, besides the suppression of names, and of incidents approaching too much to reality, the work may in a great measure be said to be new written. Several anachronisms have probably crept in during the course of these changes; and the mottoes for the Chapters have been selected without any reference to the supposed date of the incidents. For these, of course, the Editor is responsible. Some others occurred in the original materials, but they are of little consequence. In point of minute accuracy, it may be stated, that the bridge over the Forth, or rather the Avondhu, (or Black River,) near the hamlet of Aberfoil, had not an existence thirty years ago. It does not, however, become the

---

* As it may be necessary, in the present Edition, to speak upon the square, the Author thinks it proper to own, that the communication alluded to is entirely imaginary.

ADVERTISEMENT

Editor to be the first to point out these errors; and he takes this public opportunity to thank the unknown and nameless correspondent, to whom the reader will owe the principal share of any amusement which he may derive from the following pages.

1st December, 1817.

INTRODUCTION

WHEN the author projected this further encroach-
ment on the patience of an indulgent public, he
was at some loss for a title; a good name being
very nearly of as much consequence in literature
as in life. The title of ROB ROY was suggested
by the late Mr. Constable, whose sagacity and
experience foresaw the germ of popularity which
it included.

No introduction can be more appropriate to
the work than some account of the singular
character whose name is given to the title-page,
and who, through good report and bad report, has
maintained a wonderful degree of importance in
popular recollection. This cannot be ascribed to
the distinction of his birth, which, though that
of a gentleman, had in it nothing of high destination, and gave him little right to command in his
clan. Neither, though he lived a busy, restless,
and enterprising life, were his feats equal to those
of other freebooters who have been less distinguished. He owed his fame in a great measure

to his residing on the very verge of the Highlands, and playing such pranks in the beginning of the 18th century, as are usually ascribed to Robin Hood in the middle ages,—and that within forty miles of Glasgow, a great commercial city, the seat of a learned university. Thus a character like his, blending the wild virtues, the subtle policy, and unrestrained license of an American Indian, was flourishing in Scotland during the Augustan age of Queen Anne and George I. Addison, it is probable, or Pope, would have been considerably surprised if they had known that there existed in the same island with them a personage of Rob Roy's peculiar habits and profession. It is this strong contrast betwixt the civilized and cultivated mode of life on the one side of the Highland line, and the wild and lawless adventures which were habitually undertaken and achieved by one who dwelt on the opposite side of that ideal boundary, which creates the interest attached to his name. Hence it is that even yet,

> ' Far and near, through vale and hill,
> Are faces that attest the same,
> And kindle like a fire new stirr'd
> At sound of Rob Roy's name.'

There were several advantages which Rob Roy enjoyed, for sustaining to advantage the character which he assumed.

INTRODUCTION

The most prominent of these was his descent from, and connexion with, the clan MacGregor, so famous for their misfortunes, and the indomitable spirit with which they maintained themselves as a clan, linked and banded together in spite of the most severe laws, executed with unheard-of rigour against those who bore this forbidden surname. Their history was that of several others of the original Highland clans, who were suppressed by more powerful neighbours, and either extirpated, or forced to secure themselves by renouncing their own family appellation, and assuming that of the conquerors. The peculiarity in the story of the MacGregors, is their retaining, with such tenacity, their separate existence and union as a clan under circumstances of the utmost urgency. The history of the tribe is briefly as follows: But we must premise that the tale depends in some degree on tradition; therefore, excepting when written documents are quoted, it must be considered as in some degree dubious.

The sept of MacGregor claimed a descent from Gregor, or Gregorius, third son, it is said, of Alpin King of Scots, who flourished about 787. Hence their original patronymic is MacAlpine, and they are usually termed the Clan Alpine. An individual tribe of them retains the same name. They are accounted one of the most ancient clans in the

Highlands, and it is certain they were a people of original Celtic descent, and occupied at one period very extensive possessions in Perthshire and Argyleshire, which they imprudently continued to hold by the *coir a glaive*, that is, the right of the sword. Their neighbours, the Earls of Argyle and Breadalbane, in the meanwhile, managed to have the lands occupied by the MacGregors engrossed in those charters which they easily obtained from the Crown; and thus constituted a legal right in their own favour, without much regard to its justice. As opportunity occurred of annoying or extirpating their neighbours, they gradually extended their own domains, by usurping, under the pretext of such royal grants, those of their more uncivilized neighbours. A Sir Duncan Campbell of Lochow, known in the Highlands by the name of *Donacha Dhu nan Churraichd*, that is, Black Duncan with the Cowl, it being his pleasure to wear such a head-gear, is said to have been peculiarly successful in those acts of spoliation upon the clan MacGregor.

The devoted sept, ever finding themselves iniquitously driven from their possessions, defended themselves by force, and occasionally gained advantages, which they used cruelly enough. This conduct, though natural, considering the country and time, was studiously represented at the capital

INTRODUCTION

as arising from an untamable and innate ferocity, which nothing, it was said, could remedy, save cutting off the tribe of MacGregor root and branch.

In an act of Privy Council at Stirling, 22d September, 1563, in the reign of Queen Mary, commission is granted to the most powerful nobles, and chiefs of the clans, to pursue the clan Gregor with fire and sword. A similar warrant in 1563, not only grants the like powers to Sir John Campbell of Glenorchy, the descendant of Duncan with the Cowl, but discharges the lieges to receive or assist any of the clan Gregor, or afford them, under any colour whatever, meat, drink, or clothes.

An atrocity which the clan Gregor committed in 1589, by the murder of John Drummond of Drummond-ernoch, a forester of the royal forest of Glenartney, is elsewhere given, with all its horrid circumstances. The clan swore upon the severed head of the murdered man, that they would make common cause in avowing the deed. This led to an act of the Privy Council, directing another crusade against the ' wicked clan Gregor, so long continuing in blood, slaughter, theft, and robbery,' in which letters of fire and sword are denounced against them for the space of three years. The reader will find this particular fact illustrated in the Introduction to the Legend of Montrose in the present edition of these Novels.

Other occasions frequently occurred, in which the MacGregors testified contempt for the laws, from which they had often experienced severity, but never protection. Though they were gradually deprived of their possessions, and of all ordinary means of procuring subsistence, they could not, nevertheless, be supposed likely to starve for famine, while they had the means of taking from strangers what they considered as rightfully their own. Hence they became versed in predatory forays, and accustomed to bloodshed. Their passions were eager, and, with a little management on the part of some of their most powerful neighbours, they could easily be *hounded out*, to use an expressive Scottish phrase, to commit violence, of which the wily instigators took the advantage, and left the ignorant MacGregors an undivided portion of blame and punishment. This policy of pushing on the fierce clans of the Highlands and Borders to break the peace of the country, is accounted by the historian one of the most dangerous practices of his own period, in which the MacGregors were considered as ready agents.

Notwithstanding these severe denunciations, which were acted upon in the same spirit in which they were conceived, some of the clan still possessed property, and the chief of the name in 1592 is designed Allaster MacGregor of Glenstrae. He is said to have been a brave and active man; but, from the tenor of his confession at his death, appears to have been engaged in many and desperate feuds, one of which finally proved fatal to himself and many of his followers. This was the celebrated conflict at Glenfruin, near the south-western extremity of Loch Lomond, in the vicinity of which the MacGregors continued to exercise much authority by the *coir a glaive*, or right of the strongest, which we have already mentioned.

There had been a long and bloody feud betwixt the MacGregors and the Laird of Luss, head of the family of Colquhoun, a powerful race on the lower part of Loch Lomond. The MacGregors' tradition affirms that the quarrel began on a very trifling subject. Two of the MacGregors being benighted, asked shelter in a house belonging to a dependent of the Colquhouns, and were refused. They then retreated to an out-house, took a wedder from the fold, killed it, and supped off the carcass, for which (it is said) they offered payment to the proprietor. The Laird of Luss seized on the offenders, and, by the summary process which feudal barons had at their command, had them both condemned and executed. The MacGregors verify this account of the feud by appealing to a proverb current amongst them, execrating the hour (*Mult dhu an Carbail ghil*) that the black wedder with the white tail was ever lambed. To avenge this quarrel, the Laird of MacGregor assembled his clan, to the number of three or four hundred men, and marched towards Luss from the banks of Loch Long, by a pass called *Raid na Gael*, or the Highlandman's Pass.

Sir Humphrey Colquhoun received early notice of this incursion, and collected a strong force, more than twice the number of that of the invaders. He had with him the gentlemen of the name of Buchanan, with the Grahams, and other gentry of the Lennox, and a party of the citizens of Dunbarton, under command of Tobias Smollett, a magistrate, or bailie, of that town, and ancestor of the celebrated author.

The parties met in the valley of Glenfruin, which signifies the Glen of Sorrow, a name that seemed to anticipate the event of the day, which, fatal to the conquered party, was at least equally so to the victors, the 'babe unborn' of clan Alpine having reason to repent it. The MacGregors, somewhat discouraged by the appearance of a force much superior to their own, were cheered on to the attack by a Seer, or second-sighted person, who professed that he saw the shrouds of the dead wrapt around their principal opponents. The clan charged with great fury on the front of the enemy, while John MacGregor, with a strong party, made an unexpected attack on the flank. A great part of the Colquhouns' force consisted in cavalry, which could not act in the boggy ground. They were said to have disputed the field manfully, but were at length completely routed, and a merciless slaughter was exercised on the fugitives, of whom betwixt two and three hundred fell on the field, and in the pursuit. If the MacGregors lost, as is averred, only two men slain in the action, they had slight provocation for an indiscriminate massacre. It is said that their fury extended itself to a party of students for clerical orders, who had imprudently come to see the battle. Some doubt is thrown on this fact, from the indictment against the chief of the clan Gregor being silent on the subject, as is the historian Johnston, and a Professor Ross, who wrote an account of the battle twenty-nine years after it was fought. It is, however, constantly averred by the tradition of the country, and a stone where the deed was done is called *Leck-a-Mhinisteir*, the Minister or Clerk's Flag-stone. The MacGregors impute this cruel action to the ferocity of a single man of their tribe, renowned for size and strength, called Dugald, *Ciar Mhor*, or the great Mouse-coloured Man. He was Mac-Gregor's foster-brother, and the chief committed the youths to his charge, with directions to keep them safely till the affray was over. Whether fearful of their escape, or incensed by some sarcasms which they threw on his tribe, or whether out of mere thirst of blood, this savage, while the other MacGregors were engaged in the pursuit, poniarded his helpless and defenceless prisoners. When the chieftain, on his return, demanded where the youths were, the *Ciar* (pronounced Kiar) *Mhor* drew out his bloody dirk, saying in Gaelic, 'Ask that, and God save me!' The latter words allude to the exclamation which his victims used when he was murdering them. It would seem, therefore, that this horrible part of the story is founded on fact, though the number of the youths so slain is probably exaggerated in the Lowland accounts. The common people say that the blood of the Ciar Mhor's victims can never be washed off the stone. When MacGregor learnt their fate, he expressed the utmost horror at the deed, and upbraided his foster-brother with having done that which would occasion the destruction of him and his clan. This homicide was the ancestor of Rob Roy, and the tribe from which he was descended. He lies buried at the church of Fortingal, where his sepulchre, covered with a large stone,* is still shown, and where his great strength and courage are the theme of many traditions.†

MacGregor's brother was one of the very few of the tribe who was slain. He was buried near the field of battle, and the place is marked by a rude stone, called the Grey Stone of MacGregor.

Sir Humphrey Colquhoun, being well mounted, escaped for the time to the castle of Banochar, or Benechra. It proved no sure defence, however, for he was shortly after murdered in a vault of the castle, the family annals say by the MacGregors, though other accounts charge the deed upon the MacFarlanes.

This battle of Glenfruin, and the severity which the victors exercised in the pursuit, was reported to King James VI. in a manner the most unfavourable to the clan Gregor, whose general character, being that of lawless though brave men, could not much avail them in such a case. That James might fully understand the extent of the slaughter, the widows of the slain to the number of eleven score, in deep mourning, riding upon white palfreys, and each bearing her husband's bloody shirt on a spear, appeared at Stirling, in presence of a monarch peculiarly accessible to

* See Note A. The Grave of Dugald Ciar Mohr.
† See Note B. Tradition of Dugald Ciar Mohr.

such sights of fear and sorrow, to demand vengeance for the death of their husbands, upon those by whom they had been made desolate.

The remedy resorted to was at least as severe as the cruelties which it was designed to punish. By an act of the Privy Council, dated 3d April, 1603, the name of MacGregor was expressly abolished, and those who had hitherto borne it were commanded to change it for other surnames, the pain of death being denounced against those who should call themselves Gregor or MacGregor, the names of their fathers. Under the same penalty, all who had been at the conflict of Glenfruin, or accessory to other marauding parties charged in the act, were prohibited from carrying weapons, except a pointless knife to eat their victuals. By a subsequent act of Council, 24th June, 1613, death was denounced against any persons of the tribe formerly called MacGregor, who should presume to assemble in greater numbers than four. Again, by an act of Parliament, 1617, chap. 26, these laws were continued, and extended to the rising generation, in respect that great numbers of the children of those against whom the acts of Privy Council had been directed, were stated to be then approaching to maturity, who, if permitted to resume the name of their parents, would render the clan as strong as it was before.

INTRODUCTION

The execution of those severe acts was chiefly intrusted in the west to the Earl of Argyle, and the powerful clan of Campbell, and to the Earl of Athole and his followers, in the more eastern Highlands of Perthshire. The MacGregors failed not to resist with the most determined courage; and many a valley in the West and North Highlands retains memory of the severe conflicts, in which the proscribed clan sometimes obtained transient advantages, and always sold their lives dearly. At length the pride of Allaster MacGregor, the chief of the clan, was so much lowered by the sufferings of his people, that he resolved to surrender himself to the Earl of Argyle, with his principal followers, on condition that they should be sent out of Scotland. If the unfortunate chief's own account be true, he had more reasons than one for expecting some favour from the Earl, who had in secret advised and encouraged him to many of the desperate actions for which he was now called to so severe a reckoning. But Argyle, as old Birrell expresses himself, kept a Highlandman's promise with them, fulfilling it to the ear, and breaking it to the sense. MacGregor was sent under a strong guard to the frontier of England, and being thus, in the literal sense, sent out of Scotland, Argyle was judged to have kept faith with him, though the same party which took him there brought him back to Edinburgh in custody.

MacGregor of Glenstrae was tried before the Court of Justiciary, 20th January, 1604, and found guilty. He appears to have been instantly conveyed from the bar to the gallows; for Birrell, of the same date, reports that he was hanged at the Cross, and, for distinction's sake, was suspended higher by his own height than two of his kindred and friends. On the 18th of February following, more men of the MacGregors were executed, after a long imprisonment, and several others in the beginning of March.

The Earl of Argyle's service, in conducing to the surrender of the insolent and wicked race and name of MacGregor, notorious common malefactors, and in the in-bringing of MacGregor, with a great many of the leading men of the clan, worthily executed to death for their offences, is thankfully acknowledged by act of Parliament, 1607, chap. 16, and rewarded with a grant of twenty chalders of victual out of the lands of Kintire.

The MacGregors, notwithstanding the letters of fire and sword, and orders for military execution repeatedly directed against them by the Scottish legislature, who apparently lost all the calmness of conscious dignity and security, and could not even name the outlawed clan without vituperation, showed no inclination to be blotted out of the roll of clanship. They submitted to the law, indeed, so far as to take the names of the neighbouring families amongst whom they happened to live, nominally becoming, as the case might render it most convenient, Drummonds, Campbells, Grahams, Buchanans, Stewarts, and the like; but to all intents and purposes of combination and mutual attachment, they remained the clan Gregor, united together for right or wrong, and menacing with the general vengeance of their race, whomsoever committed aggressions against any individual of their number.

They continued to take and give offence with as little hesitation as before the legislative dispersion which had been attempted, as appears from the preamble to statute 1633, chapter 30, setting forth, that the clan Gregor, which had been suppressed and reduced to quietness by the great care of the late King James of eternal memory, had nevertheless broken out again, in the counties of Perth, Stirling, Clackmannan, Monteith, Lennox, Angus, and Mearns; for which reason the statute re-establishes the disabilities attached to the clan, and grants a new commission for enforcing the laws against that wicked and rebellious race.

Notwithstanding the extreme severities of King James I. and Charles I. against this unfortunate people, who were rendered furious by proscription, and then punished for yielding to the passions which had been wilfully irritated, the MacGregors to a man attached themselves during the civil war to the cause of the latter monarch. Their bards have ascribed this to the native respect of the MacGregors for the crown of Scotland, which their ancestors once wore, and have appealed to their armorial bearings, which display a pine-tree, crossed saltire wise with a naked sword, the point of which supports a royal crown. But, without denying that such motives may have had their weight, we are disposed to think, that a war which opened the low country to the raids of the clan Gregor would have more charms for them than any inducement to espouse the cause of the Covenanters, which would have brought them into contact with Highlanders as fierce as themselves, and having as little to lose. Patrick MacGregor, their leader, was the son of a distinguished chief, named Duncan Abbarach, to whom Montrose wrote letters as to his trusty and special friend, expressing his reliance on his devoted loyalty, with an assurance, that when once his Majesty's affairs were placed upon a permanent footing, the grievances of the clan MacGregor should be redressed.

At a subsequent period of these melancholy times, we find the clan Gregor claiming the immunities

INTRODUCTION

of other tribes, when summoned by the Scottish Parliament to resist the invasion of the Commonwealth's army, in 1651. On the last day of March in that year, a supplication to the King and Parliament, from Calum MacCondachie Vich Euen, and Euen MacCondachie Euen, in their own name, and that of the whole name of MacGregor, set forth, that while, in obedience to the orders of Parliament, enjoining all clans to come out in the present service under their chieftains, for the defence of religion, king, and kingdoms, the petitioners were drawing their men to guard the passes at the head of the river Forth, they were interfered with by the Earl of Athole and the Laird of Buchanan, who had required the attendance of many of the clan Gregor upon their arrays. This interference was, doubtless, owing to the change of name, which seems to have given rise to the claim of the Earl of Athole and the Laird of Buchanan to muster the MacGregors under their banners, as Murrays or Buchanans. It does not appear that the petition of the MacGregors, to be permitted to come out in a body as other clans, received any answer. But upon the Restoration, King Charles, in the first Scottish Parliament of his reign, (statute 1661, chap. 195,) annulled the various acts against the clan Gregor, and restored them to the full use of their family name, and the other privileges of liege subjects, setting forth, as a reason for this lenity, that those who were formerly designed MacGregors, had, during the late troubles, conducted themselves with such loyalty and affection to his Majesty, as might justly wipe off all memory of former miscarriages, and take away all marks of reproach for the same.

It is singular enough, that it seems to have aggravated the feelings of the non - conforming Presbyterians, when the penalties which were most unjustly imposed upon themselves were relaxed towards the poor MacGregors; so little are the best men, any more than the worst, able to judge with impartiality of the same measures, as applied to themselves, or to others. Upon the Revolution, an influence inimical to this unfortunate clan, said to be the same with that which afterwards dictated the massacre of Glencoe, occasioned the re-enaction of the penal statutes against the MacGregors. There are no reasons given why these highly penal acts should have been renewed; nor is it alleged that the clan had been guilty of late irregularities. Indeed, there is some reason to think that the clause was formed of set purpose, in a shape which should elude observation; for, though containing conclusions fatal to the rights of so many Scottish subjects, it is neither mentioned in the title nor the rubric of the Act of Parliament in which it occurs, and is thrown briefly in at the close of the statute 1693, chap. 61, entitled, an Act for the Justiciary in the Highlands.

It does not, however, appear that after the Revolution the acts against the clan were severely enforced; and in the latter half of the eighteenth century, they were not enforced at all. Commissioners of supply were named in Parliament by the proscribed title of MacGregor, and decrees of courts of justice were pronounced, and legal deeds entered into, under the same appellative. The MacGregors, however, while the laws continued in the statute book, still suffered under the deprivation of the name which was their birth-right, and some attempts were made for the purpose of adopting another, MacAlpine or Grant being proposed as the title of the whole clan in future. No agreement, however, could be entered into; and the evil was submitted to as a matter of necessity, until full redress was obtained from the British Parliament, by an act abolishing for ever the penal statutes which had been so long imposed upon this ancient race. This statute, well merited by the services of many a gentleman of the clan in behalf of their King and country, was passed, and the clan proceeded to act upon it with the same spirit of ancient times, which had made them suffer severely under a deprivation that would have been deemed of little consequence by a great part of their fellow subjects.

They entered into a deed recognising John Murray of Lanrick, Esq. (afterwards Sir John MacGregor, Baronet), representative of the family of Glencarnock, as lawfully descended from the ancient stock and blood of the Lairds and Lords of MacGregor, and therefore acknowledged him as their chief on all lawful occasions and causes whatsoever. This deed was subscribed by eight hundred and twenty-six persons of the name of MacGregor, capable of bearing arms. A great many of the clan during the last war formed themselves into what was called the Clan Alpine regiment, raised in 1799, under the command of their Chief, and his brother Colonel MacGregor.

Having briefly noticed the history of this clan, which presents a rare and interesting example of the indelible character of the patriarchal system, the author must now offer some notices of the individual who gives name to these volumes.

In giving an account of a Highlander, his pedigree is first to be considered. That of Rob Roy was deduced from Ciar Mohr, the great mouse-coloured man, who is accused by tradition of having slain the young students at the battle of Glenfruin.

Without puzzling ourselves and our readers with

INTRODUCTION

the intricacies of Highland genealogy, it is enough to say, that after the death of Allaster MacGregor of Glenstrae, the clan, discouraged by the unremitting persecution of their enemies, seem not to have had the means of placing themselves under the command of a single CHIEF. According to their places of residence and immediate descent, the several families were led and directed by *Chieftains*, which, in the Highland acceptation, signifies the head of a particular branch of a tribe, in opposition to *Chief*, who is the leader and commander of the whole name.

The family and descendants of Dugald Ciar Mohr lived chiefly in the mountains between Loch Lomond and Loch Katrine, and occupied a good deal of property there, whether by sufferance, by the right of the sword, which it was never safe to dispute with them, or by legal titles of various kinds, it would be useless to inquire and unnecessary to detail. Enough, there they certainly were; a people whom their most powerful neighbours were desirous to conciliate, their friendship in peace being very necessary to the quiet of the vicinage, and their assistance in war equally prompt and effectual.

Rob Roy MacGregor Campbell, which last name he bore in consequence of the Acts of Parliament abolishing his own, was the younger son of Donald

Mac-Gregor of Glengyle, said to have been a Lieutenant-Colonel, (probably in the service of James II.) by his wife, a daughter of Campbell of Glenfalloch. Rob's own designation was of Inversnaid; but he appears to have acquired a right of some kind or other to the property or possession of Craig Royston, a domain of rock and forest, lying on the east side of Loch Lomond, where that beautiful lake stretches into the dusky mountains of Glenfalloch.

The time of his birth is uncertain. But he is said to have been active in the scenes of war and plunder which succeeded the Revolution; and tradition affirms him to have been the leader in a predatory incursion into the parish of Kippen, in the Lennox, which took place in the year 1691. It was of almost a bloodless character, only one person losing his life; but from the extent of the depredation, it was long distinguished by the name of the Her'-ship, or devastation, of Kippen.* The time of his death is also uncertain, but as he is said to have survived the year 1733, and died an aged man, it is probable he may have been twenty-five about the time of the Her'-ship of Kippen, which would assign his birth to the middle of the 17th century.

---

* See Statistical Account of Scotland, vol. xviii. page 332. Parish of Kippen.

INTRODUCTION

In the more quiet times which succeeded the Revolution, Rob Roy, or Red Robert, seems to have exerted his active talents, which were of no mean order, as a drover or trader in cattle to a great extent. It may well be suppossed that in those days no Lowland, much less English drovers, ventured to enter the Highlands. The cattle, which were the staple commodity of the mountains, were escorted down to fairs, on the borders of the Lowlands, by a party of Highlanders, with their arms rattling around them; and who dealt, however, in all honour and good faith with their Southern customers. A fray, indeed, would sometimes arise, when the Lowlandmen, chiefly Borderers, who had to supply the English market, used to dip their bonnets in the next brook, and wrapping them round their hands, oppose their cudgels to the naked broadswords, which had not always the superiority. I have heard from aged persons, who had been engaged in such affrays, that the Highlanders used remarkably fair play, never using the point of the sword, far less their pistols or daggers; so that

> With many a stiff thwack and many a bang,
> Hard crabtree and cold iron rang.

A slash or two, or a broken head, was easily accommodated, and as the trade was of benefit to both parties, trifling skirmishes were not allowed to interrupt its harmony. Indeed it was of vital interest to the Highlanders, whose income, so far as derived from their estates, depended entirely on the sale of black cattle; and a sagacious and experienced dealer benefited not only himself, but his friends and neighbours, by his speculations. Those of Rob Roy were for several years so successful, as to inspire general confidence, and raise him in the estimation of the country in which he resided.

His importance was increased by the death of his father, in consequence of which he succeeded to the management of his nephew Gregor MacGregor of Glengyle's property, and, as his tutor, to such influence with the clan and following as was due to the representative of Dougal Ciar. Such influence was the more uncontrolled, that this family of the MacGregors seem to have refused adherence to MacGregor of Glencarnock, the ancestor of the present Sir Ewan MacGregor, and asserted a kind of independence.

It was at this time that Rob Roy acquired an interest by purchase, wadset, or otherwise, to the property of Craig Royston already mentioned. He was in particular favour, during this prosperous period of his life, with his nearest and most powerful neighbour, James first Duke of Montrose, from whom he received many marks of regard. His

INTRODUCTION

Grace consented to give his nephew and himself a right of property on the estates of Glengyle and Inversnaid, which they had till then only held as kindly tenants. The Duke, also, with a view to the interest of the country and his own estate, supported our adventurer by loans of money to a considerable amount, to enable him to carry on his speculations in the cattle trade.

Unfortunately, that species of commerce was and is liable to sudden fluctuations; and Rob Roy was — by a sudden depression of markets, and, as a friendly tradition adds, by the bad faith of a partner named MacDonald, whom he had imprudently received into his confidence, and intrusted with a considerable sum of money—rendered totally insolvent. He absconded, of course,—not empty-handed, if it be true, as stated in an advertisement for his apprehension, that he had in his possession sums to the amount of £1000 sterling, obtained from several noblemen and gentlemen under pretence of purchasing cows for them in the Highlands. This advertisement appeared in June 1712, and was several times repeated. It fixes the period when Rob Roy exchanged his commercial adventures for speculations of a very different complexion.*

He appears at this period first to have removed, from his ordinary dwelling at Inversnaid, ten or

---

* See Appendix No. I.

twelve Scots miles (which is double the number of English) farther into the Highlands, and commenced the lawless sort of life which he afterwards followed. The Duke of Montrose, who conceived himself deceived and cheated by MacGregor's conduct, employed legal means to recover the money lent to him. Rob Roy's landed property was attached by the regular form of legal procedure, and his stock and furniture made the subject of arrest and sale.

It is said that this diligence of the law, as it is called in Scotland, which the English more bluntly term distress, was used in this case with uncommon severity, and that the legal satellites, not usually the gentlest persons in the world, had insulted Mac-Gregor's wife, in a manner which would have aroused a milder man than he to thoughts of unbounded vengeance. She was a woman of fierce and haughty temper, and is not unlikely to have disturbed the officers in the execution of their duty, and thus to have incurred ill treatment, though, for the sake of humanity, it is to be hoped that the story sometimes told is a popular exaggeration. It is certain that she felt extreme anguish at being expelled from the banks of Loch Lomond, and gave vent to her feelings in a fine piece of pipe-music, still well known to amateurs by the name of 'Rob Roy's Lament.'

INTRODUCTION

The fugitive is thought to have found his first place of refuge in Glen Dochart, under the Earl of Breadalbane's protection; for though that family had been active agents in the destruction of the MacGregors in former times, they had of late years sheltered a great many of the name in their old possessions. The Duke of Argyle was also one of Rob Roy's protectors, so far as to afford him, according to the Highland phrase, wood and water —the shelter, namely, that is afforded by the forests and lakes of an inaccessible country.

The great men of the Highlands in that time, besides being anxiously ambitious to keep up what was called their Following, or military retainers, were also desirous to have at their disposal men of resolute character, to whom the world and the world's law were no friends, and who might at times ravage the lands or destroy the tenants of a feudal enemy, without bringing responsibility on their patrons. The strife between the names of Campbell and Graham, during the civil wars of the seventeenth century, had been stamped with mutual loss and inveterate enmity. The death of the great Marquis of Montrose on the one side, the defeat at Inverlochy, and cruel plundering of Lorn, on the other, were reciprocal injuries not likely to be forgotten. Rob Roy was, therefore, sure of refuge in the country of the Campbells, both

as having assumed their name, as connected by his
mother with the family of Glenfalloch, and as an
enemy to the rival house of Montrose. The extent
of Argyle's possessions, and the power of retreating
thither in any emergency, gave great encouragement to the bold schemes of revenge which he
had adopted.

This was nothing short of the maintenance of
a predatory war against the Duke of Montrose,
whom he considered as the author of his exclusion
from civil society, and of the outlawry to which
he had been sentenced by letters of horning and
caption, (legal writs so called,) as well as the seizure
of his goods, and adjudication of his landed property.
Against his Grace, therefore, his tenants, friends,
allies, and relatives, he disposed himself to employ
every means of annoyance in his power; and though
this was a circle sufficiently extensive for active
depredation, Rob, who professed himself a Jacobite,
took the liberty of extending his sphere of operations against all whom he chose to consider as
friendly to the revolutionary government, or to
that most obnoxious of measures — the Union of
the Kingdoms. Under one or other of these pre-
texts, all his neighbours of the Lowlands who had
any thing to lose, or were unwilling to compound
for security, by paying him an annual sum for protection or forbearance, were exposed to his ravages.

INTRODUCTION

The country in which this private warfare, or system of depredation, was to be carried on, was, until opened up by roads, in the highest degree favourable for his purpose. It was broken up into narrow valleys, the habitable part of which bore no proportion to the huge wildernesses of forest, rocks, and precipices by which they were encircled, and which was, moreover, full of inextricable passes, morasses, and natural strengths, unknown to any but the inhabitants themselves, where a few men acquainted with the ground were capable, with ordinary address, of baffling the pursuit of numbers.

The opinions and habits of the nearest neighbours to the Highland line were also highly favourable to Rob Roy's purpose. A large proportion of them were of his own clan of MacGregor, who claimed the property of Balquhidder, and other Highland districts, as having been part of the ancient possessions of their tribe; though the harsh laws, under the severity of which they had suffered so deeply, had assigned the ownership to other families. The civil wars of the seventeenth century had accustomed these men to the use of arms, and they were peculiarly brave and fierce from remembrance of their sufferings. The vicinity of a comparatively rich Lowland district gave also great temptations to incursion. Many belonging to other clans, habituated to contempt of industry, and to the use of arms, drew towards an unprotected frontier which promised facility of plunder; and the state of the country, now so peaceable and quiet, verified at that time the opinion which Dr. Johnson heard with doubt and suspicion, that the most disorderly and lawless districts of the Highlands were those which lay nearest to the Lowland line. There was, therefore, no difficulty in Rob Roy, descended of a tribe which was widely dispersed in the country we have described, collecting any number of followers whom he might be able to keep in action, and to maintain by his proposed operations.

He himself appears to have been singularly adapted for the profession which he proposed to exercise. His stature was not of the tallest, but his person was uncommonly strong and compact. The greatest peculiarities of his frame were the breadth of his shoulders, and the great and almost disproportioned length of his arms; so remarkable, indeed, that it was said he could, without stooping, tie the garters of his Highland hose, which are placed two inches below the knee. His countenance was open, manly, stern at periods of danger, but frank and cheerful in his hours of festivity. His hair was dark red, thick, and frizzled, and curled short around the face. His fashion of dress showed, of course, the knees and upper part of the leg, which was described to me as resembling that of a Highland bull, hirsute, with red hair, and evincing muscular strength similar to that animal. To these personal qualifications must be added a masterly use of the Highland sword, in which his length of arm gave him great advantage, and a perfect and intimate knowledge of all the recesses of the wild country in which he harboured, and the character of the various individuals, whether friendly or hostile, with whom he might come in contact.

His mental qualities seem to have been no less adapted to the circumstances in which he was placed. Though the descendant of the blood-thirsty Ciar Mohr, he inherited none of his ancestor's ferocity. On the contrary, Rob Roy avoided every appearance of cruelty, and it is not averred that he was ever the means of unnecessary bloodshed, or the actor in any deed which could lead the way to it. His schemes of plunder were contrived and executed with equal boldness and sagacity, and were almost universally successful, from the skill with which they were laid, and the secrecy and rapidity with which they were executed. Like Robin Hood of England, he was a kind and gentle robber, and, while he took from the rich, was liberal in relieving the poor. This might in part be policy; but the universal tradition of the country speaks it to have arisen from a better motive. All whom I have conversed with, and I have in my youth seen some who knew Rob Roy personally, gave him the character of a benevolent and humane man 'in his way.'

His ideas of morality were those of an Arab chief, being such as naturally arose out of his wild education. Supposing Rob Roy to have argued on the tendency of the life which he pursued, whether from choice or from necessity, he would doubtless have assumed to himself the character of a brave man, who, deprived of his natural rights by the partiality of laws, endeavoured to assert them by the strong hand of natural power; and he is most felicitously described as reasoning thus, in the high-toned poetry of my gifted friend Wordsworth:

> Say, then, that he was wise as brave,
>   As wise in thought as bold in deed;
> For in the principles of things
>   *He* sought his moral creed.
>
> Said generous Rob, 'What need of Books?
>   Burn all the statutes and their shelves!
> They stir us up against our kind,
>   And worse, against ourselves.
>
> 'We have a passion, make a law,
>   Too false to guide us or control;
> And for the law itself we fight,
>   In bitterness of soul.
>
> 'And puzzled, blinded, then we lose
>   Distinctions that are plain and few;
> These find I graven on my heart,
>   That tells me what to do.

XLVIII

INTRODUCTION

'The creatures see of flood and field,
    And those that travel on the wind;
With them no strife can last; they live
    In peace, and peace of mind.

'For why? Because the good old rule
    Sufficeth them; the simple plan,
That they should take who have the power,
    And they should keep who can.

'A lesson which is quickly learn'd,
    A signal through which all can see;
Thus, nothing here provokes the strong
    To wanton cruelty.

'And freakishness of mind is check'd,
    He tamed who foolishly aspires,
While to the measure of his might
    Each fashions his desires.

'All kinds and creatures stand and fall
    By strength of prowess or of wit;
'Tis God's appointment who must sway,
    And who is to submit.

'Since then,' said Robin, 'right is plain,
    And longest life is but a day,
To have my ends, maintain my rights,
    I'll take the shortest way.'

And thus among these rocks he lived,
    Through summer's heat and winter's snow:
The eagle, he was lord above,
    And Rob was lord below.

We are not, however, to suppose the character
of this distinguished outlaw to be that of an actual
hero, acting uniformly and consistently on such

moral principles as the illustrious bard who, standing by his grave, has vindicated his fame. On the contrary, as is common with barbarous chiefs, Rob Roy appears to have mixed his professions of principle with a large alloy of craft and dissimulation, of which his conduct during the civil war is sufficient proof. It is also said, and truly, that although his courtesy was one of his strongest characteristics, yet sometimes he assumed an arrogance of manner which was not easily endured by the high-spirited men to whom it was addressed, and drew the daring outlaw into frequent disputes, from which he did not always come off with credit. From this it has been inferred, that Rob Roy was more of a bully than a hero, or at least that he had, according to the common phrase, his fighting days. Some aged men who knew him well, have described him also as better at a *taich-tulzie*, or scuffle within doors, than in mortal combat. The tenor of his life may be quoted to repel this charge; while, at the same time, it must be allowed, that the situation in which he was placed rendered him prudently averse to maintaining quarrels, where nothing was to be had save blows, and where success would have raised up against him new and powerful enemies, in a country where revenge was still considered as a duty rather than a crime. The power of commanding his passions, on such

occasions, far from being inconsistent with the part
which MacGregor had to perform, was essentially
necessary, at the period when he lived, to prevent
his career from being cut short.

I may here mention one or two occasions on
which Rob Roy appears to have given way in the
manner alluded to. My late venerable friend, John
Ramsay of Ochtertyre, alike eminent as a classical
scholar and as an authentic register of the ancient
history and manners of Scotland, informed me,
that on occasion of a public meeting at a bonfire
in the town of Doune, Rob Roy gave some offence
to James Edmondstone of Newton, the same gentleman who was unfortunately concerned in the
slaughter of Lord Rollo, (See Maclaurin's Criminal
Trials, No. IX.,) when Edmondstone compelled
MacGregor to quit the town on pain of being
thrown by him into the bonfire. 'I broke one
of your ribs on a former occasion,' said he, 'and
now, Rob, if you provoke me farther, I will break
your neck.' But it must be remembered that
Edmondstone was a man of consequence in the
Jacobite party, as he carried the royal standard of
James VII. at the battle of Sherriff-muir, and also,
that he was near the door of his own mansion-
house, and probably surrounded by his friends and
adherents. Rob Roy, however, suffered in reputation for retiring under such a threat.

Another well-vouched case is that of Cunningham of Boquhan.

Henry Cunningham, Esq. of Boquhan, was a gentleman of Stirlingshire, who, like many *exquisites* of our own time, united a natural high spirit and daring character with an affectation of delicacy of address and manners amounting to foppery.* He chanced to be in company with Rob Roy, who, either in contempt of Boquhan's supposed effeminacy, or because he thought him a safe person to fix a quarrel on, (a point which Rob's enemies alleged he was wont to consider,) insulted him so grossly that a challenge passed between them. The goodwife of the clachan had hidden Cunningham's sword, and, while he rummaged the house in quest of his own or some other, Rob Roy went to the Shieling

---

* His courage and affectation of foppery were united, which is less frequently the case, with a spirit of innate modesty. He is thus described in Lord Binning's satirical verses, entitled 'Argyle's Levee':

> ' Six times had Harry bow'd unseen
>   Before he dared advance ;
> The Duke then, turning round well pleased,
>   Said, ' Sene you've been in France ;
> A more polite and jaunty man
>   I never saw before ';
> Then Harry bow'd, and blush'd, and bow'd,
>   And strutted to the door.'

See a Collection of Original Poems, by Scotch Gentlemen, vol. ii. page 125.

Hill, the appointed place of combat, and paraded there with great majesty, waiting for his antagonist. In the meantime, Cunningham had rummaged out an old sword, and, entering the ground of contest in all haste, rushed on the outlaw with such unexpected fury that he fairly drove him off the field, nor did he show himself in the village again for some time. Mr. MacGregor Stirling has a softened account of this anecdote in his new edition of Nimmo's Stirlingshire; still he records Rob Roy's discomfiture.

Occasionally Rob Roy suffered disasters, and incurred great personal danger. On one remarkable occasion he was saved by the coolness of his lieutenant, Macanaleister, or Fletcher, the *Little John* of his band—a fine active fellow, of course, and celebrated as a marksman. It happened that MacGregor and his party had been surprised and dispersed by a superior force of horse and foot, and the word was given to 'split and squander.' Each shifted for himself, but a bold dragoon attached himself to pursuit of Rob, and overtaking him, struck at him with his broadsword. A plate of iron in his bonnet saved the MacGregor from being cut down to the teeth; but the blow was heavy enough to bear him to the ground, crying as he fell, 'O, Macanaleister, is there naething in her?' (*i.e.* in the gun). The trooper, at the same time exclaiming, 'D—n ye, your mother never wrought your night-cap!' had his arm raised for a second blow, when Macanaleister fired, and the ball pierced the dragoon's heart.

Such as he was, Rob Roy's progress in his occupation is thus described by a gentleman of sense and talent, who resided within the circle of his predatory wars, had probably felt their effects, and speaks of them, as might be expected, with little of the forbearance with which, from their peculiar and romantic character, they are now regarded.

'This man (Rob Roy MacGregor) was a person of sagacity, and neither wanted stratagem nor address; and, having abandoned himself to all licentiousness, set himself at the head of all the loose, vagrant, and desperate people of that clan, in the west end of Perth and Stirlingshires, and infested those whole countries with thefts, robberies, and depredations. Very few who lived within his reach (that is, within the distance of a nocturnal expedition) could promise to themselves security, either for their persons or effects, without subjecting themselves to pay him a heavy and shameful tax of *black-mail*. He at last proceeded to such a degreee of audaciousness, that he committed robberies, raised contributions, and resented quarrels, at the head of a very considerable body of armed

INTRODUCTION

men, in open day, and in the face of the government.'*

The extent and success of these depredations
cannot be surprising, when we consider that the
scene of them was laid in a country where the
general law was neither enforced nor respected.

Having recorded that the general habit of cattle-
stealing had blinded even those of the better classes
to the infamy of the practice, and that as men's
property consisted entirely in herds, it was rendered
in the highest degree precarious, Mr. Grahame
adds,—

'On these accounts there is no culture of ground,
no improvement of pastures, and, from the same
reasons, no manufactures, no trade; in short, no
industry. The people are extremely prolific, and
therefore so numerous, that there is not business
in that country, according to its present order and
economy, for the one-half of them. Every place
is full of idle people, accustomed to arms, and lazy
in every thing but rapines and depredations. As
buddel or *aquavitæ* houses are to be found every
where through the country, so in these they saunter
away their time, and frequently consume there the
returns of their illegal purchases. Here the laws

* Mr. Grahame of Gartmore's Causes of the Disturbances in the
Highlands. See Jamieson's edition of Burt's Letters from the North
of Scotland, Appendix, vol. ii. p. 348.

have never been executed, nor the authority of the magistrate ever established. Here the officer of the law neither dare nor can execute his duty, and several places are about thirty miles from lawful persons. In short, here is no order, no authority, no government.'

The period of the Rebellion, 1715, approached soon after Rob Roy had attained celebrity. His jacobite partialities were now placed in opposition to his sense of the obligations which he owed to the indirect protection of the Duke of Argyle. But the desire of 'drowning his sounding steps amid the din of general war,' induced him to join the forces of the Earl of Mar, although his patron, the Duke of Argyle, was at the head of the army opposed to the Highland insurgents.

The MacGregors, a large sept of them at least, that of Ciar Mohr, on this occasion, were not commanded by Rob Roy, but by his nephew already mentioned, Gregor MacGregor, otherwise called James Grahame of Glengyle, and still better remembered by the Gaelic epithet of *Ghlune Dhu*, *i.e.* Black Knee, from a black spot on one of his knees, which his Highland garb rendered visible. There can be no question, however, that being then very young, Glengyle must have acted on most occasions by the advice and direction of so experienced a leader as his uncle.

INTRODUCTION

The MacGregors assembled in numbers at that period, and began even to threaten the Lowlands towards the lower extremity of Loch Lomond. They suddenly seized all the boats which were upon the lake, and, probably with a view to some enterprise of their own, drew them overland to Inversnaid, in order to intercept the progress of a large body of west-country whigs who were in arms for the government, and moving in that direction.

The whigs made an excursion for the recovery of the boats. Their forces consisted of volunteers from Paisley, Kilpatrick, and elsewhere, who, with the assistance of a body of seamen, were towed up the river Leven in long-boats belonging to the ships of war then lying in the Clyde. At Luss they were joined by the forces of Sir Humphry Colquhoun, and James Grant, his son-in-law, with their followers, attired in the Highland dress of the period, which is picturesquely described.* The whole party crossed to Craig-Royston, but the MacGregors did not offer combat. If we are to

---

* 'At night they arrived at Luss, where they were joined by Sir Humphry Colquhoun of Luss, and James Grant of Plascander, his son-in-law, followed by forty or fifty stately fellows in their short hose and belted plaids, armed each of them with a well-fixed gun on his shoulder, a strong handsome target, with a sharp-pointed steel of above half an ell in length screwed into the navel of it, on his left arm, a sturdy claymore by his side, and a pistol or two, with a dirk and knife, in his belt.'—*Rae's History of the Rebellion*, 4to, p. 287.

believe the account of the expedition given by the historian Rae, they leaped on shore at Craig-Royston with the utmost intrepidity, no enemy appearing to oppose them, and, by the noise of their drums, which they beat incessantly, and the discharge of their artillery and small arms, terrified the MacGregors, whom they appear never to have seen, out of their fastnesses, and caused them to fly in a panic to the general camp of the High-landers at Strath Fillan.* The low-country men succeeded in getting possession of the boats, at a great expenditure of noise and courage, and little risk of danger.

After this temporary removal from his old haunts, Rob Roy was sent by the Earl of Mar to Aberdeen, to raise, it is believed, a part of the clan Gregor, which is settled in that country. These men were of his own family (the race of the Ciar Mohr). They were the descendants of about three hundred MacGregors whom the Earl of Murray, about the year 1624, transported from his estates in Monteith to oppose against his enemies the MacIntoshes, a race as hardy and restless as they were themselves.

But while in the city of Aberdeen, Rob Roy met a relation of a very different class and character from those whom he was sent to summon

* See Note C. The Loch Lomond Expedition.

INTRODUCTION

to arms. This was Dr. James Gregory, (by descent a MacGregor,) the patriarch of a dynasty of professors distinguished for literary and scientific talent, and the grandfather of the late eminent physician and accomplished scholar, Professor Gregory of Edinburgh. This gentleman was at the time Professor of Medicine in King's College, Aberdeen, and son of Dr. James Gregory, distinguished in science as the inventor of the reflecting telescope. With such a family it may seem our friend Rob could have had little communion. But civil war is a species of misery which introduces men to strange bedfellows. Dr. Gregory thought it a point of prudence to claim kindred, at so critical a period, with a man so formidable and influential. He invited Rob Roy to his house, and treated him with so much kindness, that he produced in his generous bosom a degree of gratitude which seemed likely to occasion very inconvenient effects.

The Professor had a son about eight or nine years old,—a lively, stout boy of his age,—with whose appearance our Highland Robin Hood was much taken. On the day before his departure from the house of his learned relative, Rob Roy, who had pondered deeply how he might requite his cousin's kindness, took Dr. Gregory aside, and addressed him to this purport:—'My dear kinsman,

I have been thinking what I could do to show my sense of your hospitality. Now, here you have a fine spirited boy of a son, whom you are ruining by cramming him with your useless book-learning, and I am determined, by way of manifesting my great good-will to you and yours, to take him with me, and make a man of him.' The learned Professor was utterly overwhelmed when his warlike kinsman announced his kind purpose, in language which implied no doubt of its being a proposal which would be, and ought to be, accepted with the utmost gratitude. The task of apology or explanation was of a most delicate description; and there might have been considerable danger in suffering Rob Roy to perceive that the promotion with which he threatened the son was, in the father's eyes, the ready road to the gallows. Indeed, every excuse which he could at first think of—such as regret for putting his friend to trouble with a youth who had been educated in the Lowlands, and so on—only strengthened the chieftain's inclination to patronise his young kinsman, as he supposed they arose entirely from the modesty of the father. He would for a long time take no apology, and even spoke of carrying off the youth by a certain degree of kindly violence, whether his father consented or not. At length the perplexed Professor pleaded

INTRODUCTION

that his son was very young, and in an infirm
state of health, and not yet able to endure the
hardships of a mountain life; but that in another
year or two he hoped his health would be firmly
established, and he would be in a fitting condition to attend on his brave kinsman, and follow
out the splendid destinies to which he opened the
way. This agreement being made, the cousins
parted,—Rob Roy pledging his honour to carry
his young relation to the hills with him on his
next return to Aberdeenshire, and Dr. Gregory,
doubtless, praying in his secret soul that he might
never see Rob's Highland face again.

James Gregory, who thus escaped being his
kinsman's recruit, and in all probability his hench-
man, was afterwards Professor of Medicine in the
College, and, like most of his family, distinguished
by his scientific acquirements. He was rather of
an irritable and pertinacious disposition; and his
friends were wont to remark, when he showed any
symptom of these foibles, 'Ah! this comes of not
having been educated by Rob Roy.'

The connexion between Rob Roy and his classical kinsman did not end with the period of Rob's
transient power. At a period considerably subsequent to the year 1715, he was walking in the
Castle Street of Aberdeen, arm in arm with his
host, Dr. James Gregory, when the drums in the

barracks suddenly beat to arms, and soldiers were seen issuing from the barracks. ' If these lads are turning out,' said Rob, taking leave of his cousin with great composure, ' it is time for me to look after my safety.' So saying, he dived down a close, and, as John Bunyan says, ' went upon his way and was seen no more.'*

We have already stated that Rob Roy's conduct during the insurrection of 1715 was very equivocal. His person and followers were in the Highland army, but his heart seems to have been with the Duke of Argyle's. Yet the insurgents were constrained to trust to him as their only guide, when they marched from Perth towards Dumblane, with the view of crossing the Forth at what are called the Fords of Frew, and when they themselves said he could not be relied upon.

This movement to the westward, on the part of the insurgents, brought on the battle of Sherriffmuir, indecisive indeed in its immediate results,

---

* The first of these anecdotes, which brings the highest pitch of civilization so closely in contact with the half-savage state of society, I have heard told by the late distinguished Dr. Gregory; and the members of his family have had the kindness to collate the story with their recollections and family documents, and furnish the authentic particulars. The second rests on the recollection of an old man, who was present when Rob took French leave of his literary cousin on hearing the drums beat, and communicated the circumstance to Mr. Alexander Forbes, a connexion of Dr. Gregory by marriage, who is still alive.

but of which the Duke of Argyle reaped the whole advantage. In this action, it will be recollected that the right wing of the Highlanders broke and cut to pieces Argyle's left wing, while the clans on the left of Mar's army, though consisting of Stewarts, Mackenzies, and Camerons, were completely routed. During this medley of flight and pursuit, Rob Roy retained his station on a hill in the centre of the Highland position; and though it is said his attack might have decided the day, he could not be prevailed upon to charge. This was the more unfortunate for the insurgents, as the leading of a party of the Macphersons had been committed to MacGregor. This, it is said, was owing to the age and infirmity of the chief of that name, who, unable to lead his clan in person, objected to his heir-apparent, Macpherson of Nord, discharging his duty on that occasion; so that the tribe, or a part of them, were brigaded with their allies the MacGregors. While the favourable moment for action was gliding away unemployed, Mar's positive orders reached Rob Roy that he should presently attack. To which he coolly replied, 'No, no! if they cannot do it without me, they cannot do it with me.' One of the Macphersons, named Alexander, one of Rob's original profession, *videlicet* a drover, but a man of great strength and spirit, was so incensed at the inactivity of his temporary leader, that he threw off his plaid, drew his sword, and called out to his clansmen, 'Let us endure this no longer! if he will not lead you, I will.' Rob Roy replied, with great coolness, 'Were the question about driving Highland stots or kyloes, Sandie, I would yield to your superior skill; but as it respects the leading of men, I must be allowed to be the better judge.'—'Did the matter respect driving Glen-Eigas stots,' answered the Macpherson, 'the question with Rob would not be, which was to be last, but which was to be foremost.' Incensed at this sarcasm, MacGregor drew his sword, and they would have fought upon the spot if their friends on both sides had not interfered. But the moment of attack was completely lost. Rob did not, however, neglect his own private interest on the occasion. In the confusion of an undecided field of battle, he enriched his followers by plundering the baggage and the dead on both sides.

The fine old satirical ballad on the battle of Sherriff-muir does not forget to stigmatize our hero's conduct on this memorable occasion.

> Rob Roy he stood watch
> On a hill for to catch
>   The booty, for aught that I saw, man;
> For he ne'er advanced
> From the place where he stanced,
>   Till nae mair was to do there at a', man.

INTRODUCTION

Notwithstanding the sort of neutrality which Rob Roy had continued to observe during the progress of the Rebellion, he did not escape some of its penalties. He was included in the act of attainder, and the house in Breadalbane, which was his place of retreat, was burned by General Lord Cadogan, when, after the conclusion of the insurrection, he marched through the Highlands to disarm and punish the offending clans. But upon going to Inverary with about forty or fifty of his followers, Rob obtained favour, by an apparent surrender of their arms to Col. Patrick Campbell of Finnab, who furnished them and their leader with protections under his hand. Being thus in a great measure secured from the resentment of government, Rob Roy established his residence at Craig-Royston, near Loch Lomond, in the midst of his own kinsmen, and lost no time in resuming his private quarrel with the Duke of Montrose. For this purpose, he soon got on foot as many men, and well armed too, as he had yet commanded. He never stirred without a body-guard of ten or twelve picked followers, and without much effort could increase them to fifty or sixty.

The Duke was not wanting in efforts to destroy this troublesome adversary. His Grace applied to General Carpenter, commanding the forces in Scotland, and by his orders three parties of soldiers were directed from the three different points of Glasgow, Stirling, and Finlarig near Killin. Mr. Graham of Killearn, the Duke of Montrose's relation and factor, Sheriff-depute also of Dumbartonshire, accompanied the troops, that they might act under the civil authority, and have the assistance of a trusty guide well acquainted with the hills. It was the object of these several columns to arrive about the same time in the neighbourhood of Rob Roy's residence, and surprise him and his followers. But heavy rains, the difficulties of the country, and the good intelligence which the Outlaw was always supplied with, disappointed their well-concerted combination. The troops, finding the birds were flown, avenged themselves by destroying the nest. They burned Rob Roy's house, though not with impunity, for the MacGregors, concealed among the thickets and cliffs, fired on them, and killed a grenadier.

Rob Roy avenged himself for the loss which he sustained on this occasion by an act of singular audacity. About the middle of November, 1716, John Graham of Killearn, already mentioned as factor of the Montrose family, went to a place called Chapel Errock, where the tenants of the Duke were summoned to appear with their termly rents. They appeared accordingly, and the factor had received ready money to the amount of about £300, when Rob Roy entered the room at the head of an armed party. The steward endeavoured to protect the Duke's property by throwing the books of accounts and money into a garret, trusting they might escape notice. But the experienced freebooter was not to be baffled where such a prize was at stake. He recovered the books and cash, placed himself calmly in the receipt of custom, examined the accounts, pocketed the money, and gave receipts on the Duke's part, saying he would hold reckoning with the Duke of Montrose out of the damages which he had sustained by his Grace's means, in which he included the losses he had suffered, as well by the burning of his house by General Cadogan, as by the later expedition against Craig-Royston. He then requested Mr. Graham to attend him; nor does it appear that he treated him with any personal violence or even rudeness, although he informed him he regarded him as a hostage, and menaced rough usage in case he should be pursued, or in danger of being overtaken. Few more audacious feats have been performed. After some rapid changes of place, (the fatigue attending which was the only annoyance that Mr. Graham seems to have complained of,) he carried his prisoner to an island on Loch Katrine, and caused him to write to the Duke, to state that his ransom was fixed at 3400 merks, being the balance which MacGregor pretended remained due to him, after deducting all that he owed to the Duke of Montrose.

However, after detaining Mr. Graham five or six days in custody on the island, which is still called Rob Roy's Prison, and could be no comfortable dwelling for November nights, the Outlaw seems to have despaired of attaining further advantage from his bold attempt, and suffered his prisoner to depart uninjured, with the account-books, and bills granted by the tenants, taking especial care to retain the cash.*

Other pranks are told of Rob, which argue the same boldness and sagacity as the seizure of Killearn. The Duke of Montrose, weary of his insolence, procured a quantity of arms, and distributed them among his tenantry, in order that they might defend themselves against future violences. But they fell into different hands from those they were intended for. The MacGregors made separate attacks on the houses of the tenants, and disarmed them all one after another, not, as was supposed, without the consent of many of the persons so disarmed.

---

* The reader will find two original letters of the Duke of Montrose, with that which Mr. Graham of Killearn dispatched from his prison-house by the Outlaw's command, in the Appendix, No. II.

INTRODUCTION

As a great part of the Duke's rents were payable in kind, there were girnels (granaries) established for storing up the corn at Moulin, and elsewhere on the Buchanan estate. To these storehouses Rob Roy used to repair with a sufficient force, and of course when he was least expected, and insist upon the delivery of quantities of grain, sometimes for his own use, and sometimes for the assistance of the country people, always giving regular receipts in his own name, and pretending to reckon with the Duke for what sums he received.

In the meanwhile a garrison was established by government, the ruins of which may be still seen about half-way betwixt Loch Lomond and Loch Katrine, upon Rob Roy's original property of Inversnaid. Even this military establishment could not bridle the restless MacGregor. He contrived to surprise the little fort, disarm the soldiers, and destroy the fortification. It was afterwards re-established and again taken by the MacGregors under Rob Roy's nephew, Ghlune Dhu, previous to the insurrection of 1745-6. Finally, the fort of Inversnaid was a third time repaired after the extinction of civil discord; and when we find the celebrated General Wolfe commanding in it, the imagination is strongly affected by the variety of time and events which the circumstance brings simultaneously to recollection. It is now totally dismantled.*

It was not, strictly speaking, as a professed depredator that Rob Roy now conducted his operations, but as a sort of contractor for the police; in Scottish phrase, a lifter of black-mail. The nature of this contract has been described in the Novel of Waverley, and in the notes on that work. Mr. Grahame of Gartmore's description of the character may be here transcribed.

'The confusion and disorders of the country were so great, and the government so absolutely neglected it, that the sober people there were obliged to purchase some security to their effects by shameful and ignominious contracts of *black-mail*. A person who had the greatest correspondence with the thieves was agreed with to preserve the lands contracted for from thefts, for certain sums to be paid yearly. Upon this fund he employed one half of the thieves to recover stolen cattle, and the other half of them to steal, in order to make this agreement and black-mail contract necessary. The estates of those gentle-

---

* About 1792, when the author chanced to pass that way while on a tour through the Highlands, a garrison, consisting of a single veteran, was still maintained at Inversnaid. The venerable warder was reaping his barley croft in all peace and tranquillity; and when we asked admittance to repose ourselves, he told us we would find the key of *The Fort* under the door.

men who refused to contract, or give countenance
to that pernicious practice, are plundered by the
thieving part of the watch, in order to force them
to purchase their protection. Their leader calls
himself the *Captain of the Watch*, and his banditti
go by that name. And as this gives them a kind
of authority to traverse the country, so it makes
them capable of doing any mischief. These corps
through the Highlands make altogether a very
considerable body of men, inured from their infancy to the greatest fatigues, and very capable
to act in a military way when occasion offers.

' People who are ignorant and enthusiastic, who
are in absolute dependence upon their chief or
landlord, who are directed in their consciences by
Roman Catholic priests, or non-juring clergymen,
and who are not masters of any property, may easily
be formed into any mould. They fear no dangers,
as they have nothing to lose, and so can with ease
be induced to attempt any thing. Nothing can
make their condition worse; confusions and troubles
do commonly indulge them in such licentiousness,
that by these they better it.'*

As the practice of contracting for black-mail was
an obvious encouragement to rapine, and a great
obstacle to the course of justice, it was, by the

* Letters from the North of Scotland, vol. ii. pp. 344-5.

statute 1567, chap. 21, declared a capital crime, both on the part of him who levied and him who paid this sort of tax. But the necessity of the case prevented the execution of this severe law, I believe, in any one instance; and men went on submitting to a certain unlawful imposition rather than run the risk of utter ruin,—just as it is now found difficult or impossible to prevent those who have lost a very large sum of money by robbery, from compounding with the felons for restoration of a part of their booty.

At what rate Rob Roy levied black-mail, I never heard stated; but there is a formal contract by which his nephew, in 1741, agreed with various landholders of estates in the counties of Perth, Stirling, and Dumbarton, to recover cattle stolen from them, or to pay the value within six months of the loss being intimated, if such intimation were made to him with sufficient dispatch, in considera- tion of a payment of £5 on each £100 of valued rent, which was not a very heavy insurance. Petty thefts were not included in the contract; but the theft of one horse, or one head of black cattle, or of sheep exceeding the number of six, fell under the agreement.

Rob Roy's profits upon such contracts brought him in a considerable revenue in money or cattle, of which he made a popular use; for he was publicly

liberal, as well as privately beneficent. The minister of the parish of Balquhidder, whose name was Robison, was at one time threatening to pursue the parish for an augmentation of his stipend. Rob Roy took an opportunity to assure him that he would do well to abstain from this new exaction,— a hint which the minister did not fail to understand. But to make him some indemnification, MacGregor presented him every year with a cow and a fat sheep; and no scruples as to the mode in which the donor came by them, are said to have affected the reverend gentleman's conscience.

The following account of the proceedings of Rob Roy, on an application to him from one of his contractors, had in it something very interesting to me, as told by an old countryman in the Lennox who was present on the expedition. But as there is no point or marked incident in the story, and as it must necessarily be without the half-frightened, half-bewildered look with which the narrator accompanied his recollections, it may possibly lose its effect when transferred to paper.

My informant stated himself to have been a lad of fifteen, living with his father on the estate of a gentleman in the Lennox, whose name I have forgotten, in the capacity of herd. On a fine morning in the end of October, the period when such calamities were almost always to be apprehended, they found the Highland thieves had been down upon them, and swept away ten or twelve head of cattle. Rob Roy was sent for, and came with a party of seven or eight armed men. He heard with great gravity all that could be told him of the circumstances of the *creagh*, and expressed his confidence that the *herd-widdiefows** could not have carried their booty far, and that he should be able to recover them. He desired that two Lowlanders should be sent on the party, as it was not to be expected that any of his gentlemen would take the trouble of driving the cattle when he should recover possession of them. My informant and his father were dispatched on the expedition. They had no good-will to the journey; nevertheless, provided with a little food, and with a dog to help them to manage the cattle, they set off with MacGregor. They travelled a long day's journey in the direction of the mountain Benvoirlich, and slept for the night in a ruinous hut or bothy. The next morning they resumed their journey among the hills, Rob Roy directing their course by signs and marks on the heath, which my informant did not understand.

About noon, Rob commanded the armed party to halt, and to lie couched in the heather where it was thickest. 'Do you and your son,' he said

---

* Mad herdsmen, a name given to cattle stealers.

to the oldest Lowlander, 'go boldly over the hill.
You will see beneath you, in a glen on the other
side, your master's cattle feeding, it may be, with
others; gather your own together, taking care to
disturb no one else, and drive them to this place.
If any one speak to, or threaten you, tell them that
I am here at the head of twenty men.'—'But what
if they abuse us, or kill us?' said the Lowland
peasant, by no means delighted at finding the
embassy imposed on him and his son. 'If they
do you any wrong,' said Rob, 'I will never forgive
them as long as I live.' The Lowlander was by
no means content with this security, but did not
think it safe to dispute Rob's injunctions.

He and his son climbed the hill, therefore, found
a deep valley, where there grazed, as Rob had pre-
dicted, a large herd of cattle. They cautiously
selected those which their master had lost, and
took measures to drive them over the hill. As
soon as they began to remove them, they were
surprised by hearing cries and screams; and looking around in fear and trembling, they saw a
woman, seeming to have started out of the earth,
who *flyted* at them, that is, scolded them, in Gaelic.
When they contrived, however, in the best Gaelic
they could muster, to deliver the message Rob Roy
told them, she became silent, and disappeared without offering them any further annoyance. The

chief heard their story on their return, and spoke
with great complacency of the art which he possessed of putting such things to rights without
any unpleasant bustle. The party were now on
their road home, and the danger, though not the
fatigue, of the expedition was at an end.

They drove on the cattle with little repose until
it was nearly dark, when Rob proposed to halt for
the night upon a wide moor, across which a cold
north-east wind, with frost on its wing, was whist-
ling to the tune of the Pipers of Strath-Dearn.*
The Highlanders, sheltered by their plaids, lay
down in the heath comfortably enough, but the
Lowlanders had no protection whatever. Rob Roy
observing this, directed one of his followers to
afford the old man a portion of his plaid; 'for the
callant (boy), he may,' said the freebooter, 'keep
himself warm by walking about and watching the
cattle.' My informant heard this sentence with
no small distress; and as the frost wind grew
more and more cutting, it seemed to freeze the
very blood in his young veins. He had been
exposed to weather all his life, he said, but never
could forget the cold of that night; in so much
that, in the bitterness of his heart, he cursed the
bright moon for giving no heat with so much

---

* The winds which sweep a wild glen in Badenoch are so called.

INTRODUCTION

light. At length the sense of cold and weariness became so intolerable, that he resolved to desert his watch to seek some repose and shelter. With that purpose, he couched himself down behind one of the most bulky of the Highlanders, who acted as lieutenant to the party. Not satisfied with having secured the shelter of the man's large person, he coveted a share of his plaid, and by imperceptible degrees drew a corner of it round him. He was now comparatively in paradise, and slept sound till daybreak, when he awoke, and was terribly afraid on observing that his nocturnal operations had altogether uncovered the dhuinie-wassell's neck and shoulders, which, lacking the plaid which should have protected them, were covered with *cranreuch* (*i.e.* hoar frost). The lad rose in great dread of a beating, at least, when it should be found how luxuriously he had been accommodated at the expense of a principal person of the party. Good Mr. Lieutenant, however, got up and shook himself, rubbing off the hoar frost with his plaid, and muttering something of a *cauld neight*. They then drove on the cattle, which were restored to their owner without farther adventure. The above can hardly be termed a tale, but yet it contains materials both for the poet and artist.

It was perhaps about the same time that, by a rapid march into the Balquhidder hills at the head of a body of his own tenantry, the Duke of Montrose actually surprised Rob Roy, and made him prisoner. He was mounted behind one of the Duke's followers, named James Stewart, and made fast to him by a horse-girth. The person who had him thus in charge was grandfather of the intelligent man of the same name, now deceased, who lately kept the inn in the vicinity of Loch Katrine, and acted as a guide to visitors through that beautiful scenery. From him I learned the story many years before he was either a publican, or a guide, except to moorfowl shooters.—It was evening, (to resume the story,) and the Duke was pressing on to lodge his prisoner, so long sought after in vain, in some place of security, when, in crossing the Teith or Forth, I forget which, Mac-Gregor took an opportunity to conjure Stewart, by all the ties of old acquaintance and good-neighbourhood, to give him some chance of an escape from an assured doom. Stewart was moved with compassion, perhaps with fear. He slipped the girth-buckle, and Rob, dropping down from behind the horse's croupe, dived, swam, and escaped, pretty much as described in the Novel. When James Stewart came on shore, the Duke hastily demanded where his prisoner was; and as no distinct answer was returned, instantly suspected Stewart's conniv-ance at the escape of the outlaw; and, drawing a steel pistol from his belt, struck him down with a blow on the head, from the effects of which, his descendant said, he never completely recovered.

In the success of his repeated escapes from the pursuit of his powerful enemy, Rob Roy at length became wanton and facetious. He wrote a mock challenge to the Duke, which he circulated among his friends to amuse them over a bottle. The reader will find this document in the Appendix.* It is written in a good hand, and not particularly deficient in grammar or spelling. Our Southern readers must be given to understand that it was a piece of humour,—a *quiz*, in short,—on the part of the outlaw, who was too sagacious to propose such a rencontre in reality. This letter was written in the year 1719.

In the following year Rob Roy composed another epistle, very little to his own reputation, as he therein confesses having played booty during the civil war of 1715. It is addressed to General Wade, at that time engaged in disarming the Highland clans, and making military roads through the country. The letter is a singular composition. It sets out the writer's real and unfeigned desire to have offered his service to King George, but for his liability to be thrown into jail for a civil

* Appendix No. III.

debt, at the instance of the Duke of Montrose. Being thus debarred from taking the right side, he acknowledged he embraced the wrong one, upon Falstaff's principle, that since the King wanted men and the rebels soldiers, it were worse shame to be idle in such a stirring world, than to embrace the worst side, were it as black as rebellion could make it. The impossibility of his being neutral in such a debate, Rob seems to lay down as an undeniable proposition. At the same time, while he acknowledges having been forced into an unnatural rebellion against King George, he pleads that he not only avoided acting offensively against his Majesty's forces on all occasions, but, on the contrary, sent to them what intelligence he could collect from time to time; for the truth of which he refers to his Grace the Duke of Argyle. What influence this plea had on General Wade we have no means of knowing.

Rob Roy appears to have continued to live very much as usual. His fame, in the mean while, passed beyond the narrow limits of the country in which he resided. A pretended history of him appeared in London during his lifetime, under the title of the Highland Rogue. It is a catch-penny publication, bearing in front the effigy of a species of ogre, with a beard of a foot in length; and his actions are as much exaggerated as his personal

appearance. Some few of the best known adventures of the hero are told, though with little
accuracy; but the greater part of the pamphlet is
entirely fictitious. It is great pity so excellent a
theme for a narrative of the kind had not fallen
into the hands of De Foe, who was engaged at
the time on subjects somewhat similar, though
inferior in dignity and interest.

As Rob Roy advanced in years he became more
peaceable in his habits, and his nephew Ghlune Dhu,
with most of his tribe, renounced those peculiar
quarrels with the Duke of Montrose, by which his
uncle had been distinguished. The policy of that
great family had latterly been rather to attach this
wild tribe by kindness than to follow the mode of
violence which had been hitherto ineffectually resorted to. Leases at a low rent were granted to
many of the MacGregors, who had heretofore held
possessions in the Duke's Highland property merely
by occupancy; and Glengyle, (or Black-knee,) who
continued to act as collector of black-mail, managed
his police, as a commander of the Highland watch
arrayed at the charge of government. He is said
to have strictly abstained from the open and lawless depredations which his kinsman had practised.

It was probably after this state of temporary
quiet had been obtained, that Rob Roy began
to think of the concerns of his future state. He

had been bred, and long professed himself, a Protestant; but in his later years he embraced the
Roman Catholic faith, — perhaps on Mrs. Cole's
principle, that it was a comfortable religion for
one of his calling. He is said to have alleged as
the cause of his conversion, a desire to gratify the
noble family of Perth, who were then strict Catholics. Having, as he observed, assumed the name
of the Duke of Argyle, his first protector, he
could pay no compliment worth the Earl of Perth's
acceptance, save complying with his mode of religion. Rob did not pretend, when pressed closely
on the subject, to justify all the tenets of Catholi-
cism, and acknowledged that extreme unction
always appeared to him a great waste of *ulzie*, or
oil.*

In the last years of Rob Roy's life his clan was
involved in a dispute with one more powerful than
themselves. Stewart of Appin, a chief of the tribe
so named, was proprietor of a hill-farm in the
Braes of Balquhidder, called Invernenty. The
MacGregors of Rob Roy's tribe claimed a right
to it by ancient occupancy, and declared they
would oppose to the uttermost the settlement of
any person upon the farm not being of their own
name. The Stewarts came down with two hundred

---

* Such an admission is ascribed to the robber, Donald Bean Lean,
in Waverley, vol. ii. p. 294.

INTRODUCTION

men, well armed, to do themselves justice by main
force. The MacGregors took the field, but were
unable to muster an equal strength. Rob Roy,
finding himself the weaker party, asked a parley,
in which he represented that both clans were
friends to the *King*, and that he was unwilling
they should be weakened by mutual conflict, and
thus made a merit of surrendering to Appin the
disputed territory of Invernenty. Appin, accordingly, settled as tenants there, at an easy quit-rent,
the MacLarens, a family dependent on the Stewarts,
and from whose character for strength and bravery,
it was expected that they would make their right
good if annoyed by the MacGregors. When all
this had been amicably adjusted, in presence of
the two clans drawn up in arms near the Kirk
of Balquhidder, Rob Roy, apparently fearing his
tribe might be thought to have conceded too
much upon the occasion, stepped forward and
said, that where so many gallant men were met
in arms, it would be shameful to part without a
trial of skill, and therefore he took the freedom
to invite any gentleman of the Stewarts present
to exchange a few blows with him for the honour
of their respective clans. The brother-in-law of
Appin, and second chieftain of the clan, Alaster
Stewart of Invernahyle, accepted the challenge,
and they encountered with broad-sword and target

before their respective kinsmen.* The combat lasted till Rob received a slight wound in the arm, which was the usual termination of such a combat when fought for honour only, and not with a mortal purpose. Rob Roy dropped his point, and congratulated his adversary on having been the first man who ever drew blood from him. The victor generously acknowledged, that without the advantage of youth, and the agility accompanying it, he probably could not have come off with advantage.

This was probably one of Rob Roy's last exploits in arms. The time of his death is not known with certainty, but he is generally said to have survived 1738, and to have died an aged man. When he found himself approaching his final change, he expressed some contrition for particular parts of his life. His wife laughed at these scruples of conscience, and exhorted him to die like a man, as he had lived. In reply, he rebuked her for her violent passions, and the counsels she had given him. ' You have put strife,' he said, ' betwixt me and the best men of the country, and

---

* Some accounts state, that Appin himself was Rob Roy's antagonist on this occasion. My recollection, from the account of Invernahyle himself, was as stated in the text. But the period when I received the information is now so distant, that it is possible I may be mistaken. Invernahyle was rather of low stature, but very well made, athletic, and an excellent swordsman.

now you would place enmity between me and my God.'

There is a tradition, no way inconsistent with the former, if the character of Rob Roy be justly considered, that while on his death-bed, he learned that a person, with whom he was at enmity, proposed to visit him. 'Raise me from my bed,' said the invalid; 'throw my plaid around me, and bring me my claymore, dirk, and pistols—it shall never be said that a foeman saw Rob Roy MacGregor defenceless and unarmed.' His foeman, conjectured to be one of the MacLarens before and after mentioned, entered and paid his compliments, inquiring after the health of his formidable neighbour. Rob Roy maintained a cold, haughty civility during their short conference, and so soon as he had left the house, 'Now,' he said, 'all is over—let the piper play *Ha til mi tulidh*, (we return no more,)' and he is said to have expired before the dirge was finished.

This singular man died in bed in his own house, in the parish of Balquhidder. He was buried in the churchyard of the same parish, where his tombstone is only distinguished by a rude attempt at the figure of a broadsword.

The character of Rob Roy is, of course, a mixed one. His sagacity, boldness, and prudence, qualities so highly necessary to success in war, became in some degree vices from the manner in which they were employed. The circumstances of his education, however, must be admitted as some extenuation of his habitual transgressions against the law; and for his political tergiversations, he might in that distracted period plead the example of men far more powerful, and less excusable in becoming the sport of circumstances, than the poor and desperate outlaw. On the other hand, he was in the constant exercise of virtues, the more meritorious as they seem inconsistent with his general character. Pursuing the occupation of a predatory chieftain,—in modern phrase, a captain of banditti, — Rob Roy was moderate in his revenge, and humane in his successes. No charge of cruelty or bloodshed, unless in battle, is brought against his memory. In like manner, the formidable outlaw was the friend of the poor, and, to the utmost of his ability, the support of the widow and the orphan — kept his word when pledged—and died lamented in his own wild country, where there were hearts grateful for his beneficence, though their minds were not sufficiently instructed to appreciate his errors.

The author perhaps ought to stop here; but the fate of a part of Rob Roy's family was so extraordinary, as to call for a continuation of this somewhat prolix account, as affording an interesting chapter, not on Highland manners alone, but on every stage of society in which the people of a primitive and half-civilized tribe are brought into close contact with a nation, in which civilization and polity have attained a complete superiority.

Rob had five sons,—Coll, Ronald, James, Duncan, and Robert. Nothing occurs worth notice concerning three of them; but James, who was a very handsome man, seems to have had a good deal of his father's spirit, and the mantle of Dougal Ciar Mohr had apparently descended on the shoulders of Robin Oig, that is, young Robin. Shortly after Rob Roy's death, the ill-will which the MacGregors entertained against the MacLarens again broke out, at the instigation, it was said, of Rob's widow, who seems thus far to have deserved the character given to her by her husband, as an Até stirring up to blood and strife. Robin Oig, under her instigation, swore that as soon as he could get back a certain gun which had belonged to his father, and had been lately at Doune to be repaired, he would shoot MacLaren, for having presumed to settle on his mother's land.* He was as good as his word, and shot MacLaren when between the stilts of his plough, wounding him mortally.

---

* This fatal piece was taken from Robin Oig, when he was seized many years afterwards. It remained in possession of the magistrates, before whom he was brought for examination, and now makes part of a small collection of arms belonging to the author. It is a Spanish-barrelled gun, marked with the letters R. M. C. for Robert MacGregor Campbell.

The aid of a Highland leech was procured, who probed the wound with a probe made out of a castock, *i.e.* the stalk of a cole-wort or cabbage. This learned gentleman declared he would not venture to prescribe, not knowing with what shot the patient had been wounded. MacLaren died, and about the same time his cattle were houghed and his live stock destroyed in a barbarous manner.

Robin Oig, after this feat — which one of his biographers represents as the unhappy discharge of a gun—retired to his mother's house, to boast that he had drawn the first blood in the quarrel afore-said. On the approach of troops, and a body of the Stewarts, who were bound to take up the cause of their tenant, Robin Oig absconded, and escaped all search.

The doctor already mentioned, by name Callam MacInleister, with James and Ronald, brothers to the actual perpetrator of the murder, were brought to trial. But as they contrived to represent the action as a rash deed committed by the 'daft callant Rob,' to which they were not accessary, the jury found their accession to the crime was Not Proven. The alleged acts of spoil and violence on the MacLarens' cattle were also found to be unsupported by evidence. As it was proved, how-ever, that the two brothers, Ronald and James, were held and reputed thieves, they were appointed to find caution to the extent of £200, for their good behaviour for seven years.*

The spirit of clanship was at that time so strong —to which must be added the wish to secure the adherence of stout, able-bodied, and, as the Scotch phrase then went, *pretty* men—that the representative of the noble family of Perth condescended to act openly as patron of the MacGregors, and appeared as such upon their trial. So at least the author was informed by the late Robert MacIntosh, Esq., advocate. The circumstance may, however, have occurred later than 1736—the year in which this first trial took place.

Robin Oig served for a time in the 42d regiment, and was present at the battle of Fontenoy, where he was made prisoner and wounded. He was exchanged, returned to Scotland, and obtained his discharge. He afterwards appeared openly in the MacGregor's country; and, notwithstanding his outlawry, married a daughter of Graham of Drunkie, a gentleman of some property. His wife died a few years afterwards.

The insurrection of 1745 soon afterwards called the MacGregors to arms. Robert MacGregor of Glencarnoch, generally regarded as the chief of the whole name, and grandfather of Sir John, whom the clan received in that character, raised a Mac-

---

* See Note D. The Author's Expedition to Invernenty.

Gregor regiment, with which he joined the standard of the Chevalier. The race of Ciar Mohr, however, affecting independence, and commanded by Glengyle and his cousin James Roy MacGregor, did not join this kindred corps, but united themselves to the levies of the titular Duke of Perth, until William MacGregor Drummond of Bolhaldin, whom they regarded as head of their branch of Clan-Alpine, should come over from France. To cement the union after the Highland fashion, James laid down the name of Campbell and assumed that of Drummond, in compliment to Lord Perth. He was also called James Roy, after his father, and James Mohr, or Big James, from his height. His corps, the relics of his father Rob's band, behaved with great activity; with only twelve men he succeeded in surprising and burning, for the second time, the fort at Inversnaid, constructed for the express purpose of bridling the country of the MacGregors.

What rank or command James MacGregor had, is uncertain. He calls himself Major; and Chevalier Johnstone calls him Captain. He must have held rank under Ghlune Dhu, his kinsman, but his active and audacious character placed him above the rest of his brethren. Many of his followers were unarmed; he supplied the want of guns and swords with scythe-blades set straight upon their handles.

INTRODUCTION

At the battle of Prestonpans, James Roy distinguished himself. 'His company,' says Chevalier Johnstone, 'did great execution with their scythes.' They cut the legs of the horses in two; the riders through the middle of their bodies. MacGregor was brave and intrepid, but, at the same time, somewhat whimsical and singular. When advancing to the charge with his company, he received five wounds, two of them from balls that pierced his body through and through. Stretched on the ground, with his head resting on his hand, he called out loudly to the Highlanders of his company, 'My lads, I am not dead. By G——, I shall see if any of you does not do his duty.' The victory, as is well known, was instantly obtained.

In some curious letters of James Roy,* it appears that his thigh bone was broken on this occasion, and that he, nevertheless, rejoined the army with six companies, and was present at the battle of Culloden. After that defeat the clan MacGregor kept together in a body, and did not disperse till they had returned into their own country. They brought James Roy with them in a litter; and, without being particularly molested, he was permitted to reside in the MacGregor's country along with his brothers.

James MacGregor Drummond was attainted for

* Published in Blackwood's Magazine, vol. ii. page 228.

high treason with persons of more importance. But it appears he had entered into some communication with government, as, in the letters quoted, he mentions having obtained a pass from the Lord Justice Clerk in 1747, which was a sufficient protection to him from the military. The circumstance is obscurely stated in one of the letters already quoted, but may perhaps, joined to subsequent incidents, authorise the suspicion that James, like his father, could look at both sides of the cards. As the confusion of the country subsided, the Mac-Gregors, like foxes which had baffled the hounds, drew back to their old haunts, and lived unmolested. But an atrocious outrage, in which the sons of Rob Roy were concerned, brought at length on the family the full vengeance of the law.

James Roy was a married man, and had fourteen children. But his brother, Robin Oig, was now a widower; and it was resolved, if possible, that he should make his fortune by carrying off and marrying, by force if necessary, some woman of fortune from the Lowlands.

The imagination of the half-civilized Highlanders was less shocked at the idea of this particular species of violence, than might be expected from their general kindness to the weaker sex when they make part of their own families. But all their views were tinged with the idea that they lived in

a state of war; and in such a state, from the time
of the siege of Troy to 'the moment when Previsa
fell,'* the females captives are, to uncivilized victors,
the most valuable part of the booty.

> 'The wealthy are slaughter'd, the lovely are spared.'

We need not refer to the rape of the Sabines, or
to a similar instance in the Book of Judges, for
evidence that such deeds of violence have been
committed upon a large scale. Indeed, this sort of
enterprise was so common along the Highland line
as to give rise to a variety of songs and ballads.†
The annals of Ireland, as well as those of Scotland,
prove the crime to have been common in the more
lawless parts of both countries; and any woman
who happened to please a man of spirit who came
of a good house, and possessed a few chosen friends,
and a retreat in the mountains, was not permitted
the alternative of saying him nay. What is more,
it would seem that the women themselves, most
interested in the immunities of their sex, were,
among the lower classes, accustomed to regard such
marriages as that which is presently to be detailed
as 'pretty Fanny's way,' or rather, the way of
Donald with pretty Fanny. It is not a great many
years since a respectable woman, above the lower

---

* Childe Harold's Pilgrimage, Canto II.
† See Appendix, No. V

rank of life, expressed herself very warmly to the author on his taking the freedom to censure the behaviour of the MacGregors on the occasion in question. She said 'that there was no use in giving a bride too much choice upon such occasions; that the marriages were the happiest lang syne which had been done off hand.' Finally, she averred that her 'own mother had never seen her father till the night he brought her up from the Lennox, with ten head of black cattle, and there had not been a happier couple in the country.'

James Drummond and his brethren having similar opinions with the author's old acquaintance, and debating how they might raise the fallen fortunes of their clan, formed a resolution to settle their brother's fortune by striking up an advantageous marriage betwixt Robin Oig and one Jean Key, or Wright, a young woman scarce twenty years old, and who had been left about two months a widow by the death of her husband. Her property was estimated at only from 16,000 to 18,000 merks, but it seems to have been sufficient temptation to these men to join in the commission of a great crime.

This poor young victim lived with her mother in her own house at Edinbilly, in the parish of Balfron and shire of Stirling. At this place, in the night of 3d December 1750, the sons of Rob

Roy, and particularly James Mohr and Robin Oig, rushed into the house where the object of their attack was resident, presented guns, swords, and pistols to the males of the family, and terrified the women by threatening to break open the doors if Jean Key was not surrendered, as, said James Roy, 'his brother was a young fellow determined to make his fortune.' Having, at length, dragged the object of their lawless purpose from her place of concealment, they tore her from her mother's arms, mounted her on a horse before one of the gang, and carried her off in spite of her screams and cries, which were long heard after the terrified spectators of the outrage could no longer see the party retreat through the darkness. In her attempts to escape, the poor young woman threw herself from the horse on which they had placed her, and in so doing wrenched her side. They then laid her double over the pummel of the saddle, and transported her through the mosses and moors till the pain of the injury she had suffered in her side, augmented by the uneasiness of her posture, made her consent to sit upright. In the execution of this crime they stopped at more houses than one, but none of the inhabitants dared interrupt their proceedings. Amongst others who saw them was that classical and accomplished scholar the late Professor William Richardson of Glasgow, who used to describe as a terrible dream their violent and noisy entrance into the house where he was then residing. The Highlanders filled the little kitchen, brandishing their arms, demanding what they pleased, and receiving whatever they demanded. James Mohr, he said, was a tall, stern, and soldier-like man. Robin Oig looked more gentle; dark, but yet ruddy in complexion—a good-looking young savage. Their victim was so dishevelled in her dress, and forlorn in her appearance and demeanour, that he could hardly tell whether she was alive or dead.

The gang carried the unfortunate woman to Rowerdennan, where they had a priest unscrupulous enough to read the marriage service, while James Mohr forcibly held the bride up before him; and the priest declared the couple man and wife, even while she protested against the infamy of his conduct. Under the same threats of violence, which had been all along used to enforce their scheme, the poor victim was compelled to reside with the pretended husband who was thus forced upon her. They even dared to carry her to the public church of Balquhidder, where the officiating clergyman (the same who had been Rob Roy's pensioner) only asked them if they were married persons. Robert MacGregor answered in the affirmative; the terrified female was silent.

INTRODUCTION

The country was now too effectually subjected to the law for this vile outrage to be followed by the advantages proposed by the actors. Military parties were sent out in every direction to seize the MacGregors, who were for two or three weeks compelled to shift from one place to another in the mountains, bearing the unfortunate Jean Key along with them. In the mean while, the Supreme Civil Court issued a warrant sequestrating the property of Jean Key, or Wright, which removed out of the reach of the actors in the violence the prize which they expected. They had, however, adopted a belief of the poor woman's spirit being so far broken that she would prefer submitting to her condition, and adhering to Robin Oig as her husband, rather than incur the disgrace of appearing in such a cause in an open court. It was, indeed, a delicate experiment, but their kinsman Glengyle, chief of their immediate family, was of a temper averse to lawless proceedings;* and the captive's friends having had recourse to his advice, they feared that he would withdraw his protection if they refused to place the prisoner at liberty.

---

* Such, at least, was his general character; for when James Mohr, while perpetrating the violence at Edinbilly, called out, in order to overawe opposition, that Glengyle was lying in the moor with a hundred men to patronise his enterprise, Jean Key told him he lied, since she was confident Glengyle would never countenance so scoundrelly a business.

The brethren resolved therefore to liberate the unhappy woman, but previously had recourse to every measure which should oblige her, either from fear or otherwise, to own her marriage with Robin Oig. The cailliachs (old Highland hags) administered drugs, which were designed to have the effect of philtres, but were probably deleterious. James Mohr at one time threatened, that if she did not acquiesce in the match, she would find that there were enough of men in the Highlands to bring the heads of two of her uncles who were pursuing the civil lawsuit. At another time he fell down on his knees, and confessed he had been accessory to wronging her, but begged she would not ruin his innocent wife and large family. She was made to swear she would not prosecute the brethren for the offence they had committed; and she was obliged, by threats, to subscribe papers which were tendered to her, intimating that she was carried off in consequence of her own previous request.

James Mohr Drummond, accordingly, brought his pretended sister-in-law to Edinburgh, where, for some little time, she was carried about from one house to another, watched by those with whom she was lodged, and never permitted to go out alone, or even to approach the window. The Court of Session, considering the peculiarity of the case, and regarding Jean Key as being still under some forcible restraint, took her person under their own special charge, and appointed her to reside in the family of Mr. Wightman of Mauldsley, a gentleman of respectability, who was married to one of her near relatives. Two sentinels kept guard on the house day and night,—a precaution not deemed superfluous when the MacGregors were in question. She was allowed to go out whenever she chose, and to see whomsoever she had a mind, as well as the men of law employed in the civil suit on either side. When she first came to Mr. Wightman's house, she seemed broken down with affright and suffering, so changed in features that her mother hardly knew her, and so shaken in mind that she scarce could recognise her parent. It was long before she could be assured that she was in perfect safety. But when she at length received confidence in her situation, she made a judicial declaration, or affidavit, telling the full history of her wrongs, imputing to fear her former silence on the subject, and expressing her resolution not to prosecute those who had injured her, in respect of the oath which she had been compelled to take. From the possible breach of such an oath, though a compulsory one, she was relieved by the forms of Scottish jurisprudence, in that respect more equitable than those of England, prosecutions for crimes being always conducted at the expense and charge of the King, without inconvenience or cost to the private party who has sustained the wrong. But the unhappy sufferer did not live to be either accuser or witness against those who had so deeply injured her.

James Mohr Drummond had left Edinburgh so soon as his half-dead prey had been taken from his clutches. Mrs. Key, or Wright, was released from her species of confinement there, and removed to Glasgow, under the escort of Mr. Wightman. As they passed the Hill of Shotts, her escort chanced to say, 'This is a very wild spot; what if the MacGregors should come upon us?'—'God forbid!' was her immediate answer, 'the very sight of them would kill me.' She continued to reside at Glasgow, without venturing to return to her own house at Edinbilly. Her pretended husband made some attempts to obtain an interview with her, which she steadily rejected. She died on the 4th October 1751. The information for the crown hints that her decease might be the consequence of the usage she received. But there is a general report that she died of the small-pox.

In the meantime, James Mohr, or Drummond, fell into the hands of justice. He was considered as the instigator of the whole affair. Nay, the deceased had informed her friends that, on the night of her being carried off, Robin Oig, moved by her cries and tears, had partly consented to let her return, when James came up, with a pistol in his hand, and, asking whether he was such a coward as to relinquish an enterprise in which he had risked every thing to procure him a fortune, in a manner compelled his brother to persevere. James's trial took place on 13th July, 1752, and was conducted with the utmost fairness and impartiality. Several witnesses, all of the MacGregor family, swore that the marriage was performed with every appearance of acquiescence on the woman's part; and three or four witnesses, one of them sheriff-substitute of the county, swore she might have made her escape if she wished, and the magistrate stated that he offered her assistance if she felt desirous to do so. But when asked why he, in his official capacity, did not arrest the MacGregors, he could only answer, that he had not force sufficient to make the attempt.

The judicial declarations of Jean Key, or Wright, stated the violent manner in which she had been carried off, and they were confirmed by many of her friends, from her private communications with them, which the event of her death rendered good evidence. Indeed, the fact of her abduction (to use a Scottish law term) was completely proved by impartial witnesses. The unhappy woman admitted that she had pretended acquiescence in her fate on several occasions, because she dared not trust such as offered to assist her to escape, not even the sheriff-substitute.

The jury brought in a special verdict, finding that Jean Key, or Wright, had been forcibly carried off from her house, as charged in the indictment, and that the accused had failed to show that she was herself privy and consenting to this act of outrage. But they found the forcible marriage, and subsequent violence, was not proved; and also found, in alleviation of the panel's guilt in the premises, that Jean Key did afterwards acquiesce in her condition. Eleven of the jury, using the names of other four who were absent, subscribed a letter to the Court, stating it was their purpose and desire, by such special verdict, to take the panel's case out of the class of capital crimes.

Learned informations (written arguments) on the import of the verdict, which must be allowed a very mild one in the circumstances, were laid before the High Court of Justiciary. This point is very learnedly debated in these pleadings by Mr. Grant, Solicitor for the Crown, and the celebrated Mr. Lockhart, on the part of the prisoner; but James Mohr did not wait the event of the Court's decision.

He had been committed to the Castle of Edinburgh on some reports that an escape would be attempted. Yet he contrived to achieve his liberty even from that fortress. His daughter had the address to enter the prison, disguised as a cobbler, bringing home work as she pretended. In this cobbler's dress her father quickly arrayed himself. The wife and daughter of the prisoner were heard by the sentinels scolding the supposed cobbler for having done his work ill, and the man came out with his hat slouched over his eyes, and grumbling, as if at the manner in which they had treated him. In this way the prisoner passed all the guards without suspicion, and made his escape to France. He was afterwards outlawed by the Court of Justiciary, which proceeded to the trial of Duncan MacGregor, or Drummond, his brother, 15th January, 1753. The accused had unquestionably been with the party which carried off Jean Key; but no evidence being brought which applied to him individually and directly, the jury found him not guilty, and nothing more is known of his fate.

That of James MacGregor, who, from talent and activity, if not by seniority, may be considered as head of the family, has been long misrepresented, as it has been generally averred in Law Reports, as well as elsewhere, that his outlawry was reversed, and that he returned and died in Scotland. But the curious letters published in Blackwood's Magazine for December, 1817, show this to be an error.

The first of these documents is a petition to Charles Edward. It is dated 20th September, 1753, and pleads his service to the cause of the Stewarts, ascribing his exile to the persecution of the Hanoverian Government, without any allusion to the affair of Jean Key, or the Court of Justiciary. It is stated to be forwarded by MacGregor Drummond of Bohaldie, whom, as before mentioned, James Mohr acknowledged as his chief.

The effect which this petition produced does not appear. Some temporary relief was perhaps obtained. But, soon after, this daring adventurer was engaged in a very dark intrigue against an exile of his own country, and placed pretty nearly in his own circumstances. A remarkable Highland story must be here briefly alluded to. Mr. Campbell, of Glenure, who had been named factor for Government on the forfeited estates of Stewart of Ardshiel, was shot dead by an assassin as he passed through the wood of Lettermore, after crossing the ferry of Ballichulish. A gentleman, named James Stewart, a natural brother of Ardshiel the forfeited person, was tried as being accessory to the murder, and condemned and executed upon very doubtful evidence; the heaviest part of which only amounted to the accused person having assisted a nephew of his own, called Allan Breck Stewart, with money to escape after the deed was done. Not satisfied with this vengeance, which was obtained in a manner little to the honour of the dispensation of justice at the time, the friends of the deceased Glenure were eagerly desirous to obtain possession of the person of Allan Breck Stewart, supposed to be the actual homicide. James Mohr Drummond was secretly applied to to trepan Stewart to the sea-coast, and bring him over to Britain to almost certain death. Drummond MacGregor had kindred connexions with the slain Glenure; and, besides, the MacGregors and Campbells had been friends of late, while the former clan and the Stewarts had, as we have seen, been recently at feud; lastly, Robert Oig was now in custody at Edinburgh, and James was desirous to do some service by which his brother might be saved. The joint force of these motives may, in James's estimation of right and wrong, have been some vindication for engaging in such an enterprise, although, as must be necessarily supposed, it could only be executed by treachery of a gross description. MacGregor stipulated for a license to return to England, promising to bring Allan Breck thither along with him. But the intended victim was put upon his guard by two countrymen, who suspected James's intentions towards him. He escaped from his kidnapper, after, as MacGregor alleged, robbing his portmanteau of some clothes and four snuff-boxes. Such a charge, it may be observed, could scarce have been made unless the parties had been living on a footing of intimacy, and had access to each other's baggage.

Although James Drummond had thus missed his blow in the matter of Allan Breck Stewart, he used his license to make a journey to London, and had an interview, as he avers, with Lord Holdernesse. His Lordship, and the Under-Secretary, put many puzzling questions to him; and, as he says, offered him a situation, which would bring him bread, in the Government's service. This office was advantageous as to emolument; but in the opinion of James Drummond, his acceptance of it would have been a disgrace to his birth, and have rendered him a scourge to his country. If such a tempting offer and sturdy rejection had any foundation in fact, it probably relates to some plan of espionage on the Jacobites, which the Government might hope to carry on by means of a man who, in the matter of Allan Breck Stewart, had shown no great nicety of feeling. Drummond MacGregor was so far accommodating as to intimate his willingness to act in any station in which other gentlemen of honour served, but not otherwise; an answer which, compared with some passages of his past life, may remind the reader of Ancient Pistol standing upon his reputation.

INTRODUCTION

Having thus proved intractable, as he tells the story, to the proposals of Lord Holdernesse, James Drummond was ordered instantly to quit England.

On his return to France his condition seems to have been utterly disastrous. He was seized with fever and gravel, ill consequently in body, and weakened and dispirited in mind. Allan Breck Stewart threatened to put him to death in revenge of the designs he had harboured against him.* The Stewart clan were in the highest degree unfriendly to him; and his late expedition to London had been attended with many suspicious circumstances, amongst which it was not the slightest that he had kept his purpose secret from his chief Bohaldie. His intercourse with Lord Holdernesse was suspicious. The Jacobites were probably, like Don Bernard de Castel Blazo, in Gil Blas, little disposed to like those who kept company with Alguazils. MacDonnell, of Lochgarry, a man of unquestioned honour, lodged an information against James Drummond before the High Bailie of Dunkirk, accusing him of being a spy, so that he found himself obliged to leave that town and come to Paris, with only the sum of thirteen livres for his immediate subsistence, and with absolute beggary staring him in the face.

We do not offer the convicted common thief,

* See Note E. Allan Breck Stewart.

the accomplice in MacLaren's assassination, or the manager of the outrage against Jean Key, as an object of sympathy; but it is melancholy to look on the dying struggles even of a wolf or tiger, creatures of a species directly hostile to our own; and, in like manner, the utter distress of this man, whose faults may have sprung from a wild system of education, working on a haughty temper, will not be perused without some pity. In his last letter to Bohaldie, dated Paris, 25th September, 1754, he describes his state of destitution as absolute, and expresses himself willing to exercise his talents in breaking or breeding horses, or as a hunter or fowler, if he could only procure employment in such an inferior capacity till something better should occur. An Englishman may smile, but a Scotsman will sigh at the postscript, in which the poor starving exile asks the loan of his patron's bagpipes that he might play over some of the melancholy tunes of his own land. But the effect of music arises, in a great degree, from association, and sounds which might jar the nerves of a Londoner or Parisian, bring back to the Highlander his lofty mountain, wild lake, and the deeds of his fathers of the glen. To prove MacGregor's claim to our reader's compassion, we here insert the last part of the letter alluded to.

'By all appearance I am born to suffer crosses,

and it seems they're not at an end; for such is my wretched case at present, that I do not know earthly where to go or what to do, as I have no subsistence to keep body and soul together. All that I have carried here is about 13 livres, and have taken a room at my old quarters in Hotel St. Pierre, Rue de Cordier. I send you the bearer, begging of you to let me know if you are to be in town soon, that I may have the pleasure of seeing you, for I have none to make application to but you alone; and all I want is, if it was possible you could contrive where I could be employed without going to entire beggary. This probably is a difficult point, yet, unless it's attended with some difficulty, you might think nothing of it, as your long head can bring about matters of much more difficulty and consequence than this. If you'd disclose this matter to your friend Mr. Buttler, it's possible he might have some employ wherein I could be of use, as I pretend to know as much of breiding and riding of horses as any in France, besides that I am a good hunter, either on horseback or by footing. You may judge my reduction, as I propose the meanest things to lend a turn till better cast up. I am sorry that I am obliged to give you so much trouble, but I hope you are very well assured that I am grateful for what you have done for me, and I leave you to

ROB ROY

judge of my present wretched case.   I am, and
shall for ever continue,

'Dear Chief, your own to command,
'JAS. MACGREGOR.

'*P.S.*—If you'd send your pipes by the bearer,
and all the other little trinkims belonging to it,
I would put them in order, and play some melancholy tunes, which I may now with safety, and
in real truth.   Forgive my not going directly to
you, for if I could have borne the seeing of yourself, I could not choose to be seen by my friends
in my wretchedness, nor by any of my acquaintance.'

While MacGregor wrote in this disconsolate
manner, Death, the sad but sure remedy for
mortal evils, and decider of all doubts and uncer-
tainties, was hovering near him.   A memorandum
on the back of the letter says the writer died about
a week after, in October, 1754.

It now remains to mention the fate of Robin
Oig, for the other sons of Rob Roy seem to have
been no way distinguished.   Robin was apprehended by a party of military from the fort of
Inversnaid, at the foot of Gartmore, and was conveyed to Edinburgh 26th May, 1753.   After a
delay, which may have been protracted by the
negotiations of James for delivering up Allan

INTRODUCTION

Breck Stewart, upon promise of his brother's life, Robin Oig, on the 24th December, 1753, was brought to the bar of the High Court of Justiciary, and indicted by the name of Robert MacGregor, *alias* Campbell, *alias* Drummond, *alias* Robert Oig; and the evidence led against him resembled exactly that which was brought by the Crown on the former trial. Robert's case was in some degree more favourable than his brother's; for, though the principal in the forcible marriage, he had yet to plead that he had shown symptoms of relenting while they were carrying Jean Key off, which were silenced by the remonstrances and threats of his harder-natured brother James. Four years had also elapsed since the poor woman died, which is always a strong circumstance in favour of the accused; for there is a sort of perspective in guilt, and crimes of an old date seem less odious than those of recent occurrence. But notwithstanding these considerations, the jury, in Robert's case, did not express any solicitude to save his life, as they had done that of James. They found him guilty of being art and part in the forcible abduction of Jean Key from her own dwelling.*

Robin Oig was condemned to death, and executed on 14th February, 1754. At the place of execution

---

* The Trials of the Sons of Rob Roy, with Anecdotes of Himself and his Family, were published at Edinburgh, 1818, in 12mo.

he behaved with great decency; and professing himself a Catholic, imputed all his misfortunes to his swerving from the true church two or three years before. He confessed the violent methods he had used to gain Mrs. Key, or Wright, and hoped his fate would stop further proceedings against his brother James.*

The newspapers observe that his body, after hanging the usual time, was delivered to his friends to be carried to the Highlands. To this the recollection of a venerable friend, recently taken from us in the fulness of years, then a schoolboy at Linlithgow, enables the author to add, that a much larger body of MacGregors than had cared to advance to Edinburgh, received the corpse at that place with the coronach, and other wild emblems of Highland mourning, and so escorted it to Balquhidder. Thus, we may conclude this long account of Rob Roy and his family, with the classic phrase,

'ITE. CONCLAMATUM EST.'

I have only to add, that I have selected the above from many anecdotes of Rob Roy, which were, and may still be, current among the mountains where he flourished; but I am far from warrant-

* James died near three months before, but his family might easily remain a long time without the news of that event.

ing their exact authenticity. Clannish partialities were very apt to guide the tongue and pen as well as the pistol and claymore, and the features of an anecdote are wonderfully softened or exaggerated, as the story is told by a MacGregor or a Campbell.

APPENDIX

No. I

ADVERTISEMENT FOR APPREHENSION OF ROB ROY

(*From the Edinburgh Evening Courant, June* 18 *to June* 21, *A.D.* 1712. *No.* 1058.)

'THAT Robert Campbell, commonly known by the name of Rob Roy MacGregor, being lately intrusted by several noblemen and gentlemen with considerable sums for buying cows for them in the Highlands, has treacherously gone off with the money, to the value of £1000 sterling, which he carries along with him. All Magistrates and Officers of his Majesty's forces are intreated to seize upon the said Rob Roy, and the money which he carries with him, until the persons concerned in the money be heard against him; and that notice be given, when he is apprehended, to the keepers of the Exchange Coffee-house at Edinburgh, and the keeper of the Coffee-house at Glasgow, where the parties concerned will be advertised, and the seizers shall be very reasonably rewarded for their pains.'

It is unfortunate that this Hue and Cry, which is afterwards repeated in the same paper, contains no description of Rob Roy's person, which, of course, we must suppose to have been pretty generally known. As it is directed against Rob Roy personally, it would seem to exclude the idea of the cattle

APPENDIX TO INTRODUCTION

being carried off by his partner, MacDonald, who would certainly have been mentioned in the advertisement, if the creditors concerned had supposed him to be in possession of the money.

No. II

LETTERS

FROM AND TO THE DUKE OF MONTROSE, RESPECTING ROB ROY'S ARREST OF MR. GRAHAME OF KILLEARN

THE DUKE OF MONTROSE TO————.*

'*Glasgow, the 21st November,* 1716.

'MY LORD,—I was surprised last night with the account of a very remarkable instance of the insolence of that very notorious rogue Rob Roy, whom your lordship has often heard named. The honour of his Majesty's government being concerned in it, I thought it my duty to acquaint your lordship of the particulars by an express.

'Mr. Grahame of Killearn (whom I have had occasion to mention frequently to you, for the good service he did last winter during the rebellion) having the charge of my Highland estate, went to Monteath, which is a part of it, on Monday last, to bring in my rents, it being usual for him to be there for two or three nights together at this time of the year, in a country house, for the conveniency of meeting the tenants, upon that account. The same night, about 9 of the clock, Rob Roy, with a party of those ruffians whom he has still kept about him since the late rebellion, surrounded the house where Mr. Grahame was with some of my tenants doing his business, ordered his men to present their guns in att the windows of the room where he was sitting, while he himself

---

* It does not appear to whom this letter was addressed. Certainly from its style and tenor, it was designed for some person high in rank and office—perhaps the King's Advocate for the time.

at the same time with others entered at the door, with cocked pistols, and made Mr. Grahame prisoner, carreing him away to the hills with the money he had got, his books and papers, and my tenants' bonds for their fines, amounting to above a thousand pounds sterling, whereof the one-half had been paid last year, and the other was to have been paid now; and att the same time had the insolence to cause him to write a letter to me (the copy of which is enclosed) offering me terms of a treaty.

'That your Lordship may have the better view of this matter, it will be necessary that I should inform you, that this fellow has now, of a long time, put himself at the head of the Clan M'Gregor, a race of people who, in all ages, have distinguished themselves beyond others, by robberies, depredations, and murders, and have been the constant harbourers and entertainers of vagabonds and loose people. From the time of the Revolution he has taken every opportunity to appear against the government, acting rather as a robber than doing any real service to those whom he pretended to appear for, and has really done more mischief to the countrie than all the other Highlanders have done.

'Some three or four years before the last rebellion broke out, being overburdened with debts, he quitted his ordinary residence, and removed some twelve or sixteen miles farther into the Highlands, putting himself under the protection of the Earl of Bredalbin. When my Lord Cadogan was in the Highlands, he ordered his house att this place to be burnt, which your Lordship sees he now places to my account.

'This obliges him to return to the same countrie he went from, being a most rugged inaccessible place, where he took up his residence anew amongst his own friends and relations; but well judging that it was possible to surprise him, he, with about forty-five of his followers, went to Inverary, and made a sham surrender of their arms to Coll. Campbell of Finab, Commander of one of the Independant Companies, and returned home with his men, each of them having the Coll.'s protection. This happened in the beginning of summer last; yet not long after he appeared with his men twice in arms, in opposition to the King's troops ; and one of those times attackt them, rescued a prisoner from them, and all this while sent abroad his party through the countrie, plundering the countrie people, and amongst the rest some of my tenants.

' Being informed of these disorders after I came to Scotland, I applied to Lieut. Genll. Carpenter, who ordered three parties from Glasgow, Stirling, and Finlarig, to march in the night by different routes, in order to surprise him and his men in their houses, which would have had its effect certainly, if the great rains that happened to fall that verie night had not retarded the march of the troops, so as some of the parties came too late to the stations that they were ordered for. All that could be done upon the occasion was to burn a countrie house, where Rob Roy then resided, after some of his clan had, from the rocks, fired upon the king's troops, by which a grenadier was killed.

' Mr. Grahame, of Killearn, being my deputy-sheriff in that countrie, went along with the party that marched from Stirling; and, doubtless, will now meet with the worse treatment from that barbarous people on that account. Besides, that he is my relation, and that they know how active he has been in the service of the government—all which, your Lordship may believe, puts me under very great concern for the gentleman, while, at the same time, I can forsee no manner of way how to relieve him, other than to leave him to chance and his own management.

' I had my thoughts before of proposing to government the building of some barracks, as the only expedient for suppressing these rebels, and securing the peace of the countrie; and in that view I spoke to Genll. Carpenter, who has now a scheme of it in his hands; and I am persuaded that will be the true method for restraining them effectually; but, in the meantime, it will be necessary to lodge some of the troops in those places, upon which I intend to write to the Generall.

'I am sensible I have troubled your Lordship with a very long letter, which I should be ashamed of, were I myself singly concerned; but where the honour of the King's Government is touched, I need make no apologie, and I shall only beg leave to add, that I am, with great respect, and truth,

'My Lord,

'yr. Lords^s. most humble and

'obedient servant,

'MONTROSE.'

COPY OF GRAHAME OF KILLEARN'S LETTER ENCLOSED
IN THE PRECEDING

'*Chappellarroch, Nov.* 19*th*, 1716.

'MAY IT PLEASE YOUR GRACE,—I am obliged to give your Grace the trouble of this, by Robert Roy's commands, being so unfortunate at present as to be his prisoner. I refer the way and manner I was apprehended, to the bearer, and shall only, in short, acquaint your Grace with the demands, which are, that your Grace shall discharge him of all soumes he owes your Grace, and give him the soume of 3400 merks for his loss and damages sustained by him, both at Craigrostown and at his house, Auchinchisallen; and that your Grace shall give your word not to trouble or prosecute him afterwards; till which time he carries me, all the money I received this day, my books and bonds for entress, not yet paid, along with him, with assurances of hard usage, if any party are sent after him. The soume I received this day, conform to the nearest computation I can make before several of the gentlemen, is £3227, 2sh. 8d. Scots, of which I gave them notes. I shall wait your Grace's return, and ever am,

'Your Grace's most obedient, faithful,

'humble servant,

Sic subscribitur,   'JOHN GRAHAME.'

CXVIII

APPENDIX TO INTRODUCTION

28th Nov. 1716.—KILLEARN'S RELEASE.

' *Glasgow, 28th Nov.* 1716.

'SIR,—Having acquainted you by my last, of the 21st instant, of what had happened to my friend Mr. Grahame of Killearn, I'm very glad now to tell you, that last night I was very agreeably surprised with Mr. Grahame's coming here himself, and giving me the first account I had had of him from the time of his being carried away. It seems Rob Roy, when he came to consider a little better of it, found that he could not mend his matters by retaining Killearn his prisoner, which could only expose him still the more to the justice of the government; and therefore thought fit to dismiss him on Sunday evening last, having kept him from the Monday night before, under a very uneasy kind of restraint, being obliged to change continually from place to place. He gave him back the books, papers, and bonds, but kept the money.

    ' I am, with great truth, Sir,
       ' your most humble servant,
           ' MONTROSE.'

No. III

CHALLENGE BY ROB ROY

ROB ROY *to ain hie and mighty Prince,* JAMES DUKE OF MONTROSE.

' IN charity to your Grace's couradge and conduct, please know, the only way to retrive both is to treat Rob Roy like himself, in appointing your place and choice of arms, that at once you may extirpate your inveterate enemy, or put a period to your punny (puny ?) life in falling gloriously by his hands. That impertinent cricks or flatterers may not brand me for challenging a man that's repute of a poor dastardly soul, let such know that I admit of the two great supporters of his character and the captain of his bands to joyne with him in the combate. Then sure your Grace wont have the impudence to clamour att court for multitudes to hunt me like a fox, under pretence that I am not to be found above ground. This saves your Grace and the troops any further trouble of searching; that is, if your ambition of glory press you to embrace this unequald venture offerd of Rob's head. But if your Grace's piety, prudence, and cowardice, forbids hazarding this gentlemanly expedient, then let your design of peace restore what you have robed from me by the tyranny of your present cituation, otherwise your overthrow as a man is determined; and advertise your friends never more to look for the frequent civility payed them, of sending them home without their arms only. Even their former cravings wont purchase that favour; so your Grace by this has peace in your offer, if the sound of war be frightful, and chuse you whilk, your good friend or mortal enemy.'

[This singular rhodomontade is enclosed in a letter to a friend of Rob Roy, probably a retainer of the Duke of Argyle in Isla, which is in these words :—]

'Sir,—Receive the enclosed paper, q^n you are taking your botle; it will divert yourself and comrades. I got noa news since I saw you, only q^t we had before about the Spanyards is like to continue. If I get any account about them I'll be sure to let you hear of it, and till then I will not write any more till I have more account. I am, Sir, your affec C^n [cousin,] and most humble servant, Rob Roy.'

'*Apryle*, 1719.

Addressed, To Mr. Patrick Anderson, } at Haig—These.

The seal, a stag—no bad emblem } of a wild catteran.

APPENDIX TO INTRODUCTION

It appears from the envelope that Rob Roy still continued to act as intelligencer to the Duke of Argyle and his agents. The war he alludes to is probably some vague report of invasion from Spain. Such rumours were likely enough to be afloat, in consequence of the disembarkation of the troops who were taken at Glensheal in the preceding year, 1718.

No. IV

FROM ROBERT CAMPBELL, ALIAS M'GREGOR, COMMONLY CALLED ROB ROY, TO FIELD-MARSHAL WADE,

*Then receiving the submission of disaffected Chieftains and Clans.**

' Sir,—The great humanity with which you have constantly acted in the discharge of the trust reposed in you, and your ever having made use of the great powers with which you were vested, as the means of doing good and charitable offices to such as ye found proper objects of compassion, will, I hope, excuse my importunity in endeavouring to approve myself not absolutely unworthy of that mercy and favour which your Excellency has so generously procured from his Majesty for others in my unfortunate circumstances. I am very sensible nothing can be alledged sufficient to excuse so great a crime as I have been guilty of, that of Rebellion. But I humbly beg leave to lay before your Excellency some particulars in the circumstance of my guilt, which, I hope, will extenuate it in some measure. It was my misfortune, at the time the Rebellion broke out, to be liable to legal diligence and caption, at the Duke of Montrose's instance, for debt alledged due to him. To avoid being flung into prison, as I must certainly have been, had I followed my real inclinations in joining the King's troops at Stirling, I was forced to take party with the

---

* This curious epistle is copied from an authentic narrative of Marshal Wade's proceedings in the Highlands, communicated by the late eminent antiquary, George Chalmers, Esq., to Mr. Robert Jamieson of the Register House, Edinburgh, and published in the Appendix to an Edition of Burt's Letters from the North of Scotland. 2 vols. 8vo. Edinburgh, 1818.

adherents of the Pretender; for the country being all in arms, it was neither safe nor indeed possible for me to stand neuter. I should not, however, plead my being forced into that unnatural Rebellion against his Majesty, King George, if I could not at the same time assure your Excellency, that I not only avoided acting offensively against his Majesty's forces upon all occasions, but on the contrary, sent his Grace the Duke of Argyle all the intelligence I could from time to time, of the strength and situation of the Rebels; which I hope his Grace will do me the justice to acknowledge. As to the debt to the Duke of Montrose, I have discharged it to the utmost farthing. I beg your Excellency would be persuaded that, had it been in my power, as it was in my inclination, I should always have acted for the service of his Majesty King George, and that one reason of my begging the favour of your intercession with his Majesty for the pardon of my life, is the earnest desire I have to employ it in his service, whose goodness, justice, and humanity, are so conspicuous to all mankind.

'I am, with all duty and respect,
'Your Excellency's most, etc.
'ROBERT CAMPBELL.'

No. V

THERE are many productions of the Scottish Ballad Poets upon the lion-like mode of wooing practised by the ancient Highlanders when they had a fancy for the person (or property) of a Lowland damsel. One example is found in Mr. Robert Jamieson's Popular Scottish Songs:—

Bonny Babby Livingstone
Gaed out to see the kye,
And she has met with Glenlyon,
Who has stolen her away.

He took frae her her sattin coat,
But an her silken gown,
Syne roud her in his tartan plaid,
And happd her round and roun'.

APPENDIX TO INTRODUCTION

In another ballad we are told how

> Four-and-twenty Hieland men
>   Came doun by Fiddoch side,
> And they have sworn a deadly aith,
>   Jean Muir suld be a bride :
>
> And they have sworn a deadly aith,
>   Ilke man upon his durke,
> That she should wed with Duncan Ger,
>   Or they 'd make bloody worke.

This last we have from tradition, but there are many others in the collections of Scottish Ballads to the same purpose.

The achievement of Robert Oig, or young Rob Roy, as the Lowlanders called him, was celebrated in a ballad, of which there are twenty different and various editions. The tune is lively and wild, and we select the following words from memory :

> Rob Roy is frae the Hielands come,
>   Down to the Lowland border ;
> And he has stolen that lady away,
>   To haud his house in order.
>
> He set her on a milk-white steed,
>   Of none he stood in awe ;
> Untill they reached the Hieland hills,
>   Aboon the Balmaha' ! *
>
> Saying, Be content, be content,
>   Be content with me, lady ;
> Where will ye find in Lennox land,
>   Sae braw a man as me, lady ?
>
> Rob Roy, he was my father called,
>   MacGregor was his name, lady ;
> A' the country, far and near,
>   Have heard MacGregor's fame, lady.
>
> He was a hedge about his friends,
>   A heckle to his foes, lady ;
> If any man did him gainsay,
>   He felt his deadly blows, lady.

---

* A pass on the eastern margin of Loch Lomond, and an entrance to the Highlands.

ROB ROY

I am as bold, I am as bold,
  I am as bold and more, lady ;
Any man that doubts my word,
  May try my gude claymore, lady.

Then be content, be content,
  Be content with me, lady ;
For now you are my wedded wife,
  Until the day ye die, lady.

No. VI

GHLUNE DHU

THE following notices concerning this Chief fell under the Author's eye while the sheets were in the act of going through the press. They occur in manuscript memoirs, written by a person intimately acquainted with the incidents of 1745.

This Chief had the important task intrusted to him of defending the castle of Doune, in which the Chevalier placed a garrison to protect his communication with the Highlands, and to repel any sallies which might be made from Stirling Castle. Ghlune Dhu distinguished himself by his good conduct in this charge.

Ghlune Dhu is thus described:—' Glengyle is, in person, a tall handsome man, and has more of the mien of the ancient heroes than our modern fine gentlemen are possessed of. He is honest and disinterested to a proverb—extremely modest— brave and intrepid—and born one of the best partisans in Europe. In short, the whole people of that country declared that never did men live under so mild a government as Glengyle's, not a man having so much as lost a chicken while he continued there.'

It would appear from this curious passage that Glengyle— not Stewart of Balloch, as averred in a note on Waverley— commanded the garrison of Doune. Balloch might, no doubt, succeed MacGregor in the situation.

POSTSCRIPT

THE second article of the Appendix to the Introduction to
Rob Roy, *ante*, p. cxv, contains two curious letters respecting the arrest of Mr. Grahame of Killearn by that daring
freebooter, while levying the Duke of Montrose's rents.
These were taken from scroll copies in the possession of his
Grace the present Duke, who kindly permitted the use of
them in the present publication. Both volumes of the Novel
had but just passed through the press, when the Right
Honourable Mr. Peel—whose important state avocations do
not avert his attention from the interests of literature—
transmitted to the author copies of the original letters and
enclosure, of which he possessed only the rough draught.
The originals were discovered in the State Paper Office, by
the indefatigable researches of Mr. Lemon, who is daily
throwing more light on that valuable collection of records.
From the documents with which the author has been thus
kindly favoured, he is enabled to fill up the addresses which
were wanting in the scrolls. That of the 21st Nov. 1716, is
addressed to Lord Viscount Townshend, and is accompanied
by one of the same date to Robert Pringle, Esquire, the
Under-Secretary of State, which is here inserted, as relative
to so curious an incident.

LETTER FROM THE DUKE OF MONTROSE TO ROBERT PRINGLE, ESQ.,
UNDER-SECRETARY TO LORD VISCOUNT TOWNSHEND.

' *Glasgow*, 21 *Nov.* 1716.

' S^R,

' Haveing had so many dispatches to make this night, I
hope ye'l excuse me that I make use of another hand to
give yow a short account of the occasion of this express, by
which I have written to my Ld. Duke of Roxburgh, and my
Lord Townshend, which I hope ye'l gett carefully deleivered.

ROB ROY

'Mr. Graham, younger of Killearn, being on Munday last in Monteith att a country house, collecting my rents, was about nine o'clock that same night surprised by Rob Roy with a party of his men in arms, who, haveing surrounded the house and secured the avenues, presented their guns in at the windows, while he himself entered the room with some others with cokt pistolls, and seased Killearn with all his money, books, papers, and bonds, and carryed all away with him to the hills, at the same time ordering Killearn to write a letter to me, (of which ye have the copy inclosed,) proposeing a very honourable treaty to me. I must say this story was as surprising to me as it was insolent; and it must bring a very great concern upon me, that this gentleman, my near relation, should be brought to suffer all the barbaritys and crueltys, which revenge and mallice may suggest to these miscreants, for his haveing acted a faithfull part in the service of the government, and his affection to me in my concerns.

'I need not be more particular to you, since I know that my Letter to my Lord Townshend will come into your hands, so shall only now give you the assurances of my being, with great sincerity,

'S^r, y^r most humble servant,
(Signed) 'MONTROSE.

'I long exceedingly for a return of my former dispatches to the Secretary's about Methven and Col^{ll} Urquhart, and my wife's cousins, Balnamoon and Phinaven.

'I must beg yow'll give my humble service to Mr. Secretary Methven, and tell him that I must referr him to what I have written to My Lord Townshend in this affair of Rob Roy, believing it was needless to trouble both with letters.'

Examined, ROBT. LEMON,
Deputy Keeper of State Papers.

STATE PAPER OFFICE,
Nov. 4, 1829.

CXXVI

POSTSCRIPT

NOTE.—The enclosure referred to in the preceding letter, is another copy of the letter which Mr. Grahame of Killearn was compelled by Rob Roy to write to the Duke of Montrose, and is exactly the same as the one enclosed in his Grace's letter to Lord Townshend, dated November 21st, 1716.

R. L.

The last letter in the Appendix, p. cxix, (28th November,) acquainting the Government with Killearn's being set at liberty, is also addressed to the Under-Secretary of State, Mr. Pringle.

The author may also here remark, that immediately previous to the insurrection of 1715, he perceives, from some notes of information given to Government, that Rob Roy appears to have been much employed and trusted by the Jacobite party, even in the very delicate task of transporting *specie* to the Earl of Breadalbane, though it might have somewhat resembled trusting Don Raphael and Ambrose de Lamela with the church-treasure.

ROB ROY

CHAPTER I

How have I sinn'd, that this affliction
Should light so heavy on me ?   I have no more sons,
And this no more mine own.—My grand curse
Hang o'er his head that thus transform'd thee!—Travel ?
I'll send my horse to travel next.
                              MONSIEUR THOMAS.

You have requested me, my dear friend, to bestow
some of that leisure, with which Providence has
blessed the decline of my life, in registering the
hazards and difficulties which attended its com-
mencement. The recollection of those adventures,
as you are pleased to term them, has indeed left
upon my mind a chequered and varied feeling of
pleasure and of pain, mingled, I trust, with no
slight gratitude and veneration to the Disposer of
human events, who guided my early course through
much risk and labour, that the ease with which he
has blessed my prolonged life, might seem softer
from remembrance and contrast.   Neither is it
possible for me to doubt, what you have often
affirmed, that the incidents which befell me among a
people singularly primitive in their government and
manners, have something interesting and attractive

3

for those who love to hear an old man's stories of a past age.

Still, however, you must remember, that the tale told by one friend, and listened to by another, loses half its charms when committed to paper; and that the narratives to which you have attended with interest, as heard from the voice of him to whom they occurred, will appear less deserving of attention when perused in the seclusion of your study. But your greener age and robust constitution promise longer life than will, in all human probability, be the lot of your friend. Throw, then, these sheets into some secret drawer of your escritoir till we are separated from each other's society by an event which may happen at any moment, and which must happen within the course of a few— a very few years. When we are parted in this world, to meet, I hope, in a better, you will, I am well aware, cherish more than it deserves the memory of your departed friend, and will find in those details which I am now to commit to paper, matter for melancholy, but not unpleasing reflection. Others bequeath to the confidents of their bosom portraits of their external features —I put into your hands a faithful transcript of my thoughts and feelings, of my virtues and of my failings, with the assured hope, that the follies and headstrong impetuosity of my youth will meet the same kind construction and forgiveness which have so often attended the faults of my matured age.

One advantage, among the many, of addressing

my Memoirs (if I may give these sheets a name so imposing) to a dear and intimate friend, is, that I may spare some of the details, in this case unnecessary, with which I must needs have detained a stranger from what I have to say of greater interest. Why should I bestow all my tediousness upon you, because I have you in my power, and have ink, paper, and time before me ? At the same time, I dare not promise that I may not abuse the opportunity so temptingly offered me, to treat of myself and my own concerns, even though I speak of circumstances as well known to you as to myself. The seductive love of narrative, when we ourselves are the heroes of the events which we tell, often disregards the attention due to the time and patience of the audience, and the best and wisest have yielded to its fascination. I need only remind you of the singular instance evinced by the form of that rare and original edition of Sully's Memoirs, which you (with the fond vanity of a book-collector) insist upon preferring to that which is reduced to the useful and ordinary form of Memoirs, but which I think curious, solely as illustrating how far so great a man as the author was accessible to the foible of self-importance. If I recollect rightly, that venerable peer and great statesman had appointed no fewer than four gentlemen of his household to draw up the events of his life, under the title of Memorials of the Sage and Royal Affairs of State, Domestic, Political, and Military, transacted by Henry iv., and so forth. These grave recorders, having made their compilation, reduced the Memoirs containing all the remarkable events of their master's life into a narrative, addressed to himself *in propria persona*. And thus, instead of telling his own story, in the third person, like Julius Cæsar, or in the first person, like most who, in the hall, or the study, undertake to be the heroes of their own tale, Sully enjoyed the refined, though whimsical pleasure, of having the events of his life told over to him by his secretaries, being himself the auditor, as he was also the hero, and probably the author, of the whole book. It must have been a great sight to have seen the ex-minister, as bolt upright as a starched ruff and laced cassock could make him, seated in state beneath his canopy, and listening to the recitation of his compilers, while, standing bare in his presence, they informed him gravely, 'Thus said the duke—so did the duke infer—such were your grace's sentiments upon this important point—such were your secret counsels to the king on that other emergency,'—circumstances, all of which must have been much better known to their hearer than to themselves, and most of which could only be derived from his own special communication.

My situation is not quite so ludicrous as that of the great Sully, and yet there would be something whimsical in Frank Osbaldistone giving Will Tresham a formal account of his birth, education, and connexions in the world. I will, therefore, wrestle with the tempting spirit of P. P., Clerk of our Parish, as I best may, and endeavour to tell you nothing that is familiar to you already.

Some things, however, I must recall to your memory, because, though formerly well known to you, they may have been forgotten through lapse of time, and they afford the ground-work of my destiny.

You must remember my father well; for as your own was a member of the mercantile house, you knew him from infancy. Yet you hardly saw him in his best days, before age and infirmity had quenched his ardent spirit of enterprise and speculation. He would have been a poorer man indeed, but perhaps as happy, had he devoted to the extension of science those active energies, and acute powers of observation, for which commercial pursuits found occupation. Yet, in the fluctuations of mercantile speculation, there is something captivating to the adventurer, even independent of the hope of gain. He who embarks on that fickle sea, requires to possess the skill of the pilot and the fortitude of the navigator, and after all may be wrecked and lost, unless the gales of fortune breathe in his favour. This mixture of necessary attention and inevitable hazard,—the frequent and awful uncertainty whether prudence shall overcome fortune, or fortune baffle the schemes of prudence, affords full occupation for the powers, as well as for the feelings of the mind, and trade has all the fascination of gambling without its moral guilt.

Early in the 18th century, when I (Heaven help me) was a youth of some twenty years old, I was summoned suddenly from Bourdeaux to attend my father on business of importance. I shall never forget our first interview. You recollect the brief, abrupt, and somewhat stern mode in which he was wont to communicate his pleasure to those around him. Methinks I see him even now in my mind's eye ;—the firm and upright figure,—the step, quick and determined,—the eye, which shot so keen and so penetrating a glance,—the features, on which care had already planted wrinkles,—and hear his language, in which he never wasted word in vain, expressed in a voice which had sometimes an occasional harshness, far from the intention of the speaker.

When I dismounted from my post-horse, I hastened to my father's apartment. He was traversing it with an air of composed and steady deliberation, which even my arrival, although an only son unseen for four years, was unable to discompose. I threw myself into his arms. He was a kind, though not a fond father, and the tear twinkled in his dark eye, but it was only for a moment.

'Dubourg writes to me that he is satisfied with you, Frank.'

'I am happy, sir——'

'But I have less reason to be so,' he added, sitting down at his bureau.

'I am sorry, sir——'

'Sorry and happy, Frank, are words that, on most occasions, signify little or nothing — Here is your last letter.'

He took it out from a number of others tied up in a parcel of red tape, and curiously labelled and filed. There lay my poor epistle, written on the subject the nearest to my heart at the time, and couched in words which I had thought would work compassion, if not conviction,—there, I say, it lay, squeezed up among the letters on miscellaneous business in which my father's daily affairs had engaged him. I cannot help smiling internally when I recollect the mixture of hurt vanity, and wounded feeling, with which I regarded my remonstrance, to the penning of which there had gone, I promise you, some trouble, as I beheld it extracted from amongst letters of advice, of credit, and all the commonplace lumber, as I then thought them, of a merchant's correspondence. Surely, thought I, a letter of such importance (I dared not say, even to myself, so well written) deserved a separate place, as well as more anxious consideration, than those on the ordinary business of the counting-house.

But my father did not observe my dissatisfaction, and would not have minded it if he had. He proceeded, with the letter in his hand. ' This, Frank, is yours of the 21st ultimo, in which you advise me, (reading from my letter,) that in the most important business of forming a plan, and adopting a profession for life, you trust my paternal goodness will hold you entitled to at least a negative voice ; that you have insuperable—ay, insuperable is the word—I wish, by the way, you would write a more distinct current hand—draw a score through the tops of your t's, and open the loops of your l's— insuperable objections to the arrangements which I have proposed to you. There is much more to the same effect, occupying four good pages of paper, which a little attention to perspicuity and distinctness of expression might have comprised within as many lines. For, after all, Frank, it amounts but to this, that you will not do as I would have you.'

'That I cannot, sir, in the present instance; not that I will not.'

'Words avail very little with me, young man,' said my father, whose inflexibility always possessed the air of the most perfect calmness and self-possession. '*Can not* may be a more civil phrase than *will not*, but the expressions are synonymous where there is no moral impossibility. But I am not a friend to doing business hastily; we will talk this matter over after dinner.—Owen!'

Owen appeared, not with the silver locks which you were used to venerate, for he was then little more than fifty; but he had the same, or an exactly similar uniform suit of light-brown clothes,—the same pearl-grey silk stockings,—the same stock, with its silver buckle,—the same plaited cambric ruffles, drawn down over his knuckles in the parlour, but in the counting-house carefully folded back under the sleeves, that they might remain unstained by the ink which he daily consumed;—in a word, the same grave, formal, yet benevolent cast of features, which continued to his death to distinguish the head-clerk of the great house of Osbaldistone and Tresham.

'Owen,' said my father, as the kind old man shook me affectionately by the hand, 'you must dine with us to-day, and hear the news Frank has brought us from our friends in Bourdeaux.'

Owen made one of his stiff bows of respectful gratitude; for, in those days, when the distance between superiors and inferiors was enforced in a manner to which the present times are strangers, such an invitation was a favour of some little consequence.

I shall long remember that dinner-party. Deeply affected by feelings of anxiety, not unmingled with displeasure, I was unable to take that active share in the conversation which my father seemed to expect from me; and I too frequently gave unsatisfactory answers to the questions with which he assailed me. Owen, hovering betwixt his respect for his patron, and his love for the youth he had dandled on his knee in childhood, like the timorous, yet anxious ally of an invaded nation, endeavoured at every blunder I made to explain my no-meaning, and to cover my retreat ; manœuvres which added to my father's pettish displeasure, and brought a share of it upon my kind advocate, instead of protecting me. I had not, while residing in the house of Dubourg, absolutely conducted myself like

> A clerk condemn'd his father's soul to cross,
> Who penn'd a stanza when he should engross ;—

but, to say truth, I had frequented the counting-house no more than I had thought absolutely necessary to secure the good report of the Frenchman, long a correspondent of our firm, to whom my father had trusted for initiating me into the

11

mysteries of commerce. In fact, my principal attention had been dedicated to literature and manly exercises. My father did not altogether discourage such acquirements, whether mental or personal. He had too much good sense not to perceive, that they sate gracefully upon every man, and he was sensible that they relieved and dignified the character to which he wished me to aspire. But his chief ambition was, that I should succeed not merely to his fortune, but to the views and plans by which he imagined he could extend and perpetuate the wealthy inheritance which he designed for me.

Love of his profession was the motive which he chose should be most ostensible, when he urged me to tread the same path; but he had others with which I only became acquainted at a later period. Impetuous in his schemes, as well as skilful and daring, each new adventure, when successful, became at once the incentive, and furnished the means, for farther speculation. It seemed to be necessary to him, as to an ambitious conqueror, to push on from achievement to achievement, without stopping to secure, far less to enjoy, the acquisitions which he made. Accustomed to see his whole fortune trembling in the scales of chance, and dexterous at adopting expedients for casting the balance in his favour, his health and spirits and activity seemed ever to increase with the animating hazards on which he staked his wealth; and he resembled a sailor, accustomed to brave the billows and the foe, whose confidence rises on the eve of tempest or of battle. He was not, however, insensible to the changes which increasing age or supervening malady might make in his own constitution; and was anxious in good time to secure in me an assistant, who might take the helm when his hand grew weary, and keep the vessel's way according to his council and instruction. Paternal affection, as well as the furtherance of his own plans, determined him to the same conclusion. Your father, though his fortune was vested in the house, was only a sleeping partner, as the commercial phrase goes; and Owen, whose probity and skill in the details of arithmetic rendered his services invaluable as a head clerk, was not possessed either of information or talents sufficient to conduct the mysteries of the principal management. If my father were suddenly summoned from life, what would become of the world of schemes which he had formed, unless his son were moulded into a commercial Hercules, fit to sustain the weight when relinquished by the falling Atlas? and what would become of that son himself, if, a stranger to business of this description, he found himself at once involved in the labyrinth of mercantile concerns, without the clew of knowledge necessary for his extraction? For all these reasons, avowed and secret, my father was determined I should embrace his profession; and when he was determined, the resolution of no man was more immovable. I, however, was also a party to be consulted, and, with something of his own pertinacity, I had formed a determination precisely contrary.

It may, I hope, be some palliative for the resistance which, on this occasion, I offered to my father's wishes, that I did not fully understand upon what they were founded, or how deeply his happiness was involved in them. Imagining myself certain of a large succession in future, and ample maintenance in the meanwhile, it never occurred to me that it might be necessary, in order to secure these blessings, to submit to labour and limitations unpleasant to my taste and temper. I only saw in my father's proposal for my engaging in business, a desire that I should add to those heaps of wealth which he had himself acquired; and imagining myself the best judge of the path to my own happiness, I did not conceive that I should increase that happiness by augmenting a fortune which I believed was already sufficient, and more than sufficient, for every use, comfort, and elegant enjoyment.

Accordingly, I am compelled to repeat, that my time at Bourdeaux had not been spent as my father had proposed to himself. What he considered as the chief end of my residence in that city, I had postponed for every other, and would (had I dared) have neglected it altogether. Dubourg, a favoured and benefited correspondent of our mercantile house, was too much of a shrewd politician to make such reports to the head of the firm concerning his only child, as would excite the displeasure of both; and he might also, as you will presently hear, have views of selfish advantage in suffering me to neglect the purposes for which I was placed under his charge. My conduct was regulated by the bounds of decency

and good order, and thus far he had no evil report
to make, supposing him so disposed; but, perhaps,
the crafty Frenchman would have been equally
complaisant, had I been in the habit of indulging
worse feelings than those of indolence and aversion
to mercantile business. As it was, while I gave a
decent portion of my time to the commercial studies
he recommended, he was by no means envious
of the hours which I dedicated to other and more
classical attainments, nor did he ever find fault with
me for dwelling upon Corneille and Bcileau, in
preference to Postlethwayte, (supposing his folio to
have then existed, and Monsieur Dubourg able to
have pronounced his name,) or Savary, or any other
writer on commercial economy. He had picked
up somewhere a convenient expression, with which
he rounded off every letter to his correspondent,—
' I was all,' he said, ' that a father could wish.'

My father never quarrelled with a phrase, however frequently repeated, provided it seemed to him
distinct and expressive; and Addison himself could
not have found expressions so satisfactory to him as,
' Yours received, and duly honoured the bills enclosed,
as per margin.'

Knowing, therefore, very well what he desired
me to be, Mr. Osbaldistone made no doubt, from the
frequent repetition of Dubourg's favourite phrase,
that I was the very thing he wished to see me;
when, in an evil hour, he received my letter, containing my eloquent and detailed apology for declining a place in the firm, and a desk and stool in the
corner of the dark counting-house in Crane Alley,

surmounting in height those of Owen, and the
other clerks, and only inferior to the tripod of my
father himself. All was wrong from that moment.
Dubourg's reports became as suspicious as if his
bills had been noted for dishonour. I was summoned home in all haste, and received in the manner
I have already communicated to you.

CHAPTER II

*I begin shrewdly to suspect the young man of a terrible taint—Poetry;
with which idle disease if he be infected, there's no hope of him in a
state course.* Actum est *of him for a commonwealth's man, if he go
to't in rhyme once.*

BEN JONSON'S BARTHOLOMEW FAIR.

MY father had, generally speaking, his temper
under complete self-command, and his anger rarely
indicated itself by words, except in a sort of dry
testy manner, to those who had displeased him. He
never used threats, or expressions of loud resentment. All was arranged with him on system, and
it was his practice to do 'the needful' on every
occasion, without wasting words about it. It was,
therefore, with a bitter smile that he listened to my
imperfect answers concerning the state of commerce
in France, and unmercifully permitted me to involve
myself deeper and deeper in the mysteries of agio,
tariffs, tare and tret; nor can I charge my memory
with his having looked positively angry, until he
found me unable to explain the exact effect which
the depreciation of the louis d'or had produced on
the negotiation of bills of exchange. 'The most
remarkable national occurrence in my time,' said my
father, (who nevertheless had seen the Revolution,)
'and he knows no more of it than a post on the
quay!'

17

'Mr. Francis,' suggested Owen, in his timid and conciliatory manner, 'cannot have forgotten, that by an *arret* of the King of France, dated 1st May, 1700, it was provided that the *porteur*, within ten days after due, must make demand——'

'Mr. Francis,' said my father, interrupting him, 'will, I dare say, recollect for the moment anything you are so kind as hint to him.—But, body o' me! how Dubourg could permit him!—Hark ye, Owen, what sort of a youth is Clement Dubourg, his nephew there, in the office, the black-haired lad?'

'One of the cleverest clerks, sir, in the house; a prodigious young man for his time,' answered Owen; for the gaiety and civility of the young Frenchman had won his heart.

'Ay, ay, I suppose *he* knows something of the nature of exchange. Dubourg was determined I should have one youngster at least about my hand who understood business; but I see his drift, and he shall find that I do so when he looks at the balance-sheet. Owen, let Clement's salary be paid up to next quarter-day, and let him ship himself back to Bourdeaux in his father's ship, which is clearing out yonder.'

'Dismiss Clement Dubourg, sir?' said Owen, with a faltering voice.

'Yes, sir, dismiss him instantly; it is enough to have a stupid Englishman in the counting-house to make blunders, without keeping a sharp Frenchman there to profit by them.'

I had lived long enough in the territories of the *Grand Monarque* to contract a hearty aversion to arbitrary exertion of authority, even if it had not been instilled into me with my earliest breeding; and I could not refrain from interposing, to prevent an innocent and meritorious young man from paying the penalty of having acquired that proficiency which my father had desired for me.

'I beg pardon, sir,' when Mr. Osbaldistone had done speaking, 'but I think it but just, that if I have been negligent of my studies, I should pay the forfeit myself. I have no reason to charge Monsieur Dubourg with having neglected to give me opportunities of improvement, however little I may have profited by them; and, with respect to Monsieur Clement Dubourg——'

'With respect to him and to you, I shall take the measures which I see needful,' replied my father; 'but it is fair in you, Frank, to take your own blame on your own shoulders—very fair, that cannot be denied.—I cannot acquit old Dubourg,' he said, looking to Owen, 'for having merely afforded Frank the means of useful knowledge, without either seeing that he took advantage of them, or reporting to me if he did not. You see, Owen, he has natural notions of equity becoming a British merchant.'

'Mr. Francis,' said the head clerk, with his usual formal inclination of the head, and a slight elevation of his right hand, which he had acquired by a habit of sticking his pen behind his ear before he spoke—'Mr. Francis seems to understand the fundamental principle of all moral accounting, the great ethic rule of three. Let A do to B, as he

19

would have B do to him; the product will give the rule of conduct required.'

My father smiled at this reduction of the golden rule to arithmetical form, but instantly proceeded.

'All this signifies nothing, Frank; you have been throwing away your time like a boy, and in future you must learn to live like a man. I shall put you under Owen's care for a few months, to recover the lost ground.'

I was about to reply, but Owen looked at me with such a supplicatory and warning gesture, that I was involuntarily silent.

'We will then,' continued my father, 'resume the subject of mine of the 1st ultimo, to which you sent me an answer which was unadvised and unsatisfactory. So now, fill your glass, and push the bottle to Owen.'

Want of courage—of audacity, if you will—was never my failing. I answered firmly, 'I was sorry that my letter was unsatisfactory, unadvised it was not; for I had given the proposal his goodness had made me my instant and anxious attention, and it was with no small pain that I found myself obliged to decline it.'

My father bent his keen eye for a moment on me, and instantly withdrew it. As he made no answer, I thought myself obliged to proceed, though with some hesitation, and he only interrupted me by monosyllables.

'It is impossible, sir, for me to have higher respect for any character than I have for the commercial, even were it not yours.'

'Indeed!'

'It connects nation with nation, relieves the wants, and contributes to the wealth of all; and is to the general commonwealth of the civilized world what the daily intercourse of ordinary life is to private society, or rather, what air and food are to our bodies.'

'Well, sir?'

'And yet, sir, I find myself compelled to persist in declining to adopt a character which I am so ill qualified to support.'

'I will take care that you acquire the qualifications necessary. You are no longer the guest and pupil of Dubourg.'

'But, my dear sir, it is no defect of teaching which I plead, but my own inability to profit by instruction.'

'Nonsense; have you kept your journal in the terms I desired?'

'Yes, sir.'

'Be pleased to bring it here.'

The volume thus required was a sort of commonplace book, kept by my father's recommendation, in which I had been directed to enter notes of the miscellaneous information which I had acquired in the course of my studies. Foreseeing that he would demand inspection of this record, I had been attentive to transcribe such particulars of information as he would most likely be pleased with, but too often the pen had discharged the task without much correspondence with the head. And it had also happened, that, the book being the receptacle nearest to my hand, I had occasionally jotted down memoranda which had little regard to traffic. I now put it into my father's hand, devoutly hoping he might light on nothing that would increase his displeasure against me. Owen's face, which had looked something blank when the question was put, cleared up at my ready answer, and wore a smile of hope, when I brought from my apartment, and placed before my father, a commercial - looking volume, rather broader than it was long, having brazen clasps and a binding of rough calf. This looked businesslike, and was encouraging to my benevolent wellwisher. But he actually smiled with pleasure as he heard my father run over some part of the contents, muttering his critical remarks as he went on.

' *Brandies—Barils and barricants, also tonneaux. —At Nantz* 29—*Velles to the barique at Cognac and Rochelle* 27—*At Bourdeaux* 32—Very right, Frank —*Duties on tonnage and custom-house, see Saxby's Tables*—That's not well; you should have transcribed the passage; it fixes the thing in the memory —*Reports outward and inward—Corn debentures— Over-sea Cockets — Linens — Isingham — Gentish — Stoch-fish — Titling — Cropling—Lub-fish.* You should have noted that they are all, nevertheless, to be entered as titlings.—How many inches long is a titling ? '

Owen, seeing me at fault, hazarded a whisper, of which I fortunately caught the import.

' Eighteen inches, sir——'

' And a lub-fish is twenty-four—very right. It is important to remember this, on account of the

Portugueze trade. — But what have we here ? — *Bourdeaux founded in the year — Castle of the Trompette — Palace of Gallienus —* Well, well, that's very right too.—This is a kind of waste-book, Owen, in which all the transactions of the day, emptions, orders, payments, receipts, acceptances, draughts, commissions, and advices, are entered miscellaneously.'

'That they may be regularly transferred to the day-book and ledger,' answered Owen; 'I am glad Mr. Francis is so methodical.'

I perceived myself getting so fast into favour, that I began to fear the consequence would be my father's more obstinate perseverance in his resolution that I must become a merchant; and, as I was determined on the contrary, I began to wish I had not, to use my friend Mr. Owen's phrase, been so methodical. But I had no reason for apprehension on that score; for a blotted piece of paper dropped out of the book, and being taken up by my father, he interrupted a hint from Owen, on the propriety of securing loose memoranda with a little paste, by exclaiming, 'To the memory of Edward the Black Prince—What's all this?—verses !—By Heaven, Frank, you are a greater blockhead than I supposed you !'

My father, you must recollect, as a man of business, looked upon the labour of poets with contempt; and as a religious man, and of the dissenting persuasion, he considered all such pursuits as equally trivial and profane. Before you condemn him, you must recall to remembrance how too many

23

of the poets in the end of the seventeenth century had led their lives and employed their talents. The sect also to which my father belonged, felt, or perhaps affected, a puritanical aversion to the lighter exertions of literature. So that many causes contributed to augment the unpleasant surprise occasioned by the ill-timed discovery of this unfortunate copy of verses. As for poor Owen, could the bob-wig which he then wore have uncurled itself, and stood on end with horror, I am convinced the morning's labour of the friseur would have been undone, merely by the excess of his astonishment at this enormity. An inroad on the strong-box, or an erasure in the ledger, or a mis-summation in a fitted account, could hardly have surprised him more disagreeably. My father read the lines sometimes with an affectation of not being able to understand the sense,—sometimes in a mouthing tone of mock heroic,—always with an emphasis of the most bitter irony, most irritating to the nerves of an author.

> ' " O for the voice of that wild horn,
>   On Fontarabian echoes borne,
>   The dying hero's call,
>   That told imperial Charlemagne,
>   How Paynim sons of swarthy Spain
>   Had wrought his champion's fall."

' *Fontarabian echoes!*' continued my father, interrupting himself; 'the Fontarabian Fair would have been more to the purpose.—*Paynim?*—What's Paynim?—Could you not say Pagan as well, and write English, at least, if you must needs write nonsense?—

> "Sad over earth and ocean sounding,
>> And England's distant cliffs astounding,
>>> Such are the notes should say
>> How Britain's hope, and France's fear,
>> Victor of Cressy and Poitier,
>>> In Bourdeaux dying lay."

'Poitiers, by the way, is always spelt with an *s*, and I know no reason why orthography should give place to rhyme.—

> "'Raise my faint head, my squires,' he said,
>> 'And let the casement be display'd,
>>> That I may see once more
>> The splendour of the setting sun
>> Gleam on thy mirror'd wave, Garonne,
>>> And Blaye's empurpled shore.'"

'*Garonne* and *sun* is a bad rhyme. Why, Frank, you do not even understand the beggarly trade you have chosen.—

> "'Like me, he sinks to Glory's sleep,
>> His fall the dews of evening steep,
>>> As if in sorrow shed.
>> So soft shall fall the trickling tear,
>> When England's maids and matrons hear
>>> Of their Black Edward dead.

>> 'And though my sun of glory set,
>> Nor France, nor England shall forget
>>> The terror of my name;
>> And oft shall Britain's heroes rise,
>> New planets in these southern skies,
>>> Through clouds of blood and flame.'"

'A cloud of flame is something new — Good-morrow, my masters all, and a merry Christmas to you!—Why, the bellman writes better lines.' He then tossed the paper from him with an air of superlative contempt, and concluded,—'Upon my credit, Frank, you are a greater blockhead than I took you for.'

What could I say, my dear Tresham?—There I stood, swelling with indignant mortification, while my father regarded me with a calm but stern look of scorn and pity; and poor Owen, with uplifted hands and eyes, looked as striking a picture of horror as if he had just read his patron's name in the Gazette. At length I took courage to speak, endeavouring that my tone of voice should betray my feelings as little as possible.

'I am quite aware, sir, how ill qualified I am to play the conspicuous part in society you have destined for me; and, luckily, I am not ambitious of the wealth I might acquire. Mr. Owen would be a much more effective assistant.' I said this in some malice, for I considered Owen as having deserted my cause a little too soon.

'Owen?' said my father — 'The boy is mad, actually insane. And, pray, sir, if I may presume to inquire, having coolly turned me over to Mr. Owen, (although I may expect more attention from any one than from my son,) what may your own sage projects be?'

'I should wish, sir,' I replied, summoning up my courage, 'to travel for two or three years, should that consist with your pleasure; otherwise,

26

although late, I would willingly spend the same time at Oxford or Cambridge.'

'In the name of common sense! was the like ever heard?—to put yourself to school among pedants and Jacobites, when you might be pushing your fortune in the world! Why not go to Westminster or Eton at once, man, and take to Lilly's Grammar and Accidence, and to the birch, too, if you like it?'

'Then, sir, if you think my plan of improvement too late, I would willingly return to the Continent.'

'You have already spent too much time there to little purpose, Mr. Francis.'

'Then I would choose the army, sir, in preference to any other active line of life.'

'Choose the d—l,' answered my father, hastily, and then checking himself—'I profess you make me as great a fool as you are yourself.—Is he not enough to drive one mad, Owen?'—Poor Owen shook his head, and looked down. 'Hark ye, Frank,' continued my father, 'I will cut all this matter very short—I was at your age when my father turned me out of doors, and settled my legal inheritance on my younger brother. I left Osbaldistone Hall on the back of a broken-down hunter, with ten guineas in my purse. I have never crossed the threshold again, and I never will. I know not, and I care not, if my fox-hunting brother is alive, or has broken his neck; but he has children, Frank, and one of them shall be my son if you cross me farther in this matter.'

'You will do your pleasure,' I answered, rather, I fear, with more sullen indifference than respect, 'with what is your own.'

'Yes, Frank, what I have *is* my own, if labour in getting, and care in augmenting, can make a right of property; and no drone shall feed on my honeycomb. Think on it well; what I have said is not without reflection, and what I resolve upon I will execute.'

'Honoured sir—dear sir,' exclaimed Owen, tears rushing into his eyes, 'you are not wont to be in such a hurry in transacting business of importance. Let Mr. Francis run up the balance before you shut the account; he loves you, I am sure; and when he puts down his filial obedience to the *per contra*, I am sure his objections will disappear.'

'Do you think I will ask him twice,' said my father sternly, 'to be my friend, my assistant, and my confident?—to be a partner of my cares and of my fortune?—Owen, I thought you had known me better.'

He looked at me as if he meant to add something more, but turned instantly away, and left the room abruptly. I was, I own, affected by this view of the case, which had not occurred to me; and my father would probably have had little reason to complain of me, had he commenced the discussion with this argument.

But it was too late. I had much of his own obduracy of resolution, and Heaven had decreed that my sin should be my punishment, though not to the extent which my transgression merited.

Owen, when we were left alone, continued to look
at me with eyes, which tears from time to time
moistened, as if to discover, before attempting the
task of intercessor, upon what point my obstinacy
was most assailable. At length he began, with
broken and disconcerted accents,—'O L—d, Mr.
Francis! — Good Heavens, sir! — My stars, Mr.
Osbaldistone!—that I should ever have seen this
day—and you so young a gentleman, sir—For the
love of Heaven! look at both sides of the account
—Think what you are going to lose—a noble fortune,
sir — one of the finest houses in the City, even
under the old firm of Tresham and Trent, and now
Osbaldistone and Tresham—You might roll in gold,
Mr. Francis—And, my dear young Mr. Frank, if
there was any particular thing in the business of the
house which you disliked, I would' (sinking his
voice to a whisper) 'put it in order for you termly,
or weekly, or daily, if you will—Do, my dear Mr.
Francis, think of the honour due to your father,
that your days may be long in the land.'

'I am much obliged to you, Mr. Owen,' said I,—
'very much obliged indeed; but my father is best
judge how to bestow his money. He talks of one
of my cousins—let him dispose of his wealth as he
pleases, I will never sell my liberty for gold.'

'Gold, sir? — I wish you saw the balance-sheet
of profits at last term—It was in five figures—five
figures to each partner's sum total, Mr. Frank—
And all this is to go to a Papist, and a north-country
booby, and a disaffected person besides — It will
break my heart, Mr. Francis, that have been toiling

more like a dog than a man, and all for love of the firm.—Think how it will sound, Osbaldistone, Tresham, and Osbaldistone—or, perhaps, who knows,' (again lowering his voice,) 'Osbaldistone, Osbaldistone, and Tresham, for our Mr. Osbaldistone can buy them all out.'

'But, Mr. Owen, my cousin's name being also Osbaldistone, the name of the company will sound every bit as well in your ears.'

'O, fie upon you, Mr. Francis, when you know how well I love you — Your cousin, indeed! — a Papist, no doubt, like his father, and a disaffected person to the Protestant succession—that's another item, doubtless.'

'There are many very good men Catholics, Mr. Owen,' rejoined I.

As Owen was about to answer with unusual animation, my father re-entered the apartment.

'You were right,' he said, 'Owen, and I was wrong; we will take more time to think over this matter.—Young man, you will prepare to give me an answer on this important subject this day month.'

I bowed in silence, sufficiently glad of a reprieve, and trusting it might indicate some relaxation in my father's determination.

The time of probation passed slowly, unmarked by any accident whatever. I went and came, and disposed of my time as I pleased, without question or criticism on the part of my father. Indeed, I rarely saw him, save at meal-times, when he studiously avoided a discussion which you may well suppose I was in no hurry to press onward. Our conversation was of the news of the day, or on such general topics as strangers discourse upon to each other; nor could any one have guessed, from its tenor, that there remained undecided betwixt us a dispute of such importance. It haunted me, however, more than once, like the nightmare. Was it possible he would keep his word, and disinherit his only son in favour of a nephew, whose very existence he was not perhaps quite certain of? My grandfather's conduct, in similar circumstances, boded me no good, had I considered the matter rightly. But I had formed an erroneous idea of my father's character, from the importance which I recollected I maintained with him and his whole family before I went to France. I was not aware, that there are men who indulge their children at an early age, because to do so interests and amuses them, and who can yet be sufficiently severe when the same children cross their expectations at a more advanced period. On the contrary, I persuaded myself, that all I had to apprehend, was some temporary alienation of affection;—perhaps a rustication of a few weeks, which I thought would rather please me than otherwise, since it would give me an opportunity of setting about my unfinished version of Orlando Furioso, a poem which I longed to render into English verse. I suffered this belief to get such absolute possession of my mind, that I had resumed my blotted papers, and was busy in meditation on the oft-recurring rhymes of the Spenserian stanza, when I heard a low and cautious tap at the door of my apartment. 'Come in,' I said, and Mr. Owen entered. So regular were the motions and habits of this worthy man, that in all probability this was the first time he had ever been in the second story of his patron's house, however conversant with the first; and I am still at a loss to know in what manner he discovered my apartment.

'Mr. Francis,' he said, interrupting my expressions of surprise and pleasure at seeing him, 'I do not know if I am doing well in what I am about to say—it is not right to speak of what passes in the compting-house out of doors—one should not tell, as they say, to the post in the warehouse, how many lines there are in the ledger. But young Twineall has been absent from the house for a fortnight and more, until two days since.'

'Very well, my dear sir, and how does that concern us?'

'Stay, Mr. Francis — your father gave him a private commission; and I am sure he did not go down to Falmouth about the pilchard affair; and the Exeter business with Blackwell and company has been settled; and the mining people in Cornwall, Trevanion and Treguilliam, have paid all they are likely to pay; and any other matter of business must have been put through my books:—in short, it's my faithful belief that Twineall has been down in the north.'

'Do you really suppose so?' said I, somewhat startled.

'He has spoken about nothing, sir, since he returned, but his new boots, and his Rippon spurs, and a cock-fight at York — it's as true as the multiplication-table. Do, Heaven bless you, my dear child, make up your mind to please your father, and to be a man and a merchant at once.'

I felt at that instant a strong inclination to submit, and to make Owen happy by requesting him to tell my father, that I resigned myself to his disposal. But pride—pride, the source of so much that is good and so much that is evil in our course of life, prevented me. My acquiescence stuck in my throat; and while I was coughing to get it up, my father's voice summoned Owen. He hastily left the room, and the opportunity was lost.

My father was methodical in every thing. At the very same time of the day, in the same apartment, and with the same tone and manner which he had employed an exact month before, he recapitulated the proposal he had made for taking me into partnership, and assigning me a department in the counting-house, and requested to have my final decision. I thought at the time there was something unkind in this; and I still think that my father's conduct was injudicious. A more conciliatory treatment would, in all probability, have gained his ꞈpurpose. As it was, I stood fast, and, as respectfully as I could, declined the proposal he made to me. Perhaps,—for who can judge of their own heart?—I felt it unmanly to yield on the first summons, and expected farther ꞈsolicitation, as at least a pretext for changing my mind. If so, I was disappointed; for my father turned coolly to Owen, and only said, ' You see it is as I told you.

—Well, Frank,' (addressing me,) 'You are nearly
of age, and as well qualified to judge of what will
constitute your own happiness as you ever are
like to be; therefore, I say no more. But as I am
not bound to give in to your plans, any more than
you are compelled to submit to mine, may I ask
to know if you have formed any which depend on
my assistance?'

I answered, not a little abashed, 'That being bred
to no profession, and having no funds of my own,
it was obviously impossible for me to subsist without some allowance from my father; that my wishes
were very moderate; and that I hoped my aversion
for the profession to which he had designed me,
would not occasion his altogether withdrawing his
paternal support and protection.'

'That is to say, you wish to lean on my arm,
and yet to walk your own way? That can hardly
be, Frank;—however, I suppose you mean to obey
my directions, so far as they do not cross your own
humour?'

I was about to speak—'Silence, if you please,' he
continued. 'Supposing this to be the case, you will
instantly set out for the North of England, to pay
your uncle a visit, and see the state of his family.
I have chosen from among his sons (he has six,
I believe) one who, I understand, is most worthy
to fill the place I intended for you in the counting-house. But some farther arrangements may
be necessary, and for these your presence may be
requisite. You shall have farther instructions at
Osbaldistone Hall, where you will please to remain

until you hear from me. Every thing will be ready for your departure to-morrow morning.'

With these words my father left the apartment.

'What does all this mean, Mr. Owen?' said I to my sympathetic friend, whose countenance wore a cast of the deepest dejection.

'You have ruined yourself, Mr. Frank, that's all; when your father talks in that quiet determined manner, there will be no more change in him than in a fitted account.'

And so it proved; for the next morning, at five o'clock, I found myself on the road to York, mounted on a reasonably good horse, and with fifty guineas in my pocket; travelling, as it would seem, for the purpose of assisting in the adoption of a successor to myself in my father's house and favour, and, for aught I knew, eventually in his fortune also.

CHAPTER III

The slack sail shifts from side to side,
The boat, untrimmed, admits the tide,
Borne down, adrift, at random tost,
The oar breaks short, the rudder's lost.
GAY'S FABLES.

I HAVE tagged with rhyme and blank verse the subdivisions of this important narrative, in order to seduce your continued attention by powers of composition of stronger attraction than my own. The preceding lines refer to an unfortunate navigator, who daringly unloosed from its moorings a boat, which he was unable to manage, and thrust it off into the full tide of a navigable river. No school-boy, who, betwixt frolic and defiance, has executed a similar rash attempt, could feel himself, when adrift in a strong current, in a situation more awkward than mine, when I found myself driving, without a compass, on the ocean of human life. There had been such unexpected ease in the manner in which my father slipt a knot, usually esteemed the strongest which binds society together, and suffered me to depart as a sort of outcast from his family, that it strangely lessened the confidence in my own personal accomplishments, which had hitherto sustained me. Prince Prettyman, now a prince, and now a fisher's son, had not a more awkward sense of his degradation. We are so apt, in our engrossing egotism, to consider all those accessories which are drawn around us by prosperity, as pertaining and belonging to our own persons, that the discovery of our unimportance, when left to our own proper resources, becomes inexpressibly mortifying. As the hum of London died away on my ear, the distant peal of her steeples more than once sounded to my ears the admonitory ' Turn again,' erst heard by her future Lord Mayor; and when I looked back from Highgate on her dusky magnificence, I felt as if I were leaving behind me comfort, opulence, the charms of society, and all the pleasures of cultivated life.

But the die was cast. It was, indeed, by no means probable that a late and ungracious compliance with my father's wishes would have reinstated me in the situation which I had lost. On the contrary, firm and strong of purpose as he himself was, he might rather have been disgusted than conciliated by my tardy and compulsory acquiescence in his desire that I should engage in commerce. My constitutional obstinacy came also to my aid, and pride whispered how poor a figure I should make, when an airing of four miles from London had blown away resolutions formed during a month's serious deliberation. Hope, too, that never forsakes the young and hardy, lent her lustre to my future prospects. My father could not be serious in the sentence of foris-familiation, which he had so unhesitatingly pronounced. It must be but a trial of my disposition, which, endured with patience and steadiness on my part, would raise me in his estimation, and lead to an amicable accommodation of the point in dispute between us. I even settled in my own mind how far I would concede to him, and on what articles of our supposed treaty I would make a firm stand; and the result was, according to my computation, that I was to be reinstated in my full rights of filiation, paying the easy penalty of some ostensible compliances to atone for my past rebellion.

In the meanwhile, I was lord of my person, and experienced that feeling of independence which the youthful bosom receives with a thrilling mixture of pleasure and apprehension. My purse, though by no means amply replenished, was in a situation to supply all the wants and wishes of a traveller. I had been accustomed, while at Bourdeaux, to act as my own valet; my horse was fresh, young, and active, and the buoyancy of my spirits soon surmounted the melancholy reflections with which my journey commenced.

I should have been glad to have journeyed upon a line of road better calculated to afford reasonable objects of curiosity, or a more interesting country, to the traveller. But the north road was then, and perhaps still is, singularly deficient in these respects; nor do I believe you can travel so far through Britain in any other direction without meeting more of what is worthy to engage the attention. My mental ruminations, notwithstanding my assumed confidence, were not always of an unchequered nature. The Muse too, — the very

coquette who had led me into this wilderness,—
like others of her sex, deserted me in my utmost
need; and I should have been reduced to rather
an uncomfortable state of dulness, had it not been
for the occasional conversation of strangers who
chanced to pass the same way. But the characters
whom I met with were of a uniform and unin-
teresting description. Country parsons, jogging
homewards after a visitation; farmers, or graziers,
returning from a distant market; clerks of traders,
travelling to collect what was due to their masters
in provincial towns; with now and then an officer
going down into the country upon the recruiting
service, were, at this period, the persons by whom
the turnpikes and tapsters were kept in exercise.
Our speech, therefore, was of tithes and creeds,
of beeves and grain, of commodities wet and dry,
and the solvency of the retail dealers, occasionally varied by the description of a siege, or battle,
in Flanders, which, perhaps, the narrator only
gave me at second hand. Robbers, a fertile and
alarming theme, filled up every vacancy; and
the names of the Golden Farmer, the Flying
Highwayman, Jack Needham, and other Beggar's
Opera heroes, were familiar in our mouths as
household words. At such tales, like children
closing their circle round the fire when the ghost
story draws to its climax, the riders drew near
to each other, looked before and behind them,
examined the priming of their pistols, and vowed
to stand by each other in case of danger; an
engagement which, like other offensive and de-

fensive alliances, sometimes glided out of remembrance when there was an appearance of actual peril.

Of all the fellows whom I ever saw haunted by terrors of this nature, one poor man, with whom I travelled a day and a half, afforded me most amusement. He had upon his pillion a very small, but apparently a very weighty portmanteau, about the safety of which he seemed particularly solicitous; never trusting it out of his own immediate care, and uniformly repressing the officious zeal of the waiters and ostlers, who offered their services to carry it into the house. With the same precaution he laboured to conceal, not only the purpose of his journey, and his ultimate place of destination, but even the direction of each day's route. Nothing embarrassed him more than to be asked by any one, whether he was travelling upwards or downwards, or at what stage he intended to bait. His place of rest for the night he scrutinized with the most anxious care, alike avoiding solitude, and what he considered as bad neighbourhood; and at Grantham, I believe, he sate up all night to avoid sleeping in the next room to a thick-set squinting fellow, in a black wig, and a tarnished gold-laced waistcoat. With all these cares on his mind, my fellow traveller, to judge by his thewes and sinews, was a man who might have set danger at defiance with as much impunity as most men. He was strong, and well-built; and, judging from his gold-laced hat and cockade, seemed to have served in the army, or, at least, to belong to the military profession in one capacity or other. His conversation also, though always sufficiently vulgar, was that of a man of sense, when the terrible bugbears which haunted his imagination for a moment ceased to occupy his attention. But every accidental association recalled them. An open heath, a close plantation, were alike subjects of apprehension; and the whistle of a shepherd lad was instantly converted into the signal of a depredator. Even the sight of a gibbet, if it assured him that one robber was safely disposed of by justice, never failed to remind him how many remained still unhanged.

I should have wearied of this fellow's company, had I not been still more tired of my own thoughts. Some of the marvellous stories, however, which he related, had in themselves a cast of interest, and another whimsical point of his peculiarities afforded me the occasional opportunity of amusing myself at his expense. Among his tales, several of the unfortunate travellers who fell among thieves, incurred that calamity from associating themselves on the road with a well-dressed and entertaining stranger, in whose company they trusted to find protection as well as amusement; who cheered their journey with tale and song, protected them against the evils of overcharges and false reckonings, until at length, under pretext of showing a near path over a desolate common, he seduced his unsuspicious victims from the public road into some dismal glen, where, suddenly blowing his whistle, he assembled his comrades from their lurking-place, and displayed himself in his true colours, the captain, namely, of the band of robbers to whom his unwary fellow-travellers had forfeited their purses, and perhaps their lives. Towards the conclusion of such a tale, and when my companion had wrought himself into a fever of apprehension by the progress of his own narrative, I observed that he usually eyed me with a glance of doubt and suspicion, as if the possibility occurred to him, that he might, at that very moment, be in company with a character as dangerous as that which his tale described. And ever and anon, when such suggestions pressed themselves on the mind of this ingenious self-tormentor, he drew off from me to the opposite side of the high road, looked before, behind, and around him, examined his arms, and seemed to prepare himself for flight or defence, as circumstances might require.

The suspicion implied on such occasions seemed to me only momentary, and too ludicrous to be offensive. There was, in fact, no particular reflection on my dress or address, although I was thus mistaken for a robber. A man in those days might have all the external appearance of a gentleman, and yet turn out to be a highwayman. For the division of labour in every department not having then taken place so fully as since that period, the profession of the polite and accomplished adventurer, who nicked you out of your money at White's, or bowled you out of it at Marybone, was often united with that of the professed ruffian, who, on Bagshot Heath, or Finchley Common, commanded his brother beau to stand and deliver. There was also a touch of coarseness and hardness about the manners of the times, which has since, in a great degree, been softened and shaded away. It seems to me, on recollection, as if desperate men had less reluctance then, than now, to embrace the most desperate means of retrieving their fortune. The times were indeed past, when Anthony-a-Wood mourned over the execution of two men, goodly in person, and of undisputed courage and honour, who were hanged without mercy at Oxford, merely because their distress had driven them to raise contributions on the highway. We were still farther removed from the days of 'the mad Prince and Poins.' And yet, from the number of unenclosed and extensive heaths in the vicinity of the metropolis, and from the less populous state of remote districts, both were frequented by that species of mounted highwaymen, that may possibly become one day unknown, who carried on their trade with something like courtesy; and, like Gibbet in the Beaux Stratagem, piqued themselves on being the best-behaved men on the road, and on conducting themselves with all appropriate civility in the exercise of their vocation. A young man, therefore, in my circumstances, was not entitled to be highly indignant at the mistake which confounded him with this worshipful class of depredators.

Neither was I offended. On the contrary, I found amusement in alternately exciting, and lulling to sleep, the suspicions of my timorous companion, and in purposely so acting as still farther to puzzle a brain which nature and apprehension had combined to render none of the clearest. When my free conversation had lulled him into complete security, it required only a passing inquiry concerning the direction of his journey, or the nature of the business which occasioned it, to put his suspicions once more in arms. For example, a conversation on the comparative strength and activity of our horses took such a turn as follows:—

'O sir,' said my companion, 'for the gallop, I grant you; but allow me to say, your horse (although he is a very handsome gelding — that must be owned) has too little bone to be a good roadster. The trot, sir,' (striking his Bucephalus with his spurs,) 'the trot is the true pace for a hackney; and, were we near a town, I should like to try that daisy-cutter of yours upon a piece of level road (barring canter) for a quart of claret at the next inn.'

'Content, sir,' replied I; 'and here is a stretch of ground very favourable.'

'Hem, ahem,' answered my friend with hesitation; 'I make it a rule of travelling never to blow my horse between stages; one never knows what occasion he may have to put him to his mettle: and besides, sir, when I said I would match you, I meant with even weight; you ride four stone lighter than I.'

'Very well; but I am content to carry weight. Pray what may that portmanteau of yours weigh?'

'My p—p—portmanteau?' replied he, hesitating —'O very little—a feather—just a few shirts and stockings.'

' I should think it heavier, from its appearance. I 'll hold you the quart of claret it makes the odds betwixt our weight.'

' You 're mistaken, sir, I assure you—quite mistaken,' replied my friend, edging off to the side of the road, as was his wont on these alarming occasions.

' Well, I 'm willing to venture the wine; or, I will bet you ten pieces to five, that I carry your portmanteau on my croupe, and out-trot you into the bargain.'

This proposal raised my friend's alarm to the uttermost. His nose changed from the natural copper hue which it had acquired from many a comfortable cup of claret, or sack, into a palish brassy tint, and his teeth chattered with apprehension at the unveiled audacity of my proposal, which seemed to place the bare-faced plunderer before him in full atrocity. As he faltered for an answer, I relieved him in some degree by a question concerning a steeple, which now became visible, and an observation that we were now so near the village as to run no risk from interruption on the road. At this his countenance cleared up: but I easily perceived that it was long ere he forgot a proposal which seemed to him so fraught with suspicion as that which I had now hazarded. I trouble you with this detail of the man's disposition, and the manner in which I practised upon it, because, however trivial in themselves, these particulars were attended by an important influence on future incidents which will occur in this narrative. At the time, this person's conduct only inspired me with contempt, and confirmed me in an opinion, which I already entertained, that of all the propensities which teach mankind to torment themselves, that of causeless fear is the most irritating, busy, painful, and pitiable.

CHAPTER IV

The Scots are poor, cries surly English pride.
True is the charge; nor by themselves denied.
Are they not, then, in strictest reason clear,
Who wisely come to mend their fortunes here ?
CHURCHILL.

THERE was, in the days of which I write, an old-
fashioned custom on the English road, which I
suspect is now obsolete, or practised only by the
vulgar. Journeys of length being made on horseback, and, of course, by brief stages, it was usual
always to make a halt on the Sunday in some town
where the traveller might attend divine service,
and his horse have the benefit of the day of rest,
the institution of which is as humane to our brute
labourers as profitable to ourselves. A counter-
part to this decent practice, and a remnant of
old English hospitality, was, that the landlord of
a principal inn laid aside his character of a publican
on the seventh day, and invited the guests who
chanced to be within his walls to take a part
of his family beef and pudding. This invitation
was usually complied with by all whose distinguished rank did not induce them to think
compliance a derogation ; and the proposal of a
bottle of wine after dinner, to drink the landlord's

health, was the only recompense ever offered or accepted.

I was born a citizen of the world, and my inclination led me into all scenes where my knowledge of mankind could be enlarged; I had, besides, no pretensions to sequester myself on the score of superior dignity, and therefore seldom failed to accept of the Sunday's hospitality of mine host, whether of the Garter, Lion, or Bear. The honest publican, dilated into additional consequence by a sense of his own importance, while presiding among the guests on whom it was his ordinary duty to attend, was in himself an entertaining spectacle; and around his genial orbit, other planets of inferior consequence performed their revolutions. The wits and humorists, the distinguished worthies of the town or village, the apothecary, the attorney, even the curate himself, did not disdain to partake of this hebdomadal festivity. The guests, assembled from different quarters, and following different professions, formed, in language, manners, and sentiments, a curious contrast to each other, not indifferent to those who desired to possess a knowledge of mankind in its varieties.

It was on such a day, and such an occasion, that my timorous acquaintance and I were about to grace the board of the ruddy-faced host of the Black Bear, in the town of Darlington, and bishoprick of Durham, when our landlord informed us, with a sort of apologetic tone, that there was a Scotch gentleman to dine with us.

'A gentleman? — what sort of a gentleman?'

said my companion somewhat hastily, his mind, I suppose, running on gentlemen of the pad, as they were then termed.

'Why, a Scotch sort of a gentleman, as I said before,' returned mine host; 'they are all gentle, ye mun know, though they ha' narra shirt to back; but this is a decentish hallion—a canny North Briton as e'er cross'd Berwick bridge—I trow he's a dealer in cattle.'

'Let us have his company, by all means,' answered my companion; and then, turning to me, he gave vent to the tenor of his own reflections. 'I respect the Scotch, sir; I love and honour the nation for their sense of morality. Men talk of their filth and their poverty: but commend me to sterling honesty, though clad in rags, as the poet saith. I have been credibly assured, sir, by men on whom I can depend, that there was never known such a thing in Scotland as a highway robbery.'

'That's because they have nothing to lose,' said mine host, with the chuckle of a self-applauding wit.

'No, no, landlord,' answered a strong deep voice behind him, 'it's e'en because your English gaugers and supervisors,* that you have sent down benorth the Tweed, have taen up the trade of thievery over the heads of the native professors.'

'Well said, Mr. Campbell!' answered the landlord; 'I did nat think thoud'st been sae near us,

---

* The introduction of gaugers, supervisors, and examiners, was one of the great complaints of the Scottish nation, though a natural consequence of the Union.

mon. But thou kens I 'm an outspoken Yorkshire tyke—And how go markets in the south ? '

'Even in the ordinar,' replied Mr. Campbell; 'wise folks buy and sell, and fools are bought and sold.'

'But wise men and fools both eat their dinner,' answered our jolly entertainer; 'and here 'a comes —as prime a buttock of beef as e'er hungry mon stuck fork in.'

So saying, he eagerly whetted his knife, assumed his seat of empire at the head of the board, and loaded the plates of his sundry guests with his good cheer.

This was the first time I had heard the Scottish accent, or, indeed, that I had familiarly met with an individual of the ancient nation by whom it was spoken. Yet, from an early period, they had occupied and interested my imagination. My father, as is well known to you, was of an ancient family in Northumberland, from whose seat I was, while eating the aforesaid dinner, not very many miles distant. The quarrel betwixt him and his relatives was such, that he scarcely ever mentioned the race from which he sprung, and held as the most contemptible species of vanity, the weakness which is commonly termed family pride. His ambition was only to be distinguished as William Osbaldistone, the first, at least one of the first, merchants on Change; and to have proved him the lineal representative of William the Conqueror, would have far less flattered his vanity than the hum and bustle which his approach was wont to produce among the bulls, bears, and brokers of Stock-alley. He wished, no doubt, that I should remain in such ignorance of my relatives and descent as might insure a correspondence between my feelings and his own on this subject. But his designs, as will happen occasionally to the wisest, were, in some degree at least, counteracted by a being whom his pride would never have supposed of importance adequate to influence them in any way. His nurse, an old Northumbrian woman, attached to him from his infancy, was the only person connected with his native province for whom he retained any regard; and when fortune dawned upon him, one of the first uses which he made of her favours, was to give Mabel Rickets a place of residence within his household. After the death of my mother, the care of nursing me during my childish illnesses, and of rendering all those tender attentions which infancy exacts from female affection, devolved on old Mabel. Interdicted by her master from speaking to him on the subject of the heaths, glades, and dales of her beloved Northumberland, she poured herself forth to my infant ear in descriptions of the scenes of her youth, and long narratives of the events which tradition declared to have passed amongst them. To these I inclined my ear much more seriously than to graver, but less animated instructors. Even yet, methinks I see old Mabel, her head slightly agitated by the palsy of age, and shaded by a close cap, as white as the driven snow,—her face wrinkled, but still retaining the healthy tinge which it had acquired in rural labour,—I think I see her look around on the brick walls and narrow street which presented themselves from our windows, as she concluded with a sigh the favourite old ditty, which I then preferred, and — why should I not tell the truth ?—which I still prefer to all the opera airs ever minted by the capricious brain of an Italian Mus. D.—

> Oh, the oak, the ash, and the bonny ivy tree,
> They flourish best at home in the North Country!

Now, in the legends of Mabel, the Scottish nation was ever freshly remembered, with all the embittered declamation of which the narrator was capable. The inhabitants of the opposite frontier served in her narratives to fill up the parts which ogres and giants with seven-leagued boots occupy in the ordinary nursery tales. And how could it be otherwise ? Was it not the Black Douglas who slew with his own hand the heir of the Osbaldistone family the day after he took possession of his estate, surprising him and his vassals while solemnizing a feast suited to the occasion ? Was it not Wat the Devil who drove all the year-old hogs off the braes of Lanthorn-side, in the very recent days of my grandfather's father ? And had we not many a trophy, but, according to old Mabel's version of history, far more honourably gained, to mark our revenge of these wrongs ? Did not Sir Henry Osbaldistone, fifth baron of the name, carry off the fair maid of Fairnington, as Achilles did his Chryseis and Briseis of old, and detain her in his fortress against all the power of her friends, supported by the most mighty Scottish chiefs of warlike fame ?

And had not our swords shone foremost at most of those fields in which England was victorious over her rival? All our family renown was acquired,—all our family misfortunes were occasioned,—by the northern wars.

Warmed by such tales, I looked upon the Scottish people during my childhood, as a race hostile by nature to the more southern inhabitants of this realm; and this view of the matter was not much corrected by the language which my father sometimes held with respect to them. He had engaged in some large speculations concerning oak-woods, the property of Highland proprietors, and alleged, that he found them much more ready to make bargains, and extort earnest of the purchase-money, than punctual in complying on their side with the terms of the engagements. The Scotch mercantile men, whom he was under the necessity of employing as a sort of middle-men on these occasions, were also suspected by my father of having secured, by one means or other, more than their own share of the profit which ought to have accrued. In short, if Mabel complained of the Scottish arms in ancient times, Mr. Osbaldistone inveighed no less against the arts of these modern Sinons; and between them, though without any fixed purpose of doing so, they impressed my youthful mind with a sincere aversion to the northern inhabitants of Britain, as a people bloodthirsty in time of war, treacherous during truce, interested, selfish, avaricious, and tricky in the business of peaceful life, and having few good qualities, unless there should be accounted such, a ferocity which resembled courage in martial affairs, and a sort of wily craft, which supplied the place of wisdom in the ordinary commerce of mankind. In justification, or apology, for those who entertained such prejudices, I must remark, that the Scotch of that period were guilty of similar injustice to the English, whom they branded universally as a race of purse-proud arrogant epicures. Such seeds of national dislike remained between the two countries, the natural consequences of their existence as separate and rival states. We have seen recently the breath of a demagogue blow these sparks into a temporary flame, which I sincerely hope is now extinguished in its own ashes.*

It was, then, with an impression of dislike, that I contemplated the first Scotchman I chanced to meet in society. There was much about him that coincided with my previous conceptions. He had the hard features and athletic form, said to be peculiar to his country, together with the national intonation and slow pedantic mode of expression, arising from a desire to avoid peculiarities of idiom or dialect. I could also observe the caution and shrewdness of his country in many of the observations which he made, and the answers which he returned. But I was not prepared for the air of easy self-possession and superiority, with which he seemed to predominate over the company into which he was thrown, as it were by accident. His dress

---

* This seems to have been written about the time of Wilkes and Liberty.

was as coarse as it could be, being still decent; and, at a time when great expense was lavished upon the wardrobe, even of the lowest who pretended to the character of gentlemen, this indicated mediocrity of circumstances, if not poverty. His conversation intimated, that he was engaged in the cattle-trade, no very dignified professional pursuit. And yet, under these disadvantages, he seemed, as a matter of course, to treat the rest of the company with the cool and condescending politeness, which implies a real, or imagined, superiority over those towards whom it is used. When he gave his opinion on any point, it was with that easy tone of confidence used by those superior to their society in rank or information, as if what he said could not be doubted, and was not to be questioned. Mine host and his Sunday guests, after an effort or two to support their consequence by noise and bold averment, sunk gradually under the authority of Mr. Campbell, who thus fairly possessed himself of the lead in the conversation. I was tempted from curiosity, to dispute the ground with him myself, confiding in my knowledge of the world, extended as it was by my residence abroad, and in the stores with which a tolerable education had possessed my mind. In the latter respect, he offered no competition, and it was easy to see that his natural powers had never been cultivated by education. But I found him much better acquainted than I was myself with the present state of France, the character of the Duke of Orleans, who had just succeeded to the regency of that kingdom, and that of the statesmen by whom he was surrounded; and his shrewd, caustic, and somewhat satirical remarks, were those of a man who had been a close observer of the affairs of that country.

On the subject of politics, Campbell observed a silence and moderation which might arise from caution. The divisions of Whig and Tory then shook England to her very centre, and a powerful party, engaged in the Jacobite interest, menaced the dynasty of Hanover, which had been just established on the throne. Every alehouse resounded with the brawls of contending politicians, and as mine host's politics were of that liberal description which quarrelled with no good customer, his hebdomadal visitants were often divided in their opinion as irreconcilably as if he had feasted the Common Council. The curate and the apothecary, with a little man, who made no boast of his vocation, but who, from the flourish and snap of his fingers, I believed to have been the barber, strongly espoused the cause of high church and the Stewart line. The exciseman, as in duty bound, and the attorney, who looked to some petty office under the crown, together with my fellow-traveller, who seemed to enter keenly into the contest, stanchly supported the cause of King George and the Protestant succession. Dire was the screaming — deep the oaths! Each party appealed to Mr. Campbell, anxious, it seemed, to elicit his approbation.

'You are a Scotchman, sir: a gentleman of your country must stand up for hereditary right,' cried one party.

'You are a Presbyterian,' assumed the other class of disputants; 'you cannot be a friend to arbitrary power.'

'Gentlemen,' said our Scotch oracle, after having gained, with some difficulty, a moment's pause, 'I havena much dubitation that King George weel deserves the predilection of his friends; and if he can haud the grip he has gotten, why, doubtless, he may make the gauger, here, a commissioner of the revenue, and confer on our friend, Mr. Quitam, the preferment of solicitor-general; and he may also grant some good deed or reward to this honest gentleman who is sitting upon his portmanteau, which he prefers to a chair: And, questionless, King James is also a grateful person, and when he gets his hand in play, he may, if he be so minded, make this reverend gentleman arch-prelate of Canterbury, and Dr. Mixit, chief physician to his household, and commit his royal beard to the care of my friend Latherum. But as I doubt mickle whether any of the competing sovereigns would give Rob Campbell a tass of aquavitæ, if he lacked it, I give my vote and interest to Jonathan Brown, our landlord, to be the King and Prince of Skinkers, conditionally that he fetches us another bottle as good as the last.'

This sally was received with general applause, in which the landlord cordially joined; and when he had given orders for fulfilling the condition on which his preferment was to depend, he failed not to acquaint them, 'that, for as peaceable a gentleman as Mr. Campbell was, he was, moreover, as bold as a lion—seven highwaymen had he defeated with his single arm, that beset him as he came from Whitson-Tryste.'

'Thou art deceived, friend Jonathan,' said Campbell, interrupting him; 'they were but barely two, and two cowardly loons as man could wish to meet withal.'

'And did you, sir, really,' said my fellow-traveller, edging his chair (I should have said his portmanteau) nearer to Mr. Campbell, 'really and actually beat two highwaymen yourself alone?'

'In troth did I, sir,' replied Campbell; 'and I think it nae great thing to make a sang about.'

'Upon my word, sir,' replied my acquaintance, 'I should be happy to have the pleasure of your company on my journey—I go northward, sir.'

This piece of gratuitous information concerning the route he proposed to himself, the first I had heard my companion bestow upon any one, failed to excite the corresponding confidence of the Scotchman.

'We can scarce travel together,' he replied, dryly. 'You, sir, doubtless, are well mounted, and I, for the present, travel on foot, or on a Highland shelty, that does not help me much faster forward.'

So saying, he called for a reckoning for the wine, and throwing down the price of the additional bottle which he had himself introduced, rose as if to take leave of us. My companion made up to him, and taking him by the button, drew him aside into one of the windows. I could not help overhearing him pressing something;—I supposed his company upon the journey, which Mr. Campbell seemed to decline.

'I will pay your charges, sir,' said the traveller, in a tone, as if he thought the argument should bear down all opposition.

'It is quite impossible,' said Campbell, somewhat contemptuously; 'I have business at Rothbury.'

'But I am in no great hurry; I can ride out of the way, and never miss a day or so for good company.'

'Upon my faith, sir,' said Campbell, 'I cannot render you the service you seem to desiderate. I am,' he added, drawing himself up haughtily, 'travelling on my own private affairs, and if ye will act by my advisement, sir, ye will neither unite yourself with an absolute stranger on the road, nor communicate your line of journey to those who are asking ye no questions about it.' He then extricated his button, not very ceremoniously, from the hold which detained him, and, coming up to me as the company were dispersing, observed, 'Your friend, sir, is too communicative, considering the nature of his trust.'

'That gentleman,' I replied, looking towards the traveller, 'is no friend of mine, but an acquaintance whom I picked up on the road. I know neither his name nor business, and you seem to be deeper in his confidence than I am.'

'I only meant,' he replied hastily, 'that he seems a thought rash in conferring the honour of his company on those who desire it not.'

'The gentleman,' replied I, 'knows his own affairs

best, and I should be sorry to constitute myself a judge of them in any respect.'

Mr. Campbell made no further observation, but merely wished me a good journey, and the party dispersed for the evening.

Next day I parted company with my timid companion, as I left the great northern road to turn more westerly in the direction of Osbaldistone Manor, my uncle's seat. I cannot tell whether he felt relieved or embarrassed by my departure, considering the dubious light in which he seemed to regard me. For my own part, his tremors ceased to amuse me, and, to say the truth, I was heartily glad to get rid of him.

CHAPTER V

How melts my beating heart, as I behold
Each lovely nymph, our island's boast and pride,
Push on the generous steed, that sweeps along
O'er rough, o'er smooth, nor heeds the steepy hill,
Nor falters in the extended vale below !
THE CHASE.

I APPROACHED my native north, for such I esteemed it, with that enthusiasm which romantic and wild scenery inspires in the lovers of nature. No longer interrupted by the babble of my companion, I could now remark the difference which the country exhibited from that through which I had hitherto travelled. The streams now more properly deserved the name, for, instead of slumbering stagnant among reeds and willows, they brawled along beneath the shade of natural copsewood ; were now hurried down declivities, and now purled more leisurely, but still in active motion, through little lonely valleys, which, opening on the road from time to time, seemed to invite the traveller to explore their recesses. The Cheviots rose before me in frowning majesty ; not, indeed, with the sublime variety of rock and cliff which characterises mountains of the primary class, but huge, round-headed, and clothed with a dark robe of russet, gaining, by their extent and desolate appearance, an influence upon the imagination, as a desert district possessing a character of its own.

The abode of my fathers, which I was now approaching, was situated in a glen, or narrow valley, which ran up among those hills. Extensive estates, which once belonged to the family of Osbaldistone, had been long dissipated by the misfortunes or misconduct of my ancestors; but enough was still attached to the old mansion, to give my uncle the title of a man of large property. This he employed (as I was given to understand by some inquiries which I made on the road) in maintaining the prodigal hospitality of a northern squire of the period, which he deemed essential to his family dignity.

From the summit of an eminence I had already had a distant view of Osbaldistone Hall, a large and antiquated edifice, peeping out from a Druidical grove of huge oaks; and I was directing my course towards it, as straightly and as speedily as the windings of a very indifferent road would permit, when my horse, tired as he was, pricked up his ears at the enlivening notes of a pack of hounds in full cry, cheered by the occasional bursts of a French horn, which in those days was a constant accompaniment to the chase. I made no doubt that the pack was my uncle's, and drew up my horse with the purpose of suffering the hunters to pass without notice, aware that a hunting-field was not the proper scene to introduce myself to a keen sportsman, and determined, when they had passed on, to proceed to the mansion-house at my own pace, and there to await the return of the proprietor from his sport. I paused, therefore, on a rising ground, and, not unmoved by the sense of interest which that species of silvan sport is so much calculated to inspire, (although my mind was not at the moment very accessible to impressions of this nature,) I expected with some eagerness the appearance of the huntsmen.

The fox, hard run, and nearly spent, first made his appearance from the copse which clothed the right-hand side of the valley. His drooping brush, his soiled appearance, and jaded trot, proclaimed his fate impending; and the carrion crow, which hovered over him, already considered poor Reynard as soon to be his prey. He crossed the stream·which divides the little valley, and was dragging himself up a ravine on the other side of its wild banks, when the headmost hounds, followed by the rest of the pack in full cry, burst from the coppice, followed by the huntsman, and three or four riders. The dogs pursued the trace of Reynard with unerring instinct; and the hunters followed with reckless haste, regardless of the broken and difficult nature of the ground. They were tall, stout young men, well mounted, and dressed in green and red, the uniform of a sporting association, formed under the auspices of old Sir Hildebrand Osbaldistone. My cousins! thought I, as they swept past me. The next reflection was, what is my reception likely to be among these worthy successors of Nimrod? and how improbable is it, that I, knowing little or nothing of rural sports, shall find myself at ease, or happy, in my uncle's family. A vision that passed me interrupted these reflections.

It was a young lady, the loveliness of whose very

striking features was enhanced by the animation of
the chase and the glow of exercise, mounted on
a beautiful horse, jet black, unless where he was
flecked by spots of the snow-white foam which
embossed his bridle. She wore, what was then
somewhat unusual, a coat, vest, and hat, resembling those of a man, which fashion has since called a
riding-habit. The mode had been introduced while
I was in France, and was perfectly new to me.
Her long black hair streamed on the breeze, having
in the hurry of the chase escaped from the ribbon
which bound it. Some very broken ground, through
which she guided her horse with the most admir-
able address and presence of mind, retarded her
course, and brought her closer to me than any of
the other riders had passed. I had, therefore, a
full view of her uncommonly fine face and person,
to which an inexpressible charm was added by the
wild gaiety of the scene, and the romance of her
singular dress and unexpected appearance. As she
passed me, her horse made, in his impetuosity, an
irregular movement, just while, coming once more
upon open ground, she was again putting him to
his speed. It served as an apology for me to ride
close up to her, as if to her assistance. There was,
however, no cause for alarm; it was not a stumble,
nor a false step; and, if it had, the fair Amazon had
too much self-possession to have been deranged by
it. She thanked my good intentions, however, by
a smile, and I felt encouraged to put my horse
to the same pace, and to keep in her immediate
neighbourhood. The clamour of 'Whoop, dead,

dead!' and the corresponding flourish of the French horn, soon announced to us that there was no more occasion for haste, since the chase was at a close. One of the young men whom we had seen approached us, waving the brush of the fox in triumph, as if to upbraid my fair companion.

'I see,' she replied,—'I see; but make no noise about it; if Phœbe,' she said, patting the neck of the beautiful animal on which she rode, 'had not got among the cliffs, you would have had little cause for boasting.'

They met as she spoke, and I observed them both look at me and converse a moment in an under tone, the young lady apparently pressing the sportsman to do something which he declined shyly, and with a sort of sheepish sullenness. She instantly turned her horse's head towards me, saying,—'Well, well, Thornie, if you won't, I must, that's all.— Sir,' she continued, addressing me, 'I have been endeavouring to persuade this cultivated young gentleman to make inquiry of you, whether, in the course of your travels in these parts, you have heard any thing of a friend of ours, one Mr. Francis Osbaldistone, who has been for some days expected at Osbaldistone Hall?'

I was too happy to acknowledge myself to be the party inquired after, and to express my thanks for the obliging inquiries of the young lady.

'In that case, sir,' she rejoined, 'as my kinsman's politeness seems to be still slumbering, you will permit me (though I suppose it is highly improper) to stand mistress of ceremonies, and to

present to you young Squire Thorncliff Osbaldistone, your cousin, and Die Vernon, who has also
the honour to be your accomplished cousin's poor
kinswoman.'

There was a mixture of boldness, satire, and
simplicity in the manner in which Miss Vernon
pronounced these words. My knowledge of life
was sufficient to enable me to take up a corresponding tone as I expressed my gratitude to her for her
condescension, and my extreme pleasure at having
met with them. To say the truth, the compliment
was so expressed, that the lady might easily appro-
riate the greater share of it, for Thorncliff seemed
an arrant country bumpkin, awkward, shy, and
somewhat sulky withal. He shook hands with
me, however, and then intimated his intention of
leaving me that he might help the huntsman and
his brothers to couple up the hounds, a purpose
which he rather communicated by way of information to Miss Vernon than as apology to me.

'There he goes,' said the young lady, following
him with eyes in which disdain was admirably
painted,—'the prince of grooms and cock-fighters,
and blackguard horse-coursers. But there is not
one of them to mend another.—Have you read
Markham?' said Miss Vernon.

'Read whom, ma'am?—I do not even remember
the author's name.'

'O lud! on what a strand are you wrecked!' replied the young lady. 'A poor forlorn and ignorant
stranger, unacquainted with the very Alcoran of the
savage tribe whom you are come to reside among

ROB ROY

—Never to have heard of Markham, the most celebrated author on farriery! then I fear you are
equally a stranger to the more modern names of
Gibson and Bartlett?'

'I am, indeed, Miss Vernon.'

'And do you not blush to own it?' said Miss
Vernon. 'Why, we must forswear your alliance.
Then, I suppose, you can neither give a ball, nor a
mash, nor a horn?'

'I confess I trust all these matters to an ostler,
or to my groom.'

'Incredible carelessness!—And you cannot shoe
a horse, or cut his mane and tail; or worm a dog,
or crop his ears, or cut his dew-claws; or reclaim a
hawk, or give him his casting-stones, or direct his
diet when he is sealed; or——'

'To sum up my insignificance in one word,'
replied I, 'I am profoundly ignorant in all these
rural accomplishments.'

'Then, in the name of Heaven, Mr. Francis
Osbaldistone, what *can* you do?'

'Very little to the purpose, Miss Vernon; something, however, I can pretend to—When my groom
has dressed my horse, I can ride him, and when my
hawk is in the field I can fly him.'

'Can you do this?' said the young lady, putting
her horse to a canter.

There was a sort of rude overgrown fence crossed
the path before us, with a gate, composed of pieces
of wood rough from the forest; I was about to
move forward to open it, when Miss Vernon cleared
the obstruction at a flying leap. I was bound, in

67

point of honour, to follow, and was in a moment again at her side.

'There are hopes of you yet,' she said. 'I was afraid you had been a very degenerate Osbaldistone. But what on earth brings you to Cub-Castle?—for so the neighbours have christened this hunting-hall of ours. You might have staid away, I suppose, if you would?'

I felt I was by this time on a very intimate footing with my beautiful apparition, and therefore replied in a confidential under tone,—'Indeed, my dear Miss Vernon, I might have considered it as a sacrifice to be a temporary resident in Osbaldistone Hall, the inmates being such as you describe them; but I am convinced there is one exception that will make amends for all deficiencies.'

'O, you mean Rashleigh?' said Miss Vernon.

'Indeed I do not; I was thinking—forgive me—of some person much nearer me.'

'I suppose it would be proper not to understand your civility?—But that is not my way—I don't make a curtsey for it, because I am sitting on horseback. But, seriously, I deserve your exception, for I am the only conversible being about the Hall, except the old priest and Rashleigh.'

'And who is Rashleigh, for Heaven's sake?'

'Rashleigh is one who would fain have every one like him for his own sake.—He is Sir Hildebrand's youngest son—about your own age, but not so — not well looking, in short. But nature has given him a mouthful of common sense, and the priest has added a bushelful of learning—he is what we call a very clever man in this country, where clever men are scarce. Bred to the church, but in no hurry to take orders.'

'To the Catholic Church?'

'The Catholic Church! what Church else?' said the young lady. 'But I forgot, they told me you are a heretic. Is that true, Mr. Osbaldistone?'

'I must not deny the charge.'

'And yet you have been abroad, and in Catholic countries?'

'For nearly four years.'

'You have seen convents?'

'Often; but I have not seen much in them which recommended the Catholic religion.'

'Are not the inhabitants happy?'

'Some are unquestionably so, whom either a profound sense of devotion, or an experience of the persecutions and misfortunes of the world, or a natural apathy of temper, has led into retirement. Those who have adopted a life of seclusion from sudden and overstrained enthusiasm, or in hasty resentment of some disappointment or mortification, are very miserable. The quickness of sensation soon returns, and, like the wilder animals in a menagerie, they are restless under confinement, while others muse or fatten in cells of no larger dimensions than theirs.'

'And what,' continued Miss Vernon, 'becomes of those victims who are condemned to a convent by the will of others? what do they resemble? especially, what do they resemble, if they are born to enjoy life, and feel its blessings?'

'They are like imprisoned singing-birds,' replied I, 'condemned to wear out their lives in confinement, which they try to beguile by the exercise of accomplishments, which would have adorned society, had they been left at large.'

'I shall be,' returned Miss Vernon — 'that is,' said she, correcting herself, — 'I should be rather like the wild hawk, who, barred the free exercise of his soar through heaven, will dash himself to pieces against the bars of his cage. But to return to Rashleigh,' said she, in a more lively tone, 'you will think him the pleasantest man you ever saw in your life, Mr. Osbaldistone; that is, for a week at least. If he could find out a blind mistress, never man would be so secure of conquest; but the eye breaks the spell that enchants the ear. But here we are in the court of the old hall, which looks as wild and old-fashioned as any of its inmates. There is no great toilette kept at Osbaldistone Hall, you must know; but I must take off these things, they are so unpleasantly warm, and the hat hurts my forehead too,' continued the lively girl, taking it off, and shaking down a profusion of sable ringlets, which, half laughing, half blushing, she separated with her white slender fingers, in order to clear them away from her beautiful face and piercing hazel eyes. If there was any coquetry in the action, it was well disguised by the careless indifference of her manner. I could not help saying, 'that, judging of the family from what I saw, I should suppose the toilette a very unnecessary care.'

'That's very politely said; though, perhaps, I

ought not to understand in what sense it was meant,'
replied Miss Vernon ; ' but you will see a better
apology for a little negligence, when you meet the
Orsons you are to live amongst, whose forms no
toilette could improve. But, as I said before, the
old dinner-bell will clang, or rather clank, in a few
minutes—it cracked of its own accord on the day
of the landing of King Willie, and my uncle,
respecting its prophetic talent, would never permit
it to be mended. So do you hold my palfrey, like
a duteous knight, until I send some more humble
squire to relieve you of the charge.'

She threw me the rein as if we had been acquainted from our childhood, jumped from her
saddle, tripped across the court-yard, and entered
at a side-door, leaving me in admiration of her
beauty, and astonished with the overfrankness of
her manners, which seemed the more extraordinary,
at a time when the dictates of politeness, flowing
from the court of the Grand Monarque Louis XIV.,
prescribed to the fair sex an unusual severity of
decorum. I was left awkwardly enough stationed
in the centre of the court of the old hall,
mounted on one horse, and holding another in
my hand.

The building afforded little to interest a stranger,
had I been disposed to consider it attentively ; the
sides of the quadrangle were of various architecture,
and with their stone-shafted latticed windows, pro-
jecting turrets, and massive architraves, resembled
the inside of a convent, or of one of the older and
less splendid colleges of Oxford. I called for a

domestic, but was for some time totally unattended to; which was the more provoking, as I could perceive I was the object of curiosity to several servants, both male and female, from different parts of the building, who popped out their heads and withdrew them, like rabbits in a warren, before I could make a direct appeal to the attention of any individual. The return of the huntsmen and hounds relieved me from my embarrassment, and with some difficulty I got one clown to relieve me of the charge of the horses, and another stupid boor to guide me to the presence of Sir Hildebrand. This service he performed with much such grace and goodwill, as a peasant who is compelled to act as guide to a hostile patrol; and in the same manner I was obliged to guard against his deserting me in the labyrinth of low vaulted passages which conducted to 'Stun Hall,' as he called it, where I was to be introduced to the gracious presence of my uncle.

We did, however, at length reach a long vaulted room, floored with stone, where a range of oaken tables, of a weight and size too massive ever to be moved aside, were already covered for dinner. This venerable apartment, which had witnessed the feasts of several generations of the Osbaldistone family, bore also evidence of their success in field-sports. Huge antlers of deer, which might have been trophies of the hunting of Chevy Chace, were ranged around the walls, interspersed with the stuffed skins of badgers, otters, martins, and other animals of the chase. Amidst some remnants of old armour, which had, perhaps, served against the Scotch, hung the more valued weapons of silvan war, cross-bows, guns of various device and construction, nets, fishing-rods, otter-spears, hunting-poles, with many other singular devices and engines for taking or killing game. A few old pictures, dimmed with smoke, and stained with March beer, hung on the walls, representing knights and ladies, honoured, doubtless, and renowned in their day; those frowning fearfully from huge bushes of wig and of beard; and these looking delightfully with all their might at the roses which they brandished in their hands.

I had just time to give a glance at these matters, when about twelve blue-coated servants burst into the hall with much tumult and talk, each rather employed in directing his comrades than in discharging his own duty. Some brought blocks and billets to the fire, which roared, blazed, and ascended, half in smoke, half in flame, up a huge tunnel, with an opening wide enough to accommodate a stone-seat within its ample vault, and which was fronted, by way of chimney-piece, with a huge piece of heavy architecture, where the monsters of heraldry, embodied by the art of some Northumbrian chisel, grinned and ramped in red free-stone, now japanned by the smoke of centuries. Others of these old-fashioned serving-men bore huge smoking dishes, loaded with substantial fare; others brought in cups, flagons, bottles, yea barrels of liquor. All tramped, kicked, plunged, shouldered, and jostled, doing as little service with as much tumult as could well be imagined. At length, while the dinner was, after various efforts, in the act of being arranged upon the board, 'the clamour much of men and dogs,' the cracking of whips, calculated for the intimidation of the latter, voices loud and high, steps which, impressed by the heavy-heeled boots of the period, clattered like those in the statue of the *Festin de pierre*,* announced the arrival of those for whose benefit the preparations were made. The hubbub among the servants rather increased than diminished as this crisis approached,—some called to make haste,—others to take time,—some exhorted to stand out of the way, and make room for Sir Hildebrand and the young squires,—some to close round the table, and be *in* the way,—some bawled to open, some to shut a pair of folding-doors, which divided the hall from a sort of gallery, as I afterwards learned, or withdrawing-room, fitted up with black wainscot. Opened the doors were at length, and in rushed curs and men,—eight dogs, the domestic chaplain, the village doctor, my six cousins, and my uncle.

---

* Now called Don Juan.

CHAPTER VI

The rude hall rocks—they come, they come,—
The din of voices shakes the dome;—
In stalk the various forms, and, drest
In varying morion, varying vest,
All march with haughty step—all proudly shake the crest.

PENROSE.

IF Sir Hildebrand Osbaldistone was in no hurry to greet his nephew, of whose arrival he must have been informed for some time, he had important avocations to allege in excuse. 'Had seen thee sooner, lad,' he exclaimed, after a rough shake of the hand, and a hearty welcome to Osbaldistone Hall, 'but had to see the hounds kennelled first. Thou art welcome to the Hall, lad—here is thy cousin Percie, thy cousin Thornie, and thy cousin John—your cousin Dick, your cousin Wilfred, and —stay, where's Rashleigh—ay, here's Rashleigh— take thy long body aside, Thornie, and let's see thy brother a bit—your cousin Rashleigh.—So, thy father has thought on the old Hall, and old Sir Hildebrand at last—better late than never—Thou art welcome, lad, and there's enough.—Where's my little Die?—ay, here she comes—this is my niece Die, my wife's brother's daughter — the prettiest girl in our dales, be the other who she may—and so now let's to the sirloin.'—

To gain some idea of the person who held this language, you must suppose, my dear Tresham, a man aged about sixty, in a hunting suit which had once been richly laced, but whose splendour had been tarnished by many a November and December storm. Sir Hildebrand, notwithstanding the abruptness of his present manner, had, at one period of his life, known courts and camps; had held a commission in the army which encamped on Hounslow Heath previous to the Revolution, and, recommended perhaps by his religion, had been knighted about the same period by the unfortunate and ill-advised James II. But the Knight's dreams of further preferment, if he ever entertained any, had died away at the crisis which drove his patron from the throne, and since that period he had spent a sequestered life upon his native domains. Notwithstanding his rusticity, however, Sir Hildebrand retained much of the exterior of a gentleman, and appeared among his sons as the remains of a Corinthian pillar, defaced and overgrown with moss and lichen, might have looked, if contrasted with the rough, unhewn masses of upright stones in Stonehenge, or any other druidical temple. The sons were, indeed, heavy unadorned blocks as the eye would desire to look upon. Tall, stout, and comely, all and each of the five eldest seemed to want alike the Promethean fire of intellect, and the exterior grace and manner, which, in the polished world, sometimes supply mental deficiency. Their most valuable moral quality seemed to be the good-humour and content which was expressed in their heavy features, and their only pretence to accomplishment was their dexterity in field sports, for which alone they lived. The strong Gyas, and the strong Cloanthus, are not less distinguished by the poet, than the strong Percival, the strong Thorncliff, the strong John, Richard, and Wilfred Osbaldistones, were by outward appearance.

But, as if to indemnify herself for a uniformity so uncommon in her productions, Dame Nature had rendered Rashleigh Osbaldistone a striking contrast in person and manner, and, as I afterwards learned, in temper and talents, not only to his brothers, but to most men whom I had hitherto met with. When Percie, Thornie, and Co. had respectively nodded, grinned, and presented their shoulder, rather than their hand, as their father named them to their new kinsman, Rashleigh stepped forward, and welcomed me to Osbaldistone Hall, with the air and manner of a man of the world. His appearance was not in itself prepossessing. He was of low stature, whereas all his brethren seemed to be descendants of Anak; and, while they were handsomely formed, Rashleigh, though strong in person, was bull-necked and cross-made, and, from some early injury in his youth, had an imperfection in his gait, so much resembling an absolute halt, that many alleged that it formed the obstacle to his taking orders; the church of Rome, as is well known, admitting none to the clerical profession who labours under any personal deformity. Others, however, ascribed this unsightly defect to a mere awkward habit, and contended, that it did not amount to a personal disqualification from holy orders.

The features of Rashleigh were such, as, having looked upon, we in vain wish to banish from our memory, to which they recur as objects of painful curiosity, although we dwell upon them with a feeling of dislike, and even of disgust. It was not the actual plainness of his face, taken separately from the meaning, which made this strong impression. His features were, indeed, irregular, but they were by no means vulgar; and his keen dark eyes, and shaggy eyebrows, redeemed his face from the charge of commonplace ugliness. But there was in these eyes an expression of art and design, and, on provocation, a ferocity tempered by caution, which nature had made obvious to the most ordinary physiognomist, perhaps with the same intention that she has given the rattle to the poisonous snake. As if to compensate him for these disadvantages of exterior, Rashleigh Osbaldistone was possessed of a voice the most soft, mellow, and rich in its tones that I ever heard, and was at no loss for language of every sort suited to so fine an organ. His first sentence of welcome was hardly ended, ere I internally agreed with Miss Vernon, that my new kinsman would make an instant conquest of a mistress whose ears alone were to judge his cause. He was about to place himself beside me at dinner, but Miss Vernon, who, as the only female in the family, arranged all such matters according to her own pleasure, contrived that I should sit betwixt Thorncliff and herself; and it can scarce be doubted that I favoured this more advantageous arrangement.

'I want to speak with you,' she said, 'and I have placed honest Thornie betwixt Rashleigh and you on purpose. He will be like—

> Feather-bed 'twixt castle wall
> And heavy brunt of cannon ball;

while I, your earliest acquaintance in this intellectual family, ask of you how you like us all?'

'A very comprehensive question, Miss Vernon, considering how short while I have been at Osbaldistone Hall.'

'O, the philosophy of our family lies on the surface—there are minute shades distinguishing the individuals, which require the eye of an intelligent observer; but the species, as naturalists I believe call it, may be distinguished and characterised at once.'

'My five elder cousins, then, are, I presume, of pretty nearly the same character.'

'Yes, they form a happy compound of sot, game-keeper, bully, horse-jockey, and fool; but as they say there cannot be found two leaves on the same tree exactly alike, so these happy ingredients, being mingled in somewhat various proportions in each individual, make an agreeable variety for those who like to study character.'

'Give me a sketch, if you please, Miss Vernon.'

'You shall have them all in a family-piece, at full length—the favour is too easily granted to be refused. Percie, the son and heir, has more of the sot than of the gamekeeper, bully, horse - jockey, or fool—My precious Thornie is more of the bully than the sot, gamekeeper, jockey, or fool — John, who sleeps whole weeks amongst the hills, has most of the gamekeeper—The jockey is powerful with Dickon, who rides two hundred miles by day and night to be bought and sold at a horse-race — And the fool predominates so much over Wilfred's other qualities, that he may be termed a fool positive.'

'A goodly collection, Miss Vernon, and the individual varieties belong to a most interesting species. But is there no room on the canvas for Sir Hildebrand?'

'I love my uncle,' was her reply: 'I owe him some kindness, (such it was meant for at least,) and I will leave you to draw his picture yourself, when you know him better.'

Come, thought I to myself, I am glad there is some forbearance. After all, who would have looked for such bitter satire from a creature so young and so exquisitely beautiful?

'You are thinking of me,' she said, bending her dark eyes on me, as if she meant to pierce through my very soul.

'I certainly was,' I replied with some embarrassment at the determined suddenness of the question, and then endeavouring to give a complimentary turn to my frank avowal. 'How is it possible I should think of any thing else, seated as I have the happiness to be?'

ROB ROY

She smiled with such an expression of concentrated haughtiness as she alone could have thrown into her countenance. ' I must inform you at once, Mr. Osbaldistone, that compliments are entirely lost upon me; do not, therefore, throw away your pretty sayings — they serve fine gentlemen who travel in the country, instead of the toys, beads, and bracelets, which navigators carry to propitiate the savage inhabitants of newly discovered lands. Do not exhaust your stock in trade — you will find natives in Northumberland to whom your fine things will recommend you—on me they would be utterly thrown away, for I happen to know their real value.'

I was silenced and confounded.

' You remind me at this moment,' said the young lady, resuming her lively and indifferent manner, ' of the fairy tale, where the man finds all the money which he had carried to market suddenly changed into pieces of slate. I have cried down and ruined your whole stock of complimentary discourse by one unlucky observation. But, come, never mind it—You are belied, Mr. Osbaldistone, unless you have much better conversation than these *fadeurs*, which every gentleman with a toupet thinks himself obliged to recite to an unfortunate girl, merely because she is dressed in silk and gauze, while he wears superfine cloth with embroidery. Your natural paces, as any of my five cousins might say, are far preferable to your complimentary amble. Endeavour to forget my unlucky sex; call me Tom Vernon, if you have a mind, but speak to me as

81

you would to a friend and companion; you have no idea how much I shall like you.'

'That would be a bribe indeed,' returned I.

'Again!' replied Miss Vernon, holding up her finger; 'I told you I would not bear the shadow of a compliment. And now, when you have pledged my uncle, who threatens you with what he calls a brimmer, I will tell you what you think of me.'

The bumper being pledged by me, as a dutiful nephew, and some other general intercourse of the table having taken place, the continued and business-like clang of knives and forks, and the devotion of cousin Thorncliff on my right hand, and cousin Dickon, who sate on Miss Vernon's left, to the huge quantities of meat with which they heaped their plates, made them serve as two occasional partitions, separating us from the rest of the company, and leaving us to our *tête-à-tête*. 'And now,' said I, 'give me leave to ask you frankly, Miss Vernon, what you suppose I am thinking of you?—I could tell you what I really *do* think, but you have interdicted praise.'

'I do not want your assistance. I am conjurer enough to tell your thoughts without it. You need not open the casement of your bosom; I see through it. You think me a strange bold girl, half coquette, half romp; desirous of attracting attention by the freedom of her manners and loudness of her conversation, because she is ignorant of what the Spectator calls the softer graces of the sex; and perhaps you think I have some particular plan of storming you into admiration. I should be sorry to shock your self-opinion, but you were never more mistaken. All the confidence I have reposed in you, I would have given as readily to your father, if I thought he could have understood me. I am in this happy family as much secluded from intelligent listeners as Sancho in the Sierra Morena, and when opportunity offers, I must speak or die. I assure you I would not have told you a word of all this curious intelligence, had I cared a pin who knew it or knew it not.'

'It is very cruel in you, Miss Vernon, to take away all particular marks of favour from your communications, but I must receive them on your own terms.—You have not included Mr. Rashleigh Osbaldistone in your domestic sketches.'

She shrunk, I thought, at this remark, and hastily answered, in a much lower tone, 'Not a word of Rashleigh! His ears are so acute when his selfishness is interested, that the sounds would reach him even through the mass of Thorncliff's person, stuffed as it is with beef, venison-pasty, and pudding.'

'Yes,' I replied; 'but peeping past the living screen which divides us, before I put the question, I perceived that Mr. Rashleigh's chair was empty —he has left the table.'

'I would not have you be too sure of that,' Miss Vernon replied. 'Take my advice, and when you speak of Rashleigh, get up to the top of Otterscope-hill, where you can see for twenty miles round you in every direction—stand on the very peak, and speak in whispers; and, after all, don't be too sure that the bird of the air will not carry the matter. Rashleigh has been my tutor for four years; we are mutually tired of each other, and we shall heartily rejoice at our approaching separation.'

'Mr. Rashleigh leaves Osbaldistone Hall, then?'

'Yes, in a few days;—did you not know that?— Your father must keep his resolutions much more secret than Sir Hildebrand. Why, when my uncle was informed that you were to be his guest for some time, and that your father desired to have one of his hopeful sons to fill up the lucrative situation in his counting-house, which was vacant by your obstinacy, Mr. Francis, the good knight held a *cour plénière* of all his family, including the butler, housekeeper, and gamekeeper. This reverend assembly of the peers and household officers of Osbaldistone Hall was not convoked, as you may suppose, to elect your substitute, because, as Rashleigh alone possessed more arithmetic than was necessary to calculate the odds on a fighting-cock, none but he could be supposed qualified for the situation. But some solemn sanction was necessary for transforming Rashleigh's destination from starving as a Catholic priest, to thriving as a wealthy banker; and it was not without some reluctance that the acquiescence of the assembly was obtained to such an act of degradation.'

'I can conceive the scruples—but how were they got over?'

'By the general wish, I believe, to get Rashleigh out of the house,' replied Miss Vernon. 'Although

ROB ROY

youngest of the family, he has somehow or other got the entire management of all the others; and every one is sensible of the subjection, though they cannot shake it off. If any one opposes him, he is sure to rue having done so before the year goes about; and if you do him a very important service, you may rue it still more.'

'At that rate,' answered I, smiling, 'I should look about me; for I have been the cause, however unintentionally, of his change of situation.'

'Yes! and whether he regards it as an advantage or disadvantage, he will owe you a grudge for it—But here come cheese, radishes, and a bumper to church and king, the hint for chaplains and ladies to disappear; and I, the sole representative of womanhood at Osbaldistone Hall, retreat, as in duty bound.'

She vanished as she spoke, leaving me in astonishment at the mingled character of shrewdness, audacity, and frankness, which her conversation displayed. I despair conveying to you the least idea of her manner, although I have, as nearly as I can remember, imitated her language. In fact, there was a mixture of untaught simplicity, as well as native shrewdness and haughty boldness in her manner, and all were modified and recommended by the play of the most beautiful features I had ever beheld. It is not to be thought that, however strange and uncommon I might think her liberal and unreserved communications, a young man of two-and-twenty was likely to be severely critical on a beautiful girl of eighteen, for not observing a proper distance towards him. On the contrary, I was equally diverted and flattered by Miss Vernon's confidence; and that notwithstanding her declaration of its being conferred on me solely because I was the first auditor who occurred, of intelligence enough to comprehend it. With the presumption of my age, certainly not diminished by my residence in France, I imagined, that well-formed features, and a handsome person, both which I conceived myself to possess, were not unsuitable qualifications for the confident of a young beauty. My vanity thus enlisted in Miss Vernon's behalf, I was far from judging her with severity, merely for a frankness which, I supposed, was in some degree justified by my own personal merit; and the feelings of partiality, which her beauty, and the singularity of her situation, were of themselves calculated to excite, were enhanced by my opinion of her penetration and judgment in her choice of a friend.

After Miss Vernon quitted the apartment, the bottle circulated, or rather flew around the table in unceasing revolution. My foreign education had given me a distaste to intemperance, then and yet too common a vice among my countrymen. The conversation which seasoned such orgies was as little to my taste, and, if any thing could render it more disgusting, it was the relationship of the company. I therefore seized a lucky opportunity, and made my escape through a side-door, leading I knew not whither, rather than endure any longer the sight of father and sons practising the same degrading intemperance, and holding the same coarse and disgusting conversation. I was pursued, of course, as I had expected, to be reclaimed by force, as a deserter from the shrine of Bacchus. When I heard the whoop and hollo, and the tramp of the heavy boots of my pursuers on the winding stair which I was descending, I plainly foresaw I should be overtaken unless I could get into the open air. I therefore threw open a casement in the staircase, which looked into an old-fashioned garden; and, as the height did not exceed six feet, I jumped out without hesitation, and soon heard, far behind, the 'hey whoop! stole away! stole away!' of my baffled pursuers. I ran down one alley, walked fast up another; and then, conceiving myself out of all danger of pursuit, I slackened my pace into a quiet stroll, enjoying the cool air which the heat of the wine I had been obliged to swallow, as well as that of my rapid retreat, rendered doubly grateful.

As I sauntered on, I found the gardener hard at his evening employment, and saluted him, as I paused to look at his work. 'Good even, my friend.'

'Gude e'en—gude e'en t'ye,' answered the man, without looking up, and in a tone which at once indicated his northern extraction.

'Fine weather for your work, my friend.'

'It's no that muckle to be compleened o',' answered the man, with that limited degree of praise which gardeners and farmers usually bestow on the very best weather. Then raising his head, as if to see who spoke to him, he touched his Scotch bonnet with an air of respect, as he observed, 'Eh, gude safe us!—it's a sight for sair een, to see a gold-laced jeistiecor in the Ha' garden sae late at e'en.'

'A gold-laced what, my good friend?'

'Ou, a jeistiecor*—that's a jacket like your ain, there. They hae other things to do wi' them up yonder—unbuttoning them to make room for the beef and the bag-puddings, and the claret-wine, nae doubt—that's the ordinary for evening lecture on this side the Border.'

'There's no such plenty of good cheer in your country, my good friend,' I replied, 'as to tempt you to sit so late at it.'

'Hout, sir, ye ken little about Scotland; it's no for want of gude vivers—the best of fish, flesh, and fowl hae we, by sybos, ingans, turneeps, and other garden fruit. But we hae mense and discretion, and are moderate of our mouths; but here, frae the kitchen to the ha', it's fill and fetch mair, frae the tae end of the four-and-twenty till the tother. Even their fast days—they ca' it fasting when they hae the best o' sea-fish frae Hartlepool and Sunderland by land carriage, forbye trouts, grilses, salmon, and a' the lave o't, and so they make their very fasting a kind of luxury and abomination; and then the awfu' masses and matins of the puir deceived souls—but I shouldna speak about them, for your honour will be a Roman, I'se warrant, like the lave.'

---

* Perhaps from the French *Justaucorps*.

'Not I, my friend; I was bred an English presbyterian, or dissenter.'

'The right hand of fellowship to your honour then,' quoth the gardener, with as much alacrity as his hard features were capable of expressing, and, as if to show that his good-will did not rest on words, he plucked forth a huge horn snuff-box, or mull, as he called it, and proffered me a pinch with a most fraternal grin.

Having accepted his courtesy, I asked him if he had been long a domestic at Osbaldistone Hall?

'I have been fighting with wild beasts at Ephesus,' said he, looking towards the building, 'for the best part of these four-and-twenty years, as sure as my name's Andrew Fairservice.'

'But, my excellent friend Andrew Fairservice, if your religion and your temperance are so much offended by Roman rituals and southern hospitality, it seems to me that you must have been putting yourself to an unnecessary penance all this while, and that you might have found a service where they eat less, and are more orthodox in their worship. I dare say it cannot be want of skill which prevented your being placed more to your satisfaction.'

'It disna become me to speak to the point of my qualifications,' said Andrew, looking round him with great complacency; 'but nae doubt I should understand my trade of horticulture, seeing I was bred in the parish of Dreepdaily, where they raise lang-kale under glass, and force the early nettles for their spring kale.—And, to speak truth, I hae been flitting every term these four-and-twenty years; but when the time comes, there's aye something to saw that I would like to see sawn,—or something to maw that I would like to see mawn, —or something to ripe that I would like to see ripen,—and sae I e'en daiker on wi' the family frae year's end to year's end. And I wad say for certain, that I am gaun to quit at Cannlemas, only I was just as positive on it twenty years syne, and I find mysell still turning up the mouls here, for a' that. Forbye that, to tell your honour the even-down truth, there's nae better place ever offered to Andrew. But if your honour wad wush me to ony place where I wad hear pure doctrine, and hae a free cow's grass, and a cot, and a yard, and mair than ten punds of annual fee, and where there's nae leddy about the town to count the apples, I'se hold mysell muckle indebted t' ye.'

'Bravo, Andrew; I perceive you'll lose no preferment for want of asking patronage.'

'I canna see what for I should,' replied Andrew; 'it's no a generation to wait till ane's worth's discovered, I trow.'

'But you are no friend, I observe, to the ladies.'

'Na, by my troth, I keep up the first gardener's quarrel to them. They're fasheous bargains—aye crying for apricocks, pears, plums, and apples, summer and winter, without distinction o' seasons; but we hae nae slices o' the spare rib here, be praised for't! except auld Martha, and she's weel eneugh pleased wi' the freedom o' the berry-bushes to her sister's weans, when they come to drink tea in a holiday in the housekeeper's room, and wi' a wheen codlings now and then for her ain private supper.'

'You forget your young mistress.'

'What mistress do I forget?—whae's that?

'Your young mistress, Miss Vernon.'

'What! the lassie Vernon?—She's nae mistress o' mine, man. I wish she was her ain mistress; and I wish she mayna be some other body's mistress or it's lang—She's a wild slip that.'

'Indeed!' said I, more interested than I cared to own to myself, or to show to the fellow—'why, Andrew, you know all the secrets of this family.'

'If I ken them, I can keep them,' said Andrew; 'they winna work in my wame like barm in a barrel, I'se warrant ye. Miss Die is—but it's neither beef nor brose o' mine.'

And he began to dig with a great semblance of assiduity.

'What is Miss Vernon, Andrew? I am a friend of the family, and should like to know.'

'Other than a gude ane, I'm fearing,' said Andrew, closing one eye hard, and shaking his head with a grave and mysterious look—'something glee'd—your honour understands me?'

'I cannot say I do,' said I, 'Andrew; but I should like to hear you explain yourself'; and therewithal I slipped a crown-piece into Andrew's horn-hard hand. The touch of the silver made him grin a ghastly smile, as he nodded slowly, and thrust it into his breeches pocket; and then, like a man who well understood that there was value to be returned, stood up, and rested his arms on his spade,

ROB ROY

with his features composed into the most important
gravity, as for some serious communication.

'Ye maun ken, then, young gentleman, since it
imports you to know, that Miss Vernon is——'

Here breaking off, he sucked in both his cheeks,
till his lantern jaws and long chin assumed the
appearance of a pair of nut-crackers; winked hard
once more, frowned, shook his head, and seemed to
think his physiognomy had completed the information which his tongue had not fully told.

'Good God!' said I, 'so young, so beautiful, so
early lost!'

'Troth, ye may say sae—she's in a manner lost,
body and saul; forby being a Papist, I 'se uphaud
her for'—and his northern caution prevailed, and
he was again silent.

'For what, sir?' said I, sternly. 'I insist on
knowing the plain meaning of all this.'

'Ou, just for the bitterest Jacobite in the haill
shire.'

'Pshaw! a Jacobite?—is that all?'

Andrew looked at me with some astonishment,
at hearing his information treated so lightly; and
then muttering, 'Aweel, it's the warst thing I ken
aboot the lassie, howsoe'er,' he resumed his spade,
like the King of the Vandals, in Marmontel's late
novel.

CHAPTER VII

Bardolph. *The sheriff, with a monstrous watch, is at the door.*
HENRY IV. PART I.

I FOUND out with some difficulty the apartment which was destined for my accommodation; and, having secured myself the necessary good-will and attention from my uncle's domestics, by using the means they were most capable of comprehending, I secluded myself there for the remainder of the evening, conjecturing, from the fair way in which I had left my new relatives, as well as from the distant noise which continued to echo from the stone-hall, (as their banqueting-room was called,) that they were not likely to be fitting company for a sober man.

What could my father mean by sending me to be an inmate in this strange family? was my first and most natural reflection. My uncle, it was plain, received me as one who was to make some stay with him, and his rude hospitality rendered him as indifferent as King Hal to the number of those who fed at his cost. But it was plain my presence or absence would be of as little importance in his eyes as that of one of his blue-coated serving-men. My cousins were mere cubs, in whose company I might, if I liked it, unlearn whatever decent manners, or

93

elegant accomplishments, I had acquired, but where I could attain no information beyond what regarded worming dogs, rowelling horses, and following foxes. I could only imagine one reason, which was probably the true one. My father considered the life which was led at Osbaldistone Hall as the natural and inevitable pursuits of all country gentlemen, and he was desirous, by giving me an opportunity of seeing that with which he knew I should be disgusted, to reconcile me, if possible, to take an active share in his own business. In the meantime, he would take Rashleigh Osbaldistone into the counting-house. But he had an hundred modes of providing for him, and that advantageously, whenever he chose to get rid of him. So that, although I did feel a certain qualm of conscience at having been the means of introducing Rashleigh, being such as he was described by Miss Vernon, into my father's business—perhaps into his confidence—I subdued it by the reflection, that my father was complete master of his own affairs—a man not to be imposed upon, or influenced by any one, and that all I knew to the young gentleman's prejudice was through the medium of a singular and giddy girl, whose communications were made with an injudicious frankness, which might warrant me in supposing her conclusions had been hastily or inaccurately formed. Then my mind naturally turned to Miss Vernon herself; her extreme beauty; her very peculiar situation, relying solely upon her reflections, and her own spirit, for guidance and protection; and her whole character offering that variety and spirit which piques our curiosity, and engages our attention in spite of ourselves. I had sense enough to consider the neighbourhood of this singular young lady, and the chance of our being thrown into very close and frequent intercourse, as adding to the dangers, while it relieved the dulness, of Osbaldistone Hall; but I could not, with the fullest exertion of my prudence, prevail upon myself to regret excessively this new and particular hazard to which I was to be exposed. This scruple I also settled as young men settle most difficulties of the kind—I would be very cautious, always on my guard, consider Miss Vernon rather as a companion than an intimate; and all would do well enough. With these reflections I fell asleep, Miss Vernon, of course, forming the last subject of my contemplation.

Whether I dreamed of her or not, I cannot satisfy you, for I was tired, and slept soundly. But she was the first person I thought of in the morning, when waked at dawn by the cheerful notes of the hunting-horn. To start up, and direct my horse to be saddled, was my first movement; and in a few minutes I was in the court-yard, where men, dogs, and horses, were in full preparation. My uncle, who, perhaps, was not entitled to expect a very alert sportsman in his nephew, bred as he had been in foreign parts, seemed rather surprised to see me, and I thought his morning salutation wanted something of the hearty and hospitable tone which distinguished his first welcome. 'Art there, lad?—ay, youth's aye rathe—but look to thysell—mind the old song, lad—

ROB ROY

" He that gallops his horse on Blackstone edge
May chance to catch a fall." '

I believe there are few young men, and those very sturdy moralists, who would not rather be taxed with some moral peccadillo than with want of knowledge in horsemanship. As I was by no means deficient either in skill or courage, I resented my uncle's insinuation accordingly, and assured him he would find me up with the hounds.

'I doubtna, lad,' was his reply; 'thou'rt a rank rider, I 'se warrant thee — but take heed. Thy father sent thee here to me to be bitted, and I doubt I must ride thee on the curb, or we 'll hae some one to ride thee on the halter, if I takena the better heed.'

As this speech was totally unintelligible to me; as, besides, it did not seem to be delivered for my use, or benefit, but was spoken as it were aside, and as if expressing aloud something which was passing through the mind of my much-honoured uncle, I concluded it must either refer to my desertion of the bottle on the preceding evening, or that my uncle's morning hours being a little discomposed by the revels of the night before, his temper had suffered in proportion. I only made the passing reflection, that if he played the ungracious landlord, I would remain the shorter while his guest, and then hastened to salute Miss Vernon, who advanced cordially to meet me. Some show of greeting also passed between my cousins and me; but as I saw them maliciously bent upon criticising my dress and accoutrements, from the cap to the stirrup-irons, and sneering at whatever had a new or foreign appearance, I exempted myself from the task of paying them much attention; and assuming, in requital of their grins and whispers, an air of the utmost indifference and contempt, I attached myself to Miss Vernon as the only person in the party whom I could regard as a suitable companion. By her side, therefore, we sallied forth to the destined cover, which was a dingle or copse on the side of an extensive common. As we rode thither, I observed to Diana, that I did not see my cousin Rashleigh in the field; to which she replied,—'O no—he's a mighty hunter, but it's after the fashion of Nimrod, and his game is man.'

The dogs now brushed into the cover, with the appropriate encouragement from the hunters—all was business, bustle, and activity. My cousins were soon too much interested in the business of the morning to take any further notice of me, unless that I overheard Dickon the horse-jockey whisper to Wilfred the fool—'Look thou, an our French cousin be nat off a' first burst.'

To which Wilfred answered, 'Like enow, for he has a queer outlandish binding on's castor.'

Thorncliff, however, who, in his rude way, seemed not absolutely insensible to the beauty of his kinswoman, appeared determined to keep us company more closely than his brothers, perhaps to watch what passed betwixt Miss Vernon and me—perhaps to enjoy my expected mishaps in the chase. In the last particular he was disappointed. After beating in vain for the greater part of the morning,

a fox was at length found, who led us a chase
of two hours, in the course of which, notwithstanding the ill-omened French binding upon my hat,
I sustained my character as a horseman to the
admiration of my uncle and Miss Vernon, and the
secret disappointment of those who expected me
to disgrace it. Reynard, however, proved too wily
for his pursuers, and the hounds were at fault.
I could at this time observe in Miss Vernon's
manner an impatience of the close attendance
which we received from Thorncliff Osbaldistone;
and, as that active-spirited young lady never hesitated at taking the readiest means to gratify any
wish of the moment, she said to him, in a tone
of reproach—'I wonder, Thornie, what keeps you
dangling at my horse's crupper all this morning,
when you know the earths above Woolverton-mill
are not stopt.'

'I know no such an thing then, Miss Die, for
the miller swore himself as black as night, that he
stopt them at twelve o'clock, midnight that was.'

'O fie upon you, Thornie, would you trust to a
miller's word?—and these earths, too, where we
lost the fox three times this season, and you on
your grey mare that can gallop there and back in
ten minutes!'

'Well, Miss Die, I'se go to Woolverton then,
and if the earths are not stopt, I'se raddle Dick
the miller's bones for him.'

'Do, my dear Thornie; horsewhip the rascal to
purpose—via—fly away, and about it';—Thorncliff
went off at the gallop—'or get horsewhipt your-

self, which will serve my purpose just as well.
—I must teach them all discipline and obedience to
the word of command. I am raising a regiment,
you must know. Thornie shall be my sergeant-
major, Dickon my riding-master, and Wilfred, with
his deep dub-a-dub tones, that speak but three
syllables at a time, my kettle-drummer.'

' And Rashleigh ? '

' Rashleigh shall be my scout-master.'

' And will you find no employment for me, most
lovely colonel ? '

' You shall have the choice of being paymaster,
or plunder-master, to the corps. But see how the
dogs puzzle about there. Come, Mr. Frank, the
scent 's cold ; they won't recover it there this while ;
follow me, I have a view to show you.'

And, in fact, she cantered up to the top of a
gentle hill, commanding an extensive prospect.
Casting her eyes around, to see that no one was
near us, she drew up her horse beneath a few birch-
trees, which screened us from the rest of the hunting-field,—' Do you see yon peaked, brown, heathy
hill, having something like a whitish speck upon
the side ? '

' Terminating that long ridge of broken moorish
uplands ?—I see it distinctly.'

' That whitish speck is a rock called Hawkesmore-
crag, and Hawkesmore-crag is in Scotland.'

' Indeed ? I did not think we had been so near
Scotland.'

' It is so, I assure you, and your horse will carry
you there in two hours.'

'I shall hardly give him the trouble; why, the distance must be eighteen miles as the crow flies.'

'You may have my mare, if you think her less blown—I say, that in two hours you may be in Scotland.'

'And I say, that I have so little desire to be there, that if my horse's head were over the Border, I would not give his tail the trouble of following. What should I do in Scotland?'

'Provide for your safety, if I must speak plainly. Do you understand me now, Mr. Frank?'

'Not a whit; you are more and more oracular.'

'Then, on my word, you either mistrust me most unjustly, and are a better dissembler than Rashleigh Osbaldistone himself, or you know nothing of what is imputed to you; and then no wonder you stare at me in that grave manner, which I can scarce see without laughing.'

'Upon my word of honour, Miss Vernon,' said I, with an impatient feeling of her childish disposition to mirth, 'I have not the most distant conception of what you mean. I am happy to afford you any subject of amusement, but I am quite ignorant in what it consists.'

'Nay, there's no sound jest after all,' said the young lady, composing herself, 'only one looks so very ridiculous when he is fairly perplexed; but the matter is serious enough. Do you know one Moray, or Morris, or some such name?'

'Not that I can at present recollect.'

'Think a moment — Did you not lately travel with somebody of such a name?'

' The only man with whom I travelled for any length of time was a fellow whose soul seemed to lie in his portmanteau.'

' Then it was like the soul of the licentiate Pedro Garcias, which lay among the ducats in his leathern purse. That man has been robbed, and he has lodged an information against you, as connected with the violence done to him.'

' You jest, Miss Vernon ! '

' I do not, I assure you—the thing is an absolute fact.'

' And do you,' said I, with strong indignation, which I did not attempt to suppress, ' do you suppose me capable of meriting such a charge ? '

' You would call me out for it, I suppose, had I the advantage of being a man—You may do so as it is, if you like it—I can shoot flying, as well as leap a five-barred gate.'

' And are colonel of a regiment of horse besides,' replied I, reflecting how idle it was to be angry with her—' But do explain the present jest to me ! '

' There's no jest whatever,' said Diana ; ' you are accused of robbing this man, and my uncle believes it as well as I did.'

' Upon my honour, I am greatly obliged to my friends for their good opinion ! '

' Now do not, if you can help it, snort, and stare, and snuff the wind, and look so exceedingly like a startled horse — There's no such offence as you suppose — you are not charged with any petty larceny, or vulgar felony — by no means. This fellow was carrying money from government, both specie and bills, to pay the troops in the north; and it is said he has been also robbed of some dispatches of great consequence.'

'And so it is high treason, then, and not simple robbery, of which I am accused?'

'Certainly; which, you know, has been in all ages accounted the crime of a gentleman. You will find plenty in this country, and one not far from your elbow, who think it a merit to distress the Hanoverian government by every means possible.'

'Neither my politics nor my morals, Miss Vernon, are of a description so accommodating.'

'I really begin to believe that you are a Presbyterian and Hanoverian in good earnest. But what do you propose to do?'

'Instantly to refute this atrocious calumny.— Before whom,' I asked, 'was this extraordinary accusation laid?'

'Before old Squire Inglewood, who had sufficient unwillingness to receive it. He sent tidings to my uncle, I suppose, that he might smuggle you away into Scotland, out of reach of the warrant. But my uncle is sensible that his religion and old predilections render him obnoxious to government, and that, were he caught playing booty, he would be disarmed, and probably dismounted, (which would be the worse evil of the two,) as a Jacobite, Papist, and suspected person.'*

---

* On occasions of public alarm, in the beginning of the eighteenth century, the horses of the Catholics were often seized upon, as they were always supposed to be on the eve of rising in rebellion.

'I can conceive that, sooner than lose his hunters, he would give up his nephew.'

'His nephew, nieces, sons—daughters, if he had them, and whole generation,' said Diana; 'therefore trust not to him, even for a single moment, but make the best of your way before they can serve the warrant.'

'That I shall certainly do; but it shall be to the house of this Squire Inglewood—Which way does it lie?'

'About five miles off, in the low ground, behind yonder plantations—you may see the tower of the clock-house.'

'I will be there in a few minutes,' said I, putting my horse in motion.

'And I will go with you, and show you the way,' said Diana, putting her palfrey also to the trot.

'Do not think of it, Miss Vernon,' I replied. 'It is not—permit me the freedom of a friend—it is not proper, scarcely even delicate, in you to go with me on such an errand as I am now upon.'

'I understand your meaning,' said Miss Vernon, a slight blush crossing her haughty brow; — 'it is plainly spoken,'—and after a moment's pause she added, 'and I believe kindly meant.'

'It is indeed, Miss Vernon; can you think me insensible of the interest you show me, or ungrateful for it?' said I, with even more earnestness than I could have wished to express. 'Yours is meant for true kindness, shown best at the hour of need. But I must not, for your own sake—for the chance

of misconstruction—suffer you to pursue the dictates
of your generosity; this is so public an occasion
—it is almost like venturing into an open court
of justice.'

'And if it were not almost, but altogether
entering into an open court of justice, do you
think I would not go there if I thought it right,
and wished to protect a friend? You have no one
to stand by you—you are a stranger; and here,
in the outskirts of the kingdom, country justices
do odd things. My uncle has no desire to embroil
himself in your affair;—Rashleigh is absent, and
were he here, there is no knowing which side he
might take; the rest are all more stupid and brutal
one than another. I will go with you, and I do
not fear being able to serve you. I am no fine
lady, to be terrified to death with law books, hard
words, or big wigs.'

'But, my dear Miss Vernon——'

'But, my dear Mr. Francis, be patient and quiet,
and let me take my own way; for when I take the
bit between my teeth, there is no bridle will stop
me.'

Flattered with the interest so lovely a creature
seemed to take in my fate, yet vexed at the ridiculous appearance I should make, by carrying a
girl of eighteen along with me as an advocate, and
seriously concerned for the misconstruction to which
her motives might be exposed, I endeavoured to
combat her resolution to accompany me to Squire
Inglewood's. The self-willed girl told me roundly,
that my dissuasions were absolutely in vain; that

she was a true Vernon, whom no consideration,
not even that of being able to do but little to assist
him, should induce to abandon a friend in distress;
and that all I could say on the subject might be
very well for pretty, well-educated, well-behaved
misses from a town boarding-school, but did not
apply to her, who was accustomed to mind nobody's
opinion but her own.

While she spoke thus, we were advancing hastily
towards Inglewood-Place, while, as if to divert me
from the task of farther remonstrance, she drew a
ludicrous picture of the magistrate and his clerk.
Inglewood was, according to her description, a
white-washed Jacobite, that is, one who, having
been long a non-juror, like most of the other
gentlemen of the country, had lately qualified himself to act as a justice, by taking the oaths to
government. 'He had done so,' she said, 'in compliance with the urgent request of most of his
brother squires, who saw, with regret, that the
palladium of silvan sport, the game-laws, were likely
to fall into disuse for want of a magistrate who
would enforce them; the nearest acting justice
being the Mayor of Newcastle, and he, as being
rather inclined to the consumption of the game
when properly dressed, than to its preservation
when alive, was more partial, of course, to the
cause of the poacher than of the sportsman. Resolving, therefore, that it was expedient some one
of their number should sacrifice the scruples of
Jacobitical loyalty to the good of the community,
the Northumbrian country gentlemen imposed the

duty on Inglewood, who, being very inert in most of his feelings and sentiments, might, they thought, comply with any political creed without much repugnance. Having thus procured the body of justice, they proceeded,' continued Miss Vernon, ' to attach to it a clerk, by way of soul, to direct and animate its movements. Accordingly, they got a sharp Newcastle attorney, called Jobson, who, to vary my metaphor, finds it a good thing enough to retail justice at the sign of Squire Inglewood, and, as his own emoluments depend on the quantity of business which he transacts, he hooks in his principal for a great deal more employment in the justice line than the honest squire had ever bargained for ; so that no apple-wife within the circuit of ten miles can settle her account with a coster-monger without an audience of the reluctant Justice and his alert clerk, Mr. Joseph Jobson. But the most ridiculous scenes occur when affairs come before him, like our business of to-day, having any colouring of politics. Mr. Joseph Jobson (for which, no doubt, he has his own very sufficient reasons) is a prodigious zealot for the Protestant religion, and a great friend to the present establishment in church and state. Now, his principal, retaining a sort of instinctive attachment to the opinions which he professed openly, until he relaxed his political creed, with the patriotic view of enforcing the law against unauthorized destroyers of black-game, grouse, partridges, and hares, is peculiarly embarrassed when the zeal of his assistant involves him in judicial proceedings connected with his earlier faith ; and, instead of

seconding his zeal, he seldom fails to oppose to
it a double dose of indolence and lack of exertion.
And this inactivity does not by any means arise
from actual stupidity. On the contrary, for one
whose principal delight is in eating and drinking,
he is an alert, joyous, and lively old soul, which
makes his assumed dulness the more diverting. So
you may see Jobson on such occasions, like a bit
of a broken-down blood-tit condemned to drag an
overloaded cart, puffing, strutting, and spluttering,
to get the Justice put in motion, while, though the
wheels groan, creak, and revolve slowly, the great
and preponderating weight of the vehicle fairly
frustrates the efforts of the willing quadruped, and
prevents its being brought into a state of actual
progression. Nay more, the unfortunate pony, I
understand, has been heard to complain, that this
same car of justice, which he finds it so hard to
put in motion on some occasions, can on others
run fast enough down hill of its own accord,
dragging his reluctant self backwards along with
it, when any thing can be done of service to
Squire Inglewood's quondam friends. And then
Mr. Jobson talks big about reporting his principal
to the Secretary of State for the Home Department, if it were not for his particular regard and
friendship for Mr. Inglewood and his family.'

As Miss Vernon concluded this whimsical description, we found ourselves in front of Inglewood
Place, a handsome, though old-fashioned building,
which showed the consequence of the family.

CHAPTER VIII

' Sir,' quoth the Lawyer, ' not to flatter ye
You have as good and fair a battery
As heart could wish, and need not shame
The proudest man alive to claim.'

BUTLER.

OUR horses were taken by a servant in Sir Hilde-brand's livery, whom we found in the court-yard, and we entered the house. In the entrance-hall I was somewhat surprised, and my fair companion still more so, when we met Rashleigh Osbaldistone, who could not help showing equal wonder at our rencontre.

' Rashleigh,' said Miss Vernon, without giving him time to ask any question, 'you have heard of Mr. Francis Osbaldistone's affair, and you have been talking to the Justice about it ? '

' Certainly,' said Rashleigh, composedly, 'it has been my business here. I have been endeavour-ing,' he said, with a bow to me, 'to render my cousin what service I can. But I am sorry to meet him here.'

' As a friend and relation, Mr. Osbaldistone, you ought to have been sorry to have met me anywhere else, at a time when the charge of my reputation required me to be on this spot as soon as possible.'

' True; but, judging from what my father said,

I should have supposed a short retreat into Scotland—just till matters should be smoothed over in a quiet way——'

I answered with warmth, 'That I had no prudential measures to observe, and desired to have nothing smoothed over; on the contrary, I was come to inquire into a rascally calumny, which I was determined to probe to the bottom.'

'Mr. Francis Osbaldistone is an innocent man, Rashleigh,' said Miss Vernon, 'and he demands an investigation of the charge against him, and I intend to support him in it.'

'You do, my pretty cousin? — I should think, now, Mr. Francis Osbaldistone was likely to be as effectually, and rather more delicately, supported by my presence than by yours.'

'O certainly; but two heads are better than one, you know.'

'Especially such a head as yours, my pretty Die,' advancing, and taking her hand with a familiar fondness, which made me think him fifty times uglier than nature had made him. She led him, however, a few steps aside; they conversed in an under voice, and she appeared to insist upon some request, which he was unwilling or unable to comply with. I never saw so strong a contrast betwixt the expression of two faces. Miss Vernon's from being earnest became angry. Her eyes and cheeks became more animated, her colour mounted, she clenched her little hand, and, stamping on the ground with her tiny foot, seemed to listen with a mixture of contempt and indignation to the apologies, which, from his look of civil deference, his composed and respectful smile, his body rather drawing back than advanced, and other signs of look and person, I concluded him to be pouring out at her feet. At length she flung away from him, with ' I *will* have it so.'

' It is not in my power—there is no possibility of it.—Would you think it, Mr. Osbaldistone ? ' said he, addressing me——

' You are not mad ? ' said she, interrupting him.

' Would you think it ? ' said he, without attending to her hint—' Miss Vernon insists, not only that I know your innocence, (of which, indeed, it is impossible for any one to be more convinced,) but that I must also be acquainted with the real perpetrators of the outrage on this fellow—if, indeed, such an outrage has been committed. Is this reasonable, Mr. Osbaldistone ? '

' I will not allow any appeal to Mr. Osbaldistone, Rashleigh,' said the young lady ; ' he does not know, as I do, the incredible extent and accuracy of your information on all points.'

' As I am a gentleman, you do me more honour than I deserve.'

' Justice, Rashleigh—only justice—and it is only justice which I expect at your hands.'

' You are a tyrant, Diana,' he answered, with a sort of sigh—' a capricious tyrant, and rule your friends with a rod of iron. Still, however, it shall be as you desire. But you ought not to be here— you know you ought not—you must return with me.'

Then turning from Diana, who seemed to stand

undecided, he came up to me in the most friendly manner, and said, 'Do not doubt my interest in what regards you, Mr. Osbaldistone. If I leave you just at this moment, it is only to act for your advantage. But you must use your influence with our cousin to return; her presence cannot serve you, and must prejudice herself.'

'I assure you, sir,' I replied, 'you cannot be more convinced of this than I; I have urged Miss Vernon's return as anxiously as she would permit me to do.'

'I have thought on it,' said Miss Vernon, after a pause, 'and I will not go till I see you safe out of the hands of the Philistines. Cousin Rashleigh, I dare say, means well; but he and I know each other well.—Rashleigh, I will NOT go;—I know,' she added, in a more soothing tone, 'my being here will give you more motive for speed and exertion.'

'Stay, then, rash, obstinate girl,' said Rashleigh; 'you know but too well to whom you trust'; and hastening out of the hall, we heard his horse's feet a minute afterwards in rapid motion.

'Thank Heaven, he is gone!' said Diana. 'And now, let us seek out the Justice.'

'Had we not better call a servant?'

'O, by no means; I know the way to his den— we must burst on him suddenly—follow me.'

I did follow her accordingly, as she tripped up a few gloomy steps, traversed a twilight passage, and entered a sort of anteroom, hung round with old maps, architectural elevations, and genealogical

trees. A pair of folding-doors opened from this into
Mr. Inglewood's sitting apartment, from which was
heard the fag-end of an old ditty, chanted by a voice
which had been in its day fit for a jolly bottle-song.

> ' O, in Skipton-in-Craven,
>   Is never a haven,
>   But many a day foul weather;
>   And he that would say
>   A pretty girl nay,
>   I wish for his cravat a tether.'—

' Hey day ! ' said Miss Vernon, ' the genial Justice
must have dined already—I did not think it had
been so late.'

It was even so. Mr. Inglewood's appetite having
been sharpened by his official investigations, he
had ante-dated his meridian repast, having dined
at twelve instead of one o'clock, then the general
dining hour in England. The various occurrences
of the morning occasioned our arriving some time
after this hour, to the Justice the most important of
the four-and-twenty, and he had not neglected the
interval.

' Stay you here,' said Diana; ' I know the house,
and I will call a servant; your sudden appearance
might startle the old gentleman even to choking ';
and she escaped from me, leaving me uncertain
whether I ought to advance or retreat. It was
impossible for me not to hear some part of what
passed within the dinner apartment, and particularly
several apologies for declining to sing, expressed
in a dejected croaking voice, the tones of which, I
conceived, were not entirely new to me.

ROB ROY

'Not sing, sir? by our Lady! but you must —
What! you have cracked my silver-mounted cocoa-
nut of sack, and tell me that you cannot sing!—
Sir, sack will make a cat sing, and speak too; so up
with a merry stave, or trundle yourself out of my
doors — Do you think you are to take up all my
valuable time with your d—d declarations, and then
tell me you cannot sing?'

'Your worship is perfectly in rule,' said another
voice, which, from its pert conceited accent, might
be that of the clerk, 'and the party must be con-
formable; he hath *canet* written on his face in court
hand.'

'Up with it, then,' said the Justice, 'or, by St.
Christopher, you shall crack the cocoa-nut full of
salt-and-water, according to the statute for such
effect made and provided.'

Thus exhorted and threatened, my quondam
fellow-traveller, for I could no longer doubt that
he was the recusant in question, uplifted, with a
voice similar to that of a criminal singing his last
psalm on the scaffold, a most doleful stave to the
following effect:

'Good people all, I pray give ear,
A woful story you shall hear,
'Tis of a robber as stout as ever
Bade a true man stand and deliver.
  With his foodle doo fa loodle loo.

'This knave, most worthy of a cord,
Being arm'd with pistol and with sword,
'Twixt Kensington and Brentford then
Did boldly stop six honest men.
  With his foodle doo, etc.

113

> ' These honest men did at Brentford dine,
> Having drank each man his pint of wine,
> When this bold thief, with many curses,
> Did say, You dogs, your lives or purses.
> With his foodle doo,' etc.

I question if the honest men, whose misfortune is commemorated in this pathetic ditty, were more startled at the appearance of the bold thief, than the songster was at mine; for, tired of waiting for some one to announce me, and finding my situation as a listener rather awkward, I presented myself to the company just as my friend Mr. Morris, for such, it seems, was his name, was uplifting the fifth stave of his doleful ballad. The high tone, with which the tune started, died away in a quaver of consternation, on finding himself so near one whose character he supposed to be little less suspicious than that of the hero of his madrigal, and he remained silent, with a mouth gaping as if I had brought the Gorgon's head in my hand.

The Justice, whose eyes had closed under the influence of the somniferous lullaby of the song, started up in his chair as it suddenly ceased, and stared with wonder at the unexpected addition which the company had received, while his organs of sight were in abeyance. The clerk, as I conjectured him to be from his appearance, was also commoved; for, sitting opposite to Mr. Morris, that honest gentleman's terror communicated itself to him, though he wotted not why.

I broke the silence of surprise occasioned by my abrupt entrance. — ' My name, Mr. Inglewood, is

Francis Osbaldistone; I understand that some scoundrel has brought a complaint before you, charging me with being concerned in a loss which he says he has sustained.'

' Sir,' said the Justice, somewhat peevishly, ' these are matters I never enter upon after dinner—there is a time for every thing, and a justice of peace must eat as well as other folks.'

The goodly person of Mr. Inglewood, by the way, seemed by no means to have suffered by any fasts, whether in the service of the law or of religion.

' I beg pardon for an ill-timed visit, sir; but as my reputation is concerned, and as the dinner appears to be concluded——'

' It is not concluded, sir,' replied the magistrate; ' man requires digestion as well as food, and I protest I cannot have benefit from my victuals, unless I am allowed two hours of quiet leisure, intermixed with harmless mirth, and a moderate circulation of the bottle.'

' If your honour will forgive me,' said Mr. Jobson, who had produced and arranged his writing implements in the brief space that our conversation afforded; ' as this is a case of felony, and the gentleman seems something impatient, the charge is *contra pacem domini regis*——'

' D—n *dominie regis* !' said the impatient Justice —' I hope it's no treason to say so; — but it's enough to make one mad to be worried in this way —have I a moment of my life quiet, for warrants, orders, directions, acts, bails, bonds, and recognisances ?—I pronounce to you, Mr. Jobson, that I

115

shall send you and the justice-ship to the devil one of these days.'

'Your honour will consider the dignity of the office—one of the quorum and custos rotulorum, an office of which Sir Edward Coke wisely saith, The whole Christian world hath not the like of it, so it be duly executed.'

'Well,' said the Justice, partly reconciled by this eulogium on the dignity of his situation, and gulping down the rest of his dissatisfaction in a huge bumper of claret, 'let us to this gear then, and get rid of it as fast as we can.—Here you, sir—you, Morris—you, knight of the sorrowful countenance — is this Mr. Francis Osbaldistone the gentleman whom you charge with being art and part of felony ?'

'I, sir?' replied Morris, whose scattered wits had hardly yet re-assembled themselves—'I charge nothing—I say nothing against the gentleman.'

'Then we dismiss your complaint, sir, that's all, and a good riddance—Push about the bottle—Mr. Osbaldistone, help yourself.'

Jobson, however, was determined that Morris should not back out of the scrape so easily. 'What do you mean, Mr. Morris? — Here is your own declaration—the ink scarce dried—and you would retract it in this scandalous manner!'

'How do I know,' whispered the other, in a tremulous tone, 'how many rogues are in the house to back him?—I have read of such things in Johnson's Lives of the Highwaymen. I protest the door opens——'

And it did open, and Diana Vernon entered—

'You keep fine order here, Justice—not a servant to be seen or heard of.'

'Ah!' said the Justice, starting up with an alacrity which showed that he was not so engrossed by his devotions to Themis, or Comus, as to forget what was due to beauty — 'Ah, ha! Die Vernon, the heath-bell of Cheviot, and the blossom of the Border, come to see how the old bachelor keeps house?—Art welcome, girl, as flowers in May.'

'A fine, open, hospitable house you do keep, Justice, that must be allowed — not a soul to answer a visitor.'

'Ah! the knaves, they reckoned themselves secure of me for a couple of hours—But why did you not come earlier?—Your cousin Rashleigh dined here, and ran away like a poltroon after the first bottle was out—But you have not dined—we'll have something nice and ladylike—sweet and pretty, like yourself, tossed up in a trice.'

'I may eat a crust in the anteroom before I set out,' answered Miss Vernon—'I have had a long ride this morning; but I can't stay long, Justice—I came with my cousin, Frank Osbaldistone, there, and I must show him the way back again to the Hall, or he'll lose himself in the wolds.'

'Whew! sits the wind in that quarter?' inquired the Justice.

> "She show'd him the way, and she show'd him the way,
>   She show'd him the way to woo."

What! no luck for old fellows, then, my sweet bud of the wilderness?'

'None whatever, Squire Inglewood; but if you will be a good kind Justice, and dispatch young Frank's business, and let us canter home again, I 'll bring my uncle to dine with you next week, and we 'll expect merry doings.'

'And you shall find them, my pearl of the Tyne —Zookers, lass, I never envy these young fellows their rides and scampers, unless when you come across me. But I must not keep you just now, I suppose?—I am quite satisfied with Mr. Francis Osbaldistone's explanation — here has been some mistake, which can be cleared at greater leisure.'

'Pardon me, sir,' said I, 'but I have not heard the nature of the accusation yet.'

'Yes, sir,' said the clerk, who, at the appearance of Miss Vernon, had given up the matter in despair, but who picked up courage to press farther investigation, on finding himself supported from a quarter whence assuredly he expected no backing—'Yes, sir, and Dalton saith, That he who is apprehended as a felon shall not be discharged upon any man's discretion, but shall be held either to bail or commitment, paying to the clerk of the peace the usual fees for recognisance or commitment.'

The Justice, thus goaded on, gave me at length a few words of explanation.

It seems the tricks which I had played to this man, Morris, had made a strong impression on his imagination; for I found they had been arrayed against me in his evidence, with all the exaggerations which a timorous and heated imagination could suggest. It appeared also, that, on the day he

parted from me, he had been stopped on a solitary spot, and eased of his beloved travelling-companion, the portmanteau, by two men, well mounted and armed, having their faces covered with vizards.

One of them, he conceived, had much of my shape and air, and in a whispering conversation which took place betwixt the freebooters, he heard the other apply to him the name of Osbaldistone. The declaration farther set forth, that upon inquiring into the principles of the family so named, he, the said declarant, was informed, that they were of the worst description, the family, in all its members, having been Papists and Jacobites, as he was given to understand by the dissenting clergyman at whose house he stopped after his rencontre, since the days of William the Conqueror.

Upon all, and each of these weighty reasons, he charged me with being accessory to the felony committed upon his person; he, the said declarant, then travelling in the special employment of government, and having charge of certain important papers, and also a large sum in specie, to be paid over, according to his instructions, to certain persons of official trust and importance in Scotland.

Having heard this extraordinary accusation, I replied to it, that the circumstances on which it was founded were such as could warrant no justice, or magistrate, in any attempt on my personal liberty. I admitted that I had practised a little upon the terrors of Mr. Morris, while we travelled together, but in such trifling particulars as could have excited apprehension in no one who was one whit less timorous and jealous than himself. But I added, that I had never seen him since we parted, and if that which he feared had really come upon him, I was in nowise accessory to an action so unworthy of my character and station in life. That one of the robbers was called Osbaldistone, or that such a name was mentioned in the course of the conversation betwixt them, was a trifling circumstance, to which no weight was due. And concerning the disaffection alleged against me, I was willing to prove, to the satisfaction of the Justice, the clerk, and even the witness himself, that I was of the same persuasion as his friend the dissenting clergyman; had been educated as a good subject in the principles of the Revolution, and as such now demanded the personal protection of the laws which had been assured by that great event.

The Justice fidgeted, took snuff, and seemed considerably embarrassed, while Mr. Attorney Jobson, with all the volubility of his profession, ran over the statute of the 34 Edward III., by which justices of the peace are allowed to arrest all those whom they find by indictment or suspicion, and to put them into prison. The rogue even turned my own admissions against me, alleging, 'that since I had confessedly, upon my own showing, assumed the bearing or deportment of a robber or malefactor, I had voluntarily subjected myself to the suspicions of which I complained, and brought myself within the compass of the act, having wilfully clothed my conduct with all the colour and livery of guilt.'

I combated both his arguments and his jargon with much indignation and scorn, and observed, 'that I should, if necessary, produce the bail of my relations, which I conceived could not be refused, without subjecting the magistrate in a misdemeanour.'

'Pardon me, my good sir,—pardon me,' said the insatiable clerk, 'this is a case in which neither bail nor mainprize can be received, the felon who is liable to be committed on heavy grounds of suspicion, not being replevisable under the statute of the 3d of King Edward, there being in that act an express exception of such as be charged of commandment, or force, and aid of felony done'; and he hinted, that his worship would do well to remember that such were no way replevisable by common writ, nor without writ.

At this period of the conversation a servant entered, and delivered a letter to Mr. Jobson. He had no sooner run it hastily over, than he exclaimed, with the air of one who wished to appear much vexed at the interruption, and felt the consequence attached to a man of multifarious avocations— 'Good God!—why, at this rate, I shall have neither time to attend to the public concerns nor my own —no rest—no quiet—I wish to Heaven another gentleman in our line would settle here!'

'God forbid!' said the Justice, in a tone of *sotto-voce* deprecation; 'some of us have enough of one of the tribe.'

'This is a matter of life and death, if your worship pleases.'

'In God's name! no more justice business, I hope,' said the alarmed magistrate.

'No—no,' replied Mr. Jobson, very consequentially; 'old Gaffer Rutledge of Grime's-hill, is subpœna'd for the next world; he has sent an express for Dr. Kill-down to put in bail—another for me to arrange his worldly affairs.'

'Away with you, then,' said Mr. Inglewood hastily; 'his may not be a replevisable case under the statute, you know, or Mr. Justice Death may not like the doctor for a *main pernor*, or bailsman.'

'And yet,' said Jobson, lingering as he moved towards the door, 'if my presence here be necessary —I could make out the warrant for committal in a moment, and the constable is below—And you have heard,' he said, lowering his voice, 'Mr. Rashleigh's opinion '—the rest was lost in a whisper.

The Justice replied aloud, 'I tell thee no, man, no—we'll do nought till thou return, man; 'tis but a four-mile ride—Come, push the bottle, Mr. Morris —Don't be cast down, Mr. Osbaldistone—And you, my rose of the wilderness—one cup of claret to refresh the bloom of your cheeks.'

Diana started, as if from a reverie, in which she appeared to have been plunged while we held this discussion. 'No, Justice, I should be afraid of transferring the bloom to a part of my face where it would show to little advantage. But I will pledge you in a cooler beverage '; and, filling a glass with water, she drank it hastily, while her hurried manner belied her assumed gaiety.

I had not much leisure to make remarks upon

her demeanour, however, being full of vexation at the interference of fresh obstacles to an instant examination of the disgraceful and impertinent charge which was brought against me. But there was no moving the Justice to take the matter up in absence of his clerk, an incident which gave him apparently as much pleasure as a holiday to a schoolboy. He persisted in his endeavours to inspire jollity into a company, the individuals of which, whether considered with reference to each other, or to their respective situations, were by no means inclined to mirth. 'Come, Master Morris, you're not the first man that's been robbed, I trow —grieving ne'er brought back loss, man.—And you, Mr. Frank Osbaldistone, are not the first bully-boy that has said stand to a true man. There was Jack Winterfield, in my young days, kept the best company in the land—at horse-races and cock-fights who but he—hand and glove was I with Jack.— Push the bottle, Mr. Morris, it's dry talking—Many quart bumpers have I cracked, and thrown many a merry main with poor Jack—good family—ready wit—quick eye—as honest a fellow, barring the deed he died for—we'll drink to his memory, gentlemen —Poor Jack Winterfield—And since we talk of him, and of those sort of things, and since that d—d clerk of mine has taken his gibberish elsewhere, and since we're snug among ourselves, Mr. Osbaldistone, if you will have my best advice, I would take up this matter—the law's hard—very severe — hanged poor Jack Winterfield at York, despite family connexions and great interest—all for easing a fat west-country grazier of the price of a few beasts—Now, here is honest Mr. Morris has been frightened, and so forth—D—n it, man, let the poor fellow have back his portmanteau, and end the frolic at once.'

Morris's eyes brightened up at this suggestion, and he began to hesitate forth an assurance that he thirsted for no man's blood, when I cut the proposed accommodation short, by resenting the Justice's suggestion as an insult, that went directly to suppose me guilty of the very crime which I had come to his house with the express intention of disavowing. We were in this awkward predicament, when a servant, opening the door, announced, 'A strange gentleman to wait upon his honour'; and the party whom he thus described entered the room without farther ceremony.

CHAPTER IX

One of the thieves come back again ! I'll stand close.
He dares not wrong me now, so near the house,
And call in vain 'tis, till I see him offer it.

THE WIDOW.

'A STRANGER!' echoed the Justice,—'not upon business, I trust, for I'll be——'

His protestation was cut short by the answer of the man himself. 'My business is of a nature somewhat onerous and particular,' said my acquaintance Mr. Campbell,—for it was he, the very Scotchman whom I had seen at Northallerton,—'and I must solicit your honour to give instant and heedful consideration to it—I believe, Mr. Morris,' he added, fixing his eye on that person with a look of peculiar firmness and almost ferocity—'I believe ye ken brawly what I am—I believe ye cannot have forgotten what passed at our last meeting on the road?' Morris's jaw dropped—his countenance became the colour of tallow—his teeth chattered, and he gave visible signs of the utmost consternation. 'Take heart of grace, man,' said Campbell, 'and dinna sit clattering your jaws there like a pair of castanets! I think there can be nae difficulty in your telling Mr. Justice, that ye have seen me of yore, and ken me to be a cavalier of fortune, and a man of honour.—Ye ken fu' weel ye will be some time resident in my vicinity, when I may have the power, as I will possess the inclination, to do you as good a turn.'

'Sir—sir—I believe you to be a man of honour, and, as you say, a man of fortune.—Yes, Mr. Inglewood,' he added, clearing his voice, 'I really believe this gentleman to be so.'

'And what are this gentleman's commands with me?' said the Justice, somewhat peevishly. 'One man introduces another, like the rhymes in the "house that Jack built," and I get company without either peace or conversation!'

'Both shall be yours, sir,' answered Campbell, 'in a brief period of time. I come to release your mind from a piece of troublesome duty, not to make increment to it.'

'Body o' me! then you are welcome as ever Scot was to England, and that's not saying much —but get on, man, let's hear what you have got to say at once.'

'I presume this gentleman,' continued the North Briton, 'told you there was a person of the name of Campbell with him, when he had the mischance to lose his valise?'

'He has not mentioned such a name, from beginning to end of the matter,' said the Justice.

'Ah! I conceive—I conceive,' replied Mr. Campbell; 'Mr. Morris was kindly afeared of committing a stranger into collision wi' the judicial forms of the country; but as I understand my evidence is necessary to the compurgation of ane honest gentleman here, Mr. Francis Osbaldistone, wha has been most unjustly suspected, I will dispense with the precaution—Ye will, therefore, (he added, addressing Morris with the same determined look and accent,) please tell Mr. Justice Inglewood, whether we did not travel several miles together on the road, in consequence of your own anxious request and suggestion, reiterated ance and again, baith on the evening that we were at Northallerton, and there declined by me, but afterwards accepted, when I overtook ye on the road near Cloberry Allers, and was prevailed on by you to resign my ain intentions of proceeding to Rothbury; and, for my misfortune, to accompany you on your proposed route.'

'It's a melancholy truth,' answered Morris, holding down his head, as he gave this general assent to the long and leading question which Campbell put to him, and seemed to acquiesce in the statement it contained with rueful docility.

'And I presume you can also asseverate to his worship, that no man is better qualified than I am to bear testimony in this case, seeing that I was by you, and near you, constantly during the whole occurrence?'

'No man better qualified, certainly,' said Morris, with a deep and embarrassed sigh.

'And why the devil did you not assist him then,' said the Justice, 'since, by Mr. Morris's account, there were but two robbers; so you were two to two, and you are both stout likely men?'

'Sir, if it please your worship,' said Campbell, 'I have been all my life a man of peace and quietness, no ways given to broils or batteries. Mr. Morris, who belongs, as I understand, or hath belonged, to his Majesty's army, might have used his pleasure in resistance, he travelling, as I also understand, with a great charge of treasure; but for me, who had but my own small peculiar to defend, and who am, moreover, a man of a pacific occupation, I was unwilling to commit myself to hazard in the matter.'

I looked at Campbell as he uttered these words, and never recollect to have seen a more singular contrast than that between the strong daring sternness expressed in his harsh features, and the air of composed meekness and simplicity which his language assumed. There was even a slight ironical smile lurking about the corners of his mouth, which seemed, involuntarily as it were, to intimate his disdain of the quiet and peaceful character which he thought proper to assume, and which led me to entertain strange suspicions that his concern in the violence done to Morris had been something very different from that of a fellow-sufferer, or even of a mere spectator.

Perhaps some such suspicions crossed the Justice's mind at the moment, for he exclaimed, as if by way of ejaculation, 'Body o' me! but this is a strange story.'

The North Briton seemed to guess at what was passing in his mind; for he went on, with a change of manner and tone, dismissing from his countenance some part of the hypocritical affectation of humility which had made him obnoxious to suspicion, and

saying, with a more frank and unconstrained air,
' To say the truth, I am just ane o' those canny
folks wha care not to fight, but when they hae
gotten something to fight for, which did not chance
to be my predicament when I fell in wi' these loons.
But, that your worship may know that I am a
person of good fame and character, please to cast
your eye over that billet.'

Mr. Inglewood took the paper from his hand,
and read half aloud, ' These are to certify, that the
bearer, Robert Campbell of —— of some place which
I cannot pronounce,' interjected the Justice,—' is a
person of good lineage, and peaceable demeanour,
travelling towards England on his own proper
affairs, etc. etc. etc.   Given under our hand, at
our Castle of Inver—Invera—rara—ARGYLE.'

' A slight testimonial, sir, which I thought fit to
impetrate from that worthy nobleman, (here he
raised his hand to his head, as if to touch his hat,)
MacCallum More.'

' MacCallum who, sir ? ' said the Justice.

' Whom the Southern call the Duke of Argyle.'

' I know the Duke of Argyle very well to be
a nobleman of great worth and distinction, and a
true lover of his country.   I was one of those that
stood by him in 1714, when he unhorsed the Duke
of Marlborough out of his command.   I wish we
had more noblemen like him.   He was an honest
Tory in those days, and hand and glove with
Ormond.   And he has acceded to the present
government, as I have done myself, for the peace
and quiet of his country ; for I cannot presume

that great man to have been actuated, as violent folks pretend, with the fear of losing his places and regiment. His testimonial, as you call it, Mr. Campbell, is perfectly satisfactory; and now, what have you got to say to this matter of the robbery?'

'Briefly this, if it please your worship; that Mr. Morris might as weel charge it against the babe yet to be born, or against myself even, as against this young gentleman, Mr. Osbaldistone; for I am not only free to depone that the person whom he took him for was a shorter man, and a thicker man, but also, for I chanced to obtain a glisk of his visage, as his fause-face slipped aside, that he was a man of other features and complexion than those of this young gentleman, Mr. Osbaldistone. And I believe,' he added, turning round with a natural, yet somewhat sterner air, to Mr. Morris, 'that the gentleman will allow I had better opportunity to take cognizance wha were present on that occasion than he, being, I believe, much the cooler o' the twa.'

'I agree to it, sir—I agree to it perfectly,' said Morris, shrinking back, as Campbell moved his chair towards him to fortify his appeal—'And I incline, sir,' he added, addressing Mr. Inglewood, 'to retract my information as to Mr. Osbaldistone; and I request, sir, you will permit him, sir, to go about his business, and me to go about mine also; your worship may have business to settle with Mr. Campbell, and I am rather in haste to be gone.'

'Then, there go the declarations,' said the Justice, throwing them into the fire—'And now you are at perfect liberty, Mr. Osbaldistone—And you, Mr. Morris, are set quite at your ease.'

'Ay,' said Campbell, eyeing Morris as he assented with a rueful grin to the Justice's observations, 'much like the ease of a toad under a pair of harrows—But fear nothing, Mr. Morris; you and I maun leave the house thegither. I will see you safe—I hope you will not doubt my honour, when I say sae—to the next highway, and then we part company; and if we do not meet as friends in Scotland, it will be your ain fault.'

With such a lingering look of terror as the condemned criminal throws, when he is informed that the cart awaits him, Morris arose; but when on his legs, appeared to hesitate. 'I tell thee, man, fear nothing,' reiterated Campbell; 'I will keep my word with you—Why, thou sheep's heart, how do ye ken but we may can pick up some speerings of your valise, if ye will be amenable to gude counsel? —Our horses are ready. Bid the Justice fareweel, man, and show your southern breeding.'

Morris, thus exhorted and encouraged, took his leave, under the escort of Mr. Campbell; but, apparently, new scruples and terrors had struck him before they left the house, for I heard Campbell reiterating assurances of safety and protection as they left the anteroom—'By the soul of my body, man, thou 'rt as safe as in thy father's kail-yard— Zounds! that a chield wi' sic a black beard, should hae nae mair heart then a hen-partridge!—Come on wi' ye, like a frank fallow, ance and for aye.'

The voices died away, and the subsequent tramp-

ling of their horses announced to us that they had
left the mansion of Justice Inglewood.

The joy which that worthy magistrate received
at this easy conclusion of a matter which threatened
him with some trouble in his judicial capacity, was
somewhat damped by reflection on what his clerk's
views of the transaction might be at his return.
' Now, I shall have Jobson on my shoulders about
these d——d papers—I doubt I should not have
destroyed them, after all—But, hang it, it is only
paying his fees, and that will make all smooth—
And now, Miss Die Vernon, though I have liberated
all the others, I intend to sign a writ for committing
you to the custody of Mother Blakes, my old housekeeper, for the evening, and we will send for my
neighbour Mrs. Musgrave, and the Miss Dawkins,
and your cousins, and have old Cobs the fiddler,
and be as merry as the maids ; and Frank Osbaldistone and I will have a carouse that will make us
fit company for you in half an hour.'

' Thanks, most worshipful,' returned Miss Vernon ; ' but, as matters stand, we must return instantly to Osbaldistone Hall, where they do not
know what has become of us, and relieve my uncle
of his anxiety on my cousin's account, which is
just the same as if one of his own sons were concerned.'

' I believe it truly,' said the Justice ; ' for
when his eldest son, Archie, came to a bad end,
in that unlucky affair of Sir John Fenwick's, old
Hildebrand used to hollow out his name as readily
as any of the remaining six, and then complain that

he could not recollect which of his sons had been hanged. So, pray hasten home, and relieve his paternal solicitude, since go you must.—But, hark thee hither, heath-blossom,' he said, pulling her towards him by the hand, and in a good-humoured tone of admonition, ' another time let the law take its course, without putting your pretty finger into her old musty pie, all full of fragments of law gibberish—French and dog-Latin—And, Die, my beauty, let young fellows show each other the way through the moors, in case you should lose your own road, while you are pointing out theirs, my pretty Will o' the Wisp.'

With this admonition, he saluted and dismissed Miss Vernon, and took an equally kind farewell of me.

' Thou seems to be a good tight lad, Mr. Frank, and I remember thy father too—he was my play-fellow at school. Hark thee, lad, ride early at night, and don't swagger with chance passengers on the king's highway. What, man! all the king's liege subjects are not bound to understand joking, and it's ill cracking jests on matters of felony. And here's poor Die Vernon too—in a manner alone and deserted on the face of this wide earth, and left to ride, and run, and scamper at her own silly pleasure. Thou must be careful of Die, or, egad, I will turn a young fellow again on purpose, and fight thee myself, although I must own it would be a great deal of trouble. And now, get ye both gone, and leave me to my pipe of tobacco, and my meditations; for what says the song—

ROB ROY

'The Indian leaf doth briefly burn;
So doth man's strength to weakness turn;—
The fire of youth extinguish'd quite,
Comes age, like embers, dry and white.
Think of this as you take tobacco.'

I was much pleased with the gleams of sense and feeling which escaped from the Justice through the vapours of sloth and self-indulgence, assured him of my respect to his admonitions, and took a friendly farewell of the honest magistrate and his hospitable mansion.

We found a repast prepared for us in the ante-room, which we partook of slightly, and rejoined the same servant of Sir Hildebrand who had taken our horses at our entrance, and who had been directed, as he informed Miss Vernon, by Mr. Rashleigh, to wait and attend upon us home. We rode a little way in silence, for, to say truth, my mind was too much bewildered with the events of the morning to permit me to be the first to break it. At length Miss Vernon exclaimed, as if giving vent to her own reflections, 'Well, Rashleigh is a man to be feared and wondered at, and all but loved; he does whatever he pleases, and makes all others his puppets—has a player ready to perform every part which he imagines, and an invention and readiness which supply expedients for every emergency.'

'You think, then,' said I, answering rather to her meaning, than to the express words she made use of, 'that this Mr. Campbell, whose appearance was so opportune, and who trussed up and carried

134

off my accuser as a falcon trusses a partridge, was
an agent of Mr. Rashleigh Osbaldistone's?'

'I do guess as much,' replied Diana, 'and
shrewdly suspect, moreover, that he would hardly
have appeared so very much in the nick of time, if
I had not happened to meet Rashleigh in the hall
at the Justice's.'

'In that case, my thanks are chiefly due to you,
my fair preserver.'

'To be sure they are,' returned Diana; 'and
pray, suppose them paid, and accepted with a
gracious smile, for I do not care to be troubled
with hearing them in good earnest, and am much
more likely to yawn than to behave becoming. In
short, Mr. Frank, I wished to serve you, and I have
fortunately been able to do so, and have only one
favour to ask in return, and that is, that you will say
no more about it.—But who comes here to meet
us, "bloody with spurring, fiery-red with haste?"
It is the subordinate man of law, I think; no less
than Mr. Joseph Jobson.'

And Mr. Joseph Jobson it proved to be, in great
haste, and, as it speedily appeared, in most extreme
bad humour. He came up to us, and stopped his
horse, as we were about to pass with a slight
salutation.

'So, sir—so, Miss Vernon—ay—I see well enough
how it is—bail put in during my absence, I suppose
—I should like to know who drew the recognizance,
that's all. If his worship uses this form of procedure often, I advise him to get another clerk,
that's all, for I shall certainly demit.'

'Or suppose he get his present clerk stitched to his sleeve, Mr. Jobson,' said Diana, 'would not that do as well? And pray how does Farmer Rutledge, Mr. Jobson? I hope you found him able to sign, seal, and deliver?'

This question seemed greatly to increase the wrath of the man of law. He looked at Miss Vernon with such an air of spite and resentment, as laid me under a strong temptation to knock him off his horse with the but of my whip, which I only suppressed in consideration of his insignificance.

'Farmer Rutledge, ma'am?' said the clerk, so soon as his indignation permitted him to articulate, 'Farmer Rutledge is in as handsome enjoyment of his health as you are—it's all a bam, ma'am—all a bamboozle and a bite that affair of his illness; and if you did not know as much before, you know it now, ma'am.'

'La you there now!' replied Miss Vernon, with an affectation of extreme and simple wonder, 'sure you don't say so, Mr. Jobson?'

'But I *do* say so, ma'am,' rejoined the incensed scribe; 'and moreover I say, that the old miserly clod-breaker called me pettifogger — pettifogger, ma'am—and said I came to hunt for a job, ma'am —which I have no more right to have said to me than any other gentleman of my profession, ma'am —especially as I am clerk to the peace, having and holding said office under *Trigesimo Septimo Henricj Octavi,* and *Primo Gulielmi,*—the first of King William, ma'am, of glorious and immortal memory — our immortal deliverer from papists and pretenders, and wooden shoes and warming pans, Miss Vernon.'

'Sad things, these wooden shoes and warming pans,' retorted the young lady, who seemed to take pleasure in augmenting his wrath;—'and it is a comfort you don't seem to want a warming pan at present, Mr. Jobson. I am afraid Gaffer Rutledge has not confined his incivility to language—Are you sure he did not give you a beating?'

'Beating, ma'am!—no'—(very shortly) 'no man alive shall beat me, I promise you, ma'am.'

'That is according as you happen to merit, sir,' said I; 'for your mode of speaking to this young lady is so unbecoming, that, if you do not change your tone, I shall think it worth while to chastise you myself.'

'Chastise, sir? and—me, sir?—Do you know whom you speak to, sir?'

'Yes, sir,' I replied; 'you say yourself you are clerk of peace to the county; and Gaffer Rutledge says you are a pettifogger; and in neither capacity are you entitled to be impertinent to a young lady of fashion.'

Miss Vernon laid her hand on my arm, and exclaimed, 'Come, Mr. Osbaldistone, I will have no assaults and battery on Mr. Jobson; I am not in sufficient charity with him to permit a single touch of your whip—why, he would live on it for a term at least. Besides, you have already hurt his feelings sufficiently—you have called him impertinent.'

'I don't value his language, Miss,' said the clerk, somewhat crest-fallen; 'besides, impertinent is not an actionable word; but pettifogger is slander in the highest degree, and that I will make Gaffer Rutledge know to his cost, and all who maliciously repeat the same to the breach of the public peace, and the taking away of my private good name.'

'Never mind that, Mr. Jobson,' said Miss Vernon; 'you know, where there is nothing, your own law allows that the king himself must lose his rights; and, for the taking away of your good name, I pity the poor fellow who gets it, and wish you joy of losing it with all my heart.'

'Very well, ma'am — good evening, ma'am — I have no more to say—only there are laws against papists, which it would be well for the land were they better executed. There's third and fourth Edward vi., of antiphoners, missals, grailes, processionals, manuals, legends, pies, portuasses, and those that have such trinkets in their possession, Miss Vernon — and there's summoning of papists to take the oaths—and there are popish recusant convicts under the first of his present Majesty— ay, and there are penalties for hearing mass. See twenty-third of Queen Elizabeth, and third James First, chapter twenty-fifth.—And there are estates to be registered, and deeds and wills to be enrolled, and double taxes to be made, according to the acts in that case made and provided——'

'See the new edition of the Statutes at Large, published under the careful revision of Joseph Jobson, Gent., Clerk of the Peace,' said Miss Vernon.

'Also, and above all,' continued Jobson, — 'for I speak to your warning — you, Diana Vernon, spinstress, not being a *femme couverte*; and being a convict popish recusant, are bound to repair to your own dwelling, and that by the nearest way, under penalty of being held felon to the king—and diligently to seek for passage at common ferries, and to tarry there but one ebb and flood; and unless you can have it in such places, to walk every day into the water up to the knees, assaying to pass over.'

'A sort of Protestant penance for my Catholic errors, I suppose,' said Miss Vernon, laughing. 'Well, I thank you for the information, Mr. Jobson, and will hie me home as fast as I can, and be a better housekeeper in time coming. Good night, my dear Mr. Jobson, thou mirror of clerical courtesy.'

'Good night, ma'am, and remember the law is not to be trifled with.'

And we rode on our separate ways.

'There he goes for a troublesome mischief-making tool,' said Miss Vernon, as she gave a glance after him; 'it is hard that persons of birth and rank and estate should be subjected to the official impertinence of such a paltry pick-thank as that, merely for believing as the whole world believed not much above a hundred years ago—for certainly our Catholic faith has the advantage of antiquity at least.'

'I was much tempted to have broken the rascal's head,' I replied.

'You would have acted very like a hasty young man,' said Miss Vernon; 'and yet, had my own hand been an ounce heavier than it is, I think I should have laid its weight upon him.—Well, it does not signify complaining, but there are three things for which I am much to be pitied, if any one thought it worth while to waste any compassion upon me.'

'And what are these three things, Miss Vernon, may I ask?'

'Will you promise me your deepest sympathy, if I tell you?'

'Certainly;—can you doubt it?' I replied, closing my horse nearer to hers as I spoke, with an expression of interest which I did not attempt to disguise.

'Well, it is very seducing to be pitied, after all; so here are my three grievances—In the first place, I am a girl, and not a young fellow, and would be shut up in a mad-house, if I did half the things that I have a mind to; and that, if I had your happy prerogative of acting as you list, would make all the world mad with imitating and applauding me.'

'I can't quite afford you the sympathy you expect upon this score,' I replied; 'the misfortune is so general, that it belongs to one half of the species; and the other half——'

'Are so much better cared for, that they are jealous of their prerogatives,' interrupted Miss Vernon; 'I forgot you were a party interested. Nay,' said she, as I was going to speak, 'that soft smile is intended to be the preface of a very pretty compliment respecting the peculiar advantages which Die Vernon's friends and kinsmen enjoy, by her being born one of their Helots; but spare me the utterance, my good friend, and let us try whether we shall agree better on the second count of my indictment against fortune, as that quill-driving puppy would call it. I belong to an oppressed sect and antiquated religion, and, instead of getting credit for my devotion, as is due to all good girls beside, my kind friend, Justice Inglewood, may send me to the house of correction, merely for worshipping God in the way of my ancestors, and say, as old Pembroke did to the Abbess of Wilton,* when he usurped her convent and establishment, " Go spin, you jade,—Go spin." '

'This is not a cureless evil,' said I gravely. 'Consult some of our learned divines, or consult your own excellent understanding, Miss Vernon; and surely the particulars in which our religious creed differs from that in which you have been educated——'

'Hush!' said Diana, placing her fore-finger on her mouth,—'Hush! no more of that. Forsake the

---

* The nunnery of Wilton was granted to the Earl of Pembroke upon its dissolution, by the magisterial authority of Henry VIII., or his son Edward VI. On the accession of Queen Mary, of Catholic memory, the Earl found it necessary to reinstal the Abbess and her fair recluses, which he did with many expressions of his remorse, kneeling humbly to the vestals, and inducting them into the convent and possessions from which he had expelled them. With the accession of Elizabeth, the accommodating Earl again resumed his Protestant faith, and a second time drove the nuns from their sanctuary. The remonstrances of the Abbess, who reminded him of his penitent expressions on the former occasion, could wring from him no other answer than that in the text—' Go spin, you jade—Go spin.'

faith of my gallant fathers!—I would as soon, were I a man, forsake their banner, when the tide of battle pressed hardest against it, and turn, like a hireling recreant, to join the victorious enemy.'

'I honour your spirit, Miss Vernon; and as to the inconveniences to which it exposes you, I can only say, that wounds sustained for the sake of conscience carry their own balsam with the blow.'

'Ay; but they are fretful and irritating, for all that. But I see, hard of heart as you are, my chance of beating hemp, or drawing out flax into marvellous coarse thread, affects you as little as my condemnation to coif and pinners, instead of beaver and cockade; so I will spare myself the fruitless pains of telling my third cause of vexation.'

'Nay, my dear Miss Vernon, do not withdraw your confidence, and I will promise you, that the threefold sympathy due to your very unusual causes of distress shall be all duly and truly paid to account of the third, providing you assure me, that it is one which you neither share with all womankind, nor even with every Catholic in England, who, God bless you, are still a sect more numerous than we Protestants, in our zeal for church and state, would desire them to be.'

'It is, indeed,' said Diana, with a manner greatly altered, and more serious than I had yet seen her assume, 'a misfortune that well merits compassion. I am by nature, as you may easily observe, of a frank and unreserved disposition—a plain true-hearted girl, who would willingly act openly and honestly by the whole world, and yet fate has involved me in such a series of nets, and toils, and entanglements, that I dare hardly speak a word for fear of consequences—not to myself, but to others.'

'That is indeed a misfortune, Miss Vernon, which I do most sincerely compassionate, but which I should hardly have anticipated.'

'O, Mr. Osbaldistone, if you but knew—if any one knew, what difficulty I sometimes find in hiding an aching heart with a smooth brow, you would indeed pity me. I do wrong, perhaps, in speaking to you even thus far on my own situation; but you are a young man of sense and penetration— you cannot but long to ask me a hundred questions on the events of this day—on the share which Rashleigh has in your deliverence from this petty scrape —upon many other points which cannot but excite your attention—and I cannot bring myself to answer with the necessary falsehood and finesse—I should do it awkwardly, and lose your good opinion, if I have any share of it, as well as my own. It is best to say at once, Ask me no questions, I have it not in my power to reply to them.'

Miss Vernon spoke these words with a tone of feeling which could not but make a corresponding impression upon me. I assured her she had neither to fear my urging her with impertinent questions, nor my misconstruing her declining to answer those which might in themselves be reasonable, or at least natural.

'I was too much obliged,' I said, 'by the interest she had taken in my affairs, to misuse the opportunity her goodness had afforded me of prying into hers — I only trusted and entreated, that if my services could at any time be useful, she would command them, without doubt or hesitation.'

'Thank you—thank you,' she replied; 'your voice does not ring the cuckoo chime of compliment, but speaks like that of one who knows to what he pledges himself. If — but it is impossible — but yet, *if* an opportunity should occur, I will ask you if you remember this promise; and I assure you, I shall not be angry if I find you have forgotten it, for it is enough that you are sincere in your intentions just now—much may occur to alter them ere I call upon you, should that moment ever come, to assist Die Vernon, as if you were Die Vernon's brother.'

'And if I were Die Vernon's brother,' said I, 'there could not be less chance that I should refuse my assistance—And now I am afraid I must not ask whether Rashleigh was willingly accessory to my deliverance?'

'Not of me; but you may ask it of himself, and, depend upon it, he will say *yes*; for rather than any good action should walk through the world like an unappropriated adjective in an ill-arranged sentence, he is always willing to stand noun substantive to it himself.'

'And I must not ask whether this Campbell be himself the party who eased Mr. Morris of his portmanteau, or whether the letter, which our friend the attorney received, was not a finesse to withdraw him from the scene of action, lest he should have marred the happy event of my deliverance? And I must not ask——'

'You must ask nothing of me,' said Miss Vernon; 'so it is quite in vain to go on putting cases. You are to think just as well of me, as if I had answered all these queries, and twenty others besides, as glibly as Rashleigh could have done; and observe, whenever I touch my chin just so, it is a sign that I cannot speak upon the topic which happens to occupy your attention. I must settle signals of correspondence with you, because you are to be my confident and my counsellor, only you are to know nothing whatever of my affairs.'

'Nothing can be more reasonable,' I replied, laughing; 'and the extent of your confidence will, you may rely upon it, only be equalled by the sagacity of my counsels.'

This sort of conversation brought us, in the highest good-humour with each other, to Osbaldistone Hall, where we found the family far advanced in the revels of the evening.

'Get some dinner for Mr. Osbaldistone and me in the library,' said Miss Vernon to a servant.— 'I must have some compassion upon you,' she added, turning to me, 'and provide against your starving in this mansion of brutal abundance; otherwise I am not sure that I should show you my private haunts. This same library is my den —the only corner of the Hall-house where I am safe from the Ourang-Outangs, my cousins. They never venture there, I suppose, for fear the folios should fall down and crack their skulls; for they will never affect their heads in any other way—So follow me.'

And I followed through hall and bower, vaulted passage and winding stair, until we reached the room where she had ordered our refreshments.

CHAPTER X

In the wide pile, by others heeded not,
Hers was one sacred solitary spot,
Whose gloomy aisles and bending shelves contain
For moral hunger food, and cures for moral pain.
                                        ANONYMOUS.

THE library at Osbaldistone Hall was a gloomy room, whose antique oaken shelves bent beneath the weight of the ponderous folios so dear to the seventeenth century, from which, under favour be it spoken, we have distilled matter for our quartos and octavos, and which, once more subjected to the alembic, may, should our sons be yet more frivolous than ourselves, be still farther reduced into duode-cimos and pamphlets. The collection was chiefly of the classics, as well foreign as ancient history, and, above all, divinity. It was in wretched order. The priests, who, in succession, had acted as chaplains at the Hall, were, for many years, the only persons who entered its precincts, until Rashleigh's thirst for reading had led him to. disturb the venerable spiders, who had muffled the fronts of the presses with their tapestry. His destination for the church rendered his conduct less absurd in his father's eyes, than if any of his other descendants had betrayed so strange a propensity, and Sir Hildebrand acqui-esced in the library receiving some repairs, so as to

147

fit it for a sitting room. Still an air of dilapidation, as obvious as it was uncomfortable, pervaded the large apartment, and announced the neglect from which the knowledge which its walls contained had not been able to exempt it. The tattered tapestry, the worm-eaten shelves, the huge and clumsy, yet tottering, tables, desks, and chairs, the rusty grate, seldom gladdened by either sea-coal or fagots, intimated the contempt of the lords of Osbaldistone Hall for learning, and for the volumes which record its treasures.

'You think this place somewhat disconsolate, I suppose?' said Diana, as I glanced my eye round the forlorn apartment; 'but to me it seems like a little paradise, for I call it my own, and fear no intrusion. Rashleigh was joint proprietor with me, while we were friends.'

'And are you no longer so?' was my natural question.

Her fore-finger immediately touched her dimpled chin, with an arch look of prohibition.

'We are still *allies*,' she continued, 'bound, like other confederate powers, by circumstances of mutual interest; but I am afraid, as will happen in other cases, the treaty of alliance has survived the amicable dispositions in which it had its origin. At any rate, we live less together; and when he comes through that door there, I vanish through this door here; and so, having made the discovery that we two were one too many for this apartment, as large as it seems, Rashleigh, whose occasions frequently call him elsewhere, has generously made

148

a cession of his rights in my favour; so that I now endeavour to prosecute alone the studies in which he used formerly to be my guide.'

'And what are those studies, if I may presume to ask?'

'Indeed you may, without the least fear of seeing my fore-finger raised to my chin. Science and history are my principal favourites; but I also study poetry and the classics.'

'And the classics? Do you read them in the original?'

'Unquestionably; Rashleigh, who is no contemptible scholar, taught me Greek and Latin, as well as most of the languages of modern Europe. I assure you, there has been some pains taken in my education, although I can neither sew a tucker, nor work cross-stitch, nor make a pudding, nor, as the vicar's fat wife, with as much truth as elegance, good-will, and politeness, was pleased to say in my behalf, do any other useful thing in the varsal world.'

'And was this selection of studies Rashleigh's choice, or your own, Miss Vernon?' I asked.

'Um!' said she, as if hesitating to answer my question,—'it's not worth while lifting my finger about, after all—why, partly his, and partly mine. As I learned out of doors to ride a horse, and bridle and saddle him in case of necessity, and to clear a five-barred gate, and fire a gun without winking, and all other of those masculine accomplishments, that my brute cousins run mad after, I wanted, like my rational cousin, to read Greek and

Latin within doors, and make my complete approach to the tree of knowledge, which you men-scholars would engross to yourselves, in revenge, I suppose, for our common mother's share in the great original transgression.'

' And Rashleigh readily indulged your propensity to learning ? '

' Why, he wished to have me for his scholar, and he could but teach me that which he knew himself—he was not likely to instruct me in the mysteries of washing lace-ruffles, or hemming cambric-handkerchiefs, I suppose.'

' I admit the temptation of getting such a scholar, and have no doubt that it made a weighty consideration on the tutor's part.'

' O, if you begin to investigate Rashleigh's motives, my finger touches my chin once more. I can only be frank where my own are inquired into. But to resume—he has resigned the library in my favour, and never enters without leave had and obtained; and so I have taken the liberty to make it the place of deposit for some of my own goods and chattels, as you may see by looking round you.'

' I beg pardon, Miss Vernon, but I really see nothing around these walls which I can distinguish as likely to claim you as mistress.'

' That is, I suppose, because you neither see a shepherd or shepherdess wrought in worsted, and handsomely framed in black ebony,— or a stuffed parrot,—or a breeding-cage, full of canary-birds,— or a housewife-case, broidered with tarnished silver, — or a toilette-table, with a nest of japanned boxes, with as many angles as Christmas minced-pies,—or a broken-backed spinet,—or a lute with three strings,—or rock-work,—or shell-work,—or needle-work, or work of any kind,—or a lap-dog, with a litter of blind puppies—None of these treasures do I possess,' she continued, after a pause, in order to recover the breath she had lost in enumerating them—'But there stands the sword of my ancestor Sir Richard Vernon, slain at Shrewsbury, and sorely slandered by a sad fellow called Will Shakspeare, whose Lancastrian partialities, and a certain knack at embodying them, has turned history upside down, or rather inside out;—and by that redoubted weapon hangs the mail of the still older Vernon, squire to the Black Prince, whose fate is the reverse of his descendant's, since he is more indebted to the bard, who took the trouble to celebrate him, for good-will, than for talents,—

> " Amiddes the route you might descern one
> Brave knight, with pipes on shield, ycleped Vernon;
> Like a borne fiend along the plain he thundered,
> Prest to be carving throtes, while others plundered."

Then there is a model of a new martingale which I invented myself—a great improvement on the Duke of Newcastle's; and there are the hood and bells of my falcon Cheviot, who spitted himself on a heron's bill at Horsely-moss—poor Cheviot, there is not a bird on the perches below, but are kites and riflers compared to him; and there is my own light fowling-piece, with an improved fire-lock; with twenty other treasures, each more valuable than another—And there, that speaks for itself.'

She pointed to the carved oak-frame of a full-length portrait by Vandyke, on which were inscribed, in Gothic letters, the words *Vernon semper viret.* I looked at her for explanation—'Do you not know,' said she, with some surprise, 'our motto—the Vernon motto, where,

> " Like the solemn vice, Iniquity,
>   We moralize two meanings in one word ? "

And do you not know our cognizance, the pipes ? ' pointing to the armorial bearings sculptured on the oaken scutcheon, around which the legend was displayed.

' Pipes !—they look more like penny-whistles—But, pray, do not be angry with my ignorance,' I continued, observing the colour mount to her cheeks, ' I can mean no affront to your armorial bearings, for I do not even know my own.'

' You an Osbaldistone, and confess so much ! ' she exclaimed. ' Why, Percie, Thornie, John, Dickon—Wilfred himself, might be your instructor —Even ignorance itself is a plummet over you.'

' With shame I confess it, my dear Miss Vernon, the mysteries couched under the grim hieroglyphics of heraldry are to me as unintelligible as those of the pyramids of Egypt.'

' What ! is it possible ?— Why, even my uncle reads Gwillym sometimes of a winter night— Not know the figures of heraldry ?—of what could your father be thinking ? '

' Of the figures of arithmetic,' I answered ; ' the most insignificant unit of which he holds more highly than all the blazonry of chivalry. But, though I am ignorant to this inexpressible degree, I have knowledge and taste enough to admire that splendid picture, in which I think I can discover a family likeness to you. What ease and dignity in the attitude — what richness of colouring — what breadth and depth of shade !'

'Is it really a fine painting ? ' she asked.

'I have seen many works of the renowned artist,' I replied, 'but never beheld one more to my liking.'

'Well, I know as little of pictures as you do of heraldry,' replied Miss Vernon; 'yet I have the advantage of you, because I have always admired the painting without understanding its value.'

'While I have neglected pipes and tabors, and all the whimsical combinations of chivalry, still I am informed that they floated in the fields of ancient fame. But you will allow their exterior appearance is not so peculiarly interesting to the uninformed spectator as that of a fine painting.— Who is the person here represented ? '

'My grandfather—he shared the misfortunes of Charles I. ; and, I am sorry to add, the excesses of his son. Our patrimonial estate was greatly impaired by his prodigality, and was altogether lost by his successor, my unfortunate father. But peace be with them who have got it—it was lost in the cause of loyalty.'

'Your father, I presume, suffered in the political dissensions of the period ? '

'He did indeed ; he lost his all. And hence is

his child a dependent orphan ; eating the bread of others ; subjected to their caprices, and compelled to study their inclinations : Yet prouder of having had such a father, than if, playing a more prudent, but less upright part, he had left me possessor of all the rich and fair baronies which his family once possessed.'

As she thus spoke, the entrance of the servants with dinner cut off all conversation but that of a general nature.

When our hasty meal was concluded, and the wine placed on the table, the domestic informed us, 'that Mr. Rashleigh had desired to be told when our dinner was removed.'

'Tell him,' said Miss Vernon, 'we shall be happy to see him if he will step this way—place another wine-glass and chair, and leave the room. —You must retire with him when he goes away,' she continued, addressing herself to me ; 'even *my* liberality cannot spare a gentleman above eight hours out of the twenty-four ; and I think we have been together for at least that length of time.'

'The old scythe-man has moved so rapidly,' I answered, 'that I could not count his strides.'

'Hush !' said Miss Vernon, 'here comes Rash-leigh'; and she drew off her chair, to which I had approached mine rather closely, so as to place a greater distance between us.

A modest tap at the door,—a gentle manner of opening when invited to enter,—a studied softness and humility of step and deportment, announced that the education of Rashleigh Osbaldistone at the College of St. Omers accorded well with the ideas I entertained of the manners of an accomplished Jesuit. I need not add, that, as a sound Protestant, these ideas were not the most favourable. 'Why should you use the ceremony of knocking,' said Miss Vernon, 'when you knew that I was not alone?'

This was spoken with a burst of impatience, as if she had felt that Rashleigh's air of caution and reserve covered some insinuation of impertinent suspicion. 'You have taught me the form of knocking at this door so perfectly, my fair cousin,' answered Rashleigh, without change of voice or manner, 'that habit has become a second nature.'

'I prize sincerity more than courtesy, sir, and you know I do,' was Miss Vernon's reply.

'Courtesy is a gallant gay, a courtier by name and by profession,' replied Rashleigh, 'and therefore most fit for a lady's bower.'

'But Sincerity is the true knight,' retorted Miss Vernon, 'and therefore much more welcome, cousin. But, to end a debate not over amusing to your stranger kinsman, sit down, Rashleigh, and give Mr. Francis Osbaldistone your countenance to his glass of wine. I have done the honours of the dinner, for the credit of Osbaldistone Hall.'

Rashleigh sate down, and filled his glass, glancing his eye from Diana to me, with an embarrassment which his utmost efforts could not entirely disguise. I thought he appeared to be uncertain concerning the extent of confidence she might have reposed in me, and hastened to lead the conversation into

155

a channel which should sweep away his suspicion that Diana might have betrayed any secrets which rested between them. 'Miss Vernon,' I said, 'Mr. Rashleigh has recommended me to return my thanks to you for my speedy disengagement from the ridiculous accusation of Morris; and, unjustly fearing my gratitude might not be warm enough to remind me of this duty, she has put my curiosity on its side, by referring me to you for an account, or rather explanation, of the events of the day.'

'Indeed?' answered Rashleigh; 'I should have thought,' (looking keenly at Miss Vernon,) 'that the lady herself might have stood interpreter'; and his eye, reverting from her face, sought mine, as if to search, from the expression of my features, whether Diana's communication had been as narrowly limited as my words had intimated. Miss Vernon retorted his inquisitorial glance with one of decided scorn; while I, uncertain whether to deprecate or resent his obvious suspicion, replied, 'If it is your pleasure, Mr. Rashleigh, as it has been Miss Vernon's, to leave me in ignorance, I must necessarily submit; but, pray, do not withhold your information from me, on the ground of imagining that I have already obtained any on the subject. For I tell you as a man of honour, I am as ignorant as that picture of any thing relating to the events I have witnessed to-day, excepting that I understand from Miss Vernon, that you have been kindly active in my favour.'

'Miss Vernon has overrated my humble efforts,'

said Rashleigh, 'though I claim full credit for my zeal. The truth is, that as I galloped back to get some one of our family to join me in becoming your bail, which was the most obvious, or, indeed, I may say, the only way of serving you which occurred to my stupidity, I met the man Cawmil—Colville —Campbell, or whatsoever they call him. I had understood from Morris that he was present when the robbery took place, and had the good fortune to prevail on him, (with some difficulty, I confess,) to tender his evidence in your exculpation, which I presume was the means of your being released from an unpleasant situation.'

'Indeed?—I am much your debtor for procuring such a seasonable evidence in my behalf. But I cannot see why, (having been, as he said, a fellow-sufferer with Morris,) it should have required much trouble to persuade him to step forth and bear evidence, whether to convict the actual robber, or free an innocent person.'

'You do not know the genius of that man's country, sir,' answered Rashleigh; 'discretion, prudence, and foresight, are their leading qualities; these are only modified by a narrow-spirited, but yet ardent patriotism, which forms as it were the outmost of the concentric bulwarks with which a Scotchman fortifies himself against all the attacks of a generous philanthropical principle. Surmount this mound, you find an inner and still dearer barrier—the love of his province, his village, or, most probably, his clan; storm this second obstacle, you have a third—his attachment to his own family

—his father, mother, sons, daughters, uncles, aunts, and cousins, to the ninth generation. It is within these limits that a Scotchman's social affection expands itself, never reaching those which are outermost, till all means of discharging itself in the interior circles have been exhausted. It is within these circles that his heart throbs, each pulsation being fainter and fainter, till, beyond the widest boundary, it is almost unfelt. And what is worst of all, could you surmount all these concentric outworks, you have an inner citadel, deeper, higher, and more efficient than them all—a Scotchman's love for himself.'

'All this is extremely eloquent and metaphorical, Rashleigh,' said Miss Vernon, who listened with unrepressed impatience; 'there are only two objections to it: first, it is *not* true; secondly, if true, it is nothing to the purpose.'

'It *is* true, my fairest Diana,' returned Rashleigh; 'and moreover, it is most instantly to the purpose. It is true, because you cannot deny that I know the country and people intimately, and the character is drawn from deep and accurate consideration; and it is to the purpose, because it answers Mr. Francis Osbaldistone's question, and shows why this same wary Scotchman, considering our kinsman to be neither his countryman, nor a Campbell, nor his cousin in any of the inextricable combinations by which they extend their pedigree; and, above all, seeing no prospect of personal advantage, but, on the contrary, much hazard of loss of time and delay of business——'

'With other inconveniences, perhaps, of a nature yet more formidable,' interrupted Miss Vernon.

'Of which, doubtless, there might be many,' said Rashleigh, continuing in the same tone—'In short, my theory shows why this man, hoping for no advantage, and afraid of some inconvenience, might require a degree of persuasion ere he could be prevailed on to give his testimony in favour of Mr. Osbaldistone.'

'It seems surprising to me,' I observed, 'that during the glance I cast over the declaration, or whatever it is termed, of Mr. Morris, he should never have mentioned that Campbell was in his company when he met the marauders.'

'I understood from Campbell, that he had taken his solemn promise not to mention that circumstance,' replied Rashleigh; 'his reason for exacting such an engagement you may guess from what I have hinted — he wished to get back to his own country, undelayed and unembarrassed by any of the judicial inquiries which he would have been under the necessity of attending, had the fact of his being present at the robbery taken air while he was on this side of the Border. But let him once be as distant as the Forth, Morris will, I warrant you, come forth with all he knows about him, and, it may be, a good deal more. Besides, Campbell is a very extensive dealer in cattle, and has often occasion to send great droves into Northumberland; and, when driving such a trade, he would be a great fool to embroil himself with our Northumbrian thieves, than whom no men who live are more vindictive.'

'I dare be sworn of that,' said Miss Vernon, with a tone which implied something more than a simple acquiescence in the proposition.

'Still,' said I, resuming the subject, 'allowing the force of the reasons which Campbell might have for desiring that Morris should be silent with regard to his promise when the robbery was committed, I cannot yet see how he could attain such an influence over the man, as to make him suppress his evidence in that particular, at the manifest risk of subjecting his story to discredit.'

Rashleigh agreed with me, that it was very extraordinary, and seemed to regret that he had not questioned the Scotchman more closely on that subject, which he allowed looked extremely mysterious. 'But,' he asked, immediately after this acquiescence, 'are you very sure the circumstance of Morris's being accompanied by Campbell, is really not alluded to in his examination?'

'I read the paper over hastily,' said I; 'but it is my strong impression, that no such circumstance is mentioned; at least it must have been touched on very slightly, since it failed to catch my attention.'

'True, true,' answered Rashleigh, forming his own inference while he adopted my words; 'I incline to think with you, that the circumstance must in reality have been mentioned, but so slightly, that it failed to attract your attention. And then, as to Campbell's interest with Morris, I incline to suppose that it must have been gained by playing upon his fears. This chicken-hearted fellow, Morris, is bound, I understand, for Scotland, destined for some little employment under government; and, possessing the courage of the wrathful dove, or most magnanimous mouse, he may have been afraid to encounter the ill-will of such a kill-cow as Campbell, whose very appearance would be enough to fright him out of his little wits. You observed that Mr. Campbell has at times a keen and animated manner—something of a martial cast in his tone and bearing.'

'I own,' I replied, 'that his expression struck me as being occasionally fierce and sinister, and little adapted to his peaceable professions. Has he served in the army?'

'Yes—no—not, strictly speaking, *served*; but he has been, I believe, like most of his countrymen, trained to arms. Indeed, among the hills, they carry them from boyhood to the grave. So, if you know any thing of your fellow-traveller, you will easily judge, that, going to such a country, he will take care to avoid a quarrel, if he can help it, with any of the natives.—But, come, I see you decline your wine—and I too am a degenerate Osbaldistone, so far as respects the circulation of the bottle. If you will go to my room, I will hold you a hand at piquet.'

We rose to take leave of Miss Vernon, who had from time to time suppressed, apparently with difficulty, a strong temptation to break in upon Rashleigh's details. As we were about to leave the room, the smothered fire broke forth.

'Mr. Osbaldistone,' she said, 'your own observation will enable you to verify the justice, or injustice, of Rashleigh's suggestions concerning such individuals as Mr. Campbell and Mr. Morris. But, in slandering Scotland, he has borne false witness against a whole country; and I request you will allow no weight to his evidence.'

'Perhaps,' I answered, 'I may find it somewhat difficult to obey your injunction, Miss Vernon; for I must own I was bred up with no very favourable idea of our northern neighbours.'

'Distrust that part of your education, sir,' she replied, 'and let the daughter of a Scotchwoman pray you to respect the land which gave her parent birth, until your own observation has proved them to be unworthy of your good opinion. Preserve your hatred and contempt for dissimulation, baseness, and falsehood, wheresoever they are to be met with. You will find enough of all without leaving England.—Adieu, gentlemen,—I wish you good evening.'

And she signed to the door, with the manner of a princess dismissing her train.

We retired to Rashleigh's apartment, where a servant brought us coffee and cards. I had formed my resolution to press Rashleigh no farther on the events of the day. A mystery, and, as I thought, not of a favourable complexion, appeared to hang over his conduct; but to ascertain if my suspicions were just, it was necessary to throw him off his guard. We cut for the deal, and were soon earnestly engaged in our play. I thought I perceived in this trifling for amusement (for the stake which Rashleigh proposed was a mere trifle) something of a fierce and ambitious temper. He seemed perfectly to understand the beautiful game at which he played, but preferred, as it were on principle, the risking bold and precarious strokes to the ordinary rules of play; and neglecting the minor and better-balanced chances of the game, he hazarded every thing for the chance of piqueing, repiqueing, or capotting his adversary. So soon as the intervention of a game or two at piquet, like the music between the acts of a drama, had completely interrupted our previous course of conversation, Rashleigh appeared to tire of the game, and the cards were superseded by discourse, in which he assumed the lead.

More learned than soundly wise — better acquainted with men's minds than with the moral principles that ought to regulate them, he had still powers of conversation which I have rarely seen equalled, never excelled. Of this his manner implied some consciousness; at least, it appeared to me that he had studied hard to improve his natural advantages of a melodious voice, fluent and happy expression, apt language, and fervid imagination. He was never loud, never overbearing, never so much occupied with his own thoughts, as to outrun either the patience or the comprehension of those he conversed with. His ideas succeeded each other with the gentle but unintermitting flow of a plentiful and bounteous spring; while I have heard those of others, who aimed at distinction in conversation, rush along like the turbid gush from the sluice of a mill-pond, as hurried, and as easily exhausted. It was late at night ere I could part from a companion so fascinating; and, when I gained my own apartment, it cost me no small effort to recall to my mind the character of Rashleigh, such as I had pictured him previous to this tête-à-tête.

So effectually, my dear Tresham, does the sense of being pleased and amused blunt our faculties of perception and discrimination of character, that I can only compare it to the taste of certain fruits, at once luscious and poignant, which renders our palate totally unfit for relishing or distinguishing the viands which are subsequently subjected to its criticism.

CHAPTER XI

What gars ye gaunt, my merrymen a' ?
What gars ye look sae dreary ?
What gars ye hing your head sae sair
In the castle of Balwearie ?
OLD SCOTCH BALLAD.

THE next morning chanced to be Sunday, a day
peculiarly hard to be got rid of at Osbaldistone
Hall; for after the formal religious service of the
morning had been performed, at which all the
family regularly attended, it was hard to say upon
which individual, Rashleigh and Miss Vernon excepted, the fiend of ennui descended with the most
abundant outpouring of his spirit. To speak of
my yesterday's embarrassment amused Sir Hildebrand for several minutes, and he congratulated me
on my deliverance from Morpeth or Hexham jail,
as he would have done if I had fallen in attempting
to clear a five-barred gate, and got up without
hurting myself.

' Hast had a lucky turn, lad; but do na be over
venturous again. What, man! the king's road is
free to all men, be they Whigs, be they Tories.'

' On my word, sir, I am innocent of interrupting it; and it is the most provoking thing on earth,
that every person will take it for granted that I am
accessory to a crime which I despise and detest,

and which would, moreover, deservedly forfeit my life to the laws of my country.'

'Well, well, lad; even so be it; I ask no questions — no man bound to tell on himself — that's fair play, or the devil's in 't.'

Rashleigh here came to my assistance; but I could not help thinking that his arguments were calculated rather as hints to his father to put on a show of acquiescence in my declaration of innocence, than fully to establish it.

'In your own house, my dear sir — and your own nephew—you will not surely persist in hurting his feelings, by seeming to discredit what he is so strongly interested in affirming. No doubt, you are fully deserving of all his confidence, and I am sure, were there any thing you could do to assist him in this strange affair, he would have recourse to your goodness. But my cousin Frank has been dismissed as an innocent man, and no one is entitled to suppose him otherwise. For my part, I have not the least doubt of his innocence; and our family honour, I conceive, requires that we should maintain it with tongue and sword against the whole country.'

'Rashleigh,' said his father, looking fixedly at him, 'thou art a sly loon—thou hast ever been too cunning for me, and too cunning for most folks. Have a care thou provena too cunning for thysell —two faces under one hood is no true heraldry.— And since we talk of heraldry, I'll go and read Gwillym.'

This resolution he intimated with a yawn, resistless as that of the Goddess in the Dunciad, which was responsively echoed by his giant sons, as they dispersed in quest of the pastimes to which their minds severally inclined them—Percie to discuss a pot of March beer with the steward in the buttery, —Thorncliff to cut a pair of cudgels, and fix them in their wicker hilts,—John to dress May-flies,— Dickon to play at pitch and toss by himself, his right hand against his left,—and Wilfred to bite his thumbs, and hum himself into a slumber which should last till dinner time, if possible. Miss Vernon had retired to the library.

Rashleigh and I were left alone in the old hall, from which the servants, with their usual bustle and awkwardness, had at length contrived to hurry the remains of our substantial breakfast. I took the opportunity to upbraid him with the manner in which he had spoken of my affair to his father, which I frankly stated was highly offensive to me, as it seemed rather to exhort Sir Hildebrand to conceal his suspicions, than to root them out.

'Why, what can I do, my dear friend?' replied Rashleigh; 'my father's disposition is so tenacious of suspicions of all kinds, when once they take root, which, to do him justice, does not easily happen, that I have always found it the best way to silence him upon such subjects, instead of arguing with him. Thus I get the better of the weeds which I cannot eradicate, by cutting them over as often as they appear, until at length they die away of themselves. There is neither wisdom nor profit in disputing with such a mind as Sir Hildebrand's, which hardens itself against conviction, and believes in its own inspirations as firmly as we good Catholics do in those of the Holy Father of Rome.'

'It is very hard though, that I should live in the house of a man, and he a near relation too, who will persist in believing me guilty of a highway robbery.'

'My father's foolish opinion, if one may give that epithet to any opinion of a father's, does not affect your real innocence; and as to the disgrace of the fact, depend on it, that, considered in all its bearings, political as well as moral, Sir Hildebrand regards it as a meritorious action—a weakening of the enemy—a spoiling of the Amalekites—and you will stand the higher in his regard for your supposed accession to it.'

'I desire no man's regard, Mr. Rashleigh, on such terms as must sink me in my own; and I think these injurious suspicions will afford a very good reason for quitting Osbaldistone Hall, which I shall do whenever I can communicate on the subject with my father.'

The dark countenance of Rashleigh, though little accustomed to betray its master's feelings, exhibited a suppressed smile, which he instantly chastened by a sigh.

'You are a happy man, Frank—you go and come, as the wind bloweth where it listeth. With your address, taste, and talents, you will soon find circles where they will be more valued, than amid the dull inmates of this mansion; while I——' he paused.

'And what is there in your lot that can make you or any one envy mine,—an outcast, as I may almost term myself, from my father's house and favour ? '

' Ay, but,' answered Rashleigh, ' consider the gratified sense of independence which you must have attained by a very temporary sacrifice, for such I am sure yours will prove to be—consider the power of acting as a free agent, of cultivating your own talents in the way to which your taste determines you, and in which you are well qualified to distinguish yourself — Fame and freedom are cheaply purchased by a few weeks' residence in the North, even though your place of exile be Osbaldistone Hall.—A second Ovid in Thrace, you have not his reasons for writing Tristia.'

' I do not know,' said I, blushing as became a young scribbler, ' how you should be so well acquainted with my truant studies.'

' There was an emissary of your father's here some time since, a young coxcomb, one Twineall, who informed me concerning your secret sacrifices to the muses, and added, that some of your verses had been greatly admired by the best judges.'

Tresham, I believe you are guiltless of having ever essayed to build the lofty rhyme; but you must have known in your day many an apprentice and fellow-craft, if not some of the master-masons, in the temple of Apollo. Vanity is their universal foible, from him who decorated the shades of Twickenham, to the veriest scribbler whom he has lashed in his Dunciad. I had my own share of this common failing, and without considering how little likely this young fellow Twineall was, by taste and habits, either to be acquainted with one or two little pieces of poetry, which I had at times insinuated into Button's coffee-house, or to report the opinion of the critics who frequented that resort of wit and literature, I almost instantly gorged the bait; which Rashleigh perceiving, improved his opportunity by a diffident, yet apparently very anxious request, to be permitted to see some of my manuscript productions.

'You shall give me an evening in my own apartment,' he continued; 'for I must soon lose the charms of literary society for the drudgery of commerce, and the coarse every-day avocations of the world. I repeat it, that my compliance with my father's wishes for the advantage of my family, is indeed a sacrifice, especially considering the calm and peaceful profession to which my education destined me.'

I was vain, but not a fool, and this hypocrisy was too strong for me to swallow—'You would not persuade me,' I replied, 'that you really regret to exchange the situation of an obscure Catholic priest, with all its privations, for wealth and society, and the pleasures of the world ?'

Rashleigh saw that he had coloured his affectation of moderation too highly, and, after a second's pause, during which, I suppose, he calculated the degree of candour which it was necessary to use with me, (that being a quality of which he was never needlessly profuse,) he answered with a smile,

—'At my age, to be condemned, as you say, to wealth and the world, does not, indeed, sound so alarming as perhaps it ought to do. But, with pardon be it spoken, you have mistaken my destination — a Catholic priest, if you will, but not an obscure one—No, sir, Rashleigh Osbaldistone will be more obscure, should he rise to be the richest citizen in London, than he might have been as a member of a church, whose ministers, as some one says, " set their sandall'd feet on princes." — My family interest at a certain exiled court is high, and the weight which that court ought to possess, and does possess, at Rome, is yet higher—my talents not altogether inferior to the education I have received. In sober judgment, I might have looked forward to high eminence in the church — in the dream of fancy, to the very highest—Why might not,' (he added, laughing, for it was part of his manner to keep much of his discourse apparently betwixt jest and earnest,)—' why might not Cardinal Osbaldistone have swayed the fortunes of empires, well-born and well-connected, as well as the low-born Mazarin, or Alberoni, the son of an Italian gardener ? '

' Nay, I can give you no reason to the contrary ; but in your place I should not much regret losing the chance of such precarious and invidious elevation.'

' Neither would I,' he replied, ' were I sure that my present establishment was more certain ; but that must depend upon circumstances, which I can only learn by experience — the disposition of your father, for example.'

'Confess the truth without finesse, Rashleigh; you would willingly know something of him from me?'

'Since, like Die Vernon, you make a point of following the banner of the good knight Sincerity, I reply—certainly.'

'Well, then, you will find in my father a man who has followed the paths of thriving more for the exercise they afforded to his talents, than for the love of the gold with which they are strewed. His active mind would have been happy in any situation which gave it scope for exertion, though that exertion had been its sole reward. But his wealth has accumulated, because, moderate and frugal in his habits, no new sources of expense have occurred to dispose of his increasing income. He is a man who hates dissimulation in others; never practises it himself; and is peculiarly alert in discovering motives through the colouring of language. Himself silent by habit, he is readily disgusted by great talkers; the rather, that the circumstances by which he is most interested afford no great scope for conversation. He is severely strict in the duties of religion; but you have no reason to fear his interference with yours, for he regards toleration as a sacred principle of political economy. But if you have any Jacobitical partialities, as is naturally to be supposed, you will do well to suppress them in his presence, as well as the least tendency to the highflying or Tory principles; for he holds both in utter detestation. For the rest, his word is his own bond, and must be the law of all who act under him. He will fail in his duty to no one, and will permit no one to fail towards him; to cultivate his favour, you must execute his commands, instead of echoing his sentiments. His greatest failings arise out of prejudices connected with his own profession, or rather his exclusive devotion to it, which makes him see little worthy of praise or attention, unless it be in some measure connected with commerce.'

'O rare-painted portrait!' exclaimed Rashleigh, when I was silent—'Vandyke was a dauber to you, Frank. I see thy sire before me in all his strength and weakness; loving and honouring the King as a sort of lord mayor of the empire, or chief of the board of trade;—venerating the Commons, for the acts regulating the export trade; — and respecting the Peers, because the Lord Chancellor sits on a woolsack.'

'Mine was a likeness, Rashleigh; yours is a caricature. But in return for the *carte du pays* which I have unfolded to you, give me some lights on the geography of the unknown lands——'

'On which you are wrecked,' said Rashleigh. 'It is not worth while; it is no Isle of Calypso, umbrageous with shade and intricate with silvan labyrinth—but a bare ragged Northumbrian moor, with as little to interest curiosity as to delight the eye—you may descry it in all its nakedness in half an hour's survey, as well as if I were to lay it down before you by line and compass.'

'O, but something there is, worthy a more attentive survey—What say you to Miss Vernon?

173

Does not she form an interesting object in the landscape, were all round as rude as Iceland's coast?'

I could plainly perceive that Rashleigh disliked the topic now presented to him; but my frank communication had given me the advantageous title to make inquiries in my turn. Rashleigh felt this, and found himself obliged to follow my lead, however difficult he might find it to play his cards successfully. 'I have known less of Miss Vernon,' he said, 'for some time, than I was wont to do formerly. In early age I was her tutor; but as she advanced towards womanhood, my various avocations, — the gravity of the profession to which I was destined,—the peculiar nature of her engagements,—our mutual situation, in short, rendered a close and constant intimacy dangerous and improper. I believe Miss Vernon might consider my reserve as unkindness, but it was my duty; I felt as much as she seemed to do, when compelled to give way to prudence. But where was the safety in cultivating an intimacy with a beautiful and susceptible girl, whose heart, you are aware, must be given either to the cloister or to a betrothed husband?'

'The cloister or a betrothed husband?' I echoed— 'Is that the alternative destined for Miss Vernon?'

'It is indeed,' said Rashleigh, with a sigh. 'I need not, I suppose, caution you against the danger of cultivating too closely the friendship of Miss Vernon; you are a man of the world, and know how far you can indulge yourself in her society, with safety to yourself and justice to her. But I warn you, that, considering her ardent temper, you must let your experience keep guard over her as well as yourself, for the specimen of yesterday may serve to show her extreme thoughtlessness and neglect of decorum.'

There was something, I was sensible, of truth, as well as good sense, in all this; it seemed to be given as a friendly warning, and I had no right to take it amiss; yet I felt I could with pleasure have run Rashleigh Osbaldistone through the body all the time he was speaking.

The deuce take his insolence! was my internal meditation. Would he wish me to infer, that Miss Vernon had fallen in love with that hatchet-face of his, and become degraded so low as to require his shyness to cure her of an imprudent passion? I will have his meaning from him, was my resolution, if I should drag it out with cart-ropes.

For this purpose, I placed my temper under as accurate a guard as I could, and observed, 'That, for a lady of her good sense and acquired accomplishments, it was to be regretted that Miss Vernon's manners were rather blunt and rustic.'

'Frank and unreserved, at least, to the extreme,' replied Rashleigh; 'yet, trust me, she has an excellent heart. To tell you the truth, should she continue her extreme aversion to the cloister, and to her destined husband, and should my own labours in the mine of Plutus promise to secure me a decent independence, I shall think of renewing our acquaintance, and sharing it with Miss Vernon.'

With all his fine voice, and well-turned periods, thought I, this same Rashleigh Osbaldistone is the ugliest and most conceited coxcomb I ever met with.

'But,' continued Rashleigh, as if thinking aloud, 'I should not like to supplant Thorncliff.'

'Supplant Thorncliff!—Is your brother Thorncliff,' I inquired, with great surprise, 'the destined husband of Diana Vernon?'

'Why, ay; her father's commands, and a certain family-contract, destine her to marry one of Sir Hildebrand's sons. A dispensation has been obtained from Rome to Diana Vernon to marry *Blank* Osbaldistone, Esq., son of Sir Hildebrand Osbaldistone, of Osbaldistone Hall, Bart., and so forth; and it only remains to pitch upon the happy man, whose name shall fill the gap in the manuscript. Now, as Percie is seldom sober, my father pitched on Thorncliff, as the second prop of the family, and therefore most proper to carry on the line of the Osbaldistones.'

'The young lady,' said I, forcing myself to assume an air of pleasantry, which, I believe, became me extremely ill, 'would perhaps have been inclined to look a little lower on the family-tree, for the branch to which she was desirous of clinging.'

'I cannot say,' he replied. 'There is room for little choice in our family; Dick is a gambler, John a boor, and Wilfred an ass. I believe my father really made the best selection for poor Die, after all.'

'The present company,' said I, 'being always excepted.'

'O, my destination to the church placed me out of the question; otherwise I will not affect to say, that, qualified by my education both to instruct and guide Miss Vernon, I might not have been a more creditable choice than any of my elders.'

'And so thought the young lady, doubtless?'

'You are not to suppose so,' answered Rashleigh, with an affectation of denial, which was contrived to convey the strongest affirmation the case admitted of—'Friendship—only friendship—formed the tie betwixt us, and the tender affection of an opening mind to its only instructor—Love came not near us—I told you I was wise in time.'

I felt little inclination to pursue this conversation any farther, and, shaking myself clear of Rashleigh, withdrew to my own apartment, which I recollect I traversed with much vehemence of agitation, repeating aloud the expressions which had most offended me. 'Susceptible—ardent—tender affection—Love!—Diana Vernon, the most beautiful creature I ever beheld, in love with him, the bandy-legged, bull-necked, limping scoundrel! — Richard the Third in all but his hump-back!—And yet the opportunities he must have had during his cursed course of lectures; and the fellow's flowing and easy strain of sentiment; and her extreme seclusion from every one who spoke and acted with common sense; ay, and her obvious pique at him, mixed with admiration of his talents, which looked as like the result of neglected attachment as any thing else—

Well, and what is it to me that I should storm and rage at it? Is Diana Vernon the first pretty girl that has loved or married an ugly fellow? And if she were free of every Osbaldistone of them, what concern is it of mine?—A Catholic—a Jacobite—a termagant into the boot—for me to look that way were utter madness.'

By throwing such reflections on the flame of my displeasure, I subdued it into a sort of smouldering heart-burning, and appeared at the dinner-table in as sulky a humour as could well be imagined.

CHAPTER XII

Drunk ?—and speak parrot ?—and squabble ?—swagger ?—
Swear ?—and discourse fustian with one's own shadow ?

OTHELLO.

I HAVE already told you, my dear Tresham, what probably was no news to you, that my principal fault was an unconquerable pitch of pride, which exposed me to frequent mortification. I had not even whispered to myself, that I loved Diana Vernon; yet no sooner did I hear Rashleigh talk of her as a prize which he might stoop to carry off, or neglect, at his pleasure, than every step which the poor girl had taken, in the innocence and openness of her heart, to form a sort of friendship with me, seemed in my eyes the most insulting coquetry. 'Soh! she would secure me as a *pis aller*, I suppose, in case Mr. Rashleigh Osbaldistone should not take compassion upon her! but I will satisfy her that I am not a person to be trepanned in that manner—I will make her sensible that I see through her arts, and that I scorn them.'

I did not reflect for a moment, that all this indignation, which I had no right whatever to entertain, proved that I was any thing but indifferent to Miss Vernon's charms; and I sate down to table in high ill-humour with her and all the daughters of Eve.

Miss Vernon heard me, with surprise, return ungracious answers to one or two playful strokes of satire which she threw out with her usual freedom of speech; but, having no suspicion that offence was meant, she only replied to my rude repartees with jests somewhat similar, but polished by her good temper, though pointed by her wit. At length she perceived I was really out of humour, and answered one of my rude speeches thus:

'They say, Mr. Frank, that one may gather sense from fools—I heard cousin Wilfred refuse to play any longer at cudgels the other day with cousin Thornie, because cousin Thornie got angry, and struck harder than the rules of amicable combat, it seems, permitted. "Were I to break your head in good earnest," quoth honest Wilfred, "I care not how angry you are, for I should do it so much the more easily;—but it's hard I should get raps over the costard, and only pay you back in make-believes"—Do you understand the moral of this, Frank?'

'I have never felt myself under the necessity, madam, of studying how to extract the slender portion of sense with which this family season their conversation.'

'Necessity! and madam!—You surprise me, Mr. Osbaldistone.'

'I am unfortunate in doing so.'

'Am I to suppose that this capricious tone is serious; or is it only assumed, to make your good-humour more valuable?'

'You have a right to the attention of so many

gentlemen in this family, Miss Vernon, that it cannot be worth your while to inquire into the cause of my stupidity and bad spirits.'

' What ! ' she said, ' am I to understand, then, that you have deserted my faction, and gone over to the enemy ? '

Then, looking across the table, and observing that Rashleigh, who was seated opposite, was watching us with a singular expression of interest on his harsh features, she continued,

> ' Horrible thought !—Ay, now I see 'tis true,
> For the grim-visaged Rashleigh smiles on me,
> And points at thee for his !——

Well, thank Heaven, and the unprotected state which has taught me endurance, I do not take offence easily ; and that I may not be forced to quarrel, whether I like it or no, I have the honour, earlier than usual, to wish you a happy digestion of your dinner and your bad humour.'

And she left the table accordingly.

Upon Miss Vernon's departure, I found myself very little satisfied with my own conduct. I had hurled back offered kindness, of which circumstances had but lately pointed out the honest sincerity, and I had but just stopped short of insulting the beautiful, and, as she had said with some emphasis, the unprotected being by whom it was proffered. My conduct seemed brutal in my own eyes. To combat or drown these painful reflections, I applied myself more frequently than usual to the wine which circulated on the table.

The agitated state of my feelings combined with my habits of temperance to give rapid effect to the beverage. Habitual topers, I believe, acquire the power of soaking themselves with a quantity of liquor that does little more than muddy those intellects, which, in their sober state, are none of the clearest; but men who are strangers to the vice of drunkenness as a habit, are more powerfully acted upon by intoxicating liquors. My spirits, once aroused, became extravagant; I talked a great deal, argued upon what I knew nothing of, told stories of which I forgot the point, then laughed immoderately at my own forgetfulness; I accepted several bets without having the least judgment; I challenged the giant John to wrestle with me, although he had kept the ring at Hexham for a year, and I never tried so much as a single fall.

My uncle had the goodness to interpose and prevent this consummation of drunken folly, which, I suppose, would have otherwise ended in my neck being broken.

It has even been reported by maligners, that I sung a song while under this vinous influence; but, as I remember nothing of it, and never attempted to turn a tune in all my life before or since, I would willingly hope there is no actual foundation for the calumny. I was absurd enough without this exaggeration. Without positively losing my senses, I speedily lost all command of my temper, and my impetuous passions whirled me onward at their pleasure. I had sate down sulky and discontented, and disposed to be silent—the wine rendered me loquacious, disputatious, and quarrelsome. I contradicted whatever was asserted, and attacked, without any respect to my uncle's table, both his politics and his religion. The affected moderation of Rashleigh, which he well knew how to qualify with irritating ingredients, was even more provoking to me than the noisy and bullying language of his obstreperous brothers. My uncle, to do him justice, endeavoured to bring us to order; but his authority was lost amidst the tumult of wine and passion. At length, frantic at some real, or supposed injurious insinuation, I actually struck Rashleigh with my fist. No Stoic philosopher, superior to his own passion and that of others, could have received an insult with a higher degree of scorn. What he himself did not think it apparently worth while to resent, Thorncliff resented for him. Swords were drawn, and we exchanged one or two passes, when the other brothers separated us by main force; and I shall never forget the diabolical sneer which writhed Rashleigh's wayward features, as I was forced from the apartment by the main strength of two of these youthful Titans. They secured me in my apartment by locking the door, and I heard them, to my inexpressible rage, laugh heartily as they descended the stairs. I essayed in my fury to break out; but the window-grates, and the strength of a door clenched with iron, resisted my efforts. At length I threw myself on my bed, and fell asleep amidst vows of dire revenge to be taken in the ensuing day.

But with the morning cool repentance came. I

felt, in the keenest manner, the violence and absurdity of my conduct, and was obliged to confess that wine and passion had lowered my intellects even below those of Wilfred Osbaldistone, whom I held in so much contempt. My uncomfortable reflections were by no means soothed by meditating the necessity of an apology for my improper behaviour, and recollecting that Miss Vernon must be a witness of my submission. The impropriety and unkindness of my conduct to her personally, added not a little to these galling considerations, and for this I could not even plead the miserable excuse of intoxication.

Under all these aggravating feelings of shame and degradation, I descended to the breakfast-hall, like a criminal to receive sentence. It chanced that a hard frost had rendered it impossible to take out the hounds, so that I had the additional mortification to meet the family, excepting only Rashleigh and Miss Vernon, in full divan, surrounding the cold venison-pasty and chine of beef. They were in high glee as I entered, and I could easily imagine that the jests were furnished at my expense. In fact, what I was disposed to consider with serious pain, was regarded as an excellent good joke by my uncle, and the greater part of my cousins. Sir Hildebrand, while he rallied me on the exploits of the preceding evening, swore he thought a young fellow had better be thrice drunk in one day, than sneak sober to bed like a presbyterian, and leave a batch of honest fellows, and a double quart of claret. And to back this consolatory speech, he poured out a

large bumper of brandy, exhorting me to swallow
' a hair of the dog that had bit me.'

' Never mind these lads laughing, nevoy,' he continued; ' they would have been all as great milksops
as yourself, had I not nursed them, as one may say,
on the toast and tankard.'

Ill-nature was not the fault of my cousins in
general; they saw I was vexed and hurt at the
recollections of the preceding evening, and endeavoured, with clumsy kindness, to remove the painful
impression they had made on me. Thorncliff alone
looked sullen and unreconciled. This young man
had never liked me from the beginning; and in the
marks of attention occasionally shown me by his
brothers, awkward as they were, he alone had never
joined. If it was true, of which, however, I began
to have my doubts, that he was considered by the
family, or regarded himself, as the destined husband
of Miss Vernon, a sentiment of jealousy might have
sprung up in his mind from the marked predilection
which it was that young lady's pleasure to show for
one, whom Thorncliff might, perhaps, think likely
to become a dangerous rival.

Rashleigh at last entered, his visage as dark as
mourning weed, brooding, I could not but doubt,
over the unjustifiable and disgraceful insult I had
offered to him. I had already settled in my own
mind how I was to behave on the occasion, and had
schooled myself to believe, that true honour consisted not in defending, but in apologising for, an
injury so much disproportioned to any provocation
I might have to allege.

I therefore hastened to meet Rashleigh, and to express myself in the highest degree sorry for the violence with which I had acted on the preceding evening.

'No circumstances,' I said, 'could have wrung from me a single word of apology, save my own consciousness of the impropriety of my behaviour. I hoped my cousin would accept of my regrets so sincerely offered, and consider how much of my misconduct was owing to the excessive hospitality of Osbaldistone Hall.'

'He shall be friends with thee, lad,' cried the honest knight, in the full effusion of his heart; 'or d—n me, if I call him son more!—Why, Rashie, dost stand there like a log? *Sorry for it* is all a gentleman can say, if he happens to do any thing awry, especially over his claret.—I served in Hounslow, and should know something, I think, of affairs of honour. Let me hear no more of this, and we'll go in a body and rummage out the badger in Birkenwood-bank.'

Rashleigh's face resembled, as I have already noticed, no other countenance that I ever saw. But this singularity lay not only in the features, but in the mode of changing their expression. Other countenances, in altering from grief to joy, or from anger to satisfaction, pass through some brief interval, ere the expression of the predominant passion supersedes entirely that of its predecessor. There is a sort of twilight, like that between the clearing up of the darkness and the rising of the sun, while the swollen muscles subside, the dark eye clears, the forehead relaxes and expands itself, and the whole countenance loses its sterner shades, and becomes serene and placid. Rashleigh's face exhibited none of these gradations, but changed almost instantaneously from the expression of one passion to that of the contrary. I can compare it to nothing but the sudden shifting of a scene in the theatre, where, at the whistle of the prompter, a cavern disappears, and a grove arises.

My attention was strongly arrested by this peculiarity on the present occasion. At Rashleigh's first entrance, 'black he stood as night!' With the same inflexible countenance he heard my excuse and his father's exhortation; and it was not until Sir Hildebrand had done speaking, that the cloud cleared away at once, and he expressed, in the kindest and most civil terms, his perfect satisfaction with the very handsome apology I had offered.

'Indeed,' he said, 'I have so poor a brain myself, when I impose on it the least burden beyond my usual three glasses, that I have only, like honest Cassio, a very vague recollection of the confusion of last night—remember a mass of things, but nothing distinctly—a quarrel, but nothing wherefore—So, my dear cousin,' he continued, shaking me kindly by the hand, 'conceive how much I am relieved, by finding that I have to receive an apology, instead of having to make one—I will not have a word said upon the subject more; I should be very foolish to institute any scrutiny into an account, when the balance, which I expected to be against me, has been so unexpectedly and agreeably struck in my favour. You see, Mr. Osbaldistone, I am practising the language of Lombard Street, and qualifying myself for my new calling.'

As I was about to answer, and raised my eyes for the purpose, they encountered those of Miss Vernon, who, having entered the room unobserved during the conversation, had given it her close attention. Abashed and confounded, I fixed my eyes on the ground, and made my escape to the breakfast-table, where I herded among my busy cousins.

My uncle, that the events of the preceding day might not pass out of our memory without a practical moral lesson, took occasion to give Rashleigh and me his serious advice to correct our milksop habits, as he termed them, and gradually to inure our brains to bear a gentlemanlike quantity of liquor, without brawls or breaking of heads. He recommended that we should begin piddling with a regular quart of claret per day, which, with the aid of March beer and brandy, made a handsome competence for a beginner in the art of toping. And for our encouragement, he assured us that he had known many a man who had lived to our years without having drunk a pint of wine at a sitting, who yet, by falling into honest company, and following hearty example, had afterwards been numbered among the best good fellows of the time, and could carry off their six bottles under their belt quietly and comfortably, without brawling or babbling, and be neither sick nor sorry the next morning.

Sage as this advice was, and comfortable as was

the prospect it held out to me, I profited but little by the exhortation; partly, perhaps, because, as often as I raised my eyes from the table, I observed Miss Vernon's looks fixed on me, in which I thought I could read grave compassion blended with regret and displeasure. I began to consider how I should seek a scene of explanation and apology with her also, when she gave me to understand she was determined to save me the trouble of soliciting an interview. 'Cousin Francis,' she said, addressing me by the same title she used to give to the other Osbaldistones, although I had, properly speaking, no title to be called her kinsman, 'I have encountered this morning a difficult passage in the Divina Commedia of Dante; will you have the goodness to step to the library and give me your assistance? and when you have unearthed for me the meaning of the obscure Florentine, we will join the rest at Birkenwood-bank, and see their luck at unearthing the badger.'

I signified, of course, my readiness to wait upon her. Rashleigh made an offer to accompany us. 'I am something better skilled,' he said, 'at tracking the sense of Dante through the metaphors and elisions of his wild and gloomy poem, than at hunting the poor inoffensive hermit yonder out of his cave.'

'Pardon me, Rashleigh,' said Miss Vernon; 'but as you are to occupy Mr. Francis's place in the counting-house, you must surrender to him the charge of your pupil's education at Osbaldistone Hall. We shall call you in, however, if there is any occasion; so pray do not look so grave upon it. Besides, it is a shame to you not to understand field-sports—What will you do should our uncle in Crane-Alley ask you the signs by which you track a badger?'

'Ay, true, Die,—true,' said Sir Hildebrand, with a sigh. 'I misdoubt Rashleigh will be found short at the leap when he is put to the trial. An he would ha' learned useful knowledge like his brothers, he was bred up where it grew, I wuss; but French antics, and book-learning, with the new turnips, and the rats, and the Hanoverians, ha' changed the world that I ha' known in Old England—But come along with us, Rashie, and carry my hunting-staff, man; thy cousin lacks none of thy company as now, and I wonna ha' Die crossed—It's ne'er be said there was but one woman in Osbaldistone Hall, and she died for lack of her will.'

Rashleigh followed his father, as he commanded, not, however, ere he had whispered to Diana, 'I suppose I must in discretion bring the courtier, Ceremony, in my company, and knock when I approach the door of the library?'

'No, no, Rashleigh,' said Miss Vernon; 'dismiss from your company the false archimage Dissimulation, and it will better insure your free access to our classical consultations.'

So saying, she led the way to the library, and I followed—like a criminal, I was going to say, to execution; but, as I bethink me, I have used the simile once, if not twice before. Without any simile at all, then, I followed, with a sense of awkward and conscious embarrassment, which I would have given a great deal to shake off. I thought it a degrading and unworthy feeling to attend one on such an occasion, having breathed the air of the Continent long enough to have imbibed the notion that lightness, gallantry, and something approaching to wellbred self-assurance, should distinguish the gentleman whom a fair lady selects for her companion in a *tête-à-tête*.

My English feelings, however, were too many for my French education, and I made, I believe, a very pitiful figure, when Miss Vernon, seating herself majestically in a huge elbow-chair in the library, like a judge about to hear a cause of importance, signed to me to take a chair opposite to her, (which I did, much like the poor fellow who is going to be tried,) and entered upon conversation in a tone of bitter irony.

CHAPTER XIII

Dire was his thought, who first in poison steep'd
The weapon form'd for slaughter—direr his,
And worthier of damnation, who instill'd
The mortal venom in the social cup,
To fill the veins with death instead of life.
ANONYMOUS.

'Upon my word, Mr. Francis Osbaldistone,' said Miss Vernon, with the air of one who thought herself fully entitled to assume the privilege of ironical reproach, which she was pleased to exert, 'your character improves upon us, sir—I could not have thought that it was in you. Yesterday might be considered as your assay-piece, to prove yourself entitled to be free of the corporation of Osbaldistone Hall. But it was a masterpiece.'

'I am quite sensible of my ill-breeding, Miss Vernon, and I can only say for myself, that I had received some communications by which my spirits were unusually agitated. I am conscious I was impertinent and absurd.'

'You do yourself great injustice,' said the merciless monitor—'you have contrived, by what I saw and have since heard, to exhibit in the course of one evening a happy display of all the various masterly qualifications which distinguish your several cousins;—the gentle and generous temper of the benevolent

Rashleigh,—the temperance of Percie,—the cool courage of Thorncliff,—John's skill in dog-breaking, —Dickon's aptitude to betting,—all exhibited by the single individual Mr. Francis, and that with a selection of time, place, and circumstance, worthy the taste and sagacity of the sapient Wilfred.'

'Have a little mercy, Miss Vernon,' said I ; for I confess I thought the schooling as severe as the case merited, especially considering from what quarter it came, 'and forgive me if I suggest, as an excuse for follies I am not usually guilty of, the custom of this house and country. I am far from approving of it; but we have Shakspeare's authority for saying, that good wine is a good familiar creature, and that any man living may be overtaken at some time.'

'Ay, Mr. Francis, but he places the panegyric and the apology in the mouth of the greatest villain his pencil has drawn. I will not, however, abuse the advantage your quotation has given me, by overwhelming you with the refutation with which the victim Cassio replies to the tempter Iago. I only wish you to know, that there is one person at least sorry to see a youth of talents and expectations sink into the slough, in which the inhabitants of this house are nightly wallowing.'

'I have but wet my shoe, I assure you, Miss Vernon, and am too sensible of the filth of the puddle to step farther in.'

'If such be your resolution,' she replied, 'it is a wise one. But I was so much vexed at what I heard, that your concerns have pressed before my

ROB ROY

own.—You behaved to me yesterday, during dinner, as if something had been told you which lessened or lowered me in your opinion—I beg leave to ask you what it was?'

I was stupified—the direct bluntness of the demand was much in the style one gentleman uses to another, when requesting explanation of any part of his conduct in a good-humoured yet determined manner, and was totally devoid of the circumlocutions, shadings, softenings, and periphrasis, which usually accompany explanations betwixt persons of different sexes in the higher orders of society.

I remained completely embarrassed; for it pressed on my recollection, that Rashleigh's communications, supposing them to be correct, ought to have rendered Miss Vernon rather an object of my compassion, than of my pettish resentment; and had they furnished the best apology possible for my own conduct, still I must have had the utmost difficulty in detailing what inferred such necessary and natural offence to Miss Vernon's feelings. She observed my hesitation, and proceeded in a tone somewhat more peremptory, but still temperate and civil.

'I hope Mr. Osbaldistone does not dispute my title to request this explanation. I have no relative who can protect me; it is, therefore, just that I be permitted to protect myself.'

I endeavoured with hesitation to throw the blame of my rude behaviour upon indisposition—upon disagreeable letters from London. She suffered me to exhaust my apologies, and fairly to run myself

194

aground, listening all the while with a smile of absolute incredulity.

'And now, Mr. Francis, having gone through your prologue of excuses, with the same bad grace with which all prologues are delivered, please to draw the curtain, and show me that which I desire to see. In a word, let me know what Rashleigh says of me; for he is the grand engineer and first mover of all the machinery of Osbaldistone Hall.'

'But, supposing there was any thing to tell, Miss Vernon, what does he deserve that betrays the secrets of one ally to another?—Rashleigh, you yourself told me, remained your ally, though no longer your friend.'

'I have neither patience for evasion, nor inclination for jesting, on the present subject. Rashleigh cannot—ought not—dare not, hold any language respecting me, Diana Vernon, but what I may demand to hear repeated. That there are subjects of secrecy and confidence between us, is most certain; but to such, his communications to you could have no relation; and with such, I, as an individual, have no concern.'

I had by this time recovered my presence of mind, and hastily determined to avoid making any disclosure of what Rashleigh had told me in a sort of confidence. There was something unworthy in retailing private conversation; it could, I thought, do no good, and must necessarily give Miss Vernon great pain. I therefore replied, gravely, 'that nothing but frivolous talk had passed between Mr. Rashleigh Osbaldistone and me on the state of the family at the Hall; and I protested, that nothing had been said which left a serious impression to her disadvantage. As a gentleman, I said, I could not be more explicit in reporting private conversation.'

She started up with the animation of a Camilla about to advance into battle. 'This shall not serve your turn, sir,—I must have another answer from you.' Her features kindled — her brow became flushed—her eye glanced wild-fire as she proceeded. 'I demand such an explanation, as a woman basely slandered has a right to demand from every man who calls himself a gentleman — as a creature, motherless, friendless, alone in the world, left to her own guidance and protection, has a right to require from every being having a happier lot, in the name of that God who sent *them* into the world to enjoy and *her* to suffer. You shall not deny me —or,' she added, looking solemnly upwards, 'you will rue your denial, if there is justice for wrong either on earth or in heaven.'

I was utterly astonished at her vehemence, but felt, thus conjured, that it became my duty to lay aside scrupulous delicacy, and gave her briefly, but distinctly, the heads of the information which Rashleigh had conveyed to me.

She sate down and resumed her composure, as soon as I entered upon the subject, and when I stopped to seek for the most delicate turn of expression, she repeatedly interrupted me, with 'Go on —pray, go on; the first word which occurs to you is the plainest, and must be the best. Do not think

of my feelings, but speak as you would to an un-
concerned third party.'

Thus urged and encouraged, I stammered through
all the account which Rashleigh had given of her
early contract to marry an Osbaldistone, and of the
uncertainty and difficulty of her choice; and there
I would willingly have paused. But her penetration
discovered that there was still something behind,
and even guessed to what it related.

'Well, it was ill-natured of Rashleigh to tell this
tale on me. I am like the poor girl in the fairy tale,
who was betrothed in her cradle to the Black Bear
of Norway, but complained chiefly of being called
Bruin's bride by her companions at school. But
besides all this, Rashleigh said something of himself
with relation to me—Did he not?'

'He certainly hinted, that were it not for the
idea of supplanting his brother, he would now, in
consequence of his change of profession, be desirous
that the word Rashleigh should fill up the blank
in the dispensation, instead of the word Thorncliff.'

'Ay? indeed?' she replied; 'was he so very
condescending?—Too much honour for his humble
handmaid, Diana Vernon—And she, I suppose, was
to be enraptured with joy could such a substitute
be effected?'

'To confess the truth, he intimated as much, and
even farther insinuated——'

'What?—Let me hear it all!' she exclaimed
hastily.

'That he had broken off your mutual intimacy,

lest it should have given rise to an affection by which his destination to the church would not permit him to profit.'

'I am obliged to him for his consideration,' replied Miss Vernon, every feature of her fine countenance taxed to express the most supreme degree of scorn and contempt. She paused a moment, and then said, with her usual composure, 'There is but little I have heard from you which I did not expect to hear, and which I ought not to have expected; because, bating one circumstance, it is all very true. But as there are some poisons so active, that a few drops, it is said, will infect a whole fountain, so there is one falsehood in Rashleigh's communication, powerful enough to corrupt the whole well in which Truth herself is said to have dwelt. It is the leading and foul falsehood, that, knowing Rashleigh as I have reason too well to know him, any circumstance on earth could make me think of sharing my lot with him. No,' she continued, with a sort of inward shuddering that seemed to express involuntary horror, 'any lot rather than that—the sot, the gambler, the bully, the jockey, the insensate fool, were a thousand times preferable to Rashleigh; —the convent—the jail—the grave, shall be welcome before them all.'

There was a sad and melancholy cadence in her voice, corresponding with the strange and interesting romance of her situation. So young, so beautiful, so untaught, so much abandoned to herself, and deprived of all the support which her sex derives from the countenance and protection of female friends, and even of that degree of defence which arises from the forms with which the sex are approached in civilized life,—it is scarce metaphorical to say, that my heart bled for her. Yet there was an expression of dignity in her contempt of ceremony—of upright feeling in her disdain of falsehood—of firm resolution in the manner in which she contemplated the dangers by which she was surrounded, which blended my pity with the warmest admiration. She seemed a princess deserted by her subjects, and deprived of her power, yet still scorning those formal regulations of society which are created for persons of an inferior rank; and, amid her difficulties, relying boldly and confidently on the justice of Heaven, and the unshaken constancy of her own mind.

I offered to express the mingled feelings of sympathy and admiration with which her unfortunate situation and her high spirit combined to impress me, but she imposed silence on me at once.

'I told you in jest,' she said, 'that I disliked compliments—I now tell you in earnest, that I do not ask sympathy, and that I despise consolation. What I have borne, I have borne—What I am to bear, I will sustain as I may; no word of commiseration can make a burden feel one feather's weight lighter to the slave who must carry it. There is only one human being who could have assisted me, and that is he who has rather chosen to add to my embarrassment—Rashleigh Osbaldistone.—Yes! the time once was that I might have learned to love that man—But, great God! the purpose for which he insinuated himself into the confidence of one already so forlorn—the undeviating and continued assiduity with which he pursued that purpose from year to year, without one single momentary pause of remorse or compassion—the purpose for which he would have converted into poison the food he administered to my mind—Gracious Providence! what should I have been in this world and the next, in body and soul, had I fallen under the arts of this accomplished villain!'

I was so much struck with the scene of perfidious treachery which these words disclosed, that I rose from my chair, hardly knowing what I did, laid my hand on the hilt of my sword, and was about to leave the apartment in search of him on whom I might discharge my just indignation. Almost breathless, and with eyes and looks in which scorn and indignation had given way to the most lively alarm, Miss Vernon threw herself between me and the door of the apartment.

' Stay,' she said, — ' stay ; however just your resentment, you do not know half the secrets of this fearful prison-house.' She then glanced her eyes anxiously round the room, and sunk her voice almost to a whisper—' He bears a charmed life ; you cannot assail him without endangering other lives, and wider destruction. Had it been other-wise, in some hour of justice he had hardly been safe, even from this weak hand. I told you,' she said, motioning me back to my seat, ' that I needed no comforter—I now tell you, I need no avenger.'

I resumed my seat mechanically, musing on what she said, and recollecting also, what had escaped me in my first glow of resentment, that I had no title whatever to constitute myself Miss Vernon's champion. She paused to let her own emotions and mine subside, and then addressed me with more composure.

'I have already said, that there is a mystery connected with Rashleigh, of a dangerous and fatal nature. Villain as he is, and as he knows he stands convicted in my eyes, I cannot—dare not, openly break with or defy him. You also, Mr. Osbaldistone, must bear with him with patience, foil his artifices by opposing to them prudence, not violence; and, above all, you must avoid such scenes as that of last night, which cannot but give him perilous advantages over you. This caution I designed to give you, and it was the object with which I desired this interview; but I have extended my confidence farther than I proposed.'

I assured her it was not misplaced.

'I do not believe that it is,' she replied. 'You have that in your face and manners which authorizes trust. Let us continue to be friends. You need not fear,' she said, laughing, while she blushed a little, yet speaking with a free and unembarrassed voice, 'that friendship with us should prove only a specious name, as the poet says, for another feeling. I belong, in habits of thinking and acting, rather to your sex, with which I have always been brought up, than to my own. Besides, the fatal veil was wrapt round me in my cradle; for you may easily believe I have never thought of the detestable condition under which I may remove it. The time,' she added, 'for expressing my final determination is not arrived, and I would fain have the freedom of wild heath and open air with the other commoners of nature, as long as I can be permitted to enjoy them. And now that the passage in Dante is made so clear, pray go and see what is become of the badger-baiters—My head aches so much that I cannot join the party.'

I left the library, but not to join the hunters. I felt that a solitary walk was necessary to compose my spirits, before I again trusted myself in Rashleigh's company, whose depth of calculating villainy had been so strikingly exposed to me. In Dubourg's family, (as he was of the reformed persuasion,) I had heard many a tale of Romish priests, who gratified, at the expense of friendship, hospitality, and the most sacred ties of social life, those passions, the blameless indulgence of which is denied by the rules of their order. But the deliberate system of undertaking the education of a deserted orphan of noble birth, and so intimately allied to his own family, with the perfidious purpose of ultimately seducing her, detailed as it was by the intended victim with all the glow of virtuous resentment, seemed more atrocious to me than the worst of the tales I had heard at Bourdeaux, and I felt it would be extremely difficult for me to meet Rashleigh, and yet to suppress the abhorrence with which he impressed me. Yet this was absolutely necessary, not only on account of the mysterious charge which Diana had given me, but because I had, in reality, no ostensible ground for quarrelling with him.

I therefore resolved, as far as possible, to meet Rashleigh's dissimulation with equal caution on my part during our residence in the same family; and when he should depart for London, I resolved to give Owen at least such a hint of his character as might keep him on his guard over my father's interests. Avarice or ambition, I thought, might have as great, or greater charms, for a mind constituted like Rashleigh's, than unlawful pleasure; the energy of his character, and his power of assuming all seeming good qualities, were likely to procure him a high degree of confidence, and it was not to be hoped, that either good faith or gratitude would prevent him from abusing it. The task was somewhat difficult, especially in my circumstances, since the caution which I threw out might be imputed to jealousy of my rival, or rather my successor, in my father's favour. Yet I thought it absolutely necessary to frame such a letter, leaving it to Owen, who, in his own line, was wary, prudent, and circumspect, to make the necessary use of his knowledge of Rashleigh's true character. Such a letter, therefore, I indited, and dispatched to the post-house by the first opportunity.

At my meeting with Rashleigh, he, as well as I, appeared to have taken up distant ground, and to be disposed to avoid all pretext for collision. He was probably conscious that Miss Vernon's communications had been unfavourable to him, though he could not know that they extended to discovering his meditated villainy towards her. Our intercourse, therefore, was reserved on both sides, and turned on subjects of little interest. Indeed, his stay at Osbaldistone Hall did not exceed a few days after this period, during which I only remarked two circumstances respecting him. The first was, the rapid and almost intuitive manner in which his powerful and active mind seized upon and arranged the elementary principles necessary in his new profession, which he now studied hard, and occasionally made parade of his progress, as if to show me how light it was for him to lift the burden which I had flung down from very weariness and inability to carry it. The other remarkable circumstance was, that, notwithstanding the injuries with which Miss Vernon charged Rashleigh, they had several private interviews together of considerable length, although their bearing towards each other in public did not seem more cordial than usual.

When the day of Rashleigh's departure arrived, his father bade him farewell with indifference; his brothers, with the ill-concealed glee of schoolboys, who see their taskmaster depart for a season, and feel a joy which they dare not express; and I myself with cold politeness. When he approached Miss Vernon, and would have saluted her, she drew back with a look of haughty disdain; but said, as she extended her hand to him, 'Farewell, Rashleigh; God reward you for the good you have done, and forgive you for the evil you have meditated.'

'Amen, my fair cousin,' he replied, with an air of sanctity, which belonged, I thought, to the seminary of Saint Omers; 'happy is he whose good intentions have borne fruit in deeds, and whose evil thoughts have perished in the blossom.'

These were his parting words. 'Accomplished hypocrite!' said Miss Vernon to me, as the door closed behind him—'how nearly can what we most despise and hate approach in outward manner to that which we most venerate!'

I had written to my father by Rashleigh, and also a few lines to Owen, besides the confidential letter which I have already mentioned, and which I thought it more proper and prudent to dispatch by another conveyance. In these epistles, it would have been natural for me to have pointed out to my father and my friend, that I was at present in a situation where I could improve myself in no respect, unless in the mysteries of hunting and hawking; and where I was not unlikely to forget, in the company of rude grooms and horse-boys, any useful knowledge or elegant accomplishments which I had hitherto acquired. It would also have been natural that I should have expressed the disgust and tædium which I was likely to feel among beings, whose whole souls were centred in field-sports or more degrading pastimes—that I should have complained of the habitual intemperance of the family in which I was a guest, and the difficulty and almost resentment with which my uncle

Sir Hildebrand received any apology for deserting the bottle. This last, indeed, was a topic on which my father, himself a man of severe temperance, was likely to be easily alarmed, and to have touched upon this spring would to a certainty have opened the doors of my prison-house, and would either have been the means of abridging my exile, or at least would have procured me a change of residence during my rustication.

I say, my dear Tresham, that, considering how very unpleasant a prolonged residence at Osbaldistone Hall must have been to a young man of my age, and with my habits, it might have seemed very natural that I should have pointed out all these disadvantages to my father, in order to obtain his consent for leaving my uncle's mansion. Nothing, however, is more certain, than that I did not say a single word to this purpose in my letters to my father and Owen. If Osbaldistone Hall had been Athens in all its pristine glory of learning, and inhabited by sages, heroes, and poets, I could not have expressed less inclination to leave it.

If thou hast any of the salt of youth left in thee, Tresham, thou wilt be at no loss to account for my silence on a topic seemingly so obvious. Miss Vernon's extreme beauty, of which she herself seemed so little conscious,—her romantic and mysterious situation,—the evils to which she was exposed,—the courage with which she seemed to face them,—her manners, more frank than belonged to her sex, yet, as it seemed to me, exceeding in frankness only from the dauntless consciousness of her innocence,—above all, the obvious and flattering distinction which she made in my favour over all other persons, were at once calculated to interest my best feelings, to excite my curiosity, awaken my imagination, and gratify my vanity. I dared not, indeed, confess to myself the depth of the interest with which Miss Vernon inspired me, or the large share which she occupied in my thoughts. We read together, walked together, rode together, and sate together. The studies which she had broken off upon her quarrel with Rashleigh, she now resumed under the auspices of a tutor, whose views were more sincere, though his capacity was far more limited.

In truth, I was by no means qualified to assist her in the prosecution of several profound studies which she had commenced with Rashleigh, and which appeared to me more fitted for a churchman than for a beautiful female. Neither can I conceive with what view he should have engaged Diana in the gloomy maze of casuistry which schoolmen called philosophy, or in the equally abstruse, though more certain sciences of mathematics and astronomy; unless it were to break down and confound in her mind the difference and distinction between the sexes, and to habituate her to trains of subtile reasoning, by which he might at his own time invest that which is wrong with the colour of that which is right. It was in the same spirit, though in the latter case the evil purpose was more obvious, that the lessons of Rashleigh had encouraged Miss Vernon in setting at nought and despising the forms and ceremonial limits which are drawn round females in modern society. It is true, she was sequestered from all female company, and could not learn the usual rules of decorum, either from example or precept; yet such was her innate modesty, and accurate sense of what was right and wrong, that she would not of herself have adopted the bold uncompromising manner which struck me with so much surprise on our first acquaintance, had she not been led to conceive, that a contempt of ceremony indicated at once superiority of understanding, and the confidence of conscious innocence. Her wily instructor had, no doubt, his own views in levelling those outworks which reserve and caution erect around virtue. But for these, and for his other crimes, he has long since answered at a higher tribunal.

Besides the progress which Miss Vernon, whose powerful mind readily adopted every means of information offered to it, had made in more abstract science, I found her no contemptible linguist, and well acquainted both with ancient and modern literature. Were it not that strong talents will often go farthest when they seem to have least assistance, it would be almost incredible to tell the rapidity of Miss Vernon's progress in knowledge; and it was still more extraordinary, when her stock of mental acquisitions from books was compared with her total ignorance of actual life. It seemed as if she saw and knew every thing, except what passed in the world around her; and I believe it was this very ignorance and simplicity of thinking upon ordinary subjects, so strikingly contrasted with her fund of general knowledge and information, which rendered her conversation so irresistibly fascinating, and riveted the attention to whatever she said or did; since it was absolutely impossible to anticipate whether her next word or action was to display the most acute perception, or the most profound simplicity. The degree of danger which necessarily attended a youth of my age and keen feelings from remaining in close and constant intimacy with an object so amiable, and so peculiarly interesting, all who remember their own sentiments at my age may easily estimate.

CHAPTER XIV

Yon lamp its line of quivering light
Shoots from my lady's bower;
But why should Beauty's lamp be bright
At midnight's lonely hour?
OLD BALLAD.

THE mode of life at Osbaldistone Hall was too
uniform to admit of description. Diana Vernon and
I enjoyed much of our time in our mutual studies;
the rest of the family killed theirs in such sports
and pastimes as suited the seasons, in which we
also took a share. My uncle was a man of habits,
and by habit became so much accustomed to my
presence and mode of life, that, upon the whole, he
was rather fond of me than otherwise. I might
probably have risen yet higher in his good graces,
had I employed the same arts for that purpose
which were used by Rashleigh, who, availing himself
of his father's disinclination to business, had gradually insinuated himself into the management of his
property. But although I readily gave my uncle
the advantage of my pen and my arithmetic so often
as he desired to correspond with a neighbour, or
settle with a tenant, and was, in so far, a more
useful inmate in his family than any of his sons,
yet I was not willing to oblige Sir Hildebrand, by
relieving him entirely from the management of his

own affairs; so that, while the good knight admitted that nevoy Frank was a steady, handy lad, he seldom failed to remark in the same breath, that he did not think he should ha' missed Rashleigh so much as he was like to do.

As it is particularly unpleasant to reside in a family where we are at variance with any part of it, I made some efforts to overcome the ill-will which my cousins entertained against me. I exchanged my laced hat for a jockey-cap, and made some progress in their opinion; I broke a young colt in a manner which carried me further into their good graces. A bet or two opportunely lost to Dickon, and an extra health pledged with Percie, placed me on an easy and familiar footing with all the young squires, except Thorncliff.

I have already noticed the dislike entertained against me by this young fellow, who, as he had rather more sense, had also a much worse temper, than any of his brethren. Sullen, dogged, and quarrelsome, he regarded my residence at Osbaldistone Hall as an intrusion, and viewed, with envious and jealous eyes, my intimacy with Diana Vernon, whom the effect proposed to be given to a certain family-compact assigned to him as an intended spouse. That he loved her could scarcely be said, at least without much misapplication of the word; but he regarded her as something appropriated to himself, and resented internally the interference which he knew not how to prevent or interrupt. I attempted a tone of conciliation towards Thorncliff on several occasions; but he rejected my advances with a manner about as gracious as that of a growling mastiff, when the animal shuns and resents a stranger's attempts to caress him. I therefore abandoned him to his ill-humour, and gave myself no further trouble about the matter.

Such was the footing upon which I stood with the family at Osbaldistone Hall; but I ought to mention another of its inmates with whom I occasionally held some discourse. This was Andrew Fairservice, the gardener, who (since he had discovered that I was a Protestant) rarely suffered me to pass him without proffering his Scotch mull for a social pinch. There were several advantages attending this courtesy. In the first place, it was made at no expense, for I never took snuff; and, secondly, it afforded an excellent apology to Andrew (who was not particularly fond of hard labour) for laying aside his spade for several minutes. But, above all, these brief interviews gave Andrew an opportunity of venting the news he had collected, or the satirical remarks which his shrewd northern humour suggested.

' I am saying, sir,' he said to me one evening, with a face obviously charged with intelligence, ' I hae been doun at the Trinlay-knowe.'

' Well, Andrew, and I suppose you heard some news at the alehouse ? '

' Na, sir; I never gang to the yillhouse — that is, unless ony neighbour was to gie me a pint, or the like o' that; but to gang there on ane's ain coat tail, is a waste o' precious time and hard-won siller. —But I was doun at the Trinlay-knowe, as I was

saying, about a wee bit business o' my ain wi' Mattie Simpson, that wants a forpit or twa o' peers, that will never be missed in the Ha'-house—and when we were at the thrangest o' our bargain, wha suld come in but Pate Macready the travelling merchant?'

'Pedlar, I suppose you mean?'

'E'en as your honour likes to ca' him; but it's a creditable calling and a gainfu', and has been lang in use wi' our folk. Pate's a far-awa cousin o' mine, and we were blythe to meet wi' ane anither.'

'And you went and had a jug of ale together, I suppose, Andrew?—For Heaven's sake, cut short your story.'

'Bide a wee — bide a wee; you southrons are aye in sic a hurry, and this is something concerns yoursell, an ye wad tak patience to hear't—Yill? —deil a drap o' yill did Pate offer me; but Mattie gae us baith a drap skimmed milk, and ane o' her thick ait jannocks, that was as wat and raw as a divot. — O, for the bonnie girdle cakes o' the North!—and sae we sat doun and took out our clavers.'

'I wish you would take them out just now. Pray, tell me the news, if you have got any worth telling, for I can't stop here all night.'

'Than, if ye maun hae't, the folk in Lunnun are a' clean wud about this bit job in the north here.'

'Clean wood! what's that?'

'Ou, just real daft—neither to haud nor to bind —a' hirdy-girdy — clean through ither — the deil's over Jock Wabster.'

'But what does all this mean? or what business have I with the devil or Jack Webster?'

'Umph!' said Andrew, looking extremely knowing, 'it's just because—just that the dirdum's a' about yon man's pokmanty.'

'Whose portmanteau? or what do you mean?'

'Ou, just the man Morris's, that he said he lost yonder; but if it's no your honour's affair, as little is it mine; and I maunna lose this gracious evening.'

And, as if suddenly seized with a violent fit of industry, Andrew began to labour most diligently.

My attention, as the crafty knave had foreseen, was now arrested, and unwilling, at the same time, to acknowledge any particular interest in that affair, by asking direct questions, I stood waiting till the spirit of voluntary communication should again prompt him to resume his story. Andrew dug on manfully, and spoke at intervals, but nothing to the purpose of Mr. Macready's news; and I stood and listened, cursing him in my heart, and desirous, at the same time, to see how long his humour of contradiction would prevail over his desire of speaking upon the subject, which was obviously uppermost in his mind.

'Am trenching up the sparry-grass, and am gaun to saw sum Misegun beans; they winna want them to their swine's flesh, I 'se warrant — muckle gude may it do them. And sicklike dung as the grieve has gien me; it should be wheat-strae, or aiten at the warst o't, and it's pease-dirt, as fizzenless as chuckie-stanes. But the huntsman guides a' as he

likes about the stable-yard, and he's selled the best
o' the litter, I'se warrant. But, howsoever, we
maunna lose a turn o' this Saturday at e'en, for
the wather's sair broken, and if there's a fair day
in seven, Sunday's sure to come and lick it up—
Howsomever, I'm no denying that it may settle,
if it be Heaven's will, till Monday morning, and
what's the use o' my breaking my back at this
rate—I think, I'll e'en awa' hame, for yon's the
curfew, as they ca' their jowing-in bell.'

Accordingly, applying both his hands to his spade,
he pitched it upright in the trench which he had
been digging, and, looking at me with the air of
superiority of one who knows himself possessed of
important information, which he may communicate
or refuse at his pleasure, pulled down the sleeves
of his shirt, and walked slowly towards his coat,
which lay carefully folded up upon a neighbouring
garden-seat.

I must pay the penalty of having interrupted the
tiresome rascal, thought I to myself, and even
gratify Mr. Fairservice by taking his communication on his own terms. Then raising my voice, I
addressed him,—' And after all, Andrew, what are
these London news you had from your kinsman,
the travelling merchant ? '

' The pedlar, your honour means ? ' retorted
Andrew—' but ca' him what ye wull, they're a
great convenience in a country-side that's scant o'
borough-towns, like this Northumberland—That's
no the case, now, in Scotland—There's the kingdom o' Fife, frae Culross to the East Nuik, it's

215

just like a great combined city—Sae mony royal
boroughs yoked on end to end, like ropes of
ingans, with their hie-streets, and their booths, nae
doubt, and their kræmes, and houses of stane and
lime and forestairs—Kirkcaldy, the sell o't, is langer
than ony town in England.'

'I dare say it is all very splendid and very fine
—but you were talking of the London news a little
while ago, Andrew.'

'Ay,' replied Andrew; 'but I dinna think your
honour cared to hear about them—howsoever,' (he
continued, grinning a ghastly smile,) 'Pate Macready does say, that they are sair mistrysted yonder
in their Parliament-House about this rubbery o'
Mr. Morris, or whatever they ca' the chiel.'

'In the House of Parliament, Andrew! How
came they to mention it there?'

'Ou, that's just what I said to Pate; if it like
your honour, I'll tell you the very words; it's no
worth making a lie for the matter—"Pate," said
I, "what ado had the lords and lairds and gentles
at Lunnun wi' the carle and his walise?—When we
had a Scotch Parliament, Pate," says I, (and deil
rax their thrapples that reft us o't!) "they sate
dousely down and made laws for a haill country
and kinrick, and never fashed their beards about
things that were competent to the judge ordinar o'
the bounds; but I think," said I, "that if ae kail-
wife pou'd aff her neighbour's mutch, they wad hae
the twasome o' them into the Parliament-House o'
Lunnun. It's just," said I, "amaist as silly as our
auld daft laird here and his gomerils o' sons, wi' his

216

huntsmen and his hounds, and his hunting cattle and horns, riding haill days after a bit beast that winna weigh sax punds when they hae catched it."'

'You argued most admirably, Andrew,' said I, willing to encourage him to get into the marrow of his intelligence; 'and what said Pate?'

'Ou,' he said, 'what better could be expected of a wheen pock-pudding English folk?—But as to the robbery, it's like that when they're a' at the thrang o' their Whig and Tory wark, and ca'ing ane anither, like unhanged blackguards — up gets ae lang-tongued chield, and he says, that a' the north of England were rank Jacobites, (and, quietly, he wasna far wrang maybe,) and that they had levied amaist open war, and a king's messenger had been stoppit and rubbit on the highway, and that the best bluid o' Northumberland had been at the doing o't—and mickle gowd ta'en aff him, and mony valuable papers; and that there was nae redress to be gotten by remeed of law, for the first justice o' the peace that the rubbit man gaed to, he had fund the twa loons that did the deed birling and drinking wi' him, wha but they; and the justice took the word o' the tane for the compearance o' the tither; and that they e'en gae him leg-bail, and the honest man that had lost his siller was fain to leave the country for fear that waur had come of it.'

'Can this be really true?' said I.

'Pate swears it's as true as that his ellwand is a yard lang—(and so it is, just bating an inch, that it may meet the English measure)—And when the

chield had said his warst, there was a terrible cry
for names, and out comes he wi' this man Morris's
name, and your uncle's, and Squire Inglewood's,
and other folk's beside,' (looking sly at me)—'And
then another dragon o' a chield got up on the other
side, and said, wad they accuse the best gentlemen
in the land on the oath of a broken coward,—for
it 's like that Morris had been drummed out o' the
army for rinning awa in Flanders; and he said, it
was like the story had been made up between the
minister and him or ever he had left Lunnun; and
that, if there was to be a search-warrant granted,
he thought the siller wad be fund some gate near
to St. James's Palace.   Aweel, they trailed up
Morris to their bar, as they ca't, to see what he
could say to the job; but the folk that were again
him, gae him sic an awfu' throughgaun about his
rinnin' awa, and about a' the ill he had ever dune or
said for a' the forepart o' his life, that Patie says, he
looked mair like ane dead than living; and they
cou'dna get a word o' sense out o' him, for down-
right fright at their gowling and routing.—He maun
be a saft sap, wi' a head nae better than a fozy
frosted turnip—it wad hae ta'en a hantle o' them
to scaur Andrew Fairservice out o' his tale.'

'And how did it all end, Andrew? did your
friend happen to learn?'

'Ou, ay; for as his walk's in this country, Pate
put aff his journey for the space of a week or thereby,
because it wad be acceptable to his customers to
bring down the news.   It just a' gaed aff like moon-
shine in water.   The fallow that began it drew in

his horns and said, that though he believed the man had been rubbit, yet he acknowledged he might hae been mista'en about the particulars. And then the other chield got up, and said, he cared na whether Morris was rubbit or no, provided it wasna to become a stain on ony gentleman's honour and reputation, especially in the north of England; for, said he before them, I come frae the north mysell, and I carena a boddle wha kens it. And this is what they ca' explaining—the tane gies up a bit, and the tither gies up a bit, and a' friends again. Aweel, after the Commons' Parliament had tuggit, and rived, and ruggit at Morris and his rubbery till they were tired o't, the Lords' Parliament they behoved to hae their spell o't. In puir auld Scotland's Parliament they a' sate thegither, cheek by choul, and than they didna need to hae the same blethers twice ower again. But till't their lordships went wi' as muckle teeth and gude-will, as if the matter had been a' speck and span new. Forbye, there was something said about ane Campbell, that suld hae been concerned in the rubbery, mair or less, and that he suld hae had a warrant frae the Duke of Argyle, as a testimonial o' his character. And this put MacCallum More's beard in a bleize, as gude reason there was; and he gat up wi' an unco bang, and garr'd them a' look about them, and wad ram it even doun their throats, there was never ane o' the Campbells but was as wight, wise, warlike, and worthy trust, as auld Sir John the Græme. Now, if your honour's sure ye arena a drap's bluid a-kin to a Campbell, as I am nane mysell, sae far as I can count my kin, or hae had it counted to me, I 'll gie ye my mind on that matter.'

'You may be assured I have no connexion whatever with any gentleman of the name.'

'Ou, than we may speak it quietly amang oursells. There's baith gude and bad o' the Campbells, like other names. But this MacCallum More has an unco sway and say baith, amang the grit folk at Lunnun even now; for he canna preceesely be said to belang to ony o' the twa sides o' them, sae deil ane o' them likes to quarrel wi' him; sae they e'en voted Morris's tale a fause calumnious libel, as they ca't, and if he hadna gien them leg-bail, he was likely to hae ta'en the air on the pillory for leasing-making.'

So speaking, honest Andrew collected his dibbles, spades, and hoes, and threw them into a wheelbarrow,—leisurely, however, and allowing me full time to put any farther questions which might occur to me before he trundled them off to the tool-house, there to repose during the ensuing day. I thought it best to speak out at once, lest this meddling fellow should suppose there were more weighty reasons for my silence than actually existed.

'I should like to see this countryman of yours, Andrew; and to hear his news from himself directly. You have probably heard that I had some trouble from the impertinent folly of this man Morris,' (Andrew grinned a most significant grin,) 'and I should wish to see your cousin the merchant, to ask him the particulars of what he heard in London, if it could be done without much trouble.'

'Naething mair easy,' Andrew observed; 'he had but to hint to his cousin that I wanted a pair or twa o' hose, and he wad be wi' me as fast as he could lay leg to the grund.'

'O yes, assure him I shall be a customer; and as the night is, as you say, settled and fair, I shall walk in the garden until he comes; the moon will soon rise over the fells. You may bring him to the little back-gate; and I shall have pleasure, in the meanwhile, in looking on the bushes and evergreens by the bright frosty moon-light.'

'Vara right—vara right—that's what I hae aften said; a kail-blaid, or a colliflour, glances sae glegly by moonlight, it's like a leddy in her diamonds.'

So saying, off went Andrew Fairservice with great glee. He had to walk about two miles, a labour he undertook with the greatest pleasure, in order to secure to his kinsman the sale of some articles of his trade, though it is probable he would not have given him sixpence to treat him to a quart of ale. The good-will of an Englishman would have displayed itself in a manner exactly the reverse of Andrew's, thought I, as I paced along the smooth-cut velvet walks, which, embowered with high hedges of yew and of holly, intersected the ancient garden of Osbaldistone Hall.

As I turned to retrace my steps, it was natural that I should lift up my eyes to the windows of the old library; which, small in size, but several in number, stretched along the second story of that side of the house which now faced me. Light glanced from their casements. I was not surprised at this, for I knew Miss Vernon often sate there of an evening, though from motives of delicacy I put a strong restraint upon myself, and never sought to join her at a time when I knew, all the rest of the family being engaged for the evening, our interviews must necessarily have been strictly *tête-à-tête*. In the mornings we usually read together in the same room; but then it often happened that one or other of our cousins entered to seek some parchment duo-decimo that could be converted into a fishing-book, despite its gildings and illumination, or to tell us of some 'sport toward,' or from mere want of know-ing where else to dispose of themselves. In short, in the mornings the library was a sort of public room, where man and woman might meet as on neutral ground. In the evening it was very dif-ferent; and, bred in a country where much attention is paid, or was at least then paid, to *bienséance*, I was desirous to think for Miss Vernon concerning those points of propriety where her experience did not afford her the means of thinking for herself. I made her therefore comprehend, as delicately as I could, that when we had evening lessons, the presence of a third party was proper.

Miss Vernon first laughed, then blushed, and was disposed to be displeased; and then, suddenly checking herself, said, ' I believe you are very right; and when I feel inclined to be a very busy scholar, I will bribe old Martha with a cup of tea to sit by me and be my screen.'

Martha, the old housekeeper, partook of the taste of the family at the Hall. A toast and tankard would have pleased her better than all the tea in China. However, as the use of this beverage was then confined to the higher ranks, Martha felt some vanity in being asked to partake of it; and by dint of a great deal of sugar, many words scarce less sweet, and abundance of toast and butter, she was sometimes prevailed upon to give us her countenance. On other occasions, the servants almost unanimously shunned the library after nightfall, because it was their foolish pleasure to believe that it lay on the haunted side of the house. The more timorous had seen sights and heard sounds there when all the rest of the house was quiet; and even the young squires were far from having any wish to enter these formidable precincts after nightfall without necessity.

That the library had at one time been a favourite resource of Rashleigh—that a private door out of one side of it communicated with the sequestered and remote apartment which he chose for himself, rather increased than disarmed the terrors which the household had for the dreaded library of Osbaldistone Hall. His extensive information as to what passed in the world,— his profound knowledge of science of every kind,—a few physical experiments which he occasionally showed off, were, in a house of so much ignorance and bigotry, esteemed good reasons for supposing him endowed with powers over the spiritual world. He understood Greek, Latin, and Hebrew; and, therefore, according to the apprehension, and in the phrase, of his brother Wilfred, needed not to care ' for ghaist or barghaist, devil or dobbie.' Yea, the servants persisted that they had heard him hold conversations in the library, when every varsal soul in the family were gone to bed; and that he spent the night in watching for bogles, and the morning in sleeping in his bed, when he should have been heading the hounds like a true Osbaldistone.

All these absurd rumours I had heard in broken hints and imperfect sentences, from which I was left to draw the inference; and, as easily may be supposed, I laughed them to scorn. But the extreme solitude to which this chamber of evil fame was committed every night after curfew time, was an additional reason why I should not intrude on Miss Vernon when she chose to sit there in the evening.

To resume what I was saying, I was not surprised to see a glimmering of light from the library windows; but I was a little struck when I distinctly perceived the shadows of two persons pass along and intercept the light from the first of the windows, throwing the casement for a moment into shade. It must be old Martha, thought I, whom Diana has engaged to be her companion for the evening, or I must have been mistaken, and taken Diana's shadow for a second person. No, by Heaven! it appears on the second window,— two figures distinctly traced; and now it is lost again—it is seen on the third—on the fourth—the darkened forms of two persons distinctly seen in each window as they pass along the room, betwixt the windows and the lights. Whom can Diana have got for a companion?

—The passage of the shadows between the lights and the casements was twice repeated, as if to satisfy me that my observation served me truly; after which the lights were extinguished, and the shades, of course, were seen no more.

Trifling as this circumstance was, it occupied my mind for a considerable time. I did not allow myself to suppose, that my friendship for Miss Vernon had any directly selfish view; yet it is incredible the displeasure I felt at the idea of her admitting any one to private interviews, at a time, and in a place, where, for her own sake, I had been at some trouble to show her, that it was improper for me to meet with her.

'Silly, romping, incorrigible girl!' said I to myself, 'on whom all good advice and delicacy are thrown away! I have been cheated by the simplicity of her manner, which I suppose she can assume just as she could a straw bonnet, were it the fashion, for the mere sake of celebrity. I suppose, notwithstanding the excellence of her understanding, the society of half a dozen of clowns to play at whisk and swabbers would give her more pleasure than if Ariosto himself were to awake from the dead.'

This reflection came the more powerfully across my mind, because, having mustered up courage to show to Diana my version of the first books of Ariosto, I had requested her to invite Martha to a tea-party in the library that evening, to which arrangement Miss Vernon had refused her consent, alleging some apology which I thought frivolous at the time. I had not long speculated on this disagreeable subject, when the back garden-door opened, and the figures of Andrew and his countryman, bending under his pack, crossed the moonlit alley, and called my attention elsewhere.

I found Mr. Macready, as I expected, a tough, sagacious, long-headed Scotchman, and a collector of news both from choice and profession. He was able to give me a distinct account of what had passed in the House of Commons and House of Lords on the affair of Morris, which, it appears, had been made by both parties a touchstone to ascertain the temper of the Parliament. It appeared also, that, as I had learned from Andrew by second hand, the ministry had proved too weak to support a story, involving the character of men of rank and importance, and resting upon the credit of a person of such indifferent fame as Morris, who was, moreover, confused and contradictory in his mode of telling the story. Macready was even able to supply me with a copy of a printed journal, or News-Letter, seldom extending beyond the capital, in which the substance of the debate was mentioned; and with a copy of the Duke of Argyle's speech, printed upon a broadside, of which he had purchased several from the hawkers, because, he said, it would be a saleable article on the north of the Tweed. The first was a meagre statement, full of blanks and asterisks, and which added little or nothing to the information I had from the Scotchman; and the Duke's speech, though spirited and eloquent, contained chiefly a panegyric on his country, his family, and his clan, with a few compliments, equally sincere, perhaps, though less glowing, which he took so favourable an opportunity of paying to himself. I could not learn whether my own reputation had been directly implicated, although I perceived that the honour of my uncle's family had been impeached, and that this person Campbell, stated by Morris to have been the most active robber of the two by whom he was assailed, was said by him to have appeared in the behalf of a Mr. Osbaldistone, and by the connivance of the Justice, procured his liberation. In this particular, Morris's story jumped with my own suspicions, which had attached to Campbell from the moment I saw him appear at Justice Inglewood's. Vexed upon the whole, as well as perplexed with this extraordinary story, I dismissed the two Scotchmen, after making some purchases from Macready, and a small compliment to Fairservice, and retired to my own apartment to consider what I ought to do in defence of my character thus publicly attacked.

CHAPTER XV

Whence, and what art thou ?
MILTON.

AFTER exhausting a sleepless night in meditating on the intelligence I had received, I was at first inclined to think that I ought, as speedily as possible, to return to London, and by my open appearance repel the calumny which had been spread against me. But I hesitated to take this course on recollection of my father's disposition, singularly absolute in his decisions as to all that concerned his family. He was most able, certainly, from experience, to direct what I ought to do, and from his acquaintance with the most distinguished Whigs then in power, had influence enough to obtain a hearing for my cause. So, upon the whole, I judged it most safe to state my whole story in the shape of a narrative, addressed to my father; and as the ordinary opportunities of intercourse between the Hall and the post-town recurred rarely, I determined to ride to the town, which was about ten miles' distance, and deposit my letter in the post-office, with my own hands.

Indeed I began to think it strange, that though several weeks had elapsed since my departure from home, I had received no letter, either from my father or Owen, although Rashleigh had written to

Sir Hildebrand of his safe arrival in London, and of the kind reception he had met with from his uncle. Admitting that I might have been to blame, I did not deserve, in my own opinion at least, to be so totally forgotten by my father; and I thought my present excursion might have the effect of bringing a letter from him to hand more early than it would otherwise have reached me. But before concluding my letter concerning the affair of Morris, I failed not to express my earnest hope and wish that my father would honour me with a few lines, were it but to express his advice and commands in an affair of some difficulty, and where my knowledge of life could not be supposed adequate to my own guidance. I found it impossible to prevail on myself to urge my actual return to London as a place of residence, and I disguised my unwillingness to do so under apparent submission to my father's will, which, as I imposed it on myself as a sufficient reason for not urging my final departure from Osbaldistone Hall, would, I doubted not, be received as such by my parent. But I begged permission to come to London, for a short time at least, to meet and refute the infamous calumnies which had been circulated concerning me in so public a manner. Having made up my packet, in which my earnest desire to vindicate my character was strangely blended with reluctance to quit my present place of residence, I rode over to the post - town, and deposited my letter in the office. By doing so, I obtained possession, somewhat earlier than I should otherwise have done, of the following letter from my friend Mr. Owen.

'DEAR MR. FRANCIS,

'Yours received per favour of Mr. R. Osbaldistone, and note the contents. Shall do Mr. R. O. such civilities as are in my power, and have taken him to see the Bank and Custom-house. He seems a sober, steady young gentleman, and takes to business; so will be of service to the firm. Could have wished another person had turned his mind that way; but God's will be done. As cash may be scarce in those parts, have to trust you will excuse my enclosing a goldsmith's bill at six days' sight, on Messrs. Hooper and Girder of Newcastle, for £100, which I doubt not will be duly honoured.—I remain, as in duty bound, dear Mr. Frank, your very respectful and obedient servant, JOSEPH OWEN.

'*Postscriptum.*—Hope you will advise the above coming safe to hand. Am sorry we have so few of yours. Your father says he is as usual, but looks poorly.'

From this epistle, written in old Owen's formal style, I was rather surprised to observe that he made no acknowledgment of that private letter which I had written to him, with a view to possess him of Rashleigh's real character, although, from the course of post, it seemed certain that he ought to have received it. Yet I had sent it by the usual conveyance from the Hall, and had no reason to suspect that it could miscarry upon the road. As it comprised matters of great importance, both to my father and to myself, I sat down in the post-office, and again wrote to Owen, recapitulating the heads of my former letter, and requesting to know, in course of post, if it had reached him in safety. I also acknowledged the receipt of the bill, and promised to make use of the contents, if I should have any occasion for money. I thought, indeed, it was odd that my father should leave the care of supplying my necessities to his clerk; but I concluded it was a matter arranged between them. At any rate, Owen was a bachelor, rich in his way, and passionately attached to me, so that I had no hesitation in being obliged to him for a small sum, which I resolved to consider as a loan, to be returned with my earliest ability, in case it was not previously repaid by my father; and I expressed myself to this purpose to Mr. Owen. A shopkeeper in a little town, to whom the post-master directed me, readily gave me in gold the amount of my bill on Messrs. Hooper and Girder, so that I returned to Osbaldistone Hall a good deal richer than I had set forth. This recruit to my finances was not a matter of indifference to me, as I was necessarily involved in some expenses at Osbaldistone Hall; and I had seen, with some uneasy impatience, that the sum which my travelling expenses had left unexhausted at my arrival there, was imperceptibly diminishing. This source of anxiety was for the present removed. On my arrival at the Hall, I found that Sir Hildebrand

and all his offspring had gone down to the little hamlet, called Trinlay-Knowes, 'to see,' as Andrew Fairservice expressed it, 'a wheen midden cocks pike ilk ither's harns out.'

'It is indeed a brutal amusement, Andrew; I suppose you have none such in Scotland?'

'Na, na,' answered Andrew boldly; then shaded away his negative with, 'unless it be on Fastern's-e'en, or the like o' that—But, indeed, it's no muckle matter what the folk do to the midden pootry, for they haud siccan a skarting and scraping in the yard, that there's nae getting a bean or pea keepit for them.—But I am wondering what it is that leaves that turret-door open; now that Mr. Rashleigh's away, it canna be him, I trow.'

The turret-door, to which he alluded, opened to the garden at the bottom of a winding-stair, lead-ing down from Mr. Rashleigh's apartment. This, as I have already mentioned, was situated in a sequestered part of the house, communicating with the library by a private entrance, and by another intricate and dark vaulted passage with the rest of the house. A long narrow turf-walk led, between two high holly hedges, from the turret-door to a little postern in the wall of the garden. By means of these communications, Rashleigh, whose move-ments were very independent of those of the rest of his family, could leave the Hall or return to it at pleasure, without his absence or presence attract-ing any observation. But during his absence the stair and the turret-door were entirely disused, and this made Andrew's observation somewhat remarkable.

'Have you often observed that door open?' was my question.

'No just that often neither; but I hae noticed it ance or twice. I'm thinking it maun hae been the priest, Father Vaughan, as they ca' him. Ye'll no catch ane o' the servants ganging up that stair, puir frightened heathens that they are, for fear of bogles and brownies, and lang-nebbit things frae the neist warld. But Father Vaughan thinks him-sell a privileged person—set him up and lay him down!—I'se be caution the warst stibbler that ever stickit a sermon out ower the Tweed yonder, wad lay a ghaist twice as fast as him, wi' his holy water and his idolatrous trinkets. I dinna believe he speaks gude Latin neither; at least he disna take me up when I tell him the learned names o' the plants.'

Of Father Vaughan, who divided his time and his ghostly care between Osbaldistone Hall, and about half-a-dozen mansions of Catholic gentlemen in the neighbourhood, I have as yet said nothing, for I had seen but little. He was aged about sixty, of a good family, as I was given to understand, in the north; of a striking and imposing presence, grave in his exterior, and much respected among the Catholics of Northumberland, as a worthy and upright man. Yet Father Vaughan did not alto-gether lack those peculiarities which distinguish his order. There hung about him an air of mystery, which, in Protestant eyes, savoured of priestcraft. The natives (such they might be well termed) of Osbaldistone Hall looked up to him with much more fear, or at least more awe, than affection. His condemnation of their revels was evident, from their being discontinued in some measure when the priest was a resident at the Hall. Even Sir Hildebrand himself put some restraint upon his conduct at such times, which, perhaps, rendered Father Vaughan's presence rather irksome than otherwise. He had the well-bred, insinuating, and almost flattering address, peculiar to the clergy of his persuasion, especially in England, where the lay Catholic, hemmed in by penal laws, and by the restrictions of his sect and recommendation of his pastor, often exhibits a reserved, and almost a timid manner, in the society of Protestants; while the priest, privileged by his order to mingle with persons of all creeds, is open, alert, and liberal in his intercourse with them, desirous of popularity, and usually skilful in the mode of obtaining it.

Father Vaughan was a particular acquaintance of Rashleigh's, otherwise, in all probability, he would scarce have been able to maintain his footing at Osbaldistone Hall. This gave me no desire to cultivate his intimacy, nor did he seem to make any advances towards mine; so our occasional intercourse was confined to the exchange of mere civility. I considered it as extremely probable that Mr. Vaughan might occupy Rashleigh's apartment during his occasional residence at the Hall; and his profession rendered it likely that he should occasionally be a tenant of the library. Nothing was more probable than that it might have been his candle which had excited my attention on a preceding evening. This led me involuntarily to recollect that the intercourse between Miss Vernon and the priest was marked with something like the same mystery which characterized her communications with Rashleigh. I had never heard her mention Vaughan's name, or even allude to him, excepting on the occasion of our first meeting, when she mentioned the old priest and Rashleigh as the only conversible beings, besides herself, in Osbaldistone Hall. Yet although silent with respect to Father Vaughan, his arrival at the Hall never failed to impress Miss Vernon with an anxious and fluttering tremor, which lasted until they had exchanged one or two significant glances.

Whatever the mystery might be which overclouded the destinies of this beautiful and interesting female, it was clear that Father Vaughan was implicated in it; unless, indeed, I could suppose that he was the agent employed to procure her settlement in the cloister, in the event of her rejecting a union with either of my cousins,—an office which would sufficiently account for her obvious emotion at his appearance. As to the rest, they did not seem to converse much together, or even to seek each other's society. Their league, if any subsisted between them, was of a tacit and understood nature, operating on their actions without any necessity of speech. I recollected, however, on reflection, that I had once or twice discovered signs pass betwixt them, which I had at the time supposed to bear reference to some hint concerning Miss Vernon's religious observances, knowing how artfully the Catholic clergy maintain, at all times and seasons, their influence over the minds of their followers. But now I was disposed to assign to these communications a deeper and more mysterious import. Did he hold private meetings with Miss Vernon in the library? was a question which occupied my thoughts; and if so, for what purpose? And why should she have admitted an intimate of the deceitful Rashleigh to such close confidence?

These questions and difficulties pressed on my mind with an interest which was greatly increased by the impossibility of resolving them. I had already begun to suspect that my friendship for Diana Vernon was not altogether so disinterested as in wisdom it ought to have been. I had already felt myself becoming jealous of the contemptible lout Thorncliff, and taking more notice, than in prudence or dignity of feeling I ought to have done, of his silly attempts to provoke me. And now I was scrutinizing the conduct of Miss Vernon with the most close and eager observation, which I in vain endeavoured to palm on myself as the offspring of idle curiosity. All these, like Benedick's brushing his hat of a morning, were signs that the sweet youth was in love; and while my judgment still denied that I had been guilty of forming an attachment so imprudent, she resembled those ignorant guides, who, when they have led the traveller and themselves into irretrievable error, persist in obstinately affirming it to be impossible that they can have missed the way.

CHAPTER XVI

It happened one day about noon, going to my boat, I was exceedingly surprised with the print of a man's naked foot on the shore, which was very plain to be seen on the sand.'

ROBINSON CRUSOE.

WITH the blended feelings of interest and jealousy which were engendered by Miss Vernon's singular situation, my observations of her looks and actions became acutely sharpened, and that to a degree, which, notwithstanding my efforts to conceal it, could not escape her penetration. The sense that she was observed, or, more properly speaking, that she was watched by my looks, seemed to give Diana a mixture of embarrassment, pain, and pettishness. At times it seemed that she sought an opportunity of resenting a conduct which she could not but feel as offensive, considering the frankness with which she had mentioned the difficulties that surrounded her. At other times she seemed prepared to expostulate upon the subject. But either her courage failed, or some other sentiment impeded her seeking an eclaircissement. Her displeasure evaporated in repartee, and her expostulations died on her lips. We stood in a singular relation to each other, spending, and by mutual choice, much of our time in close society with each other, yet disguising our mutual sentiments, and jealous of, or offended by, each other's actions. There was betwixt us intimacy without confidence; on one side love without hope or purpose, and curiosity without any rational or justifiable motive; and on the other embarrassment and doubt, occasionally mingled with displeasure. Yet I believe that this agitation of the passions, such is the nature of the human bosom, as it continued by a thousand irritating and interesting, though petty circumstances, to render Miss Vernon and me the constant objects of each other's thoughts, tended, upon the whole, to increase the attachment with which we were naturally disposed to regard each other. But although my vanity early discovered that my presence at Osbaldistone Hall had given Diana some additional reason for disliking the cloister, I could by no means confide in an affection which seemed completely subordinate to the mysteries of her singular situation. Miss Vernon was of a character far too formed and determined, to permit her love for me to overpower either her sense of duty or of prudence, and she gave me a proof of this in a conversation which we had together about this period.

We were sitting together in the library. Miss Vernon, in turning over a copy of the Orlando Furioso, which belonged to me, shook a piece of written paper from between the leaves. I hastened to lift it, but she prevented me.

'It is verse,' she said, on glancing at the paper; and then unfolding it, but as if to wait my answer before proceeding—'May I take the liberty?—

nay, nay, if you blush and stammer, I must do violence to your modesty, and suppose that permission is granted.'

'It is not worthy your perusal—a scrap of a translation—My dear Miss Vernon, it would be too severe a trial, that you, who understand the original so well, should sit in judgment.'

'Mine honest friend,' replied Diana, 'do not, if you will be guided by my advice, bait your hook with too much humility; for, ten to one, it will not catch a single compliment. You know I belong to the unpopular family of Tell-truths, and would not flatter Apollo for his lyre.'

She proceeded to read the first stanza, which was nearly to the following purpose:—

'Ladies, and knights, and arms, and love's fair flame,
    Deeds of emprize and courtesy, I sing;
What time the Moors from sultry Africk came,
    Led on by Agramant, their youthful king—
He whom revenge and hasty ire did bring
    O'er the broad wave, in France to waste and war;
Such ills from old Trojano's death did spring,
    Which to avenge he came from realms afar,
And menaced Christian Charles, the Roman Emperor.

Of dauntless Roland, too, my strain shall sound,
    In import never known in prose or rhyme,
How He, the chief, of judgment deem'd profound,
    For luckless love was crazed upon a time—'

'There is a great deal of it,' said she, glancing along the paper, and interrupting the sweetest sounds which mortal ears can drink in,—those of a youthful poet's verses, namely, read by the lips which are dearest to them.

'Much more than ought to engage your attention, Miss Vernon,' I replied, something mortified; and I took the verses from her unreluctant hand —'and yet,' I continued, 'shut up as I am in this retired situation, I have felt sometimes I could not amuse myself better than by carrying on, merely for my own amusement you will of course understand, the version of this fascinating author, which I began some months since, when I was on the banks of the Garonne.'

'The question would only be,' said Diana, gravely, 'whether you could not spend your time to better purpose?'

'You mean in original composition,' said I, greatly flattered; 'but, to say truth, my genius rather lies in finding words and rhymes than ideas; and, therefore, I am happy to use those which Ariosto has prepared to my hand. However, Miss Vernon, with the encouragement you give——'

'Pardon me, Frank; it is encouragement not of my giving, but of your taking. I meant neither original composition nor translation, since I think you might employ your time to far better purpose than in either. You are mortified,' she continued, 'and I am sorry to be the cause.'

'Not mortified,—certainly not mortified,' said I, (with the best grace I could muster, and it was but indifferently assumed;) 'I am too much obliged by the interest you take in me.'

'Nay, but,' resumed the relentless Diana, 'there

is both mortification and a little grain of anger in that constrained tone of voice; do not be angry if I probe your feelings to the bottom—perhaps what I am about to say will affect them still more.'

I felt the childishness of my own conduct, and the superior manliness of Miss Vernon's, and assured her, that she need not fear my wincing under criticism which I knew to be kindly meant.

'That was honestly meant and said,' she replied; 'I knew full well that the fiend of poetical irritability flew away with the little preluding cough which ushered in the declaration. And now I must be serious.—Have you heard from your father lately?'

'Not a word,' I replied; 'he has not honoured me with a single line during the several months of my residence here.'

'That is strange;—you are a singular race, you bold Osbaldistones. Then you are not aware that he has gone to Holland, to arrange some pressing affairs which required his own immediate presence?'

'I never heard a word of it until this moment.'

'And farther, it must be news to you, and I presume scarcely the most agreeable, that he has left Rashleigh in the almost uncontrolled management of his affairs until his return?'

I started, and could not suppress my surprise and apprehension.

'You have reason for alarm,' said Miss Vernon, very gravely; 'and were I you, I would endeavour to meet and obviate the dangers which arise from so undesirable an arrangement.'

'And how is it possible for me to do so?'

'Every thing is possible for him who possesses courage and activity,' she said, with a look resembling one of those heroines of the age of chivalry, whose encouragement was wont to give champions double valour at the hour of need; 'and to the timid and hesitating every thing is impossible, because it seems so.'

'And what would you advise, Miss Vernon?' I replied, wishing, yet dreading, to hear her answer.

She paused a moment, then answered firmly,— 'That you instantly leave Osbaldistone Hall, and return to London. You have perhaps already,' she continued, in a softer tone, 'been here too long; that fault was not yours. Every succeeding moment you waste here will be a crime. Yes, a crime: for I tell you plainly, that if Rashleigh long manages your father's affairs, you may consider his ruin as consummated.'

'How is this possible?'

'Ask no questions,' she said; 'but, believe me, Rashleigh's views extend far beyond the possession or increase of commercial wealth: He will only make the command of Mr. Osbaldistone's revenues and property the means of putting in motion his own ambitious and extensive schemes. While your father was in Britain this was impossible; during his absence, Rashleigh will possess many opportunities, and he will not neglect to use them.'

'But how can I, in disgrace with my father, and divested of all control over his affairs, prevent this danger by my mere presence in London?'

' That presence alone will do much. Your claim to interfere is a part of your birthright, and is inalienable. You will have the countenance, doubtless, of your father's head - clerk, and confidential friends and partners. Above all, Rashleigh's schemes are of a nature that '—(she stopped abruptly, as if fearful of saying too much) — ' are, in short,' she resumed, ' of the nature of all selfish and unconscientious plans, which are speedily abandoned as soon as those who frame them perceive their arts are discovered and watched. Therefore, in the language of your favourite poet—

" To horse ! to horse ! urge doubts to those that fear." '

A feeling, irresistible in its impulse, induced me to reply, — ' Ah ! Diana, can *you* give me advice to leave Osbaldistone Hall ?—then indeed I have already been a resident here too long ! '

Miss Vernon coloured, but proceeded with great firmness : ' Indeed, I do give you this advice—not only to quit Osbaldistone Hall, but never to return to it more. You have only one friend to regret here,' she continued, forcing a smile, ' and she has been long accustomed to sacrifice her friendships and her comforts to the welfare of others. In the world you will meet a hundred whose friendship will be as disinterested—more useful—less encumbered by untoward circumstances—less influenced by evil tongues and evil times.'

' Never ! ' I exclaimed, 'never ! the world can afford me nothing to repay what I must leave behind me.' Here I took her hand, and pressed it to my lips.

'This is folly!' she exclaimed — 'This is madness!' and she struggled to withdraw her hand from my grasp, but not so stubbornly as actually to succeed, until I had held it for nearly a minute. 'Hear me, sir!' she said, 'and curb this unmanly burst of passion. I am, by a solemn contract, the bride of Heaven, unless I could prefer being wedded to villainy in the person of Rashleigh Osbaldistone, or brutality in that of his brother. I am, therefore, the bride of Heaven, betrothed to the convent from the cradle. To me, therefore, these raptures are misapplied—they only serve to prove a farther necessity for your departure, and that without delay.' At these words she broke suddenly off, and said, but in a suppressed tone of voice, 'Leave me instantly—we will meet here again, but it must be for the last time.'

My eyes followed the direction of hers as she spoke, and I thought I saw the tapestry shake, which covered the door of the secret passage from Rashleigh's room to the library. I conceived we were observed, and turned an inquiring glance on Miss Vernon.

'It is nothing,' said she, faintly; 'a rat behind the arras.'

'Dead for a ducat,' would have been my reply, had I dared to give way to the feelings which rose indignant at the idea of being subjected to an eavesdropper on such an occasion. Prudence, and the necessity of suppressing my passion, and obeying Diana's reiterated command of 'Leave me! leave me!' came in time to prevent any rash action. I left the apartment in a wild whirl and giddiness of mind, which I in vain attempted to compose when I returned to my own.

A chaos of thoughts intruded themselves on me at once, passing hastily through my brain, intercepting and overshadowing each other, and resembling those fogs which in mountainous countries are wont to descend in obscure volumes, and disfigure or obliterate the usual marks by which the traveller steers his course through the wilds. The dark and undefined idea of danger arising to my father from the machinations of such a man as Rashleigh Osbaldistone,—the half-declaration of love which I had offered to Miss Vernon's acceptance, — the acknowledged difficulties of her situation, bound by a previous contract to sacrifice herself to a cloister, or to an ill-assorted marriage, — all pressed themselves at once upon my recollection, while my judgment was unable deliberately to consider any of them in their just light and bearings. But chiefly, and above all the rest, I was perplexed by the manner in which Miss Vernon had received my tender of affection, and by her manner, which, fluctuating betwixt sympathy and firmness, seemed to intimate that I possessed an interest in her bosom, but not of force sufficient to counterbalance the obstacles to her avowing a mutual affection. The glance of fear, rather than surprise, with which she had watched the motion of the tapestry over the concealed door, implied an apprehension of danger which I could not but suppose well-grounded; for Diana Vernon was little subject to the nervous emotions of her sex, and totally unapt to fear without actual and rational cause. Of what nature could those mysteries be with which she was surrounded as with an enchanter's spell, and which seemed continually to exert an active influence over her thoughts and actions, though their agents were never visible? On this subject of doubt my mind finally rested, as if glad to shake itself free from investigating the propriety or prudence of my own conduct, by transferring the inquiry to what concerned Miss Vernon. I will be resolved, I concluded, ere I leave Osbaldistone Hall, concerning the light in which I must in future regard this fascinating being, over whose life frankness and mystery seem to have divided their reign, the former inspiring her words and sentiments, the latter spreading in misty influence over all her actions.

Joined to the obvious interests which arose from curiosity and anxious passion, there mingled in my feelings a strong, though unavowed and undefined, infusion of jealousy. This sentiment, which springs up with love as naturally as the tares with the wheat, was excited by the degree of influence which Diana appeared to concede to those unseen beings by whom her actions were limited. The more I reflected upon her character, the more I was internally though unwillingly convinced, that she was formed to set at defiance all control, excepting that which arose from affection; and I felt a strong, bitter, and gnawing suspicion, that such was the foundation of that influence by which she was overawed.

These tormenting doubts strengthened my desire to penetrate into the secret of Miss Vernon's conduct, and in the prosecution of this sage adventure I formed a resolution, of which, if you are not weary of these details, you will find the result in the next Chapter.

CHAPTER XVII

I hear a voice you cannot hear,
   Which says, I must not stay;
I see a hand you cannot see,
   Which beckons me away.

TICKELL.

I HAVE already told you, Tresham, if you deign
to bear it in remembrance, that my evening visits
to the library had seldom been made except by
appointment, and under the sanction of old Dame
Martha's presence. This, however, was entirely a
tacit conventional arrangement of my own institut-
ing. Of late, as the embarrassments of our relative
situation had increased, Miss Vernon and I had
never met in the evening at all. She had therefore
no reason to suppose that I was likely to seek a
renewal of these interviews, and especially without
some previous notice or appointment betwixt us,
that Martha might, as usual, be placed upon duty;
but, on the other hand, this cautionary provision
was a matter of understanding, not of express
enactment. The library was open to me, as to the
other members of the family, at all hours of the day
and night, and I could not be accused of intrusion,
however suddenly and unexpectedly I might make
my appearance in it. My belief was strong, that in
this apartment Miss Vernon occasionally received

Vaughan, or some other person, by whose opinion she was accustomed to regulate her conduct, and that at the times when she could do so with least chance of interruption. The lights which gleamed in the library at unusual hours, — the passing shadows which I had myself remarked,—the foot-steps which might be traced in the morning dew from the turret-door to the postern-gate in the garden, — sounds and sights which some of the servants, and Andrew Fairservice in particular, had observed and accounted for in their own way,—all tended to show that the place was visited by some one different from the ordinary inmates of the hall. Connected as this visitant must probably be with the fates of Diana Vernon, I did not hesitate to form a plan of discovering who or what he was,— how far his influence was likely to produce good or evil consequences to her on whom he acted,—above all, though I endeavoured to persuade myself that this was a mere subordinate consideration, I desired to know by what means this person had acquired or maintained his influence over Diana, and whether he ruled over her by fear or by affection. The proof that this jealous curiosity was uppermost in my mind, arose from my imagination always ascribing Miss Vernon's conduct to the influence of some one individual agent, although, for aught I knew about the matter, her advisers might be as numerous as Legion. I remarked this over and over to myself, but I found that my mind still settled back in my original conviction, that one single individual, of the masculine sex, and in all probability young and handsome, was at the bottom of Miss Vernon's conduct; and it was with a burning desire of discovering, or rather of detecting, such a rival, that I stationed myself in the garden to watch the moment when the lights should appear in the library windows.

So eager, however, was my impatience, that I commenced my watch for a phenomenon, which could not appear until darkness, a full hour before the daylight disappeared, on a July evening. It was Sabbath, and all the walks were still and solitary. I walked up and down for some time, enjoying the refreshing coolness of a summer evening, and meditating on the probable consequences of my enterprise. The fresh and balmy air of the garden, impregnated with fragrance, produced its usual sedative effects on my over-heated and feverish blood; as these took place, the turmoil of my mind began proportionally to abate, and I was led to question the right I had to interfere with Miss Vernon's secrets, or with those of my uncle's family. What was it to me whom my uncle might choose to conceal in his house, where I was myself a guest only by tolerance? And what title had I to pry into the affairs of Miss Vernon, fraught, as she had avowed them to be, with mystery, into which she desired no scrutiny?

Passion and self-will were ready with their answers to these questions. In detecting this secret, I was in all probability about to do service to Sir Hildebrand, who was probably ignorant of the intrigues carried on in his family; and a still more important service to Miss Vernon, whose frank simplicity of character exposed her to so many risks in maintaining a private correspondence, perhaps with a person of doubtful or dangerous character. If I seemed to intrude myself on her confidence, it was with the generous and disinterested (yes, I even ventured to call it the *disinterested*) intention of guiding, defending, and protecting her against craft,—against malice,—above all, against the secret counsellor whom she had chosen for her confident. Such were the arguments which my will boldly preferred to my conscience, as coin which ought to be current; and which conscience, like a grumbling shopkeeper, was contented to accept, rather than come to an open breach with a customer, though more than doubting that the tender was spurious.

While I paced the green alleys, debating these things *pro* and *con*, I suddenly lighted upon Andrew Fairservice, perched up like a statue by a range of bee-hives, in an attitude of devout contemplation; one eye, however, watching the motions of the little irritable citizens, who were settling in their straw-thatched mansion for the evening, and the other fixed on a book of devotion, which much attrition had deprived of its corners, and worn into an oval shape; a circumstance, which, with the close print and dingy colour of the volume in question, gave it an air of most respectable antiquity.

'I was e'en taking a spell o' worthy Mess John Quackleben's Flower of a Sweet Savour sawn on the Middenstead of this World,' said Andrew, closing his book at my appearance, and putting his horn spectacles, by way of mark, at the place where he had been reading.

'And the bees, I observe, were dividing your attention, Andrew, with the learned author?'

'They are a contumacious generation,' replied the gardener; 'they hae sax days in the week to hive on, and yet it's a common observe that they will aye swarm on the Sabbath-day, and keep folk at hame frae hearing the word—But there's nae preaching at Graneagain Chapel the e'en—that's aye ae mercy.'

'You might have gone to the parish church as I did, Andrew, and heard an excellent discourse.'

'Clauts o' cauld parritch—clauts o' cauld parritch,' replied Andrew, with a most supercilious sneer,—'gude aneuch for dogs, begging your honour's pardon—Ay! I might nae doubt hae heard the curate linking awa at it in his white sark yonder, and the musicians playing on whistles, mair like a penny wedding than a sermon—and to the boot of that, I might hae gane to even-song, and heard Daddie Docharty mumbling his mass—muckle the better I wad hae been o' that!'

'Docharty!' said I, (this was the name of an old priest, an Irishman, I think, who sometimes officiated at Osbaldistone Hall,) 'I thought Father Vaughan had been at the Hall. He was here yesterday.'

'Ay,' replied Andrew; 'but he left it yestreen, to gang to Greystock, or some o' thae west-country

haulds. There's an unco stir amang them a' e'enow.
They are as busy as my bees are—God sain them!
that I suld even the puir things to the like o'
papists. Ye see this is the second swarm, and
whiles they will swarm off in the afternoon. The
first swarm set off sune in the morning. But I am
thinking they are settled in their skeps for the
night. Sae I wuss your honour good-night, and
grace, and muckle o't.'

So saying, Andrew retreated; but often cast a
parting glance upon the *skeps*, as he called the bee-
hives.

I had indirectly gained from him an important
piece of information, that Father Vaughan, namely,
was not supposed to be at the Hall. If, therefore, there appeared light in the windows of the
library this evening, it either could not be his, or he
was observing a very secret and suspicious line of
conduct. I waited with impatience the time of
sunset and of twilight. It had hardly arrived, ere
a gleam from the windows of the library was seen,
dimly distinguishable amidst the still enduring light
of the evening. I marked its first glimpse, however, as speedily as the benighted sailor descries
the first distant twinkle of the light-house which
marks his course. The feelings of doubt and propriety, which had hitherto contended with my
curiosity and jealousy, vanished when an opportunity of gratifying the former was presented to me.
I re-entered the house, and, avoiding the more
frequented apartments with the consciousness of one
who wishes to keep his purpose secret, I reached

the door of the library,—hesitated for a moment as my hand was upon the latch,—heard a suppressed step within,—opened the door,—and found Miss Vernon alone.

Diana appeared surprised,—whether at my sudden entrance, or from some other cause, I could not guess; but there was in her appearance a degree of flutter, which I had never before remarked, and which I knew could only be produced by unusual emotion. Yet she was calm in a moment; and such is the force of conscience, that I, who studied to surprise her, seemed myself the surprised, and was certainly the embarrassed person.

' Has any thing happened ?' said Miss Vernon. ' Has any one arrived at the Hall ?'

' No one that I know of,' I answered, in some confusion; ' I only sought the Orlando.'

' It lies there,' said Miss Vernon, pointing to the table.

In removing one or two books to get at that which I pretended to seek, I was, in truth, meditating to make a handsome retreat from an investigation to which I felt my assurance inadequate, when I perceived a man's glove lying upon the table. My eyes encountered those of Miss Vernon, who blushed deeply.

' It is one of my relics,' she said, with hesitation, replying not to my words, but to my looks; ' it is one of the gloves of my grandfather, the original of the superb Vandyke which you admire.'

As if she thought something more than her bare assertion was necessary to prove her statement true, she opened a drawer of the large oaken table, and, taking out another glove, threw it towards me. When a temper naturally ingenuous stoops to equivocate or to dissemble, the anxious pain with which the unwonted task is laboured, often induces the hearer to doubt the authenticity of the tale. I cast a hasty glance on both gloves, and then replied gravely—'The gloves resemble each other, doubtless, in form and embroidery; but they cannot form a pair, since they both belong to the right hand.'

She bit her lip with anger, and again coloured deeply.

'You do right to expose me,' she replied, with bitterness; 'some friends would have only judged from what I said, that I chose to give no particular explanation of a circumstance which calls for none —at least to a stranger. You have judged better, and have made me feel, not only the meanness of duplicity, but my own inadequacy to sustain the task of a dissembler. I now tell you distinctly, that that glove is not the fellow, as you have acutely discerned, to the one which I just now produced. It belongs to a friend yet dearer to me than the original of Vandyke's picture—a friend by whose counsels I have been, and will be, guided— whom I honour—whom I'—She paused.

I was irritated at her manner, and filled up the blank in my own way. 'Whom she *loves*, Miss Vernon would say.'

'And if I do say so,' she replied, haughtily, 'by whom shall my affection be called to account?'

'Not by me, Miss Vernon, assuredly. I entreat you to hold me acquitted of such presumption. *But*,' I continued, with some emphasis, for I was now piqued in return, 'I hope Miss Vernon will pardon a friend, from whom she seems disposed to withdraw the title, for observing——'

'Observe nothing, sir,' she interrupted, with some vehemence, 'except that I will neither be doubted nor questioned. There does not exist one by whom I will be either interrogated or judged; and if you sought this unusual time of presenting yourself, in order to spy upon my privacy, the friendship or interest with which you pretend to regard me, is a poor excuse for your uncivil curiosity.'

'I relieve you of my presence,' said I, with pride equal to her own; for my temper has ever been a stranger to stooping, even in cases where my feelings were most deeply interested—'I relieve you of my presence. I awake from a pleasant, but a most delusive dream; and — but we understand each other.'

I had reached the door of the apartment, when Miss Vernon, whose movements were sometimes so rapid as to seem almost instinctive, overtook me, and, catching hold of my arm, stopped me with that air of authority which she could so whimsically assume, and which, from the naiveté and simplicity of her manner, had an effect so peculiarly interesting.

'Stop, Mr. Frank,' she said; 'you are not to leave me in that way neither; I am not so amply

provided with friends, that I can afford to throw away even the ungrateful and the selfish. Mark what I say, Mr. Francis Osbaldistone. You shall know nothing of this mysterious glove,' and she held it up as she spoke — ' nothing — no, not a single iota more than you know already; and yet I will not permit it to be a gauntlet of strife and defiance betwixt us. My time here,' she said, sinking into a tone somewhat softer, 'must necessarily be very short; yours must be still shorter: We are soon to part, never to meet again; do not let us quarrel, or make any mysterious miseries the pretext for farther embittering the few hours we shall ever pass together on this side of eternity.'

I do not know, Tresham, by what witchery this fascinating creature obtained such complete management over a temper, which I cannot at all times manage myself. I had determined, on entering the library, to seek a complete explanation with Miss Vernon. I had found that she refused it with indignant defiance, and avowed to my face the preference of a rival; for what other construction could I put on her declared preference of her mysterious confident? And yet, while I was on the point of leaving the apartment, and breaking with her for ever, it cost her but a change of look and tone, from that of real and haughty resentment to that of kind and playful despotism, again shaded off into melancholy and serious feeling, to lead me back to my seat, her willing subject, on her own hard terms.

' What does this avail?' said I, as I sate down.

'What can this avail, Miss Vernon? Why should I witness embarrassments which I cannot relieve, and mysteries which I offend you even by attempting to penetrate? Inexperienced as you are in the world, you must still be aware that a beautiful young woman can have but one male friend. Even in a male friend I will be jealous of a confidence shared with a third party unknown and concealed; but with *you*, Miss Vernon——'

'You are, of course, jealous, in all the tenses and moods of that amiable passion? But, my good friend, you have all this time spoke nothing but the paltry gossip which simpletons repeat from play-books and romances, till they give mere cant a real and powerful influence over their minds. Boys and girls prate themselves into love; and when their love is like to fall asleep, they prate and teaze themselves into jealousy. But you and I, Frank, are rational beings, and neither silly nor idle enough to talk ourselves into any other relation, than that of plain honest disinterested friendship. Any other union is as far out of our reach as if I were man, or you woman.—To speak truth,' she added, after a moment's hesitation, 'even though I am so complaisant to the decorum of my sex as to blush a little at my own plain dealing, we cannot marry, if we would; and we ought not, if we could.'

And certainly, Tresham, she did blush most angelically as she made this cruel declaration. I was about to attack both her positions, entirely forgetting those very suspicions which had been confirmed in the course of the evening, but she proceeded with a cold firmness which approached to severity.

' What I say is sober and indisputable truth, on which I will neither hear question nor explanation. We are therefore friends, Mr. Osbaldistone—are we not ? ' She held out her hand, and taking mine, added,—' And nothing to each other now, or henceforward, except as friends.'

She let go my hand. I sunk it and my head at once, fairly *overcrowed*, as Spenser would have termed it, by the mingled kindness and firmness of her manner. She hastened to change the subject.

' Here is a letter,' she said, ' directed for you, Mr. Osbaldistone, very duly and distinctly ; but which, notwithstanding the caution of the person who wrote and addressed it, might perhaps never have reached your hands, had it not fallen into the possession of a certain Pacolet, or enchanted dwarf of mine, whom, like all distressed damsels of romance, I retain in my secret service.'

I opened the letter and glanced over the contents — the unfolded sheet of paper dropped from my hands, with the involuntary exclamation of ' Gracious Heaven ! my folly and disobedience have ruined my father ! '

Miss Vernon rose with looks of real and affectionate alarm—' You grow pale—you are ill—shall I bring you a glass of water ? Be a man, Mr. Osbaldistone, and a firm one. Is your father—is he no more ? '

'He lives,' said I, 'thank God! but to what distress and difficulty——'

'If that be all, despair not. May I read this letter?' she said, taking it up.

I assented, hardly knowing what I said. She read it with great attention.

'Who is this Mr. Tresham, who signs the letter?'

'My father's partner,' (your own good father, Will,) 'but he is little in the habit of acting personally in the business of the house.'

'He writes here,' said Miss Vernon, 'of various letters sent to you previously.'

'I have received none of them,' I replied.

'And it appears,' she continued, 'that Rashleigh, who has taken the full management of affairs during your father's absence in Holland, has some time since left London for Scotland, with effects and remittances to take up large bills granted by your father to persons in that country, and that he has not since been heard of.'

'It is but too true.'

'And here has been,' she added, looking at the letter, 'a head-clerk, or some such person,—Owenson—Owen—dispatched to Glasgow, to find out Rashleigh, if possible, and you are entreated to repair to the same place, and assist him in his researches.'

'It is even so, and I must depart instantly.'

'Stay but one moment,' said Miss Vernon. 'It seems to me that the worst which can come of this matter will be the loss of a certain sum of money;

and can that bring tears into your eyes ? For shame, Mr. Osbaldistone ! '

' You do me injustice, Miss Vernon,' I answered. ' I grieve not for the loss, but for the effect which I know it will produce on the spirits and health of my father, to whom mercantile credit is as honour ; and who, if declared insolvent, would sink into the grave, oppressed by a sense of grief, remorse, and despair, like that of a soldier convicted of cowardice, or a man of honour who had lost his rank and character in society. All this I might have prevented by a trifling sacrifice of the foolish pride and indolence which recoiled from sharing the labours of his honourable and useful profession. Good Heaven ! how shall I redeem the consequences of my error ! '

' By instantly repairing to Glasgow, as you are conjured to do by the friend who writes this letter.'

' But if Rashleigh,' said I, ' has really formed this base and unconscientious scheme of plundering his benefactor, what prospect is there that I can find means of frustrating a plan so deeply laid ? '

' The prospect,' she replied, ' indeed, may be uncertain ; but, on the other hand, there is no possibility of your doing any service to your father by remaining here.—Remember, had you been on the post destined for you, this disaster could not have happened ; hasten to that which is now pointed out, and it may possibly be retrieved.—Yet stay— do not leave this room until I return.'

She left me in confusion and amazement ; amid

which, however, I could find a lucid interval to admire the firmness, composure, and presence of mind, which Miss Vernon seemed to possess on every crisis, however sudden.

In a few minutes she returned with a sheet of paper in her hand, folded and sealed like a letter, but without address. 'I trust you,' she said, 'with this proof of my friendship, because I have the most-perfect confidence in your honour. If I understand the nature of your distress rightly, the funds in Rashleigh's possession must be recovered by a certain day — the 12th of September, I think, is named—in order that they may be applied to pay the bills in question; and, consequently, that, if adequate funds be provided before that period, your father's credit is safe from the apprehended calamity.'

'Certainly—I so understand Mr. Tresham '— I looked at your father's letter again, and added, 'There cannot be a doubt of it.'

'Well,' said Diana, 'in that case my little Pacolet may be of use to you.—You have heard of a spell contained in a letter. Take this packet; do not open it until other and ordinary means have failed; if you succeed by your own exertions, I trust to your honour for destroying it without opening or suffering it to be opened. But if not, you may break the seal within ten days of the fated day, and you will find directions which may possibly be of service to you.—Adieu, Frank; we never meet more—but sometimes think on your friend Die Vernon.'

She extended her hand, but I clasped her to my bosom. She sighed as she extricated herself from the embrace which she permitted, escaped to the door which led to her own apartment, and I saw her no more.

NOTES

Note A, p. xxvii.—The Grave of Dugald Ciar Mohr.

I have been informed, that, at no very remote period, it was proposed to take this large stone, which marks the grave of Dugald Ciar Mohr, and convert it to the purpose of the lintel of a window, the threshold of a door, or some such mean use. A man of the clan MacGregor, who was somewhat deranged, took fire at this insult; and when the workmen came to remove the stone, planted himself upon it, with a broad axe in his hand, swearing he would dash out the brains of any one who should disturb the monument. Athletic in person, and insane enough to be totally regardless of consequences, it was thought best to give way to his humour; and the poor madman kept sentinel on the stone day and night, till the proposal of removing it was entirely dropped.

Note B, p. xxvii.—Tradition of Dugald Ciar Mohr.

The above is the account which I find in a manuscript history of the clan MacGregor, of which I was indulged with a perusal by Donald MacGregor, Esq., late Major of the 33d regiment, where great pains have been taken to collect traditions and written documents concerning the family. But an ancient and constant tradition, preserved among the inhabitants of the country, and particularly those of the clan MacFarlane, relieves Dugald Ciar Mohr of the guilt of murdering the youths, and lays the blame on a certain Donald or Duncan Lean, who performed the act of cruelty, with the assistance of a gillie who attended him, named Charlioch, or Charlie. They say that the homicides dared not again join their clan, but that they resided in a wild and solitary state as outlaws, in an unfrequented part of the MacFarlanes' territory. Here they lived for some time undisturbed, till they committed an act of brutal violence on two defenceless women, a mother and daughter of the MacFarlane clan. In revenge of this atrocity, the MacFarlanes hunted them down and shot them. It is said the younger ruffian, Charlioch,

265

might have escaped, being remarkably swift of foot. But his crime became his punishment, for the female whom he had outraged had defended herself desperately, and had stabbed him with his own dirk in the thigh. He was lame from the wound, and was the more easily overtaken and killed. I incline to think that this last is the true edition of the story, and that the guilt was transferred to Dugald Ciar Mohr, as a man of higher name. Or it is possible these subordinate persons had only executed his orders.

Note C, p. lviii.—THE LOCH LOMOND EXPEDITION.

The Loch Lomond expedition was judged worthy to form a separate pamphlet, which I have not seen, but, as quoted by the historian Rae, it must be delectable.

'On the morrow, being Thursday the 13th, they went on their expedition, and about noon came to Inversnaid, the place of danger, where the Paisley men and those of Dumbarton, and several of the other companies, to the number of an hundred men, with the greatest intrepidity leapt on shore, got up to the top of the mountains, and stood a considerable time, beating their drums all the while; but no enemy appearing, they went in quest of their boats, which the rebels had seized, and having casually lighted on some ropes and oars hid among the shrubs, at length they found the boats drawn up a good way on the land, which they hurled down to the loch. Such of them as were not damaged they carried off with them, and such as were, they sank and hewed to pieces. That same night they returned to Luss, and thence next day to Dumbarton, from whence they had first set out, bringing along with them the whole boats they found in their way on either side of the loch, and in the creeks of the isles, and mooring them under the cannon of the castle. During this expedition the pinnaces discharging their patararoes, and the men their small-arms, made such a thundering noise, through the multiplied rebounding echoes of the vast mountains on both sides of the loch, that the MacGregors were cowed and frighted away to the rest of the rebels who were encamped at Strath Fillan.'— *Rae's History of the Rebellion,* 4to, p. 287.

Note D, p. lxxxix.—THE AUTHOR'S EXPEDITION TO INVERNENTY.

The author is uncertain whether it is worth while to mention, that he had a personal opportunity of observing even in his own time, that the king's writ did not pass quite current in the Braes of Balquhidder. There were very considerable debts due by

NOTES

Stewart of Appin (chiefly to the author's family), which were likely to be lost to the creditors, if they could not be made available out of this same farm of Invernenty, the scene of the murder done upon MacLaren.

His family, consisting of several strapping deer-stalkers, still possessed the farm, by virtue of a long lease, for a trifling rent. There was no chance of any one buying it with such an encumbrance, and a transaction was entered into by the MacLarens, who, being desirous to emigrate to America, agreed to sell their lease to the creditors for £500, and to remove at the next term of Whitsunday. But whether they repented their bargain, or desired to make a better, or whether from a mere point of honour, the MacLarens declared they would not permit a summons of removal to be executed against them, which was necessary for the legal completion of the bargain. And such was the general impression that they were men capable of resisting the legal execution of warning by very effectual means, no king's messenger would execute the summons without the support of a military force. An escort of a sergeant and six men was obtained from a Highland regiment lying in Stirling; and the author, then a writer's apprentice, equivalent to the honourable situation of an attorney's clerk, was invested with the superintendence of an expedition, with directions to see that the messenger discharged his duty fully, and that the gallant sergeant did not exceed his part by committing violence or plunder. And thus it happened, oddly enough, that the author first entered the romantic scenery of Loch Katrine, of which he may perhaps say he has somewhat extended the reputation, riding in all the dignity of danger, with a front and rear guard, and loaded arms. The sergeant was absolutely a Highland Sergeant Kite, full of stories of Rob Roy and of himself, and a very good companion. We experienced no interruption whatever, and when we came to Invernenty, found the house deserted. We took up our quarters for the night, and used some of the victuals which we found there. On the morning we returned as unmolested as we came.

The MacLarens, who probably never thought of any serious opposition; received their money and went to America, where, having had some slight share in removing them from their *paupera regna*, I sincerely hope they prospered.

The rent of Invernenty instantly rose from £10 to £70 or £80; and when sold, the farm was purchased (I think by the late Laird of MacNab) at a price higher in proportion than what even the modern rent authorised the parties interested to hope for.

ROB ROY

Allan Breck Stewart was a man likely in such a matter to keep his word. James Drummond MacGregor and he, like Katherine and Petruchio, were well matched ' for a couple of quiet ones.' Allan Breck lived till the beginning of the French Revolution. About 1789, a friend of mine, then residing at Paris, was invited to see some procession which was supposed likely to interest him, from the windows of an apartment occupied by a Scottish Benedictine priest. He found, sitting by the fire, a tall, thin, raw-boned, grim-looking old man, with the petit croix of St. Louis. His visage was strongly marked by the irregular pro-jections of the cheek-bones and chin. His eyes were grey. His grizzled hair exhibited marks of having been red, and his complexion was weather-beaten, and remarkably freckled. Some civilities in French passed between the old man and my friend, in the course of which they talked of the streets and squares of Paris, till at length the old soldier, for such he seemed, and such he was, said with a sigh, in a sharp Highland accent, ' Deil ane o' them a' is worth the Hie street of Edinburgh !' On inquiry, this admirer of Auld Reekie, which he was never to see again, proved to be Allan Breck Stewart. He lived decently on his little pension, and had, in no subsequent period of his life, shown any thing of the savage mood, in which he is generally believed to have assassinated the enemy and oppressor, as he supposed him, of his family and clan.

GLOSSARY

a', *all.*
aboot, *about.*
abune, *above.*
ado, *concern, business,* 216.
ae, *one.*
aff, *off.*
again, *against.*
ain, *own.*
ait, *oat*; aiten, *oaten.*
amaist, *almost.*
amang, *among.*
an, *if.*
ane, *one*; ance, *once.*
aneuch, *enough.*
anither, *another.*
Apryle, *April,* cxx.
aquavitæ, *whisky.*
arena, *are not.*
auld, *old.*
Auld Reekie, *Edinburgh.*
awa, *away.*
aweel, *well.*
awfu', *awful.*
aye, *always.*

baith, *both.*
bang, *bound,* 219.
barghaist, *wraith, hobgoblin,* 223.
barm, *yeast.*
belang, *belong.*
bide, *stay, wait.*
birling, *carousing,* 217.
bit, *(diminutive),* e.g. *bit beast,* 217.
bleize, *blaze.*
blethers, *idle talk,* 219.

blythe, *glad,* 213.
boddle, *a copper coin of two pennies Scots* = $\frac{1}{6}$th *of a penny English,* 219.
bogle, *spectre, ghost,* 224.
bonnie, *fine.*
brawly, *finely.*
brownies, *fairy-goblins,* 233.
buddel-house(*bottle-house*), *tavern,*lv.
burn, *brook.*
by, *besides,* 88.

ca', *call.*
ca'ing, *abusing,* 217.
cailliachs, (gael.), *old women, hags,* xcviii.
callant, *lad,* lxxvi.
Cannlemas, *Candlemas,* 90.
canny, *gentle, cautious.*
caption, (legal), *judicial order for apprehension for non-payment of a debt or non-fulfilment of an obligation,* cxxi.
carena, *care not.*
carle, *fellow, churl.*
castock, *cabbage-stalk,* lxxxviii.
cauld, *cold.*
chiel, chield, *fellow.*
chowl, *jowl.*
chuckie-stanes, *pebbles,* 214.
clauts, *scrapings,* 252.
clavers, *gossip,* 213.
close, *alley, narrow street,* lxii.
coat-tail, on ane's ain, *at one's own expense,* 212.

269

ROB ROY

compearance, (legal), *appearance in a court of justice*, 217.

compleened, *complained*.

compurgation, (legal), *testimony borne as to the credibility of another*, 126.

coronach, (gael.), *dirge*, cxii.

cou'dna, *could not*.

coup, *capsize*.

cranreuch, (gael.), *hoar-frost*, lxxvii.

creagh, (gael.), *raid*, lxxiv.

daft, *sportive, lawless*, lxxxviii ; *crazy*, 213.

daiker, *toil*, 90.

deil, *devil*.

deil's over Jock Wabster, *the devil to pay*, 213.

dhuinie-wassell, (gael.), *gentleman*, lxxvii.

didna, *did not*.

diligence, (legal), *execution of decree of court*, cxxi.

dinna, *do not*.

dirdum, *tumult, uproar*, 214.

disna, *does not*.

divot, *turf*, 213.

dobbie, *sprite, apparition*, 224.

doun, *down*.

dousely, *quietly, sedately*, 216.

drap, *drop*.

dune, *done*.

durke, *dirk, highland dagger*.

een, *eyes*.

e'en, the, *this evening*, 252.

e'enow, (*even now*), *just now*.

ellwand, *Scots yardstick* = 37.2 *imperial inches*, 217.

eneugh, enow, *enough*.

even, *equal*, 253.

even-down, *straight, honest*, 90.

fallow, *fellow*.

far-awa, *distantly related*, 213.

fareweel, *farewell*.

fashed, *troubled*, 216.

fasheous, *troublesome*, 90.

Fastern's E'en, *Shrove Tuesday*, 232.

fause, *false*.

fause-face, *mask*, 130.

fearing, *afraid*, 91.

fee, *wages, hire*, 90.

fizzenless, *weak, useless*, 214.

flyted, *scolded*, lxxv.

forbye, *besides*, 88.

forestairs, *outside stair to the front of a house*, 216.

forpit, *the fourth part of a peck*, 213.

fozy, *soft and spongy*, 218.

frae, *from*.

fu', *full*.

gae, *gave*.

gaed, *gone, went*, cxxii.

gars, garr'd, *makes, made*.

gate, *place*, 218.

gauger, *exciseman*, 49.

gaun, *going*.

gaunt, *yawn*, 165.

gentles, *gentlefolk*, 216.

ghaist, *ghost*.

gie, *give* ; gien, *given*.

girnel, *granary*, lxix.

glee'd, *twisted*, 91.

glegly, *brightly*, 221.

glisk, *glimpse*, 130.

gomeril, *fool, idiot*, 216.

gotten, *got*.

gowd, *gold*, 217.

gowling, *storming, scolding*, 218.

Græme, Sir John the, *a Scottish patriot, killed at the battle of Falkirk, 1298*, 219.

grieve, *farm-steward*, 214.

grit, *great*.

grund, *ground*.

GLOSSARY

gude, *good.*
guides, *directs,* 214.

ha', *hall.*
hae, *have.*
haill, *whole.*
hallion, *worthless fellow.*
hame, *home.*
hantle, (*handful*), *great many of,* 218.
happed, *wrapped warmly,* cxxii.
harns, *brains,* 232.
haud, *hold.*
haulds, *places of resort,* 253.
havena, *have not.*
heckle, lit. *a comb;* by met. *that which teases or irritates,* cxxiii.
herd-widdiefows, (gael.), *mad herdsmen, a name given to cattle-stealers,* lxxiv.
her'ship, *plunder, devastation,* xxxviii.
hie, *high.*
himsell, *himself.*
hing, *hang.*
hirdy-girdy, *topsy-turvy; in reckless confusion,* 213.
horning, letters of, (legal), *a judicial order to pay a debt or to perform an act under penalty of outlawry and forfeiture for non-performance. The proclamation of the order was formerly preceded by the blast of a horn,* xliv.

ilk, *each,* cxxiii.
ingans, *onions,* 88.
I 'se, *I shall, I would.*
ither, *other.*

jannock, *loaf of oaten bread,* 213.
jeistiecor, *waistcoat with sleeves, ('juste au corps'),* 88.
jowin'-in, *tolling,* 215.

judge ordinar o' the bounds, *judge of that particular jurisdiction,* 216.

kail-blade, *cabbage-leaf,* 221.
kail-yard, *cabbage-garden,* 131.
kale, *cabbage,* 89.
keepit, *kept.*
ken, *know.*
kinrick, *kingdom,* 216.
knowe, *knoll.*
kræmes, *warehouses where goods are packed; range of booths for the sale of goods,* 216.
kye, *kine,* cxxii.
kyloes, *highland cattle,* lxiv.

lairds, *landowners.*
lang, *long.*
lang-kale, *full-grown colewort,* 89.
lang-nebbit, *long-nosed,* 233.
lang syne, *long ago,* xciv.
lang-tongued, *loquacious,* 217.
lave, *remainder,* 88.
leasing-making, (legal), *calumniating the king to the subjects or the subjects to the king,* 220.
leddy, *lady.*
leg-bail, gae him, *absconded,* 217.
like o', *such as,* 253.
linking, *repeating rapidly,* 252.
loon, *fellow, lout,* 58.
Lunnun, *London,* 213.

mair, *more.*
maun, *must;* maunna, *must not,* 214.
maw, *mow.*
mayna, *may not.*
mense, *prudence, discretion,* 88.
merk, 13s. 4d. *Scots* = 1s. 1⅓d. *of English money,* 251.
Mess John, (*Mass John*), *parish minister,* 251.

271

mickle, *much.*
midden, *dunghill,* 232.
middenstead, *dunghill site,* 252.
mistrysted, *alarmed,* 216.
mony, *many.*
mouls, *mould, earth,* 90.
muckle, *much.*
mutch, *a woman's cap,* 216.
mysell, *myself.*

na, nae, *no.*
naething, *nothing.*
nane, *none.*
narra, *never a.*
neist, *next.*
nevoy, *nephew,* 185.
no, *not.*
nuik, *nook, corner,* 215.

o', *of;* o't, *of it.*
observe, *observation,* 252.
ony, *any.*
or, *ere, before,* 91.
oursells, *ourselves.*
out ower, *beyond,* 233.
ower, *over.*

parritch, *porridge,* 252.
peers, *pears,* 213.
penny wedding, *wedding party to which the guests contribute money for the entertainment, the surplus being given to the newly married pair,* 252.
pike, *pick,* 232.
pinners, *cap with lappets formerly worn by women of rank,* 142.
pock-pudding, (lit. *pudding-bag*); *contemptuously applied to Englishmen, as being fond of their food,* 217.
pokmanty, *portmanteau,* 214.
pootry, *poultry,* 232.

pou'd, *pulled.*
preceesely, *precisely.*
pretty, *gallant, soldier-like,* lxxxix.
puir, *poor.*
pund, *pound.*

rax, *draw, stretch,* 216.
remeed, *remedy;* remeed of law, *obtaining of justice,* 217.
rinning, *running.*
rived, *torn,* 219.
roud, *rolled,* cxxii.
routing, *roaring, ranting.*
rubbery, *robbery.*
rubbit, *robbed.*
ruggit, *pulled roughly,* 219.

sae, *so.*
saft, *soft.*
sair, *sore, entirely,* 215.
sang, *song.*
sap, *ninny,* 218.
sark, *shirt, contemptuously applied to a surplice,* 252.
saul, *soul.*
saw, *sow.*
sax, *six.*
say, *voice, influence,* 220.
scaur, *scare, frighten,* 218.
sell, *self.*
selled, *sold.*
shelty, *pony,* 58.
sheriff-substitute, *resident county magistrate,* ci.
shouldna, *should not.*
sic, siccan, *such;* sicklike, *suchlike.*
siller, *money,* 212.
skarting, *scratching,* 232.
skeps, *beehives,* 253.
sparry-grass, *asparagus,* 214.
speck and span new, *entirely new,* 219.
speerings, *tidings, information,* 131.

GLOSSARY

stibbler, *a term applied in ridicule to a probationer*, i.e. *a candidate for a clerical benefice*, 233.

stickit, *stuck*.

stoppit, *stopped*.

strae, *straw*.

suld, *should*.

sum, *some*.

sune, *soon*.

sybos, *onions*, 88.

syne, *then*, cxxii.

tae, *one*.

taich-tulzie, (gael.), *scuffle within doors*, l.

tane, *the one*, 217.

tass, *cup, goblet*, 57.

thae, *these*.

than, *then*.

thegither, *together*.

thrang, *bustle*, 217 ; thrangest, *busiest*, 213.

thrapple, *throat*, 216.

throughgaun, *rebuke, 'wigging,'* 218.

through ither, *confused*, 213.

till, *to*.

tither, *the other*, 217.

trailed, *haled*, 218.

tryste, *market*, 58.

tuggit, *tugged*.

turneeps, *turnips*.

twa, twasome, *two*.

ulzie, *oil*, lxxxii.

unco, *very, extraordinary, great*.

uphaud, *uphold, maintain*.

vera, *very*.

vivers, *victuals*, 88.

wad, *would*.

wadset, (*pledged-lease*); *a conveyance of land in pledge for a debt or obligation but redeemable in the event of satisfying the obligation*, xl.

walise, *valise*.

wame, *belly*, 91.

wark, *work*.

warld, *world*.

warst, *worse*.

wasna, *was not*.

wat, *wet*.

wather, *weather*.

waur, *worst*.

weans, (*wee ones*), *children*, 90.

wee, *little*.

weel, *well*.

wha, whae, *who*.

what for, *why*, 90.

wheen, *few*, 91.

whiles, *sometimes*.

whilk, *which*.

wi', *with*.

wight, *stout*, 219.

winna, wonna, *will not*.

wrang, *wrong*.

wud, *crazy, mad*, 213.

wull, *will*.

wush, *wish*.

yestreen, (*yester even*), *yesterday*, 252.

yillhouse, *alehouse*, 212.

This book was designed by William B. Taylor
for Heron Books, London

Printed in Switzerland